Acknowledging Our Sponsors

As author of **"RONNIE"**, I have traveled across the USA and have spoken with thousands of people concerning the issue of **underage drinking and alcohol abuse** among our young people. Without exception, everyone has expressed their absolute approval and personal belief in the message that is advocated through this book and our program, **"A Message from RONNIE"**.

There are many Rotarians and their friends who have joined with us to provide financial assistance so that complimentary copies of **RONNIE** may be distributed in communities like yours in our effort to **make a difference** in the lives of our young people.

If this book was given to you as a complimentary copy, I sincerely ask that you take a moment and contact the sponsor named below and express your appreciation for the tremendous financial assistance that has been given this program.

Our Fabulous Endorsements

I am immensely pleased that *"RONNIE"* has been endorsed and sanctioned by U.S. Presidents, Senators, Congressmen, the President of the U.S. Senate, the Speaker of the U.S. House, Governors, State Education Commissioners, Education Associations, college coaches and many other influential men and women who understand the problem associated with the horrors of under-age drinking and alcohol abuse. It is my firm belief that you will not find another book that carries the magnitude and clout of those who have endorsed *RONNIE.* I have posted one of these extraordinary endorsements, or comments, at the end of each chapter. Please take a few minutes to pay special attention to each comment.

I urge you to visit our website at **www.fatherson.com** where you will find an array of information. On our home page, just click on the jacket cover of *RONNIE* for a complete menu.

Bill Williams, Author

As author of **"RONNIE"** I am extremely pleased that **RONNIE** and our program, *"A Message from RONNIE"*, has been licensed by Rotary International for the purpose of marketing to Rotary Clubs around the world.

The primary reason for this endeavor is to enable clubs to educate their community"s youth, teenagers and young adults about the perils of **underage drinking and alcohol abuse**. Together, we can make a vast difference in the lives of countless thousands of young people. However, if we succeed in having a positive influence in the life of **only one youth**, all of our efforts, cost and time will remain totally insignificant.

Our RI Licensing agreement affords us the opportunity to bring to Rotarians worldwide our high visibility, immensely effective and vastly important program that will have a positive and lasting affect on thousands, perhaps millions, of young people. The program is from the pages of Ronnie's true-to-life story.

Secondary to that purpose, the program will assist Rotary in its efforts to provide humanitarian service all over the world. I believe that your participation in this program will quickly become one of the most effective and meaningful programs undertaken by any club or individual Rotarian.

If you will access our website at **www.fatherson.com** and click on the jacket cover of **RONNIE**, you will find an array of information. I would be delighted to personally bring our story to your club as a guest speaker. On our website you will find an email address and phone contacts for this purpose.

I look forward to working with every Rotary Club as we spread our message of how quickly and disastrous, alcohol can ruin the life of the most unsuspecting young person.

Bill Williams, Author

RONNIE
"there just ain't no light"

by

Bill Williams

BADM BOOKS
Pensacola, Florida

www.fatherson.com
(click on jacket cover of Ronnie)

RONNIE is the true story and life experiences faced by a most unique athlete. Much of the story took place during the mid-1950s. In order to tell the story properly and accurately, I have done so in the vernacular of the language of those days and times past. Such comments and jargon of that period have been used sparingly; however, when used, the language was necessary to tell the story factually. If you wish to make a comment to the author, you may do so by mail at: Post Office Box 9728, Pensacola, FL 32513-9728. Be sure to visit our website at www.fatherson.com.

The views expressed in this book are those of the author and not necessarily those of Rotary International or the Rotary Foundation.

Rotary International and the Rotary emblem ® are registered trademarks of Rotary International and are used here with the permission of Rotary International.

08 07 06 05 04 / 10 9 8 7 6 5 4

Manufactured in the United States of America
by

FATHER & SON
PUBLISHING, INC.

4909 N. Monroe Street • Tallahassee, Florida 32303
http://fatherson.com
800-741-2712

This book is dedicated to:

**THE MEMORY OF
MALCOLM RONALD "RONNIE" WILLIAMS**

"To live in hearts we leave behind, is not to die"

AND

**THE 1953 PENSACOLA HIGH SCHOOL FIGHTING TIGER
FOOTBALL TEAM**
Head Coach Jim Scoggins

**THE 1954 AND 1955 JONES COUNTY JUNIOR
COLLEGE FOOTBALL TEAM**
Head Coach Jim Clark
Coach A. B. Howard

**THE 1956 AND 1957 FLORIDA STATE UNIVERSITY
FOOTBALL TEAM**
Head Coach Tom Nugent

And to Ronnie's teammates and their wives who have graciously given of their time to recall many of the stories found herein. And to Ronnie's very special friend, Red West.

I also want to recognize Pete Flemming, Tony Roper, Gayle Winchester, Don Scoggins, Mary Schulte, Tracey Stites, Teenie Armstrong Barnett and Pat Hogan.

And a very special thanks to my long-time friend B.J. Peters of Tallahassee who was instrumental in many ways in the completion of this book.

And a heartfelt thanks to Florida State Seminoles' Head Football Coach Bobby Bowden. His winning attitude, but more so his personal character, has been the guiding light for countless numbers of players, parents, students and fans throughout his very successful career.

I appreciate each and every one of you very much.

"Alcohol abuse among our youth is a continuing problem and often leads to tragic results, as you have illustrated in the telling of **RONNIE'S** story. The pressures faced by our young people are immense, and it is vitally important that they are given the tools to assist them in overcoming these temptations and challenges. Your message through RONNIE will serve as a tool and, hopefully, have a positive and lasting impact on the reader. Thank you for your dedication to helping our youth. Best wishes as you continue your work educating our young people and their families about the dangers of abusive substances such as alcohol."

Governor Jeb Bush, Florida

"Alcohol is the number-one problem on our college campuses today and apparently **RONNIE** had problems with both alcohol and a sense of identity when his athletic career was over. This book can help young people see that preparation for life after athletics is very important."

Congressman Tom Osborne, Former coach
Nebraska Cornhuskers

FOREWORD

by
FSU Head Football Coach
Bobby Bowden

Although I never stood eyeball to eyeball with **"RONNIE,"** I did make his acquaintance. It was on a cold Saturday night in Ellisville, Mississippi, during my maiden coaching year at South Georgia. We went there undefeated, chest-pounding proud, and returned to Georgia with our tails between our legs. That night I experienced the worse defeat of my coaching career. Jones County Junior College led at the half 33-0 and before it was over humiliated us 60-13.

"RONNIE" scored twice. His first, a 39-yard dash around right end, then a reception for a 45-yard touchdown. They out-rushed us 415 yards to 105 and out-passed us 128 yards to 87.

Jones finished the year undefeated and was invited to Pasadena to play Compton, California, in the Rose Bowl for the National Junior College Championship. The game held the significance of being the very first time any sports team from the state of Mississippi would play against an integrated opponent. Although the political atmosphere was boiling over, the president of Jones elected to accept the invitation against the wishes of the Legislature and all major newspapers. Perhaps all the turmoil played a part in JCJC's 22-13 loss.

"RONNIE" scored both of Jones's touchdowns, which caught the attention of many senior college head coaches. Eventually he was sweet-talked into coming to FSU by **Coach Tom Nugent**. It was during his two years in Tallahassee that his life started to unravel.

The story of **"RONNIE"** will enlighten you about one of the major problems of today's athlete: those who do not prepare properly for real life after the glory days of sports are behind them.

"RONNIE" continued to live in the world that he had already known, live with accomplishments of the past as if they were his meal ticket to the future. After the flash bulbs and newspaper articles were over, he was totally lost, completely unprepared.

Although the temptations of the drug scene as the world knows it today did not exist back in 1956-1957, alcohol, its equally crippling predecessor, dominated and claimed many lives.

The author of **"RONNIE"** is his younger brother, a staunch supporter of FSU and its sports programs. You will enjoy reading of the times and events scattered throughout the book which touched **"RONNIE'S"** life: his friendship with Burt Reynolds while at FSU, his brush with Elvis Presley, the real Hank Williams, Lee Corso and others who played an important role in his personal life.

"RONNIE" carried with him a crutch throughout his life, something unknown and unseen by others, a memory to lean on when times got rough. The book reveals his crutch to be the very first guitar that Elvis Presley's parents gave to him when he was eleven years old. The surfacing of the "lost guitar" will create worldwide interest when revealed for the first time in **"RONNIE."**

This story was written in the hope that the thousands of athletes who annually aspire to conquer the sports world will prepare themselves for the real world outside, the real world that each one of them must face sooner of later. I believe you will enjoy reading **"RONNIE."**

Coach Bobby Bowden
Florida State Seminoles
Tallahassee, Florida

CONTENTS

A Message From The Author

I wrote **"RONNIE"** for one reason - to combat under-age drinking and alcohol abuse among our young people. Alcohol affects the rich and poor, the good and bad, men and women, boys and girls, black and white, Republicans, Democrats and Independents. The atrocity of alcohol abuse happens to people without concern for their personal status in life, *Simply because that demon shows no favoritism — there are no exemptions or exceptions.*

Several years had passed since Ronnie's sad and lonely death and with the dawn of every new day, I became more obsessed with the cause and circumstances of his demise. As difficult as it would be, I knew I had to write his story; a story that I am sure will prevent others from falling into the miserable and pathetic pit that took his life.

You see, Ronnie is my brother and I watched him deteriorate from an outstanding athlete into someone who literally gave up on life. He was a fine young man who lost all self worth, self-control and then forfeited his life to alcohol abuse that started with social drinking in high school and escalated until his horrendous death. After all the glory days of sports were no more, it left him an empty shell of a man who was convinced there remained no real purpose for his life.

If this story has a positive influence on the life of just one young person, then I will have been successful with my goal. I intend to *make a difference* and I sincerely ask you to join me in this effort. Please make contact with your friends and associates and ask them to visit our website, **www.fatherson.com,** where they can learn about our program and how together we can make a difference through Ronnie's story.

I would sincerely like to have your comments. Please drop me a line at Post Office Box 9728, Pensacola, Florida 32513.

Bill Williams, Author

1

WHY'D THEY SHOOT ME?
I DID NOTHING WRONG.

A BARRAGE OF explosive, rapid-fire Magnum shots echoed loud and clear, breaking the silence of an older section of the quaint northeast side neighborhood on the eve of the day of love, Valentine's 1980.

The 44-year-old man lay crumpled in a grotesque position on the cold, hard winter ground, which was bare of grass but now covered with wilted, dried, blood-stained leaves. Falling face down, his chin was buried deep into his chest.

His right arm, as if broken, lay under and across his body. Both arms were fully extended, stretched outward to his left. His bluish-grey hands lay silently within inches of each other. Both legs were positioned as though his torso had been thrown from a high building, crushing all life from its limbs.

He died alone, collapsed on the frigid, crusty ground while his family, who loved him dearly, had no earthly idea of his dreadful dilemma. There, all alone, light years away from the crowds of fans who always marveled, cheered and praised his athletic prowess.

Policemen cluttered around, gawking at the motionless figure more like sightseers than law enforcement officials. No one even had the decency to take the time to cover the remains of what was once an outstanding, fine-tuned athlete.

Like the magnificent eagle whose elegant wings evermore

seek to catch updrafts of warm air currents in search of a more splendid ride across the heavens, to portray its mastery of flight is to liken it to a star athlete who shines in his chosen field of excellence. An athlete who demands perfection of himself and displays his precision skills for thousands each year who are astonished and pleased with his performances.

And when the life is squelched from the monarch of the sky, there is nothing sadder or more demeaning than to see its crumpled, limp, lifeless body fall to the earth. When its performance of an elegant, beautiful flight is fatally interrupted, there is little to compare with the remains. So it was with Ronnie.

"I COULD NOT believe what my eyes and ears were telling me. From a not-too-distant height I could clearly see my body lying on the cold, damp earth. "Why did they shoot me? I did nothing wrong. Boo, why did they shoot me? All I did was run from the burglars. Run away from the man coming through my bedroom window. All I did was run. Why did they have to shoot me?

"Why isn't anyone doing anything? Squad car after car of police officials are here. Why are they converging around me? Why are they just standing there ogling over me? Why don't they help? Why don't they do something for me? Am I going to die lying here on this cold hard ground? What about my mother? What will she think? My family? My children?

"I can see clearly all about me. Is this the end? Is this all there is going to be to life? Am I to die like the vagrant I am being called by the officers?

"Life has not been fulfilled for me. It's passed me by. I want to go back. I want to go back to the golden days, back to the beginning. Where are all my friends? Fred, are you here? Tony? Ben? Red, where are you? Hubie? Alibi? Pinky? Boo? Boo, are you here? Boo? Where are all of them? Why am I alone?

"Why do I feel alone, yet know I'm in the comfort of a warm glow of a gentle spirit?

"All my life I have always felt alone, even in a crowd of hundreds. Even with someone that I loved dearly, loneliness was always close at hand.

"Boo, why do I feel alone but sense the warm, comforting, sparkling light which surrounds and beckons to me?

"Still, I want to drift back into the real world, the world I knew before all the depressions of my life. Before all the hardships and failures. Back when the days were filled with fun things to do, and the nights were shared with friends, many friends who had thoughts, feelings and desires in common. Back when we all dared to dream of a bright future. A fantastically bright future.

"I want to go back to sleep and dream of the days of the past when life was easy as a child. Back when Mom took care of us and Dad made the living for the family. Back when times were easy and I could enjoy just being a child with no responsibilities."

I'VE BEEN AROUND this old world a long, long time— seems like almost forever. I never sleep. Never take a day off. I know no holidays, no vacations. Perhaps you will recognize me; if not, then maybe a member of your family will or someone very close to you. I'm everywhere.

I have a lot of friends. Perhaps ten million times ten million. I have rich friends and poor friends, women and men, black and white, young and old, smart and dumb, gay and straight. I like them all, but I have to confess I'm partial to the older teen-agers. Those who have demonstrated they will be outstanding and successful in what ever direction they choose to take their lives, especially athletes because they are, by and large, natural leaders. Their friendship seems to last forever.

It just seems right that, when you start out with a young friend and the two of you stick together over the years, there really isn't anything that can take its place. Sure, you meet new companions daily, and while they are nice and responsive they still can't take the place of an old friend. That's the way it was between me and my friend "Ronnie."

After we became close, we talked often, many times every day. Together, just him and me. We shared all of his friends and acquaintances, and no one ever had an clue. While I was never at his side, I was always a constant companion within his mind, within his brain, within his memory. I was there every hour of every day, constantly wrapped up completely in his every thought pattern. After we became close, he started calling me "Boo," the nickname he gave me many years ago.

I first met Ronald at a beach party in the summer after his sophomore year at Pensacola High. That was back in '52, perhaps a year before his friends started calling him Ronnie. A great athlete and such a splendid guy. Quick-witted, funny, handsome. As a matter of fact, he was voted best looking in both his junior high and high school classes.

Ronald was for sure a ladies' man even at the spry young age of 13 or 14. By the time he was in the eighth grade, all the girls made sure he was on their invitation list for all their birthday parties. Before any of them were old enough to drive, they would go with their parents when he was to be picked up and insisted that he was always the last one they dropped off after their parties.

Although sometimes shy, he was still the life of the party. The young ladies were always delighted when he accepted their invitations. While traces shown through at this early age, it really wasn't until he reached high school and on into college when some of the ladies would think of him as conceited. His standard and quick reply was always "If you can perform, it's not bragging."

THROUGH THE YEARS I learned much about Ronald's family. Their upbringing, lifestyle, bloodline and genes attest to a family where each was far above average in intelligence. And they all, each in his or her own way, had a built-in stubborn streak three miles wide. Each one, in a differing degree, possessed an almost uncontrollable passionate jealousy, often smothering those they loved with way too much kindness and affection.

And each one had a tendency to keep it all in, all to themselves. To hold their feelings inside and not to discuss anything with anyone. Rather than twist or distort true facts, which perhaps would enhance his personal opinion of himself, his self-image or self-worth, Ronald, much more so than other family members, chose to keep it all bottled up inside. He would open up only to me and to no one else.

His parents were the salt of the earth. His mom, a wonderful housewife, accepted her duties of taking care of her family most seriously. Back then a woman loved to show her devotion to her husband and family by making sure everything was just right at home. Making sure the meals were prepared and served on time and that the family had their hour together at the end of each day.

Family meals have all but become a thing of the past in today's family structure. But Ronald's family was assured they would all be together at the end of every day. All three children were expected to be at the table on time or have a very good excuse acceptable to both Mom and Dad if they were late.

Ronald's mom was a delightfully warm, devoutly religious, strong and forceful lady, mother and wife. Seldom did she raise her voice, but when she did the law was laid down hard and firm. When she spoke, everyone paid attention.

Every Sunday morning without exception, Ronald and his younger brother and sister, Billy and Sandi, were awakened early, bathed, had their breakfast, dressed, and as a family left home together, walking the four blocks to Brownsville Baptist Church. As the children went their separate ways to their Sunday School classes, their mom would take her position and fill her role as teacher for the largest class of grade school kids.

She had little concern for any parent who would preach one thing six days a week but then not attend worship services on Sunday. She made sure that if she was going to lead her family in the ways of the church, she, herself, had to play a part and do exactly what she was teaching and preaching. There simply was no other way.

Now their dad, although it was often said by many that he was the second greatest man who ever walked the face of the earth, was somewhat deficient in his church attendance. Although a man of profound and abiding faith, he was also a man who had a built-in resentment for those whom he would often see at church glad-handing everyone, playing the role. Showing themselves to be someone that he knew for sure they were not, then reverting to their real-to-life-character Monday through Saturday.

If there could be just one description of his dad, it would have to be said that he was not a hypocrite. While he did not attend church regularly, he was truly a man among men, a man who, when given his word, you could always take it to the bank. A man, who in his very on intimate way worshipped the way he felt most comfortable and at ease with himself. There was never a question as to his personal beliefs.

He financially supported the church, and in later years, after going into business for himself, was able to give considerably more to the church's daily operations, ministeries and missions. There is no doubt in my mind that both of Ronald's parents are at this very moment sitting at the head table in the Kingdom of God.

Years before I came to know Ronald as I did, I was a long-time friend of his father. Shortly after Sandi was born, his dad kicked me out, and our friendship ended abruptly. After that things were never the same between us. We never visited again.

IN 1946 WHEN Ronald was eleven, his family finally settled in Pensacola after countless numbers of moves across the Southeast. His father worked for an asphalt paving company and was forever on the move. Constantly relocating from city to city and from state to state during the war years building military bases for the government. By the time the family settled in Pensacola, the children had attended eight different schools in the last three years.

After renting a home for two years, the family decided to purchase a small, three bedroom, one bath home less than a block from Allie Yniestra Elementary School on West Jackson Street.

Becoming a homeowner for the first time was big business for the Williams family. When the parents decided to purchase, they called the kids together for a family discussion. It mattered not that they were too young to really understand; their parents just wanted them included. It was almost as if they wanted their children's approval just in case they made a mistake with their decision.

The kids were told the family was going to commit to a mortgage. A mortgage of 25 years to purchase their new home, and the payments would be $23.87 each and every month. Quite a taxing amount for the weekly earnings of only one bread winner, but by today's standards this amount may pay for a tank of gas for the family car. It was not until January first of 1956, eight years later, that Mr. Williams went into business for himself, and for the first time in his life earned $100 per week as steady income. Things were certainly beginning to look up.

WITH NO TELEVISION, computers or video games to rob them of their precious, valuable childhood time, Ronald, his brother and the boys of the neighborhood spent countless hours playing ball on the school grounds.

During the early years not a day went by when the kids were not either playing baseball or a simple game of pitch and catch. Often, even alone, Ronald could be found throwing a ball high against the school's brick wall, catching and throwing, catching and throwing.

In their small back yard their Dad assembled a pole vault. Daily, the neighborhood kids would gather, and soon someone would be crowned the champion pole vaulter of the block. And for those not big enough to vault, their dad hand crafted a see-saw, a teeter-totter.

Soon added to the games were boxing gloves, then a basket-ball goal was erected in the drive way, and finally their first foot-ball. The boys were so protective and proud of that ball they were reluctant to take it from their room in fear of getting it dirty and most definitely would not take it outside when threatened by rain.

ABOUT THIS SAME time in another tiny, sleepy, Southern town a slender kid of Ronnie's age experienced perhaps his first real life disappointment. The only child of hard-working par-ents was sorely disappointed that his family could not financially afford to buy him the .22 rifle he had wanted for his eleventh birthday. Although he begged and pleaded, he had to settle for the only gift his folks could afford, a $7.75 guitar. Times were tough not only in the South but across the entire nation.

Little did he or anyone else in Tupelo, Mississippi, know that "The Unwanted Gift" would ignite the first spark of reality in his, thus far, dull life. It would prove to be the initial opportu-nity and contribute immensely to the future career of this young-ster, who was still two years shy of being a teen-ager. The gift would create within him a purpose which would quickly propel him into America's spotlight and earn for him multi-millions of dollars as he became the world's best-known entertainer.

And obviously, no one had an inkling of an idea that The Un-wanted Gift would someday play a significant role in Ronnie's life.

2

JUST KIDS—JUST TEENAGERS

THERE WERE FEW organized sports for kids until they reached junior high school. The Williams boys and their neighborhood friends attended Blount Junior High on West Gregory Street. In Ronald's first year, the seventh grade, all of his friends went out for football. All but one made the team.

In 1948 there were only two junior high schools within the city limits of Pensacola: Blount on the west side and Clubbs on 12th Avenue, the east side of town. Annually, Coach Jimmy Reece and his Blount Panthers battled Clubbs for the city championship, and, generally speaking, it was always a toss-up as to which would be crowned champion.

During the junior high school years, times were slow and easy. The boys of the neighborhood searched diligently for new things to do, new experiences for their curious minds. They were soon to find a new brand of excitement.

Two or three times each year, for a week at a time, a young evangelist would bring his tent revival to West Pensacola. He always came to the same corner, Pace Boulevard and Strong Street. His exhibitions and showmanship were new to the kids. The carryings on inside the tent were like something they had never witnessed. It sounded more like a circus than the Baptist church the boys attended.

A very young Oral Roberts had started down the long road to establish himself as a world renowned faith healing minister. For those attending these revivals, mainly the downtrodden and elderly, the tremendous heat captured within the tent on hot, steamy summer days was miserable. More often than not, the scheduled daytime meetings had to be rescheduled for early evenings in order to endure the torture of the summer heat.

In the evenings the temperature would drop a bit, but it was always miserably uncomfortable inside the tent. And to make things even worse, you could always smell the vapors from the heat bouncing off the canvas and mixing with the packed-in crowds of sweaty men and women.

Inside, the congregation sat on folding wooden chairs and made great use of the ample supply of cardboard fans, both provided by local funeral homes in exchange for the reverend mentioning their businesses by name.

During the seven days of the revival, Ronald and friends were most anxious to know what the commotion, loud shouting and off-key music coming from the canvas walls was all about. For better ventilation purposes all four sides of the tent would be rolled up about a foot and tied off. The kids would lay in the tall, uncut grass and gaze under raised sides. While they would get an ear full of what was being said, their view usually was nothing more than dusty shoes and dirty socks.

Until they got too big for such nonsense, the youngsters looked forward to the annual shouting event. In the summer of the third year after a session on a Thursday evening, Bobby Hattaway's dad warned him, and it quickly spread through the neighborhood, that some of those evangelists made a habit of worshiping snakes. He told how they would handle them, letting them encircle their arms, neck and body. He warned that they had better be careful laying in the grass because some might get loose. The previous night marked their last visit to the Reverend Roberts' tent revival.

In the heat of midsummer the boys had a routine habit of blowing their entire weekly allowance of 25 cents in a single day. They would ride their bikes to the Palmetto Motel on West Cervantes, and for a quarter they could swim in the pool from sunrise to sundown. Occasionally, they ventured east on Cervantes and down 19th Avenue to Bayview Park where they tested their swimming skills by making it all the way across to the east side of Bayou Texar.

Any week they chose not to swim up their allowance, on Saturday they would take in a movie which always included a double feature, a continuing weekly serial, a comic strip and the RKO news reel.

There were two theaters within walking distance of their home: the Gulf on Strong Street at Pace Boulevard and the Sky Chief on West Cervantes near "V" Street. The Sky Chief was quite different, a normal theater in every respect except it had no roof. It was advertised as open-air. The owners were trying hard to capitalize on the popularity of drive-in theaters, but with a brand new twist.

Sometimes, the kids would go downtown for a movie. The main drag, Palafox Street, offered three theaters within four blocks: the Florida, Isis and Saenger. The black community had its own theater. However, the Saenger allowed blacks to attend, but they were confined to the balcony. They had to purchase tickets at an outside booth, then climb an outside metal staircase, resembling a fire escape route, to the balcony area.

Admission tickets were only nine cents, and most candy bars were a nickel except Mounds, which cost a dime. Popcorn was also ten cents, and a drink, any flavor, just a nickel.

With a quarter per week allowance, the kids would take in a movie, have a coke and two candy bars and leave the theater with a penny, which was spent on the way home at Dr. Bland's Pharmacy, always on a Big Jack's Cookie. Never did any part of their allowance ever see the sunrise of Sunday morning.

Only a block from the Gulf Theater, a family friend owned a Pure Oil service station on the corner of Cervantes and Pace Boulevard. If the kids attended the five o'clock movie, they would not get out until around seven, and during the short days it was already dark.

The station closed promptly at six each evening, and with no one around minor mischief certainly prevailed. On the outside of the building under the station's high canopy sat its cold drink box, the type which resembled a chest. Its top lid was hinged on the rear and, when lifted, exposed the cold drinks. All drinks were in bottles which hung freely by their neck between flat strips of shiny metal. You made your selection by sliding the drink of your choice along the strips toward the left end where you moved it into a receptacle large enough for only one bottle at a time. After you deposited a nickel, the passage would allow you to lift the bottle straight up from the cooler.

While this was a modern day invention, it only took the neighborhood kids a short time to quickly find a means of having all the free cola they could drink. Before leaving for the movie, they would borrow a "church key" from their moms kitchen, and with this marvelous tool they would pop off the tops, exposing the inviting liquid while leaving the bottles hanging in the cooler.

When finished, hanging in front of them remained a cooler full of cold drinks of which many had lost their tops. With the straws they'd kept from their drink purchased in the theater, they would bend over the cooler and suck the liquid from as many drinks as their small tummies could hold. Which was not too much, with the exception of Johnny Watson whose tummy could never be considered as small. Most Monday mornings Ben Fillingem, the station owner, would find at least two racks of cold drink bottles hanging empty.

These days were good days, good times for everyone. Slipping and sipping cold drinks and such was just about as much minor trouble as the kids ever got into. Or perhaps trivial things like throwing small brown bags filled with sand onto someone's front porch on Halloween night should they choose to ignore their plea for trick or treats.

Minor trouble, that is with maybe a couple of exceptions. South of their home was a large track of undeveloped land. The area lay roughly between Jackson Street on the north, Navy Boulevard on the south, Pace Boulevard on the east and Bayou Chico on the west.

Ronald and his friends often "went into the woods to play." They would shoot birds with their BB guns, fish in the streams of the bayou, climb trees and do the usual things done by most young boys.

Often they would climb a small, tall and tender, skinny pine tree. With the weight of three or four of them at the top of the tree it would bend slowly to the ground. Next, they would tie a rope to the tip top and while all but one held the rope, the remaining trooper would straddle tightly around the top limbs. When the chief of the ground crew thought the timing right, all would let go of the rope. This always provided a wild ride for the boy still on the tree as it swished back and forth. Never did they realize just how very lucky they were that no one was ever hurt.

One day little Gail Hardy followed them into the woods and simply wanted to be part of the boys' play. Not meaning any harm, they tied her to a tree, piled brush and pine straw around her feet and did a "burning at the stake" routine. The fire almost got out of control but they were able to cut her free before she suffered any damage. The only real damage occurred when her parents came calling on the parents of the boys that evening.

They were sworn never to carry matches again, although they confessed their only purpose had been to start a fire so they could skewer the bluebirds and robins they had shot or bream they had caught. Now they found new ways to get in a little deeper trouble.

A much-disliked neighborhood kid, "Horse Face Couch," was finally permitted to go with them into the woods. Over the previous week they had dug a tunnel, not too wide but perhaps 20 feet long. They had quickly tired of using it and contrived a plan to really scare old Horse Face.

They invited him to come into the woods and be part of their gang. They concocted a reason for him to be in the tunnel, all alone. The rest of the plan concluded when Ronald, Billy, Ronnie Shaw and Bobby Hattaway jumped over the top of the tunnel to purposely cause it to collapse. Again, they were lucky. Digging frantically, they finally pulled him to safety. Needless to say, old Horse Face never again wanted to go into the woods.

Oh yeah, sure, there were times the kids got in minor trouble. Like when Shaw knew the time had arrived for him to fire his dad's shotgun. Knowing the neighbors would object if done outside, he decided on an interior blast. In the back side of his bedroom closet, he stacked three Sears catalogs on top of each other and opened fire. Not only did it disintegrate the catalogs but also blasted a four-foot hole through the closet and into his parents bedroom on the opposite side of the wall. His mother's only pair of Sunday dress shoes were totally demolished. His parents were not pleased.

And once, three days after Easter, Billy took all ten of the small, colored biddies which were given to him, Ronnie and Sandi and lined them up neatly, different colors between each, in the octagon squares of a chicken fence and neatly squeezed the flexible wire around their dainty little necks. He thought the artistry that he made with the array of colors was quite impressive. Daddy Williams had a whole different idea.

Around their neighborhood, parents did not need to be told how to raise their kids. The Williams boys got more than their share of ass whuppings. Daddy Williams was a large man with a great girth; therefore, a long and wide belt was always handy.

Today's liberal society of do-gooders mixed with their liberal judges and social agencies surely would have put him behind bars for child abuse. In fact, Sing Sing, Folsom or Alcatraz may have been his destination. He had no qualms in believing the old saying, "Spare the rod and spoil the child". If parents today felt more like Mr. Williams did then, perhaps our world would be a much safer place to live and raise our families.

Oh, well, for the minor skirmishes as kids! But remember, never did the kids ever break any laws. All their fun was clean, although sometimes dangerous, but always within the law.

EACH SUMMER MOST of the neighborhood kids would participate in Midget or Little League Baseball, often hanging around Baliss Park to hone their skills. From the west side of Pensacola came some rather good ball players, Gabby and Bubba Gibson, Donnie Tidwell, Marshall Renfroe, Jerry Hudson and Jerry Miller. And the Cobb brothers, William, Lamar and David, who lived maybe six blocks east of Allie Yniestra School.

The Cobb family was well-known throughout Escambia County and had bushels of relatives scattered in every direction. Mr. Allison Cobb owned a grocery store on Cervantes Street and served the citizens for many years as a county commissioner, often being elected its chairman. Of the Cobb brothers, it appeared that David probably had the most baseball talent, but after his teen years he gave up any future dreams of developing it as a career. Unfortunately, in the prime of his young life, he succumbed to a tragic automobile accident.

DURING THE SUMMER the kids would hang around Legion Field to watch Pensacola's pro team, "The Pensacola Flyers." Their all-time favorite player was hard hitting, left fielder Neb Wilson. They would delight in watching him send home run balls soaring across the left field fence and into the living rooms of "G" Street homes or into the plate glass window of Paulk's Poultry Store at the corner of Gregory Street.

Wally Dashiels' Pensacola Flyers were in the old Southern League and played on the road an equal number of days as they did at home. When they traveled, it was common for these young friends to gather around a radio at one of their homes and listen to the game on WCOA or WBSR, local AM radio stations.

When you listened to the radio, you really had to pay attention. You had to formulate in your mind what was happening on the field without the benefit of having a television picture and an announcer telling you what you should see, think and feel about the game. It was much more fun back then just sitting around home listening to the game and filling Coke bottles with peanuts and in general just being kids.

AS GRADUATION FROM junior high neared, the boys all knew they were going to miss the school that started them on their athletic journey. And for sure, they were going to miss the after school walks to downtown where they hung out at Walgreen's Drug Store, then hustled up Palafox Street hill where they played basketball at the YMCA until dark, then wandered next door to Hoppy's for a soda. And surely they would miss walking by Polar Dairy where milk shakes were two for a quarter, the quarter they saved rather than spend it on the awful school cafeteria food that day.

Finally, the big day came, the second Friday of the month of June 1951. Graduation was here. During the ceremonies Ronnie and his teammates had a grand ole time making fun of one of their own. Jerry Miller had the courage, more so than perhaps all of them put together, to take part in the program by standing before his classmates and singing a song. However, for sure, his rendition of "IF" wouldn't propel him into a singing career.

THE SKINNY KID from Tupelo, a person who through a series of strange circumstances would eventually play an enormous role in Ronnie's personal life, was also losing some of his shyness by muddling through a few verses of songs in front his classmates.

Young Elvis Presley, now a tenth-grader at Humes High School in Memphis, began some form of personal transformation from his reserved timid self into a kid with a bit more confidence. Confidence if nothing more than to at least appear and behave different than all of his high school buddies.

After the summer of 1951, Ronald and his friends convinced themselves they were ready for Big Time Sports at the high school level. At Pensacola High he and his Blount Panther teammates soon met and became good friends with many players from their former arch rival, Clubbs. One player who quickly became one of Ronald's best friends was Lonnie Webster, a tough lineman who would soon distinguish himself on the PHS team.

TWO MONTHS AFTER Ronald entered the tenth grade as a sophomore at PHS, he turned sixteen and earned his driver's license. This new freedom had much to do with our first meeting. He never owned a car until after his college days, but his dad's was available most nights.

By the time Ronnie was a senior, brother Bill, two years younger, had bought a used 1950 Pontiac sedan. Ronnie often sweet-talked him into letting him use it for the evening. He would promise a full tank of gas as payback, and he most often made good his promise. Around the city there were several service station owners who were more than willing to contribute because of their fondness for his football feats.

IN THE BEGINNING we were just casual friends hanging together with the cream of the crop, the most popular boys and girls of the school. All the top athletes, cheerleaders and other popular students who chose not to participate in sports.

Ronnie, a year-around athlete, had to have something to do with every minute of his time. After football and baseball seasons ended, he opted to join the track team. Under the coaching of John Paul Jones, a part-time coach and great financial supporter of PHS track, he won and held the 100 yard sprint record for the state of Florida for two consecutive years.

Each weekend when the sports events were over, he, his buddies and I would frequent Mamma's Drive-In, Nob Hill Lounge, Jerry's Drive In and Scenic Terrace, all located in East Pensacola

Heights along beautiful Scenic Highway. Ronnie and his under-age teammates felt at ease at these eastside hangouts because most of them lived on the west side of the city. Sometimes their playground moved much closer to home. This always presented a problem and made their evenings on the town considerably more tense.

A couple of times each year a friend of Ronnie's, Fred Levin, another person who would continue to play a significant role in his personal life, would rent the Osceola Golf Clubhouse for an evening and throw quite a party. The facility, a west side, city-owned course, was at that time, "way out on Mobile Highway."

Not understanding high finance, these high school students, of whom some were just now learning how to calculate after missing the opportunity to grasp it at the junior high level, had a hard time comprehending just how Fred could come up with $500 or $600 to pay for such exclusive and expensive parties. He often laid out another $200 or more for the band of Walley "The Cat" Mercer and another $50 or $60 for intermission entertainment by "Snapper the Tapper."

They never stopped having fun long enough to realize that, when Fred threw the parties there would be 300 couples or more at $5 per head on most occasions. And that was just the cost of a ticket to get in the door. Perhaps this is where Fred began his pathway to wealth.

During the summers Pensacola Beach was the destination of this group of popular, fun-and-sun-seeking athletes. The beach on Santa Rosa Island was just starting to develop. The Island Authority started a promotion development package and was giving away one hundred foot waterfront lots, either on the Gulfside or Soundside, to those who would go over and build a home. Some of Pensacola's more affluent citizens accepted the offer and built three bedroom, one bath, block homes, most costing less than $5,000.

It had long been a popular belief that the primary reluctance of the public to go to the island in the early days was the necessity of having to cross the only bridge, an old wooden, rickety, high rise that swayed when each vehicle crossed. Many were the times when we knew for sure that our car, packed solid with guys and gals, was headed into the drink.

As the public began to focus on weekend trips to the island, an enterprising entrepreneur built a casino at the south end of the only road where it dead-ended at the Gulf. There were showers, concession stands, short order food and, obviously, beer. Everything needed to entice the public to visit the beach.

This area was the original, the beginning, of what today is a fantastic commercial development throughout all of Santa Rosa Island. But back then "The Casino" was the one and only meeting place. The only place the kids would hangout, the only place on the entire island that was of any interest to them.

Soon after, a long fishing pier extending far into the Gulf was added just to the west of The Casino. From day one it attracted thousands of visitors who longed to fish in deep water; however, fishing was of no interest to Ronnie's group as they willingly settled for beach blankets, radios and cold beer.

AT THE END of his sophomore year, the third day after school was out for the summer, June of '52, began the annual house parties at the beach. As usual, they would start at noon on Friday and end at noon the following Sunday week, thus a full nine days of around the clock partying.

Pensacola High School outlawed fraternities and sororities, but that meant little to these celebrated teens. There were two male and two female "outlaw clubs" which counted as members the most popular boys and girls of the school.

Around midyear the club presidents would get together and agree on the best dates, and when that time arrived each club had rented their own beach house. Dozens of cots and pads were strewn everywhere leaving little walking-around room. But as it seemed, the more crowded the better everyone like it.

Nightly, much of the entertainment at the two fraternity houses centered around card games of blackjack and poker. It was not unusual to find the young men still dealing with the rising sun.

Each evening the sorority sisters fixed something that occasionally resembled a meal. The visiting boys always questioned what was served, but, not being able to decipher, they readily came up with their own name and description for each dish. Most were unmentionable.

Beer, for the most part, was the number one choice, but there was always Early Times, Southern Comfort and Ten High. All was mixed with Coke, never water. Premium booze, such as Jack Daniels, Dewar's, Absolute or Crown Royal, was way too expensive for these $1.00 per hour part-time folks. Even the price of Bud and Miller often forced the students to purchase a cheaper brand. Some had to settle for popular local brews, such as Spearman Beer & Ale or Black Label.

Throughout the day and night the boys would visit back and forth at the two sorority houses. The muffins, very wisely, had adopted a rule among themselves that they would not go to the fraternity houses. It was very simple: if the boys wanted to see them, they would have to come calling.

Every night each sorority had an overnight chaperon who most often was a mother of one of the girls. At the end of each house party season, the girls graded the chaperons and only asked back the following year those who seemed to be most liberal with time limits and rules in general.

It didn't take the boys long to understand just exactly how that worked. They immediately made great friends with every chaperon. Ronnie was always a favorite with these women. Every night he would sketch a freehand drawing of the chaperon on duty and add some personal touch, perhaps an outlandish look or personal trait. He had perfected his drawing talent, but neither he nor his family had any clue from whence it came. Years later, his only son, Vince, would inherit his talent.

Ronnie's persona and outgoing personality gave him the ability to quickly maneuver those around him to his persuasive way of thinking. About this time this special characteristic began to develop at a rapid pace. He impressed the chaperons.

With the constant roaring of rock and roll music from the likes of Little Richard, Clyde McPhatter, The Drifters, Fats Domino, Bo Diddley, Bill Haley and the Comets and dozens of teen-agers trying to be heard above each other, the assigned chaperon would always make an early retreat into her private bedroom and was not seen until time to leave the following morning.

IN THE FIFTIES I had little, if any, drugs to compete with. This would become a massive, an enormous problem in the sixties with the hippy generation, but in the fifties I had the teen-agers all to myself. Back then, as you may imagine, it was much easier to become friends without drugs as competition.

I could consistently count on a long and lasting relationship with the vast majority of those who were starting to party at a young age. Those whom I chose to take under my wing were of my own preference. I could select at will and choose only those I was assured could and would make the very best companions for a long, lasting and continued relationship. I wanted leaders.

Ronnie fought me long and hard over several months. His parents gave up the use of alcohol and partying many years ago and would not have approved had they known of their kids or friends of their kids participating in such.

They believed the atmosphere which they provided within their home was sufficient and all that was necessary for their young, energetic family. Certainly, they would not approve a social life at such an early age, knowing it was absolutely out of the question. This was the viewpoint of many of those I met that summer; consequently, all the partying had to be done away from home. Out of sight and sound of suspicious, prying parents.

I could not comprehend that Ronnie's dad was not aware of some of the partying going on. While he had given up on such, in his heyday he was a tough hombre. After dropping out of high school, he and a long time friend, Wilbur Stokes from Leesburg, had participated in their share of the rough and tumble outside world.

They both were scrappers. Real men, tough as nails. Back in 1932 at the ripe old age of 18, they put together a boxing promotion tour. They traveled the South where they would box any man who would dare get in the ring with them. Depending on what condition they were in after the previous day's bout, the one who had fared best would first crawl into the ring the next day. While one boxed, the other acted as promoter and ticket seller. This duo held the distinction of promoting the very first prize fight ever held in the great state of Texas. While Don King would never have to be concerned about this competition, they were pioneers as such in the boxing world.

Perhaps this trait carried over into Ronnie's genes, a trait that led him, from time to time, to believe he was much tougher than his weight of 145 pounds.

Occasionally, he and a few of his friends would drive over to Gulf Shores for an afternoon of checking out the muffins on the Alabama beach. Their route would take them west on Highway 98 through Foley, then south down a lonely single-lane road to the Gulf.

One very hot Saturday afternoon in July, after a couple of brews in transit, Ronnie and his three buddies arrived at their destination. While they were never interested in starting a commotion, they also never shied away from one. They were always alert, and as it would sometimes happen, not often, but sometimes, they took things out of context way too quickly.

On this steamy day, during a light summer shower, they had gathered under the roof edge of a concession stand. While not meaning to offend anyone, a local beach bum made a comment that was not taken lightly by the visitors. Ronnie, never really hot tempered but often quick to respond, and sometimes in a mouthy way said, "Man, I'll drop you like last week's girl friend if you don't get yore rump outta here."

Now this caused quite a stir among the south Alabama natives who greatly outnumbered the visiting Floridians. Given the seriousness of the situation, our boys decided, very wisely, to bring it on back across the state line to their familiar and more friendly shores. The incident ended just about as quickly as it had began; otherwise, it could have boiled over into a major skirmish very easily. Our boys decided that the Alabama muffins were no better or worse than those on their home turf and certainly not worth a rumble.

IT WAS THIS summer that Ronnie and friends found a brand new place to be entertained. A place that was for sure off limits, including the format which would be completely unacceptable to their families had they known. Pensacola, like all Southern cities, was totally segregated. The city had one black high school, Booker T. Washington, all black, no whites. Pensacola High was all white, no blacks. Everything was segregated with little regard for the phrase, "separate but equal," that would soon become popular jargon among all liberal politicians, but yet not accepted by those of the Deep South.

Anyway, the kids were introduced to a couple of night clubs

around Alcaniz, Belmont and DeVilliers Streets, dead centered in the middle of colored town. While Ronnie's choice of music was geared around his most favorite singer, Hank Williams, another person who would drastically influence his future life, he was always amenable to expanding his preference.

Hubie Brahan had quickly spread the word that black entertainers who were well-known outside of Pensacola were being booked at Abe's 506 club and performing to a packed house each night. The boys just had to be in on this action. During their three visits, and with much concern each time, the group of young white boys ventured into the club and gathered around a table in the very back.

Over the weeks they enjoyed the sounds of Al Hibbler, Roy Hamilton and Louis "Satchmo" Armstrong. While they loved hearing this new and different kind of music, they never totally relaxed enough to enjoy themselves. The tenseness of the atmosphere, whether actual or not, gave them reason to abandon any future performances.

ALTHOUGH WE HAD been friends throughout his last two years of high school, it was not until the summer after he graduated that we started talking almost daily. At first he always called me "Booze," but one night after a long discussion he shortened it to "Boo." From then on "Boo" was the only name he ever used.

WHETHER YOU'RE YOUNG or old it matters not. When a life is suddenly taken from the earth, a life which may have meant little to you until it happened, the feelings and sadness of those left behind are the same.

When someone you loved or admired passes away, someone who had made an impression on your life, either of gigantic proportions or just an insignificant passing moment, when they are no longer around, it begins to register.

Guilt feelings often creep into your waking hours and sometimes haunts your dreams. Could you have done things different around them? Could you have been more attentive towards them? What could you have done better?

If someone dies that you admire and if they are a national

figure, then what if anything could you have done differently? Ronnie's dad had a perspective on death and dying perhaps totally different than many. He absolutely hated going to funerals and always proclaimed that "If you are going to show your respect for someone, do it while they are living, don't wait until their dead." Makes a lot of sense to me.

While much of the country was "sleeping-in" after last night's New Year's Eve celebrations, when they finally began to stir, the morning papers and radios brought the sad news. The world learned of the loss of a 29-year-old entertainer who had earned the respect of millions over the last few short years. While traveling in West Virginia to do a New Year's Eve show, Hank Williams died in the back seat of his Cadillac.

The entertainer was well-known across the coast of northwest Florida as he came here often to fish the lakes and rivers, most of the time with nothing more than a cane pole and rusty coffee can full of silty soil and red wigglers. It was not surprising that he sometimes dropped in at honky-tonks to have a few drinks with the locals. And when not slumming somewhere, he as likely as not was seen hanging out at the San Carlos Hotel in downtown Pensacola, a longtime favorite of his.

Just a few weeks before Hank's death, a local radio celebrity, four-hundred-and-fifty-eight-pound LeRoy Morris, had announced that the entertainer would be appearing at Irwin's Record Shop and would be signing autographs. That afternoon Ronnie and his brother had walked the few blocks to the corner of Garden and Pace Boulevard in hopes of seeing their idol and perhaps getting his signature.

Sure enough there he was. Big as life. The man that every radio station and country deejay across America was talking about. They both were mesmerized, maybe Ronnie more so than Billy, but you would never know because he always kept his feelings and emotions so well hidden. The tall, slim gentleman with sunken cheek bones, wearing a big white hat looked more like a movie star cowboy than a singer. He talked freely with the small crowd, most of whom were much older than the two young boys.

After a few minutes of milling around the store as if looking for a record selection and often stealing glances in his direction, they finally got up the courage to approached him. They offered a nervous hand shake and then stuck a small piece of paper in front of him hoping he would sign. He told them how delighted he was to see them and urged them to tell all their friends about the popularity of his country music. He graciously signed his name and thanked them for purchasing his latest record, a sixty-nine-cent 45 RPM version of "Cold, Cold Heart."

HANK WILLIAMS HAD been a favorite of Ronnie's for a long time. Over the next 27 years Hank Williams would be a constant companion in Ronnie's memory. During the last years of Ronnie's life, he would make many trips to Montgomery to visit Hank's burial site.

LURKING JUST AROUND the corner was the skinny young entertainer who would soon capture the heart and soul of America's youth. It was almost as if a replacement for Hank had been assigned to take his place. Ronnie thought at first that Elvis would never surpass his adulation for the late and great Hank Williams, but very soon he would learn otherwise.

"Virtually every problem that I have observed among youth has been precipitated by alcohol. It is our role to guide, lead and direct our youth to positive and consistent solutions to the major problem in our country. I am grateful that you, through your book "RONNIE," have chosen to do just that.

Coach Bill Snyder, Kansas State

3

THAT MAGIC SEASON OF 1953

RONNIE AND FRED Levin spent the first two weeks of the summer of 1953 doing little more than loafing; going to the beach, getting tanned and generally just having a grand time. Their parents, as if in cahoots with each other and jointly orchestrated, although it wasn't, made their feelings known the Sunday afternoon of the second week of vacation. This year both of these very able young men would indeed find themselves a summer job.

By mid-morning on Monday Ronnie had talked Billy into driving him to Fred's home where they would set out to find employment. This was most certainly going to be a work of art as neither had a real desire to find a job, let alone actually work at one.

It just so happened that the Levin's maid had overheard the dictates of Fred's father demanding he find summer employment. And the day before, she had heard her husband speaking to his nephew about a new, small company which was looking for two strong young men. Thus, the first opportunity of the season for Ronnie and Fred.

They placed a call to Howard's Honey Dipper Service to set up an interview. Bobby Joe Howard insisted that a face-to-face interview was not necessary, that if they wanted the job they were to report to his yard promptly at 8:00 the following morning. When he inquired about dress code requirements, Fred was told that old work clothes would do just fine.

After Fred picked Ronnie up, they set out to find the home office of their new employer. During the ride the conversation of the morning dealt primarily with the question of what in the world was a "honey dipping service." Neither had the faintest idea.

The directions given the previous day were to come to the south end of "C" Street, down to the water's edge, and look to the right. There they would find a small wooden building and a couple of trucks. Arriving a few minutes before the appointed hour, they introduced themselves to Bobby Joe who in turn introduced them to someone he called "Moppy."

With this seeming not to be the best neighborhood in the city, Fred was skeptical about leaving his mother's car, a huge '52 black four-door Buick sedan complete with five big designer holes in the side of each fender, unattended. However, he had little choice.

Still unfazed and completely in the dark as to the duties of an "assistant honey dipper," the boys climbed into the passenger's side of the worn out truck, whose seat springs had found their way through the dirty brown imitation leather covers. But Moppy had seen to it that their pale rear ends were properly protected by a half dozen or more dingy towels strategically placed thereon.

The first call of the day was in the Ensley area of Escambia County. After locating the home, Moppy knocked on the front door and informed a teen-age girl to let her folks know they had arrived and would be working in the yard on the east side of the house.

He backed the truck down the driveway and told the boys to get the two flat-edged shovels that were hanging upside down behind a metal band on the passenger side of the truck. One was for Fred and one for Ronnie.

With a quarter-inch metal rod, perhaps three feet long, Moppy located the four corners of the concrete slab and instructed the boys to shovel off the grass which had grown over the top. Suddenly, it became quite clear to these two new entrepreneurs exactly what their job duties entailed.

Within minutes the six inches of grass and dirt had been removed. Moppy then backed the truck closer and swung a small boom mounted on the rear of the truck into place directly over the slab. He next connected two cables, one to each end of steel sleeves that had been built into the concrete top and protruded outward for the purpose intended. The heavy concrete lid was slowly lifted and set aside on the ground.

"Now, you boys get hold o' that rubber hose and bring it over here."

"You mean the whole thing?" inquired Fred.

"Well, no. Just the end of it. Unroll it, and bring the end here."

They did exactly what was asked of them, then took several steps backward, completely out of the way. To the fullest measure they both now knew for certain their duties as an "assistant honey dipper."

Their observation and personal predicament was nauseating, but the sounds they heard were even more so than the sight. The old gas engine, with its busted exhaust pipe, coupled with the grunts and groans coming from the sucking action of the eight-inch "honey dipper" hose was almost unbearable.

When the machine had removed all the sludge that it was capable of getting, next came an unbelievable task. Moppy slid into a pair of what the boys only recognized to be waders for the purpose of fly fishing. Then, very carefully, he sat on the ground at the edge of the open hole and rotated his body so that both legs were hanging over the side and into the almost empty concrete septic tank.

With his strong hands resting on the ground on each side of his body, he eased himself down into the tank where the remaining thicker sludge completely covered the top of both boots.

"Ronnie, go to the back of the truck, and bring me that galvanized metal bucket. It's in the wooden box just on the front side of the pump engine."

Ronnie hastened to do just as directed but had little interest in whatever the next step would be.

Moppy took the bucket and, bending over, scrapped it along the bottom of the tank, making a dreadful, muffled, echoing sound. With the bucket full, he lifted it upwards and said, "Fred, take this and pour it into the top of the drum on the back of the truck."

"No. No, no, no. That's it, man. I quit. There ain't no way I'm gonna let nobody hand me any crap."

Within seconds the boys bolted from the yard and were last seen hitchhiking south toward town.

Two days later both of them found part-time work as salesmen at the National Shirt Shop on the corner of Palafox and Garden Streets in Downtown Pensacola.

EVERY ONE OF the PHS Tiger team mates suffered long and hard through their sophomore and junior years. They practiced intensely, gave it their all and paid their dues. Still, their playing time was limited. But this year Head Coach Jim Scoggins and his two top assistants, Shorty Sneed and Punk Gorday, knew the patience and persistence of the players had paid off; their time was nearing. They had a gut feeling down deep inside that the 1953 team was going to be something special. They thought there was an opportunity to go all the way.

In the spring of that year, I was most pleased to read in the *Pensacola News* where sports columnist Jerry Mock in his column, "The Mocking Word," predicted that the 1953 Pensacola High School football team had tremendous potential. His comments came on the heel of their spring intrasquad contest.

In that game on April 17th, Ronnie, my new friend, did himself proud. His Maroon squad beat the White team 21-7. Ronnie scored two of the three touchdowns, one an 85-yard kick-off return and threw the third, a fancy-dan, Harry Gilmore style jump pass to Pee Wee Cain. He rushed for 73 yards and completed four of six passes for another 59, for a total of 217 yards. Head Coach Jim Scoggins noted, "A game like this can make a boy into a man overnight. He played a great game tonight."

While the paper heaped praise on little Eddie Gebara for his ball-carrying ability and the extra point plunge by fullback Ed Sears, their dual combination did not generate enough power to keep their White team in the game. The paper equally touted the effort of Oliver Nellums for completing all three PAT's for the Maroon team.

The game was much better played than was last year's with several freshmen giving good accounts of themselves. David Hudson, Manning Hitt, Lamar Rawson, Leo Flynn and Marvin Cornwell all performed well.

Over the summer the small group of close-knit friends partied hard at the beach but kept in mind a commitment to themselves. They had made a pact that they were going to be a great football team. A team with a single goal. And that goal was to accept nothing from themselves short of winning the state championship. The 1953 season might very well be the magic year that Coach Scoggins had been dreaming about for his Pensacola High School Fighting Tigers. A dream that had been with him since leaving the coaching ranks of Vanderbilt University four years earlier.

THREE WEEKS BEFORE the beginning of the new school year the team was well into long afternoon practices. After two weeks of conditioning and individual work, the players had launched into their scrimmage sessions in earnest. They would face their opening opponent on September 18th, Bolles Academy of Jacksonville.

The afternoon of the game the students gathered at a pep rally in the stadium, a great turnout. You could feel the excitement, the electricity; the smell of fall football was in the air. The band played, cheerleaders pumped up the crowd and the majorettes were at their best. Mr. McCord, the principal, quieted the students and after a few remarks introduced Coach Scoggins. Being a man of action but few words, his remarks were more brief than the principal's.

"Thank you Mr. McCord. Your comments were most kind. And thank each of you for being with us today. The band, the majorettes, the cheerleaders, we are all a team. A team if we work together, and I mean work hard together, we can be successful not only tonight but the entire season."

The crowd of students went wild with his comments. He continued, "We have a tough schedule this year. But our team is ready. We are up for the occasion." Again, another standing ovation. "If we can stay healthy, keep our boys off the injury list, we have the potential of going all the way. Thank you for being here. I hope to see all of you tonight".

With that, the principal made a final comment and dismissed the students for the day. But the band continued its play, and most of the students hung around to listen. The players and coaches, sitting as a group, remained for a few minutes in appreciation of the band, then filed off into the dressing room for a final skull session before the opening game of the magic season.

THE TIGERS WOULD be operating from the split "T." Their veteran club, sprinkled with a new, well-polished group of young freshmen up from the junior high ranks, was roaring to get it on. Among the freshmen who were expected to add much this year was Manning Hitt, a 200-pound center from Warrington Junior High, David Hudson, a 182-pound end from Clubbs, and Lamar Rawson, a 157-pound halfback from Brent.

Coach Scoggins was pleased that Ronnie, his starting quarterback, was again in shape and weighing in at 147 pounds after being down to a puny 137 over the summer. In the morning paper the coach described his line as big and strong and the backfield as very, very potent. The running game would be led by huge, hard-running fullback Ed Sears and the passing attack by Ronnie. Other offensive backs, with great potential and who were primed and expected to have a good game, were Eddie Gebara, Clyde Vaughn, Gayle Winchester, Glen Barton, David Telhiard and Harold Bell.

THE *PENSACOLA JOURNAL* reported in its headline, "Tigers Take Smashing Victory Over Bolles Academy." All in all, it wasn't much of a game, but in classic form Pensacola High won 44-0.

After the first string backfield of Ed Sears, Ronnie and Clyde Vaughn all scored in the first quarter, the reserves began taking the field. Gayle Winchester tossed a perfect touchdown pass to Lamar Rawson, Ronnie returned to complete one to David Hudson for a another score and Rawson scampered down the sideline for still another. The final score came near the end of the game when Glen Barton scored on a ten-yard option run around his right end.

Coach Scoggins was pleased with what he saw but was quick to point out, "That was just our first game. We got a long way to go. If you don't think so, look at who we will be facing in the coming weeks."

Ronnie and friends were pleased with their performance but concerned for one of their own. Lonnie Webster had to be carried from the field late in the game. Still, the adrenalin was flowing, and they all were sky high. For those who had been members of the conquering Maroon squad during the spring game, it was just a continuation of the winning spirit they had already experienced, except on a much higher scale. The entire team was cocky and ready to take on the world.

After the game the athletes headed out Scenic Highway to Mamma's Drive Inn. Marie Enzor, the owner, and Maude, her trusted friend and right hand assistant, always listened to the game on the radio and waited patiently to welcome the players and their muffins, the finest muffins on campus. Some were cheerleaders, some majorettes; all were the cream of the crop. Only the choicest of ladies for these special young men. With a few beers under their belt and a couple of hours of conversation, sprinkled with a bit of bragging while completely replaying the game, they headed down the road to the Scenic Terrace where they again would have to convince Mr. Jordan they were of age.

THE PANAMA CITY Bay High Tornadoes felt they had the right stuff to defeat the Tigers, but their hopes were short-lived. In an overflowed stadium of more than 7,500, the Pensacola Tigers continued their winning streak by handing the Tornadoes a 27-6 thrashing at Tiger Stadium.

The *Pensacola Journal* headlined its sports page with "Sears & Company Wreck Bay High Tornadoes." Giant fullback Ed Sears scored two touchdowns, one a 71-yard romp inside the right end and a 49-yard gallop straight up the middle. He set up a third touchdown by rushing over center for 37 yards. Swift halfback Eddie Gebara returned a kick for a 75-yard touchdown just three minutes before the end of the game, sending the PHS fans home happy. They were also both pleased and disappointed with his 57-yard touchdown earlier in the game that was called back because of an offensive penalty on the Bengals.

It wasn't much of a game for my buddy Ronnie. He fumbled three times.

During the next week the confidence was evident. Every team member knew they were on a roll. A roll that just might win them the state championship if they could keep focused and stay healthy. Time and again the coaches continued to warn them not to get too cocky, warning over and over that "Any old mule can kick down a barn."

A small inner circle of teammates was always found together; hardly would you see one without the others. But now, something was changing; something new had been added. Their walk, a new mannerism magnified, a new and different step, a new gait. It mattered not where they were seen—in the halls of school or mingling in their social life—everywhere they ventured, their walk seemed to take on a new special form, a new perspective, a cock-of-the-walk attitude. The walk of a big, spry, patriarchal and well-seasoned Rhode Island Red Rooster.

I made it my business to keep an eye on every last one of them. Throughout the day they would strut down the halls between classes and at noon saunter into the cafeteria where they and their muffins would gather at their own designated table. Everywhere they went, they strutted. What a perfect name, "the strutters."

WITH NO LOSSES to fret over, the Tigers were awaiting the Louisville, Kentucky, Colonels. Again, Pensacola High School stadium was packed. After a fierce offensive attack the Tigers came away dominating their visitors, 42-6. As usual, the offensive backs got all the press, but the coaches knew their defense was awesome, especially the efforts of massive Max Baxter. Big Ed Sears really romped, scoring three touchdowns, one a 19-yard trot, another for 54 yards and still a third, a beautiful sprint of 60 yards. Eddie Gebara was again outstanding with two touchdowns, and Tiger defensive back Frank Martin intercepted a pass and returned it 33 yards for still another score. The educated toe of Oliver Nellums was perfect all evening. All six extra points were dead center of the uprights.

Ronnie completed three of five passes for a total of 90 yards, a respectable showing for the quarterback who turned eighteen the day before.

The Tigers were still undefeated. Throughout the week, over and over, at practice or while passing the players in the hall, the coaches continued to preach and to warn them about not letting their heads get too big. The season was a long way from being over, and it only took one loss and they would be back among those just dreaming of winning the state title.

Ronnie's perception of Pensacola High School Coaches "Punk" Gorday and Shorty Sneed after Coach Gorday's squad defeated Coach Sneed's in the 1953 spring game.

Ronnie as quarterback of PHS in 1953.

The 1953 PHS football team.

Above: The coaches of 1953: Ralph Sneed, Bryant "Punk" Gorday, Head Coach Jim Scoggins, John Johnson and Bill Showalter. Left: Ronnie's sketch of PHS Head Coach Jim Scoggins.

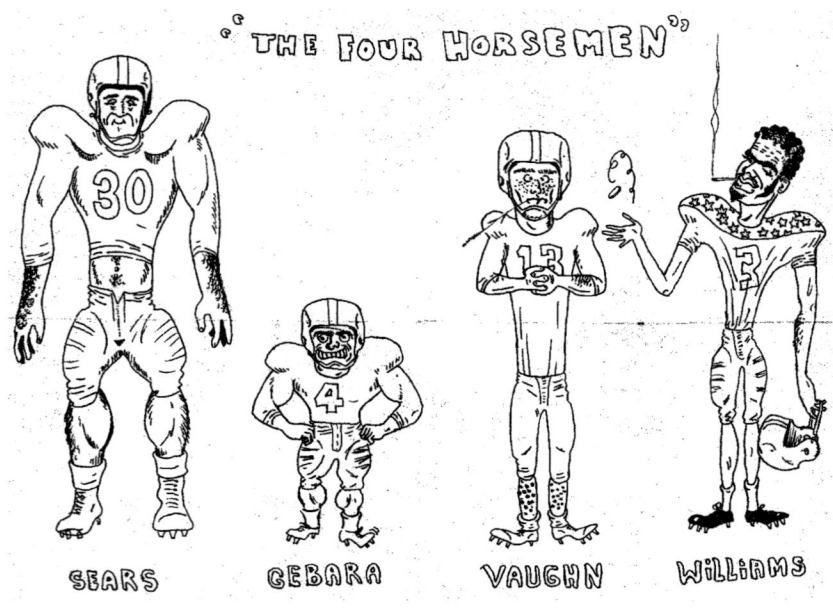

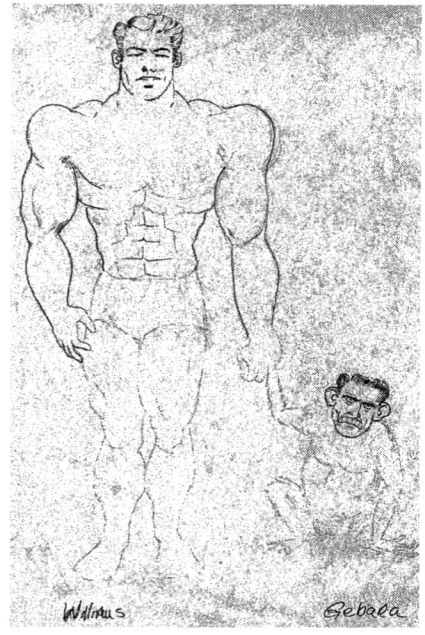

Above: Self sketch of the Four Horsemen of the 1953 PHS State Champion Football Team. Left: A self sketch of himself holding PHS teammate Eddie Gebera's hand.

He Ran 68 Yards of Tiger History

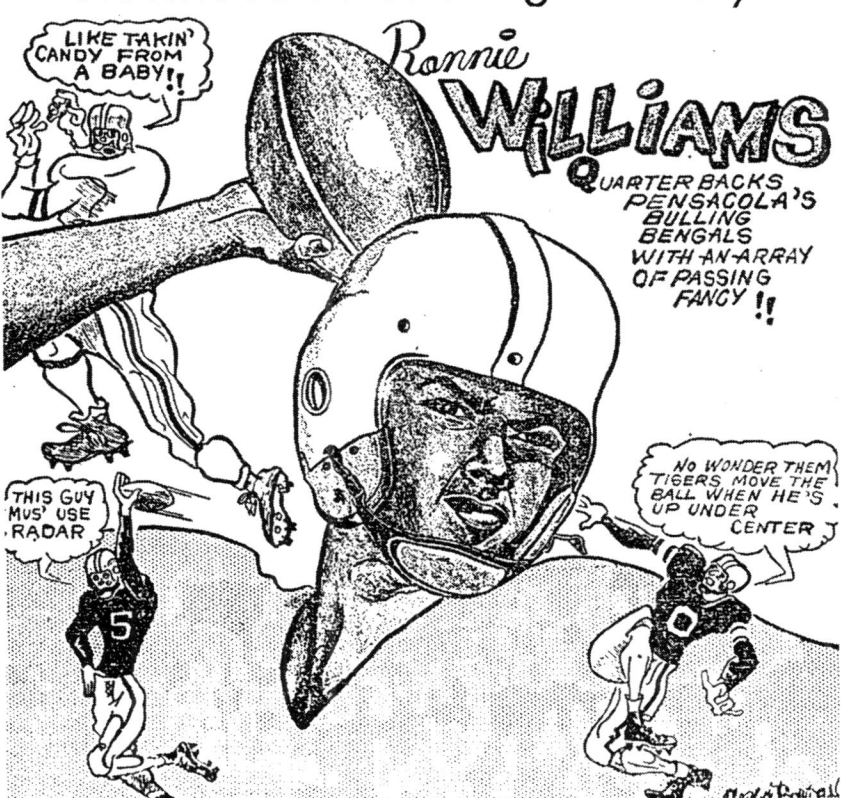

A drawing by Earl Bowden in the November 10, 1953,
Pensacola News Journal.

Self sketch of himself carrying the ball.

Above: Ronnie winning the 100-yard dash at the PHS track in 1954. Left: Ronnie's 1952 sketch of Abe Levin, Fred's father. Mr. Levin was a favorite of Ronnie's. As noted, he dubbed him "The Prince of Palafox."

Although the game was three weeks away, Coach Scoggins was much concerned and afraid that his team was looking ahead to the mighty showdown with the dreaded Jesuit Blue Jays from New Orleans, the state of Louisiana champions. He feared his team was not mentally or physically preparing itself smartly for the next opponent. And to make things worse, during the week of practice three key players were injured and not expected to see action. Eddie Gebara, Frank Martin and Hurley Langford were all sidelined.

HOWEVER, AS WAS becoming commonplace, the Tigers romped again, beating the Dothan High Eagles 39-0. This week's sports page headlines read, "RONNIE WILLIAMS STEALS SPOTLIGHT."

Sears took the kickoff on his 30 and returned it to his 41. Ronnie ran a couple of sneaks, then tossed to Gayle Winchester, making his first appearance as a starter, for 19 yards and a first down. Sears picked up another first on a 13-yard plunge inside his left end.

Rawson took a pitch-out for four, Sears went over the left side for six and Ronnie, on the option, kept the ball, swept shallow around his left end and with excellent blocking went 21 yards for the first score. Nellums' extra point was wide. Only five minutes had been used on the clock.

Dothan was unable to get any offense going and booted the ball dead on Pensacola's 20. After good gains by Vaughn and Winchester, Sears galloped 48 yards. Vaughn scored from the five, and Nellums' kick was good. Sears did not have near as good a game as in previous contests but did score twice. One was a touchdown pass from Ronnie, and a few plays later he set up a third touchdown with a 30-yard gallop straight up the middle of the Eagle line.

Ronnie passed for a total of 77 yards, one for a touchdown thrown to Pee Wee Cain. Freshman Lamar Rawson intercepted a pass and carried it 48 yards for a touchdown, and Clyde Vaughn completed the Tiger scoring with a five-yard plunge.

About the middle of the following week, a call came to Coach Scoggins from the Associated Press. The *Miami Herald* had voted his Tigers the number one high school football team in the state.

When he announced the result in the dressing room before the day's practice, the term went wild. Ronnie and his strutters could hardly contain themselves. Scoggins gave them a few minutes to celebrate, then quickly made them understand their poll position could be short-lived.

This was the first time in the history of the state poll that the Pensacola High School Tigers had been ranked number one, and the big show was just around the corner. Their number one ranking set up the next game between the top ranked team in Florida and the top ranked team in Louisiana.

The afternoon pep rally was enormous. Every student in school was squarely behind the Tigers and was eager to show it. The band was performing at top notch perfection. The majorettes had put together a brand new routine, and the cheerleaders seemed even more energized, if that was possible. School officials were expecting more than 10,000, an overflow crowd. If their prediction came true, it would be the largest turnout for a high school game in the history of Pensacola, the oldest city in the United States.

The Blue Jays arrived in town Thursday evening. The two high school football giants were prepared and anxious for the showdown. Since being named Florida's top high school team by both the *Miami Herald* and the Dunkel system, the Tigers were on top of the world. Ready for bear. But were they ready for Louisiana's best, the Jesuit High School Blue Jays?

The two teams had met on seven previous occasions over the years, and the Tiger had yet to come away victorious. The Blue Jays had won 24-6 in 1946, 19-0 in 1947, 33-7 in 1949, 8-7 in 1950, 33-7 in 1951 and 20-7 last year.

Only the most avid of local fans gave Scoggins's team an even chance for victory. The downtown Pensacola armchair quarterbacks had predicted the Tigers to be a thirteen-point underdog.

THE PENSACOLA HIGH fans knew they had witnessed one of the best, if not the best, game ever played by a high school in the state of Florida. The Saturday morning edition of the *Pensacola News* told the story. A great defensive battle. Both teams in the finest of shape. The story was long, but the only part that really mattered was the touchdown and extra point by PHS.

"From his own 40-yard line, quarterback Ronnie Williams took the snap, turned and faked the ball to his right halfback, Eddie Gebara, then scampered down the left side hugging the white chalk line for 68 yards. As the maroon and white jerseys began to gather, each Jesuit High player, one by one, found themselves grounded as if a giant bowling ball were attacking a line of pins. The blocking was led by fullback Ed Sears, Y.B. Patterson and Lonnie Webster. With the path being cleared, the PHS quarterback knew that he was on his way to pay dirt.

"Crossing into the end zone, the game was then tied at 6 to 6. Pensacola High School was back in the game against their annual arch rival.

"With time running out, if the game was to be won it would have to come from the toe of Oliver Nellums. The snap. The ball spiraled towards the holder, reserve quarterback Harold Bell, who was kneeling and patiently awaiting the pigskin. The kick. Up and away, somewhat wobbling and near the left side upright. Good! Pensacola High 7, Jesuit 6. Ninety-three seconds remained on the clock. The Tigers would defeat Louisiana's best."

The crowd simply went wild! Coach Scoggins and his assistant coaches led the excitement. Every fan in the stadium was on his feet. And none could have been more jubilant than Ronnie's brother and his seatmate friend, Jere Tolton. Both were ecstatic. The crowd had exceeded the expected sellout prediction of more than 10,000 in attendance, including 1,000 tickets designated for standing room only. And everyone was up and roaring.

This was a normal fall football evening at Tiger Stadium. Northwest Florida, as did all of the deep South, staunchly supported local high school football teams. In Escambia County there were only two other high schools, Pensacola Catholic and Tate High in Gonzalez. Although each was much smaller than PHS, their supporters were equally energetic and gave fantastic and faithful support to all of their sports programs.

The following week Jesuit remained atop its state poll even after the disappointing loss to the Tigers. The *New Orleans Times-Picayune* even named Dominic "Mickey" LaNass, who succeeded in peeling off impressive yardage against the Tigers, as the player of the week.

AFTER THE GAME it was a time to celebrate. The strutters and their friends again headed for Mamma's. Ronnie and Fred Levin, being the gamblers they were, had decided to stake their evening chances on their luck and did so this night without a muffin in tow. As anticipated, their gamble soon paid off when they saw two of the cheerleaders driving slowly down the dirt drive and headed to a favorite parking place under a giant oak tree overlooking the bluffs of Escambia Bay. After the group tired of visiting back and forth between vehicles, they talked the girls into going with them down the road to the Scenic Terrace. They agreed but insisted on taking their own car.

As it would happen, and I learned early on it happened quite often, Ronnie made a comment to his date that did not sit too well with her. Never being someone to back down from a confrontation from another man, he was always quick to walk away from any adversity between himself and a muffin. He told her to kiss off and abruptly left the table, headed for the water front patio for a Pall Mall and another Lord Calvert.

"What you doing out here all alone by yourself?" I asked.

Quickly turning around, he questioned, "Who is that? Who said that?"

"It's just me. I want to be your friend," I responded.

From the dark patio Ronnie asked, "Who said that? Fred, you out here?" At once he realized that he was by himself but asked again, "Who was that?"

"Listen, Ronnie, I just want to be your friend. You can't see me. Just be quiet and listen."

"Man, are you like that rabbit in that stupid movie? You know, the one that Jimmy Stewart talked to all the time."

"You could say that. So you didn't like the movie, huh?"

"No, I didn't. I met that Stewart person at an open house at Eglin Air Force Base a couple of years ago. You know that he was a general in the Air Force and flew those big old airplanes?"

"I know that. I know a lot. I will teach you a lot."

"Man, I can't believe that I am talking with someone that isn't here. This is silly. This is sick."

"Ronnie, relax. I will be your friend. Just pay attention to me. And for sure, don't tell anyone, don't ever tell anyone that we have talked. Is that a deal?"

"I don't know. This is weird. Man, this is really weird."

"You got to promise me that you will not tell anyone. I will be your friend and help you, but you have got to promise me that you will not tell anyone of our secret. Agreed?"

"Yeah. Yeah, I guess so."

"Okay. That's great. Now, go back inside and behave yo'self. That's a great looking lady you're with tonight. You need to be nicer to Tennie. She's special. Be kind to her; be kind to all your friends. That's the only way to get to the top in this world. Let that be my first lesson to you."

AFTER AN OPEN date weekend the Tigers traveled to Birmingham to meet the Ensley High Yellow Jackets. The game was played at Legion Field with fewer than 2,500 in attendance. Perhaps the lack of local fans was due to the Tigers remaining atop the Florida poll, although by only three points due to an idle week. The local Birmingham quarterback club had given the winning nod to Ensley simply because the members were under the impression that Alabama high school football was stronger than what was played in Florida. Their suspicions and predictions were short-lived.

The Tigers were at full strength with Lonnie Webster and Gayle Winchester coming off the injured list. Ensley's record was 4 and 4 against teams in the same league as PHS. Twice in previous years the Tigers with an unbeaten record had faced the Yellow Jackets, and both times the Birmingham team had spoiled the season for the Bengals.

The game was played in almost perfect weather. The powerful Tigers scored points in every quarter and were victorious to the tune of 22-0. They rolled up an impressive 240 yards on the ground and 65 by air while holding Ensley to 69 on the ground and 54 through passes.

Midway of the first quarter the Tigers ate up 82 yards in 12 hungry gulps. After two passes, a 25-yarder to Eddie Gebara and a 22-yarder to Pee Wee Cain, Ronnie scored on a quarterback sneak from the one, and Oliver Nellums' kick was good. Max Baxter recovered a fumble, then big Ed Sears found pay dirt with only seconds remaining on the clock before the half. Nellums' kick missed the mark. Early in the third quarter lineman Y.B. Patterson, a ball hawk all year, recovered a fumble at the six and, as is every lineman's dream, crossed into the end zone for a touchdown. Nellums booted his second point of the night, and the Tigers led 20-0. A safety in the final minutes gave PHS the win, 22-0.

The Tigers remained undefeated not only due to their dynamic offense but also their time-proven stingy defense. After disposing of Ensley High, the Tigers were now undefeated in seven straight games. Their final test would come the last weekend of November in Tallahassee at Doak Campbell Stadium.

THE TIGERS WOULD face the Leon Lions and their great quarterback Bud Williamson, who many say is the best signal caller Leon High has ever fielded. Aiding Williamson in the backfield would be a trio of halfbacks, Jack Givens, Blair Culpepper and Billy Watson. These potent and talented players were the reason for the success of Leon throughout the year. They had a 7-1-1 record with their single loss at the hands of the Tornadoes of Panama City Bay.

Head Coach Bill Armstrong had his team prepared for the visiting Tigers and was quoted earlier in the week, "We want to score on the Tigers so the emphasis this week in practice has been on polishing our running and passing game."

Before 6,500 fans the Lions played the Tigers hard throughout the first half. Within four minutes of the first period Bud Williamson slipped around right end and raced 35 yards into the end zone. Laurie Hosford's point after was wide. Leon led 6-0.

The Tigers came right back with Ronnie throwing to Eddie Gebara, who took the ball down inside the Lions' 20. Sears carried to the one, and Ronnie bucked center for the score. Nellums' kick was good, and the Tigers led for the first time, 7-6.

Showing little effectiveness by either club, each turned the ball over twice. Then Ronnie, almost caught 20 yards behind the line, passed to Sears who toted the pigskin into glory land. Nellums' kick was wide, but the Tigers had increased their lead to 13-6.

Williamson returned the Tigers kick-off back to their 35, and after nine plays they were again knocking on the Tigers' door. The Leon quarterback completed a nice screen pass to Bill Watson for the touchdown. The point after was missed. The Tigers led 13-12 at half.

Leading by only a single point, the Tigers were headed for mental castigation and perhaps light bruises from their coaches. In the dressing room Scoggins laid it on the line. Play better or lose the state title. The tongue trashing apparently had a positive impact. The Tigers were a different breed when they returned to the field. This half they completely outclassed Leon, a very good team, by leaps and bounds.

Lamar Rawson got it in gear with an 80-yard reverse run around left end for a touchdown, Nellums' kick was good. A Leon pass by Jack Givens, intended for Bobby Malloy, was intercepted by the Tigers' Leo Flynn, who raced 24 yards into the end zone; the kick was wide.

PENSACOLA HIGH SCHOOL Tigers left the field that glorious evening as proud owners of a perfect undefeated season. Their explosive offense had generated a total of 227 points for the season while their frugal defense had allowed only 37.

"Thank you for your concern regarding an issue that is important to the welfare of both young and old. It is critical that we eliminate this tragic disruption of life from the habits of the young. Alcohol abuse is a no-win situation for all involved, so I share your call to action. I have always asked young persons to inform me of what it is that they can perform better intoxicated than sober. To this day, other than foolish behavior, they have not given me anything positive. Alcohol abuse does not allow you to move forward in life, and if that is the case, we are better off avoiding its deadly trap. I hope this short statement will provide you with ammunition to enlighten one person to save a precious life. Please continue your valuable work."

Coach Tyrone Willingham, University of Notre Dame

4

HEARING VOICES

THE 1953 SEASON had truly been a magic year for the fighting Tigers. At season's end they were crowned the state of Florida High School Champions. The Tigers received 16 first place votes out of a possible 27 and rolled up 242 total points in the poll. In second place was Jacksonville Jackson, which drew only two first place votes and finished with 231 total points. Coming in third was unbeaten Manatee High of Bradenton with six first place votes and 211 points.

This special team had a multitude of stars. Four of the starters made All State, two from the backfield and two from the line. Fullback Ed Sears won additional honors by being named to the Little All American High School Team.

These were sincerely exciting times for this talented group of athletes, both on the field and in their personal lives. They were pursued continuously by the prettiest, most popular muffins on campus and invariably had all the attention they could possibly want. And after this season's performance, the attention was probably deserved, Strutters or not.

With each win, Pensacola merchants freely awarded gifts to the players who were most instrumental for the week's victory, those who displayed outstanding performance during the game. Items of clothes, sports equipment, meals and often an automobile dealer would loan the use of a convertible for a full week. You name it, and they received. All were spoiled.

This was a place in time when few concerned themselves with

all the rules and regulations which now have plagued, confused and in general ruined the spirit of high school sports, not to mention college athletic programs.

After days of receiving countless accolades from the city of Pensacola, businessmen and women, social and professional clubs, the magic season of 1953 and its celebrations finally came to an end.

Throughout their lives this group of young, outstanding athletes and their seasoned coaches would cherish these precious memories. Embedded deep in a warm and very special mental compartment, they would forever stay. No one could ever take away this genuinely exceptional and extraordinary experience. Hundreds of interesting stories would be treasured and some day shared with their children and grandchildren.

THE WEEK BEFORE PHS let out for the Christmas Holiday Season, three of the four All State Players had signed their college scholarships. On Tuesday, December 15th, Y.B. Patterson committed to attend the University of Florida. On the same day the University of Alabama head recruiting coach, Bubber Nesbitt, signed six players from Panama City. The next day while working his way across the Florida Panhandle he inked Max Baxter to a four-year commitment. On Thursday Florida Head Coach Bob Woodruff flew into Pensacola, and in front of *Pensacola News Journal* sportswriters and cameramen signed fullback Ed Sears.

Ronnie still had not made his choice among those who had shown an interest. With Christmas vacation starting the next day, he promised himself to make a decision before returning to school on January 4th, but for now he had seventeen days of party time.

Over the next three nights he had been invited to five parties and additionally had promised, although he could change his mind as easy as a check off play at the line of scrimmage, to take a muffin to the Annual Noel Dance.

ON TUESDAY, THREE days before Christmas, he, as he would sometimes do—and do even more in later years—took an afternoon all to himself. This day he would borrow his brother's Pontiac and drive out old Gulf Beach Highway and sit awhile at a small, friendly lounge. A quiet place that he and his friends had frequented many times earlier in the year before the start of football practice.

The lounge, Jerry Jordan's Nut Club, sometimes was open, sometimes closed. Obviously, the choice of hours was that of the owner and depended on whether or not he wanted to work that day. Just behind the lounge was a long, single-story, dingy, yellow, concrete block building that appeared to be divided into six motel rooms. It too was open on occasion.

This afternoon Ronnie was in luck. When he pulled off the highway onto the dirt parking area on the southwest side of the building, he saw two cars. At least he wouldn't be alone. One of the cars was parked in an awkward position to give the driver a better opportunity of perhaps not drowning when he stepped from his vehicle near one of the many mud holes. The second, a newly repainted bright red 1948 Cadillac four-door sedan, complete with a Rebel flag tied to its antenna, was parked parallel to the building. It almost blocked the only entrance.

With all the windows down in his brother's car, he knew immediately from the piano racket escaping from the open front door that one of his summertime acquaintances was in the midst of entertaining whoever would listen. Putting two and two together, the Caddy had to be his.

Over the past summer, Ronnie and friends had enjoyed spending a few hours at the Nut Club, a name that fit perfectly well with the entertainment. They got a real kick from this man of the South, a heavy cigarette smoking, hard drinking, singing, joke-telling piano player who would sit around with them telling stories and occasionally joining them in a game of pool.

During the last few years Dave had been meandering across the upper Gulf Coast from Texas to Panama City playing for anyone who would gather around. And most of the time just for the cost of a fresh drink or a pack of smokes. As long as he had these two crutches, he would play for hours on end. His variety of songs, few serious, most not, mixed well with his down-home stories, fables, myths and Southern humor. In a few years his brand of comedy would find its proper place on several LP albums which gained heavy air play on radio stations throughout the South. "Brother Dave" Gardner had arrived!

After a couple of hours of steady piano banging, Brother Dave let the thin crowd of two know that he was going to take a short break but with a promise that he would, like MacArthur, return. He sauntered down to the southernmost end unit of the motel, leaving his Caddy, his rolling billboard, parked haphazardly at the front door.

The barkeep, who liked to be called "H.D.," short for Haroldean, although the regulars was sure it stood for "heavy duty," was a short, plump woman of about 50 and the perfect fit for a leading character in any Western movie which might feature a shotgun-totin' granny. Her nerves, perhaps understandably, couldn't stand the sounds of silence after the piano commotion was over, so she lifted a few coins from the cash register and slipped them into an old amber-colored, plastic-faced and somewhat corroded Wurlitzer. Her selections were a mix of pure country with artists like Red Foley, Faron Young, Hank Snow, Sonny James, Kitty Wells and, of course, Hank Williams.

After the last song, a scratchy rendition of Foley's "Peace In The Valley," with little more to do, Ronnie picked up a cue stick, then rearranged the triangle of loosely racked balls. The old table had almost seen its better days. You couldn't place your finger on any spot around the green padded bumper rail without touching a brown cigarette burn mark, some deep. Occasionally, a ball would begin a stroll on its own with no obvious destination.

The only other customer, a rancher type, maybe a young 40ish, wearing dirty, high heel boots and paint-spattered blue jeans, introduced himself as "Dub." He challenged Ronnie to shoot a game for a beer. It was an even toss up after a six pack of games when Dub suddenly announced that he thought he had heard his wife calling.

Not quite ready to go home and certainly not in the mood to get into heavy conversation with H.D., Ronnie chose to linger a bit longer. Since no one was spending the afternoon on the worn out sofa, just scarcely out of reach of the end of a cue stick should someone feel the need to challenge the table, he made himself at home. He slipped two buffalos into the jukebox and selected a couple of tear-jerkers. Hank belting out "Your Cheating Heart" followed by Kitty Wells letting loose with "I Didn't Know God Made Honky Tonk Angels."

With his old brown leather slouch hat shading his eyes and a dingy, off-white pillow, proclaiming in bright red letters "Jesus Saves," resting between his head and the wooden arm of the sofa, he finally found a relaxing spot and even appeared to be comfortable. Maybe he would go to the Noel dance after all came his first real thought of the day.

After Hank and Kitty put everyone to sleep, the place fell quiet at last. Ronnie's mind went immediately into gear. "Boo, where'm I going to go to college? I gotta make up my mind and quick."

"Where you wanna go? LSU? Florida? Memphis State? Furman? Alabama? Where?"

"I don't want to go anywhere that I'll have to warm the bench. I want to go where I can play. You know that. I'm not into sitting around on some old cold bench for two or three years."

"What about those three junior college schools you looked at out in Mississippi? You interested in those?"

"Don't really care to be in Mississippi. Nowhere in Mississippi. I thought the letter from Furman was somewhat interesting. You know that part where the coach said, "They'll take care of anything I need. Just ask.""

"Yeah, that was something. Why not try them?"

"We'll see, Boo. We'll see."

RONNIE CAVED IN, as few thought he would, and took Teenie, his front-runner, number one muffin to the dance. He and his buddies looked like fashion models, dressed properly for the occasion in formal tux. Throughout the evening the Strutters had great laughs each time big Ed Sears wandered anywhere close to little Eddie Gebara. The big man and the little man looked completely out of place dressed in their penguin suits.

CHRISTMAS MORNING CAME early at the Williams' home. Ronnie, Billy and Sandi were awake before dawn, just moments after Santa had left, leaving his half-eaten cookie and an empty glass which had held warm milk. Although Sandi was eleven years old, Daddy Williams thrilled at continuing the ritual of ole Saint Nick.

The close family, as usual, genuinely enjoyed their traditional Christmas Day festivities. After opening their gifts around the tree, a call would be placed to both sets of grandparents and to a few close friends. Coffee, milk, sweets and ambrosia would be the breakfast menu followed by a huge lunch at high noon. Nearing mid-afternoon the first of two annual knocks which Daddy Williams always anticipated was finally heard at the back door. The first to arrive was "Raspberry," a colored man who had worked for his company many years. Within the hour came the second knock, another colored employee, Robert Williams, with yet a longer employment history.

Each year Daddy Williams knew they would show up just like clockwork. They came around for their gifts, always something to eat, something that their entire family could enjoy. The basket would include a ham, turkey, fruit cake, fresh fruits and nuts and always several links of country smoked sausage.

THE STRUTTERS ENJOYED the Holidays and didn't look forward to the 4th of January. This year they knew they had earned a long Christmas vacation since each of them had really put out a tremendous effort throughout the football season.

New Year's Eve would find the close group of friends at a beach house they rented to celebrate the coming of 1954. They and their favorite muffins would celebrate with loud music, drinks and a cookout on the white pristine sands of the Gulf of Mexico. For several hours toasts were offered by one and then another. They toasted everything that you could possibly imagine. It would be the start of a great new year, and everyone was looking forward to taking the next step out into the big wide world that awaited them.

THE FOLLOWING JUNE Ronnie and his teammates graduated from Pensacola High, few with scholastic honors, but one hundred percent graduated. As noted in the school annual, Ronnie's classmates had voted him "best looking."

I knew I was on the right track. What more could I want in a friend? A high school All State Quarterback, superb baseball player, holder of the record as the fastest sprinter in the state in the 100 yard dash, witty, receiver of nine scholarship offers, popular with all the girls. Yes, he would be one of my special friends, one of my main goals. I planned for us to be together until the end.

   ALTHOUGH THE ENTIRE team, the starters and reserves, had an outstanding year that magic year of 1953, still some of the more-fortunate players received even more accolades during the summer. I was very pleased that the four players who had won scholarships were also selected to represent Pensacola High in the sixth annual Florida High School All Star game. The game this year was to be played for the first time at Florida Field on the University of Florida campus in Gainesville.

   Big Fullback Ed Sears, who also received additional honors by being named the state of Florida's top prep gridder for 1953, and scrappy guard Y.B. Patterson should feel right at home on Florida Field as that will be their home field for the next four years.

   Huge lineman, Max Baxter, a work horse all three years at Pensacola High, signed with Bear Bryant and the University of Alabama Crimson Tide.

   Rounding out the elite four was my friend Ronnie who would attend Jones County Junior College in tiny Ellisville, Mississippi.

   While his three teammates and other friends from Catholic High and Tate High would accept four-year scholarships, he simply was not interested in warming the bench a couple or three years before he got the chance to play, no matter how prestigious the school may have been. He did his homework and visited three schools in the powerful Mississippi Junior College Conference. The school he favored and the coach that seemed to have the most on the ball was Head Coach Jim Clark of JCJC.

   Through all the trials and tribulations that would haunt Ronnie over his entire life, no one ever hinted that he wasn't highly intelligent. However, most would agree that he simply would not apply himself, would not adapt. His decision to attend a good junior college with a great football team and his choice of signing with JCJC proved to one and all that he made the right selection.   How many of you, or how many football players have you known, have scored two touchdowns in the Granddaddy of all bowls, the Rose Bowl, while playing for a national champi-

*Four players from PHS, Y.B. Patterson, Max Baxter, Ed
Sears and Ronnie leave on August 5, 1954, for the Florida
All Star Game in Gainesville.*

The 1953 Florida High School All State South Team: front row, left to rright: Coach Ralph Davis, Reynolds, Westbrook, Tanner, Wilkes, Coach Charlie Tate, Baker, Hinds, Renaud; second row, left to right, McGhee, Studstill, Weaver, Kelley, Keneipp, Durrance, Strickland, Williams, Harrell, Rountree; top row, left to right: Mitchell, Windham, Bailey, Carter, Fort, Hicks, Gill, Tracy, Mooneyham, Rose.

Note: #22 is Burt Reynolds of movie fame.

The 1953 Florida High School All State North Team: front row, left to right: Coach Earl Bert, Baggatt, Morris, Bryant, Marshall, Priest, Ritch, Woodard, Hemmingway, Williams, Coach Ed Stack; second row, left to right: Tredwell, Brown, Abood, Daniels, Sears, Mann, Edwards, Seymore, May, Thieman; top row, left to right: Mincey, Tenney, Whittington, Stewart, Zier, Patterson, Strom, Baxter, Fetchtel.

Above: Ronnie's senior picture at Pensacola High School. Right: His 1954 Pensacola High School graduation picture.

onship? Ronnie was to claim this feat, but next on his agenda was the Florida All Star Game.

ON THE SECOND Thursday night of August, a scorching hot night with suffocating, hellish, high humidity, the pride of Florida's best high school players squared off. The game was reported in every paper across the state on Friday morning. Bodie McCrory of the *Pensacola News-Journal* and Ray Charleston of the *Jacksonville Times-Union* filed their reports.

"A savage South football squad, after watching their Confederate brothers suffer humiliation in Wednesday night's All State basketball game, brought smiles back to Dixie Thursday night with a decisive 33-7 victory over the pride of North Florida.

"It was a small, ferret-like halfback named Dick McGehee that was the special fly in the North's ointment. The 143-pound speedster from Miami Edison showed his heels to the losers on runs of 56, 2, and 13 yards. He also caught a pass from Jim Roundtree for 62 yards to set up the South's first score.

"McGehee, a little flash who wasn't there when North tacklers tried to get to him, sparked the South's efforts in the sixth annual state prep football classic.

"It was the second straight triumph for the South team. They won last year 33-6. This year's match could have been by a much wider margin because the southerners had two touchdowns called back due to offensive penalties.

"Lightning fast runs and sensational passes in the first half placed the Northerners at a disadvantage they couldn't overcome. The 150 pounder, running like an elusive ghost, streaked for three touchdowns while carrying the ball only four times.

"After McGehee had put the ball inside the North ten yard line with his reception of the 62 yard aerial, Ellis Baker of Miami High shot over for the score. Minutes later Roundtree, A Miami Jackson product, fired a 14 yard scoring pass putting the South two-up. McGehee then collected the first of his touchdowns, giving the South a 20-0 half time lead.

"Early in the first quarter Roundtree gave the 8,000 fans a sample of his exceptional speed when he broke over right tackle and went 63 yards across the North's goal line, but the play was nullified by an offside penalty.

"The North got a scoring chance shortly thereafter when Leo Baggett of Panama City recovered Bill Weaver's fumble on the South's 36-yard line. The North made a couple of yards but the threat was wiped out when Jim Hinds of Miami High intercepted Ronnie Williams pass on the South's 30.

"Midway of the fourth quarter Williams brought new life to the humbled Northers by sparking a 70-yard drive. It was sluggish progress, taking all of seven minutes, but they made it although Williams had to go to the air to get the job done.

"Ed Sears, Jim Marshall and Williams ate up most of the yardage, but the closer they got to the South goal line the tougher the opposition. With the ball on the 17 and fourth down, Williams found Marshall standing in the end zone. Billy Bryant added the extra point.

In the losing effort Ed Sears carried the ball nine times for 43 total yards. Marshall picked up 20 yards in four carries and Dick Wiggington from Jacksonville Jackson added 19 yards in six attempts.

"It was the highest scoring game in the history of the contest. The North was simply on the wrong end of the score."

DURING THE GAME Ronnie had no clue that a player on the South team would eventually become a teammate of his and play a significant role in his personal life. Buddy Reynolds, from Palm Beach, would sign with the Florida State Seminoles where eventually Ronnie would play his last two years of eligibility on the same team. Within three years Reynolds would abandon football, change his name to Burt Reynolds and head for Hollywood for a long shot career in the movies.

I HAD ASKED Ronnie not to tell anyone that we had been talking, thinking it best be kept between the two of us. For the most part, my friends and I talk only with each other without bringing in outsiders. But he was determined to talk with Fred Levin, one of his closest, non-teammate friends.

Saturday morning shortly after 10:00, the phone rang in the Levin's home on East LaRua Street.

"Hello."

"Fred?"

"No. This is Stanley. Just a minute."

"Hello."

"Fred. That you?"

"Yeah, man, what's up?"

"What you doing after lunch?"

"Thought about going downtown and shooting some pool. Wanna go?"

"Naw, man. Listen I need to talk with you. I may need your help."

"What's the matter? Something wrong?"

"Well, nothing serious. I just need to talk."

"Okay, where you want to meet?"

"Billy is going to Cotton's to get a haircut. I'll ride with him and meet you at the pool hall, say around 1:00. That good for you?"

"Yeah. See you then."

"Great. So long."

On Saturdays, during off season, most of the Strutters spent considerable time between Cotton's Barber Shop, where "Cotton," a wise old barber of black and Cajun ancestry, specialized in flat top cuts, the craze of day, and the pool hall which was immediately next door. After parking, the two Williams brothers went separate way as they most always did.

"You gonna get a ride home?" Billy asked.

"Sure. Fred will drop me off. See you later."

Hanging loosely outside the pool hall was "Kid Booker," a permanent downtown sidewalk fixture, always with a well-soaked cigar dangling from his lip, never lit but genuinely chewed, shaggy clothing, tattered and worn shoes, no socks. The same greeting for all of the boys. Every time. "I see ya', kid."

"How you doing, Booker?" Ronnie nodded. "Is Fred inside?"

"Yeah, he just came in."

After a couple of semi-cold beers, Ronnie suggested they ride over to the Surf Club at the north end of the toll bridge leading onto Santa Rosa Island. They and most of their friends spent several hours a week at the "Club," owned by Fred's Uncle Bennie. Ronnie and Bennie had become great pals and had jointly and severally consumed their share of spirits and wild times.

"What's on your mind, pal?" Levin asked.

"Listen, I'm kinda confused. You won't think I'm goofy for asking you something that actually sounds really crazy, will you?"

"Of course not. What are friends for? What's the matter?"

"Well, I don't know exactly how to begin. Let me ask you something. In your mind have you ever thought that you could talk with someone? Someone who seems to be in your mind but is not really around? KnowwhatImean? I mean talk with someone who is not with you, but just in your mind? I'm probably not making much sense, am I?"

"You mean like you hear voices inside your head?" Fred asked.

"Yeah, kinda like that. Voices. Like someone is talking to me. And damned if I ain't starting to talk back to him. I mean like answering him within my mind, not out loud. Have you ever done that?"

"Well, no, I don't guess I have. Maybe its your conscience talking with you. Done anything bad lately?"

"Fred, don't start that crap. Man, I'm serious. Listen, if I can't talk with you about it, just forget it."

"Hey, I'm just pulling your string. Tell me about what's going on. Tell me about these voices."

"Are you on my side, or are you going to be your usual smart-ass self?" Ronnie scolded.

"Listen, Ronnie, tell me. I was just joking with you. Really. Lets talk. Tell me about this voice you hear."

"Well, then how about taking me serious. Okay?"

"Sure, now tell me. Talk to me. How long has this been going on?"

"Just a few weeks now. I think it started the weekend after it was announced that we had won the state title. You remember that night we left Mamma's and took those two muffins to the Terrace?"

"Yeah, I remember. Was that the first time you heard the voice?"

"Yes. That night when I walked out on the back porch. I stood there looking across the bay, and this voice started talking to me. This was the very first time I ever heard the voice. And, Fred, it was as real as I am talking with you right now."

"Since then, when and where have you heard it again?"

"Many places, many times. At the beach, driving a car, at a party. Sometime with friends and sometime when I am alone. It doesn't seem to matter."

"Is it always the same voice? Is it the same person all the time?"

"Yeah, always the same person, the same voice."

"A man? A woman? Who is it that you hear?"

"A man. Like I say it's always the same person, the same voice. The same man."

"And what's the subject? What you hearing? What do you talk about?"

"Just anything. Family, school, football, dating, friends. Just anything. He says, I mean the voice says, that he wants to be my friend and not to worry, he will always be around."

"Listen, and don't get teed with me when I say this. You had a hell of a great football season. Do you think that a hard hit, a tackle or something like that, could have had an effect on your body? Your head? Your mental attitude? And I'm not being cute. Perhaps you should talk with your folks and tell them about this. You may need to see a doctor. Maybe something could be more serious than either of us would want to believe."

"Yeah, I've thought of that. But, Fred, I only hear this voice after I've had a few beers or two or three drinks. Let's just drop it for now. Let's just wait and see what happens next."

"No, wait a minute. You've opened up a new can of worms. You only hear this voice after having a few drinks. Is that what you're telling me?"

"That's right"

"Never at any other time?" Fred questioned.

"Well, sometimes we talk when I'm stressed out. KnowwhatImean?

"Yeah I think so. But tell me anyway. Talk about stress."

"You know, when there's a big game or a school test coming, something I gotta do well. A decision to make, like where to go to college. Or when some muffin starts pulling my string. KnowwhatImean?"

"Yeah, I think I'm getting the picture."

They left the beach and returned to the pool hall, had a couple of beers and decided to call some muffins and take in the early movie at the Twin Air Drive-In. The "passion pit," as their teachers were fond of calling it, was always a place to dump tensions and stress. Tonight, through heavily fogged windows, they would occasionally get a glimpse of Gary Cooper starring in "High Noon."

OVER THE SUMMER Ronnie received loads of attention, admiring comments written in many letters from head coaches across the Southeast who offered scholarships. But he had made up his mind for sure after we had our in-depth discussion. He would attend Jones Junior College in Ellisville, Mississippi.

Life this summer was different from those of the past. It seemed as though the old gang was breaking up. Knowing each would be going his separate way in the fall, they hung closer together than usual. During midsummer they enjoyed driving down to the Shalimar Club in Fort Walton to watch Andy Griffith perform his act. He had released his hit comedy record, "What It Was, Was Football," and the story was hilarious.

And somehow it came to be that some of the Strutters fancied themselves as fine roller skaters. During this summer of contentment they would often show off their new found skills in front of their favorite muffins at the Silver Dome Skating Rink in downtown Pensacola. Most were lucky they made it to fall practice with both arms and legs intact.

"Goals set early in life can be destroyed when a person's judgement is led astray due to drug dependency...RONNIE is the story of how early success can ultimately lead to the ending of a life after being unable to adjust to the pressures of life after fame."

Coach Tommy Bowden, Clemson University

5

ELVIS, RED AND LIFE

THE TWO YEARS spent at JCJC were enjoyable. Head Coach Jim Clarke thought the world of Ronnie as he did all of his players. He took all of them under his wing and constantly advised, taught and cared for each as if all were his own boys. He and his able assistants, Coach A.B. Howard and Coach Milton White, offered everyone an at-home atmosphere, a true home away from home.

The junior college circuit in Mississippi was and is one of the toughest conferences in the country. The rules and by-laws of the conference state that no more than ten players from outside Mississippi could participate on a team. The Jones' coaches did their homework well. From Tennessee they chose Red West and Paul Hathcock out of Memphis and John Wayne Williams from Martel. And leading the Bobcats was quarterback Ken Schulte from New Orleans. From LeRoy, Alabama, came Ed Garris. And five of the ten came from Florida. Scrappy Sam Burkett, an outstanding lineman, was from Panama City. The remaining four, Gayle Winchester, Pete Flemming, Eddie Gebera and Ronnie all hailed from Pensacola High.

The reputation and outstanding achievements of past seasons certainly played a part in the decision of these out-of-staters to choose Jones. They were well aware that a large percent of former athletes who performed admirably during their two-year stint there were regarded as prime players and most were rewarded with scholarships to a major four-year college for the remaining two years of their eligibility.

During the two seasons Ronnie attended JCJC, the team lost only one game while outscoring their opponents 669 to 228, a winning ratio of nearly 3 to 1. Their only loss was to Hinds Junior College, 20 to 14 his first year in 1954. That year Hinds went to the Rose Bowl and won the Junior College National Championship. The Jones' boys had their chance the following year.

Life at JCJC suited Ronnie just fine. He was, as was the rest of the country, very much aware of the multitude of gorgeous, simply beautiful Southern belles who came from every nook and cranny of the great state of Mississippi. Many graced the JCJC campus. For years on end Mississippi led all other states in numbers of strikingly beautiful Miss America finalists. However, the gorgeous and exquisite ladies of JCJC had to contend with the muffins who came from the players' hometowns for weekend visits. By Sunday afternoon the hometown ladies had hit the road, and the JCJC charmers were more than eager to again accept their place at the head of the table, especially since they had total control of the situation at least five days of every week. For sure, there was never a shortage of great looking muffins in and around Ellisville and Laurel, Mississippi!

Ronnie had a flair for making friends quickly and easily. He was popular and well-liked by his team mates and other students across campus. These two years would acquaint him with several who would become lifelong, very special friends, but sadly, in memory only.

Blended deep within the Williams' family genes has long lived a trait that demands when someone is your friend, he remains your friend. When he is your enemy, he remains your enemy. In every case it is either black or white with very little gray. When they like you, they like you totally and completely. No questions asked. And when they love, they love dearly and unconditionally, almost to the point of a jealous and smothering love. Seldom, if ever, did any of them ever "kinda like" anyone.

This is how it was between Ronnie and his JCJC teammates, including his three longtime friends who came to Ellisville with him from Pensacola High. Two of his teammates that he really enjoyed spending free time with were Bobby "Red" West, who shared duties at center with scrappy Don Scoggins, and tackle Tony Roper. Rough and tumble, they both were. As rough a pair as you would want to anchor the offensive line, especially with you running from the backfield. Red was the lightest man on the line but knew no fear. Ronnie would often say that he expected that Red would stand toe to toe and slap a grizzly without giving it a second thought. He was one hundred percent total kick ass.

Red didn't show up at JCJC until the fall of 1955 and shortly after returning from the Rose Bowl left for other more exciting fields of dreams. However, the five months they were together made an impact, an indelible impression on Ronnie's life like no other person he had ever met.

Tony and Red were Ronnie's kind of men. Down to earth, quick witted, men who told it exactly like it was. Men among men, men you could trust and count on. Always stand-up kind of guys, no matter the situation. As former President Lyndon Johnson was fond of saying, they were the kind of men who "would go to the well with you". The three became close friends. When Ronnie was a junior at Pensacola High, his friends shortened his name to "Ron." Shortly after Red arrived on campus, he took it on himself to change it again. From now on while at JCJC he would be known as "Rod." Among those who knew him best, there should be little speculation as to why!

Red would soon become known to the world as the first person at Humes High School in Memphis who took up for and made friends with Elvis Presley. A lot was going on during the fall of 1955. While attending JCJC, Red had two best friends. When time permitted, he would return to Memphis and hang with Elvis, who was determined to get his singing career off the ground; then he would return to school where he spent his leisure hours with Ronnie. As Elvis became more and more popular, Ronnie would reminisce about such times. Each memory would bring to him a very special and sincere satisfaction. But at the same time, conflicting thoughts clashed within his mind about what perhaps could have been.

With his formal education behind him, Red became Elvis' personal bodyguard, his chief protector and director of security. He would remain his oldest and closest friend, confidant and insider for more than 25 years. There was a special bond between these two men, although it was bumpy and argumentative from time to time, until August 16, 1977, when Presley died within the walls of Graceland, his cherished mansion in Memphis.

Over the years Red would write a number of songs that were recorded by Elvis, Pat Boone, Ricky Nelson and Johnny Rivers. Elvis recorded his song, "If Every Day Was Like Christmas," along with several others he wrote with co-authors, including "If You Think I Don't Need You," "Holly Leaves And Christmas Trees," "If You Talk In Your Sleep," "That's Someone You'll Never Forget," "Seeing Is Believing," "You'll Be Gone" and perhaps Ronnie's most favorite, "Separate Ways."

After Elvis' passing, Red would move on to Hollywood where he soon became a television and movie actor in his own right. For several seasons he co-stared with Robert Conrad in the television series, "Baa Baa Black Sheep." His character was the cigar smoking, tough talking airplane mechanic, Sgt. Andy Micklin.

He also had great roles in two other Conrad series, "The Wild, Wild West" and "The Duke." And along the way he made a couple of appearances in the "Hardcastle and McCormick" adventures.

Later, one of his favorite roles was a character in the movie, "Roadhouse," starring Patrick Swazey. He would find work in both made for television and big screen movies, including the role of father of the sick boy in John Grisham's, "Rainmaker."

RED WEST IS as tough as they come, a former Golden Gloves champion of Tennessee who was selected to both the All Memphis High School Football Team and the Tennessee All-State Team playing at center. It had been only a few short weeks into his junior year when he encountered a situation concerning a slim, frightened young boy when he walked into the men's room at Humes High School. He told the story many times over the years.

"The place was full of smoke; you could hardly see your hand in front of you. But I could see far enough to notice that Elvis was in a whole heap of trouble again. About four or five guys had him cornered, holding him up against the wall. They were carrying on, yelling and laughing and ridiculing him about his long hair. They had made a decision to cut it.

"I knew all of them; they were football team members. When

I saw "E's" face, it just set off an emotion inside of me. These were good kids, good old boys just having fun. They meant no harm; they were not going to hurt him, just relieve him of some of his hair. But the fear in his eyes, the fear on his young face was horrendous. He looked like a scared animal, and I could not just stand by and let it happen.

"When you come from public housing, you generally let everyone take care of his own problems, but something came over me and I just had to help him. Since that day I have seen that same scared face of his, time and again over the years. He was a frightened cat. The face of a kid that was asking for help.

"I tried to calm the boys down. This ain't going to do any good, I preached. If the kid likes his hair long, then leave it be. Let him alone. It's his hair, for God's sake. Now, if you insist on cutting his hair, then you may as well be prepared to cut mine. And that probably will develop into something you're not really interested in."

RED WOULD PLAY a big part in Ronnie's life as would Elvis Presley, Burt Reynolds, Hank Williams, Sr., and hometown friend Fred Levin. And to a much lesser extent, so did Lee Corso and comedian Brother Dave Gardner. However, after the race of life had been run, none of these distinguished and famous men would ever have an inkling of an idea just what prominent, important and impressionable roles that each actually did play throughout Ronnie's short life of only 44 years and four months.

THE SUMMER BEFORE the '55 school year began, Red was traveling with Elvis, meeting scheduled appearances in many small towns across the South. Earlier during the year Elvis had played shows with such stars as Hank Snow, Marty Robbins and Andy Griffith. A few months later he would tour with Johnny Cash, Bill Haley, Roy Acuff and Kitty Wells.

The first week of August he signed on as a part of a package deal headlined by Webb Pierce. This tour would take them to a number of cities and towns across Tennessee and Mississippi and would end in Gulfport. Leaving the Gulf Coast about midmorning on Monday, Elvis and Red again hit the road, burning rubber toward Memphis.

Approaching the outskirts of Corinth, Mississippi, Elvis spotted a black Model "A" Ford sedan with a newly painted sign inside the window that read "For Sale By Owner." While still struggling to get a real start in the tough world of music, that Monday afternoon he set a precedent that soon would be known to his fans around the globe.

He hit the brakes, almost throwing Red into the dash, did a "U" turn in the middle of Highway 72 and returned to the front lawn of an old two-story farm house, an aged home that for sure needed the attention of a good house painter. While Red waited patiently, Elvis hustled to the front door. Finding no door bell, he knocked loudly on the weather-beaten side panel. Hearing no response from within, he scooted around the left side of the home and spotted an elderly couple sitting under a great magnolia tree. She, in her bright yellow apron, was snapping beans into a large blue and white speckled dish pan. He, with a razor sharp knife, was gently shearing white corn from its cob.

After stating the purpose of his stop, they, with absolutely no knowledge whatsoever of who the visitor was, returned to the front yard to show the car. Elvis asked all the ordinary questions while kicking both tires on the left side. Being satisfied, he paid the farmer cash for his asking price. Returning to his car he tossed the keys to Red, telling him that he would need some form of transportation when he left for college in a few days.

This proved to be the first automobile ever given away by Elvis Presley. And it established a precedent that he would choose to continue. And indeed a very expensive precedent it would soon become. As his career bloomed, it afforded him the opportunity to bestow Cadillacs, Lincolns, Mercedeses and other very expensive cars and fine gifts on friends, family and total strangers throughout the last half of his 42-year life.

Red made great use of the Model A. It played a significant part in his social activities while at Jones.

AFTER WINNING THE first four games of the 1955 season, one a 34 to 28 defeat of Hinds, the 1954 National Champion, the team had its second open date of the year. It happened to fall on Ronnie's twentieth birthday, October 15th.

Red had suggested that Ronnie, Tony and he make another trip back to Memphis. He recalled a club they had missed when visiting during their first open date. It seems that the "Jungle Club," in West Memphis near the Arkansas line, would offer some real entertainment. He spoke of how everyone was searched at the door for a gun or a knife, and, if he had neither, one or the other would be issued to him for the evening. Not knowing if this was true or not, Ronnie and Tony voted to stay closer to home.

The three decided their weekend would be in beautiful downtown Laurel, less than ten minutes northeast of Ellisville. They celebrated his birthday in good-ole-boy fashion, making all the stops, squiring around the city in Red's black Model A sedan. But most of the afternoon was spent at their very favorite hangout, Nub's Steak House, just outside the Laurel city limits on the Ellisville Road.

Since none of the other unmarried players had a car, Ronnie felt special and pleased to be friends with a teammate who had his own set of wheels. Little did any of them know at the time, although Red had a strange suspicion, just what a magnificent performer and movie actor the giver of the Model A would become. And become so very, very quickly.

SHE WAS A magnificent, majestic muffin with medium length amber hair, hazy blue eyes deep seated as if constantly seeing right through you. A birthday present supreme! Her lips were beautiful when covered with commercial paint but, when lacking, seemed to beg for medical attention. A lady whose dignity, presence, and demeanor were more than any man could ask for and certainly acceptable and worthy of the gods, that is, when she was made up. But without, Ronnie quickly learned that beauty is only a light switch away. At times she appeared as if she were a farm worker who had returned from a hot day of toiling in the field. Or a next-door neighbor who labored hour upon hour in her yard during the scorching heat of the summer.

At times she dressed as though a street woman in shabby clothes, a heinous looking specimen that no man could possibly crave. But when the muffin wanted, she presented herself in a most powerful and exquisite manner. She had the absolute, God-given ability to always make a person feel completely comfortable, at ease, and never alone. Never alone as in Ronnie's deepest fear.

6

UNDEFEATED—AGAIN

THERE WAS LITTLE to do around Ellisville during the off season. Taking in a movie was about it, so much of their entertainment had to be created by themselves. While other students would settle for a much lower-keyed variety of fun, you could always count on the ball players generating a bit more excitement in their spare time.

Members of the local VFW welcomed the players, although they were not old enough to purchase alcohol. Most members were delighted to spend time celebrating with them, whether or not there was a reason to commemorate anything in the first place.

Occasionally, after such a visit on a Saturday afternoon, a handful of the more daring ones like Roper, Ronnie, Red, Flemming and Burkett were off to other adventures. They would pile into Red's Model A and make a quick trip out State Road 588 towards Tuckers Crossing to an old farm house they had visited frequently. Parking down the road they would sneak through the heavy woods then attempt to creep silently around the back of the barn and borrow three or four of the farmer's fattest chickens. The farmer never had a clue as to the true culprits. He always blamed it on "ole Blue," a hound owned by his down-the-road neighbor.

Back in Ellisville they had a classmate who worked part time at a small family restaurant and would gladly fry the chickens provided they were plucked and cleaned before being brought to the back door. Of these fearless young men possibly Ronnie was the only one who had no experience whatsoever in plucking chickens. His sole education being that of an observer when his maternal grandmother, Viola Smith, would do the honors by grabbing a hen by the neck and swiftly whirling it around until the chicken gave up and rendered its wrung neck into her hand.

Somehow or another, these spirited young men managed to penknife the chicken's neck, releasing it from its misery as well as its body. How they plucked the birds was anyone's guess. Be that as it may, from time to time they would enjoy a fine chicken dinner. The mashed potatoes and turnip greens were always on the house!

FROM THE BULLPEN came many happy memories. After Coach Clark came by for his nightly bed check, the men were assured his task was finished when they no longer heard his ever present flip-flops beating against the floor. Now it was time to haul buggy for some late night fun. They delighted themselves by introducing all the new players, one by one, to "Miss Lilly." She, a delightful, well-proportioned woman, specialized in soothing all the problems, cares and sore spots of the young athletes.

About twice a week the leaders of the pack would make proper arrangements, then select an uninitiated player who was to be offered the treat. Being told that Miss Lilly was there to take care of his every need, she, as often found in Southern tradition, expected her caller to come to her dressed in coat and tie. With everything on ready, a couple of the boys would accompany the excited freshman to Miss Lilly's home for proper introduction.

After leaving a paved road, they traveled down a muddy lane to the seemingly deserted home, explaining as they approached how Miss Lilly delighted in having the house dark until her caller was at her front door, pointing out to the freshman this was one of her less kinky traits.

Well before the three stepped on the porch, Larry Kelly was already strategically placed inside the old house. With the first knock, he opened up with a blast from his shotgun and loudly proclaimed, "So you're the scamp that's been fooling with my wife." With this, one of the escorts screamed and fell to the ground. As usual, the freshman hauled it back to the paved road and was always the first to arrive at Red's Model A.

Legend has it that one time the boys initiated a set of twins, freshmen who had just arrived on campus from Texas. The two were outstanding running backs who were expected to play a lot of ball at JCJC. Immediately after the shotgun blast was the last time anyone in Mississippi ever saw the pair again. Leaving their clothing at the dorm, they apparently returned to Texas and matriculated at some other school.

THERE WERE MANY good times and fond memories around the Jones campus. The small, laid-back town offered little recreation other than their beloved football during the fall. Loneliness often came calling, and the players seemed to be its primary target. Years later teammates would recall how Red would often take his cornet and, while sitting on a car hood late at night, play some of the sweetest melodies they had ever heard. Tearjerking renditions that always brought memories of their special muffin back at home. Ronnie would speak of the many talents which Red had mastered but couldn't believe that during home games at Humes High he sometimes would change into a band uniform and perform at halftime, then slide back into his sweaty football outfit to finish the game.

Seldom do you find a football player who loved his music as much as did Red. Years later his brother Tom would tell stories of how Red taught Elvis how to read music. While having all the rhythm and movements, Elvis had no formal training in music. Red would coax him to sing high here and low there. A most talented and special person indeed was Red West.

FOLLOWING THEIR TREMENDOUS win over Hinds, the only school that defeated them last year, Coach Clark heaped praise on his team and bragged about their toughness. But he was quick to point out they would be facing an undefeated team from South Georgia after their open date the following week. He warned that while they were victorious over South Georgia last year by a tune of 51-12, this year South Georgia had a new coach who had yet to lose a game.

After light practices throughout the week and before the men left for their open weekend, the coach decided to read aloud the story of the Hinds victory which appeared in the school newspaper on Wednesday. He was thinking it might help bolster and maintain their resolve to continue their winning attitude.

The article headlined: "Bobcats End Jinx, Beat Hinds 34-28."

"Fighting an inspired battle all the way, the Jones Junior College Bobcats scored three second half touchdowns to come from behind and defeat the Hinds Junior College Eagles last Saturday night in a thrilling game played in overflowing Bush-Young Stadium. The victory was sweet revenge for the Bobcats who dropped a heart breaking 20-14 decision to the Eagles last year, the only loss on their otherwise perfect record.

"The Bobcats played inspired ball throughout the night in maintaining their undefeated record and holding on to a first place tie with the Copiah-Lincoln Wolves in the Mississippi Junior College Conference. The win was a great team effort with every player performing brilliantly in the winning cause.

"Eddie Gebara put the Bobcats into an early lead when he raced 22 yards in the first quarter on a double reverse. Hamburger Harrison's try for the extra point veered to the right of the bar. Hinds came back and scored in just two plays on a 23-yard aerial from Harvey to Frank Drummonds. Hard charging fullback Jimmy Taylor added the extra point, the first of four for the night, giving the Eagles a 7-6 lead.

"Taylor placed the Eagles in a greater advantage by scoring from one yard out in the second period, after personally spearheading a march which originated on the Hinds 24. The Bobcats scored in the last minute of the half on a 23-yard scoring aerial from Schulte to Williams. Sammy Stribling added the conversion, his first of four. Halftime ended with Hinds enjoying a lead by a 14-13 count.

"The Jones boys went to work after the halftime intermission. Gebara scored again in the third period on a nine-yard dash around his own left end after taking a handoff from Schulte. On the first play of the final period Schulte heaved a 29 yard pass to Edward Garris for another tally, giving the Bobcats a 27-14 advantage.

"The Eagles of Hinds kept the tension up and came right back to score on a ten yard throw from Harvey to Willie Eldridge narrowing the lead to 27-21.

"The Bobcats were not to be denied, however, and matched the Eagles touchdown by scoring another to take a 34-21 lead when Jerry Johnston climaxed the Jones scoring for the night on a smash off tackle from one yard out. Gayle Winchester added his fourth consecutive conversion.

"It made little difference that the Eagles tallied once more in the final minute of play on a 21 yard pass from Harvey to Olin Renfroe, All-American junior college halfback. The Bobcats had the ball game in their grasp, and when the final buzzer sounded seconds later a jubilant crew of Bobcat football players carried coach Jim Clark off the field on their shoulders.

"The brilliant team play of the entire Jones eleven offset the one-man efforts of substitute quarterback Junior Harvey of Hinds. Harvey came into the game replacing injured Ernest Breithaupt and passed the Eagles, defending state champs, to three touchdowns, hitting a different receiver each time.

"The Bobcats also produced their share of backfield stars. Ken Schulte, an All-State choice at quarterback last season, tossed two touchdown passes, one to Ronnie Williams and another to Ed Garris. Eddie Gebara tallied two touchdowns on runs of 22 and 9 yards, and Jerry Johnston, the workhorse fullback of the backfield, racked up a total of 109 yards rushing for the night, including one touchdown. Williams, in addition to his touchdown grab, made a beautiful catch of another aerial, good for 40 yards, to set up his touchdown.

"The Jones line, bolstered by ends Ed Garris and Pete Flemming; tackles Tony Roper, Hamburger Harrison and Connie Boykin; guards Paul Hathcock and John Perkins; and centers Red West, Don Scoggins and Buck Anderson formed an impenetrable barrier of human flesh and muscle. They piled up every offensive thrust the Eagles could make and held the highly touted Hinds offense to a net of but 126 yards on the ground.

"Penalties kept the Bobcats in the hole for the first half. On a number of occasions, potential scoring marches were washed away by erroneous play.

"The win gave the Bobcats their first victory over their traditional rivals since 1951 when the Bobcats went on to an undefeated season and the state championship. This win shoved the

Bobcats into the lead in the series between these two powerful schools. Jones has now won ten games compared to nine victories for Hinds. Four games have ended in a tie since the inauguration of the Jones-Hinds rivalry back in 1930. The game also established a new scoring record for the series with a total of 62 points scored.

"Well men, that is what the papers are saying about you. It was a good game but you mustn't let up. South Georgia and their new coach will be gunning for you. Have a good weekend and be careful. I'll see you Monday."

BEFORE PRACTICE ON Monday Ken Schulte, the Team Captain, called his teammates together. "Men, we did good against Hinds, but we are facing an undefeated team on Saturday. We must win. Coach Clark read the account of the Hinds game to us last week. Give me a few minutes and let me read to you about our last year's win over South Georgia. You new guys pay special attention.

"The headlines read: 'Jones Jr. College Bobcats Overwhelmed South Georgia Jr. College Tigers, 51-12.'

"Scoring almost at will, the Jones Junior College Bobcats overwhelmed the South Georgia Junior College Tigers by the score of 51-12 in a game played in South Georgia College Stadium in Douglas, Georgia.

"The Bobcats scored at least once in each quarter in rolling to a total of eight touchdowns. The Bobcats scored once in the first quarter, broke loose for four touchdowns in the second stanza, scored twice again in the third period, and closed out the evening's scoring with a final tally in the fourth quarter. South Georgia scored in the second and third quarters.

"The Bobcats made a total of twelve first downs during the night. They marked up eight first downs rushing, two passing and two from penalties.

"The Jones team showed from the beginning that they were out for victory. On the first play from scrimmage, halfback Ronnie Williams broke into the clear and raced 73 yards for the score. Aubrey Wade's try for the extra point was no good. Seconds later Co-Captain Harold Clark blocked a South Georgia punt with JCJC recovering on the Tigers' 27 yard line. Jones failed to

The 1955 Jones County Junior College Bobcat Squad.

Above: The 1955 coaches of JCJC: End Coach A.B. Howard, Head Coach Jim Clark and Backfield Coach Milton White. Left: Ronnie at JCJC in 1954.

School picture of Ronnie in his 1955 JCJC jacket.

Above: Football action shot at a 1955 JCJC game: # 65 John Perkins, # 54 Red West, # 30 Ronnie, and # 47 Pete Flemming. Below: Red West, Ronnie and Ken Schulte taken in a 25-cent arcade at the Jones County Fairground in 1955.

A self sketch of himself with his "Elvis Do." He wrote on the back, "Don't worry Baby, I'll get a haircut before I come up to see you."

Sketches of JCJC teammates Eddie Gebara, Red West and others.

make enough yardage for a first down and South Georgia took over on downs at their own nineteen yard line.

"South Georgia tied the game up in the early moments of the second quarter when quarterback Dean Madray scored. Jones then struck back with Ronnie Williams running 60 yards for a touchdown on the first play of the series. The extra point attempt was again not good.

"The Bobcats added to their lead moments later. Bobby Banna drove to the one yard line where he fumbled, but Grady Woodard picked up the ball and crossed the goal line for the touchdown. A pass interception by Ken Schulte set up Jones fourth touchdown. Schulte intercepted the pass on his own 28-yard line and ran to the South Georgia 22-yard marker before he was brought down. From that point halfback Eddie Gebara raced all the way for the tally. Jay Mason kicked the extra point for the Bobcats, making the score 25-6 in favor of Jones.

"Jones scored again just before the half ended. The Bobcats took over on their own 40-yard line. After a 15-yard penalty moved the ball back to the 25, fullback Jerry Johnston ran one in for a 75-yard touchdown. Jay Mason added the conversion on a perfect kick. The half ended seconds later with the score reading Jones 32 and South Georgia 6.

"South Georgia scored their last touchdown of the night in the opening minutes of the third period. After intercepting a JCJC pass, the Tigers then threw an aerial to halfback Ronnie Kelly for the touchdown. Their conversion attempt failed.

"Taking the kickoff on their own 31-yard line, the Jones Bobcats began a march for another score. They drove to the Tigers' 45 where they were stalled, but on fourth down a penalty against the Georgia team for roughing the kicker gave Jones a first down at the Georgia 30-yard stripe.

"Two plays later the strong and accurate arm of quarterback Schulte, the largest man in the JCJC backfield, passed to Aubrey Wade for the touchdown. Wade's try for the extra point missed its mark. The Bobcats further increased their lead in the waning moments of the third stanza when Dick Priester drove over from the eight yard marker after the Bobcats had driven from their own 47. Mason's attempt for the extra point failed.

"Midway of the last quarter Jones picked up their final seven points of the evening when Lamar Green climaxed a 68-yard drive with a powerful run. Mack McInnis added the extra point.

"As the game ended, the Bobcats were again on the march at the South Georgia 28-yard line as a result of a pass from Ray Merritt to Dick Priester.

"Now, guys that's what we did last year. Over the last few days, we've heard a lot from Coach Clark about South Georgia coming to visit us with an undefeated record, and we've heard quite a bit about their new head coach. But let me tell you something. We have what it takes to win on Saturday. Let's take this week serious and prepare ourselves for another victory. Now, let's go get 'em."

ON SUNDAY MORNING the local newspaper told the story in detail with stunning headlines: "Bobcats Trounce South Georgia."

"The Jones County Bobcats added a perfect climax in a day of colorful Homecoming celebration at JCJC as they scored often to trounce previously unbeaten South Georgia College into submission by a top heavy score of 60-13 in a game played before a near capacity crowd in their home stadium. The Bobcats sent the Tigers from Douglas, Georgia, slinking home with a humiliating defeat as their reward for their second venture into Mississippi for a football contest. The victory kept Jones prestige high in national junior college football circles.

"Saturday night was the first time this season that the Georgia eleven, who came to Mississippi with an unblemished record, had scored less than four touchdowns in a game. The hard-charging Jones line bottled up the South Georgia ground game and also the supposedly strong aerial attack.

"Jones scored three touchdowns in the initial quarter, tallied twice more in the second period for a 33-0 halftime advantage. Scored a single TD in the third period and burst back for three more in the fourth quarter. South Georgia scored both of their touchdowns in the third quarter.

"Ronnie Williams, Lamar Green and Gayle Winchester all scored a duo of touchdowns each for the winning cause, with Ken Schulte, Jerry Johnston and Eddie Gebara adding single tallies. Williams scored on a 39-yard dash off tackle and on a 45-

yard pass from Schulte. Green scored touchdowns in the second and fourth periods on runs of one and ten yards. Winchester's scores came in the final quarter on a one-yard buck and on an eight-yard pass from Sammy Stribling. Schulte scored on a four-yard option play and Johnston went five yards off tackle for his touchdown.

"Eddie Gebara raced 81 yards in the second period for a touchdown, his run being the longest of the night. Earlier in the same period Gebara had sprinted 80 yards for an apparent score only to have it called back because of a holding penalty. Winchester added three extra points, and Gebara, Stribling and 'Hamburger' Harrison added single conversions.

"South Georgia scored both of their touchdowns in the third period. Roger Wilkinson scored the first on a quarterback keeper from the one. Billy Thornton ran three yards for the other score late in the period. Homer Sowell added the conversion after the second TD. His first attempt was 'wide right,' perhaps sending a signal of things to come for their new coach.

"Jones marked up fifteen first downs during the evening, eleven on the ground and four via the airways. South Georgia's Tigers made ten first downs, five by rushing, two through the air and three on penalties.

"The Bobcats ground out a net of 415 yards rushing for the game, and their rugged defense held South Georgia to only 105 yards on the ground. Gebara was the big ground gainer with 96 yards in only four carries. Following him came Winchester with 91, Johnston with 85 and Williams with 60.

"Jones gained 128 yards through the air, with the Georgia Tigers gaining 87. Ken Schulte connected on three out of five aerials for 77 yards and one TD. Sammy Stribling completed two of four for 38 yards and a touchdown. Ray Merritt hit on one of three for 13 yards. Ed Garris led the JCJC receivers with three receptions.

APPARENTLY, SCHULTE'S READING of last year's account had motivated the Jones Boys to out-do their former teammates. The lopsided score would be the most embarrassing game of the season for the South Georgia Tigers and, as time would prove, the most lopsided loss of a lifetime for their new coach.

After being warned and preached to throughout the week about the strength of their undefeated opponent, the Jones boys were delighted with their overpowering victory.

When the game was over, Pete Flemming was overheard saying to John Perkins, "Well, I guess their new coach, what was his name? Wasn't it Bowden, Bobby Bowden? He might just have to look for a job selling cars or something. It don't look like he'll make it coaching college football."

"RONNIE" obviously packs a wallop regarding the dangers faced by so many athletes who foolishly feel that they will be a sports hero all their life and that the thrill of the game and fan adoration are all important. I admire your willingness to put so many memories, some of which must have been painful, on paper. The letters written by well known coaches were interesting to read as they understand the need for athletes to learn appropriate values in addition to honing their athletic skills. It was most appropriate to have Bobby Bowden write the Foreword, since his personal value system is admired by all who know him. I hope the message of RONNIE will be shared with many inspiring, young athletes and students."

Tom Gallagher, Florida Chief Financial Officer

7

THE ROSE BOWL—
MUST WE PLAY AGAINST
BLACKS?

WHILE THE GREAT majority of the Jones County Junior College Bobcats were oblivious to the concerns of playing against blacks, nevertheless, some did have a personal opinion. Unlike today where every sneeze or every rumor, whether true or not, is broadcast instantly around the globe with little concern for credibility, it wasn't that way back in 1955.

Television was still in its infancy, just coming of age. Only a small percent of families had this new, marvelous invention in their homes or businesses. At that time there were only three major networks, ABC, NBC and CBS. No one had ever heard of Ted Turner, CNN, or any other of the numerous new channels which now inundate our entire life from birth to the grave.

The Jones Boys, as they were now being called, had little access to the news—nor did they give much concern to any they happened to hear. Among the Bobcat players, perhaps the only two who had any previous experience playing against blacks were Red West and Paul Hathcock. Each played at Humes High School in Memphis where sports integration had already become common practice. The upcoming Rose Bowl and the blacks on the opposing team presented little if any concern at all. But make no mistake about it, the Jones boys were going to California to play rough and tough football and cared less who might or might not be on the receiving end of a punishing day. They were unfazed about whoever might get in their way, either black or white.

A LARGE PERCENT of Mississippians, and for sure a good number of Jones Countians, a county known to some as "The Free State Of Jones" as depicted in the book *The Echo Of The Black Horn,* were of different and varied opinions. The sentiments and attitudes of many of Jones residents were much the same as their ancestors. Those whose opinions jelled around the mid 1860s during and after the Civil War when Captain Newton Knight tried relentlessly to crown himself as "Governor Of The Free State Of Jones." As the book notes, the Captain assembled a band of soldiers, men who had deserted the Confederate Army and formed their own unit which was known far and wide as "The Deserter Band."

During the war almost every family in Jones County, even the families of the men who were fighting for the Confederacy, looked up to Captain Knight with respect and admiration. Often he was spoken of as the greatest man that ever lived because many of these people believed that the Captain's Company was fighting both the Yankee and the Confederate armies to keep them from stealing from the widows and orphans of men who had already lost their lives in battle.

The descendants of hundreds tell how Captain Knight kept their ancestors from starvation, which he did. However, little is mentioned about just how he acquired help for those families. But on the other hand, no praise came from the families of other areas who were robbed by the Deserter Band so that a precious few chosen families might be fed.

Early during the war the Captain was truly a man honored by countless numbers across Jones County. Nevertheless, that would soon drastically change as citizens of the county would tell how Captain Knight forever ruined the good name of Jones County.

While there were many slaveowners in the county, there was absolutely no social or personal relationship between whites and blacks. Slaveowners were known to be friendly towards those who worked their lands, but friendly only in the scantiest of terms. Time and again, any white person who was known to have any degree of "nigger blood" was run from the county.

At the end of the war, the Union was in command of Jones County. During Reconstruction martial law was proclaimed throughout the South, which was divided into five military districts. To escape from the drudgery of military law, the states had to reconstruct according to the Federal congressional plan.

Those men of the Knight Company in Jones County, and even some from adjoining counties, came forward as the qualified electors, along with every Negro in the county. This was not only in Jones County but throughout Mississippi, which explains how the state came under "Negro Rule."

Reconstruction marked the first time blacks were extended the same legal rights as whites. Yet it was a turbulent and violent period of American history as the opposition of whites to allowing blacks the same freedoms eventually doomed the attempt.

During this time the Mississippi State Government was practically run by Negroes who were placed in powerful positions by Carpetbaggers, Northerners who had come to the South in search of economic opportunity and who supposedly could fit all their belongings into a single suitcase. And Scalawags, Southern whites who strongly supported the Republican created Reconstruction Government. Joining in were countless numbers of dishonest politicians who were hellbent on holding the South in ruin and disgrace.

Mississippi, at this time, had nine Negro senators, fifty-five Negro members of the House, the Lieutenant Governor was a Negro, as was the Superintendent of Education, Secretary of State and Agriculture Commissioner. The appointment and/or election of these were through the efforts of shrewd and unscrupulous white men who had something to gain personally as most of the Negro officials could neither read nor write. This would remain so until gradually the state began a movement of progress to relieve itself from the yoke of oppression. The new law disenfranchised most all of the white men who were known leaders across the South and placed the ballot in the hands of the Negro. Carpetbag Rule existed twelve years, until 1877.

The people of Jones County reacted indifferently when learning that Captain Knight had been appointed by the Union to the position of provost marshall. Many sought to have their names added to his former muster roll, thinking in terms of favors that could be forthcoming.

Because of his change in tactics and goals during the later months of the war and due to his appointment as provost marshall by the Union forces, most families living in Jones became stand-offish to the captain as well as every member of his Deserter Band Company. Few would have anything to do with them and absolutely no association whatsoever with Captain Knight after the war finally came to an end. After years of being admired by almost everyone, now his was a sad and lonely life.

Before the war, several years earlier, the captain had bought a slave family, a mulatto woman and her two small children. The woman could have almost passed for white as she appeared to have but a trace of "nigger blood." After the war the captain took up with the family of blacks and was entirely shunned by the upper crust citizens of Jones County. Many assumed over the years she had always been his mistress; however, apparently this was not the case.

The citizens of Jones County looked upon the captain's own children as they did him. No one would associate with any member of his family. The captain spent countless days and nights in deep thought searching for a way, a means, to improve his children's, and some day his grandchildren's, station in life in their home county. Presently, there was no way on earth that any of his children would ever be accepted into Jones County society. Because of the hatred of the captain, he feared that none of his children would ever be acceptable to others as a wife or husband.

The captain finally conjured up a plan that he thought was the answer. He had arranged for both of his sons and his only daughter to marry one of the "white niggers" of the mulatto woman. By this time she had seven or eight children, all by different men, of whom more were white that black. Some of her children looked "white" and carried all the "white characteristics" including long blonde hair and blue eyes.

Since it was obvious that the captain's children were not going to become a part of the Jones social community, then his plan would be to marry them off to the children of his slave family and start a breed of off-springs who would eventually become a pure white clan.

Two of his children, a son and his daughter, went along with the idea. The captain saw to it the marriages were performed. However, his third child, a son named Tom, balked at his father's plan and absolutely refused to marry "a nigger." A horrible fight between the two erupted which saw Tom running for his life at the threat of his father's attempt to kill him only to have a bullet from the Captain's rifle miss its human target.

Later, Tom's faith in God lifted him triumphantly from the depths of despair and released him from a life of bitterness and anguish. At first his life was a turmoil of hate, humiliation and racial intolerance. As an innocent man he was made to suffer untold agonies, mistreated and abused and shamefully discriminated against because he was the son of the leader of the Deserter Band. He would, in time, overcome his inferiority complex and concern himself only slightly about what the public thought about his personal situation.

"Uncle Tom," as he came to be known, told Ethel Knight, the author of *The Echo Of The Black Horn,* "That's all in the past now, but I never would have made it if it hadn't been for my God. He has led me through it all—the disgrace and the shame that my father heaped upon me when he went to the Niggers. Since I've lived it down, and I'm soon to die, I'd like to tell it all, the whole truth about my father."

SINCE THE WAR years, feelings over race relations in Jones County had been a bitter pill for many to accept. The Ku Klux Klan, having been formed in Tennessee in 1866, and other hatemongers—although the players may not have been aware of their tactics—would try as hard as they could to see to it that the people of Jones County would come to hate the thought of JCJC facing blacks across the line of scrimmage in a football game. Not only in California but any and everywhere.

One afternoon Ronnie had taken some clothes to the local laundry and was approached by someone who only identified himself as a member of the Klan.

"Understand you Jones boys want to play against those niggers out there in California. You gonna do that?"

"Pardon me!" came Ronnie's reply.

"Y'all gonna play against those niggers in that Rose Bowl?"

"Sir, I don't believe that we should be having this conversation. Decisions such as those are made by our coaches. You best take your comments to Coach Clark."

"Ain't you one of the players?"

"Well, yeah, I play on the team."

"Ain't you number 30? Ain't you Williams?"

"That's right. But you need to be talking with someone else, not me. Please excuse me. I have to leave."

"Now, Williams, don't go away mad. Listen, have you even thought about how it will be? All those niggers slobbering and dripping their sweat and juices all over you. What about it when you're tackled? You want a big ass nigger laying on top of you?"

"Sir, I've got to go. You need to call Coach Clark and talk with him. So long."

THE SPORTS WORLD would soon recognize that in every major sport around the globe, the black athlete felt his time had come. He would not be satisfied as being just a factor to deal with but would become an equal with the whites and in most cases overshadowed them in competitive sports programs. Coaches and recruiters began taking serious note of the load of talent they had been, until now, overlooking. For the most part the black athlete was bigger, stronger and faster.

And as Bear Bryant would later say about the white player, "Percentage wise, you don't find as many who want to sacrifice and be dedicated because they've already got too much. Having a chance to get something that he never had, has a lot to do with making a winner. That's why the blacks are doing so well now. They're hungry for recognition, for something better, the way we were when I was in school. The blacks will stick it out; they won't quit on you. They know this may be their only chance to make something of themselves. The great majority have no other place to start."

THE HARSH WINTER winds were blowing briskly on the 6th of December when the 37-member Jones County Junior College Bobcats left by bus for their short trip to Jackson. There they would board a Delta Convair on the first leg of their trip to sunny California, their trip to the Junior Rose Bowl in Pasadena.

Most of the players did not own appropriate attire to make a trip of such importance, so each had been outfitted in a wool tweed suit for the purpose. Neither the coaches, the athletic director nor other school officials realized that, despite freezing temperatures being experienced in Mississippi, when they arrived in California the temperature would be nearing 90 degrees.

After an undefeated season JCJC was ranked number two in the nation and was headed for a showdown with number one, Compton Junior College of Compton, California. Everyone traveling from Mississippi was looking forward to a visit to the big state.

THIS WAS A time in Mississippi when people seldom locked their doors, when Sundays were spent in church, when Southern tradition still meant something, and "yes" and "no" were freely followed by "sir" or "ma'am," when saddle shoes, poodle skirts and bobby socks made fashion statements. A time when some of the players were attempting to sing along with Fats Domino and his latest hit, "Blueberry Hill." A time when the current number one song on the charts was Bill Haley's "Shake, Rattle and Roll." The school paper and the local radio station published the other top four songs sweeping the country; "If I Give My Heart To You," "Honey Love," "I Understand" and "I'm Gonna Sit Right Down And Cry Over You."

In an interview with the school paper about the upcoming game, Red West got in a plug for his buddy, Elvis. He cautiously advised the writer for the The Radionian to be aware of and keep an eye on his slim friend from Memphis who was attempting to bust on the scene with his fresh, innovative style of music. "Elvis," said Red, "may well be a newcomer of some distinction, and you just may want to pay him a bit of attention."

The players and the 110 band members making the trip were filled with excitement. For most it was their first flight and for many their very first trip outside the borders of the great state of Mississippi. These 147 young folks, accompanied by coaches and staff, had set off on what was to be the trip of their lives. Among the band members was the shinning personality of tuba player Terrell Tisdale who in later years would become Dr. Tisdale, President of Jones County Junior College.

The players, for the most part, were 17-to-20-year-old kids from rural areas of Mississippi where teen-agers seldom went beyond a high school education. A junior or senior college degree was seldom accomplished. The game of football in Mississippi was and is serious business and could be compared to the atmosphere of basketball in the state of Indiana. The players, family and fans took football to the highest level of competition.

Arriving in Dallas where the plane refueled, the players deplaned thinking a few challenging runs up and down the stairs inside the airport corridors would do them good. It just so happened the airport was showcasing its newest invention for moving people at a more rapid pace. The day of the escalator had arrived. For the Jones boys this was their first glimpse at a set of "moving steps."

Here, according to schedule, the group divided. Half took one flight and half another. While no one wanted to discuss the reason, all were in agreement that should some unforseen tragedy occur, it would not affect the entire entourage.

This was the second year in a row that a Mississippi junior college team had represented its state by playing in the Rose Bowl for the Junior College National Championship. The previous year Hinds Junior College had defeated El Camino Junior College 13-7. However, this year had already proven itself to be genuinely different from last year. Representing Mississippi as the first team to play against an integrated opponent would indeed be very, very different.

WHEN JCJC ACCEPTED the invitation to play, it would become the first Mississippi team in any sport to play a racially integrated team. The first ever. During 1955 the norm in Mississippi, as it was throughout the Deep South, was all segregated sports teams. However, JCJC President Dr. J.N. Young decided to defy not only the rules of the day but also a large percentage of the political structure and its powerful supporters across the state. His decision ignited editorials in most of the larger newspapers. The papers steadfast warning was that if the school played the game then it would be in direct violation of Mississippi state laws. They urged all concerned not to accept the bid to play, to promptly decline the invitation.

Those Bobcats Fly !!

1955

FOOTBALL SCHEDULE

• Sept. 10	—	Ellisville	32	Perkinston	0		• Ellisville	60	South Georgia	13 — Oct. 22
• Sept. 24	—	Ellisville	43	East Mississippi	6		• Ellisville	32	Pearl River	12 — Oct. 29
• Oct. 1	—	Ellisville	26	Northeast	12		• Ellisville	26	Southwest	21 — Nov. 5
• Oct. 8	—	Ellisville	34	Hinds	28		• Ellisville	39	Copiah Lincoln	6 — Nov. 12
							• Ellisville	34	East Central	12 — Nov. 19

JUNIOR ROSE BOWL

Ellisville 13 Compton, Calif. 22

*The 1955 JCJC Bobcat schedule and their group picture
en route to the Rose Bowl in Pasadena, California.*

A photo in the Los Angeles Mirror-News *on December 7, 1955, of Red West, Pete Fleming, Rose Bowl Queen Barbara Wilson and John Perkins.*

The date of the game was just a year after the Supreme Court struck down "separate but equal" treatment of white people and black people. Many Southerners wanted to fight the court and preserve segregation as the South had known forever.

The players were drawn into a political situation which they not only wanted to avoid, but one which they cared little about. When anyone asked their opinion, they, one and all, stated emphatically that "They were just a group of country boys who wanted to play football. To play in the Rose Bowl in the big state of California for the National Championship." The team members showed little concern that Compton had eight blacks, five of whom were starters. The color of the skin of those who would be on the other side of the ball made little difference to the players, those who were actually going to play the game. They did not really understand, or care, about the historical precedent which was to take place on December 10, 1955.

Perhaps no newspaper was more vocal than Mississippi's largest, The *Jackson Daily News*. The very day the 37-member team boarded the plane their headline read: "CANCEL THAT CALIFORNIA TRIP." The editorial writers warned "that a violation of the ban we have declared on social equality would lead the state legislature to eliminate funding for the junior college in future years." And as predicted, such a bill was introduced in the next legislative session.

The paper continued, "If the authorities of Jones County Junior College permit their football team to journey to California to play in the Junior Rose Bowl Game with a team having five Negroes in its lineup, it can, with equal reason permit the team to play the all black teams of Tougaloo College or Alcorn A&M College in our home state.

"Surely the Jones County school authorities realize there is no middle ground on the subject of segregation, nor should any exceptions be made.

"Mississippi is officially on record, through the voice of its legislature, approved by the Governor and Attorney General, to oppose the integration order of the United States Supreme Court to the utmost limit. It would be glaringly inconsistent, to say the least of it, for Mississippi to send a junior college football team all the way to California to play a game against a team that has Negroes.

"There is no escaping the cold fact that a game between Mississippi junior collegians and a California team having Negroes in its organization would not only be a violation of the ban we have declared on social equality but would be an acceptance of social equality. Argue until you are black in the face but there is no way to escape that conclusion. Self respect demands that we do not temporize or compromise in dealing with this problem."

The editor, Major Frederick Sullens, still angry about the decision to go, published an editorial hoping the Jones team would go down in defeat. He wrote, "A defeat will not cause mourning in our home state. The decision to play against Negroes is the most unfortunate thing that has happened since the infamous Supreme Court ruling. Nothing but avarice and cold-blooded greed for a share of the monetary receipts could have prompted such action."

THINGS WERE BEGINNING to heat up across Mississippi at a scorching temperament. This was seven years before James Meredith's attempts to become the first black University of Mississippi student. It was a decade before three civil rights workers were slain in Philadelphia, Mississippi. It was sixteen years before court-ordered desegregation was instituted across the state. When word spread that the JCJC team was serious in its consideration of accepting the invitation and the reality of Mississippi boys actually lining up face to face with blacks, hatred began to rise in many communities.

An alumnus of JCJC, and for many years one of its biggest financial supporters, Lieutenant Governor Carroll Gartin, announced that he would fly to California and be the "number one booster." However, after learning of the black players and after Dr. Young announced his acceptance of the invitation, Gartin divorced himself from all support and announced that he would not attend the game as planned. Governor-Elect J.P. Coleman declined comment, stating it was a matter for the Junior College Board of Trustees.

The commissioners of a neighboring county withdrew their financial support for sending the team and band to the game. But to a person, the team and band members voted to go and represent the state of Mississippi in its quest for the national championship.

Much of the resentment of playing against "niggers" was generated by the Ku Klux Klan, a very powerful organization throughout Mississippi during the 1950s. To them, this was serious business, deadly serious business. They were not going to take this plunge towards integration without a good fight. And because of the pressures of the Klan, even eight years later Mississippi State's basketball team had to sneak out of the state to play an integrated opponent in the NCAA Tournament.

At the same time all the fuss was brewing over the Rose Bowl, another dispute was boiling over in the state of Georgia. Governor Marvin Griffin had demanded that Georgia Tech turn down its Sugar Bowl invitation to play Pitt because Pitt had a black fullback.

It was evidently clear that the Jones boys came to sunny California to play football. To play without any of the distractions which were occurring back home in Mississippi. While a few of the players were aware of all of the commotion, most were either completely in the dark or could care less about the controversy.

PERHAPS ALL THE fuss over playing against a team with Negro players did not really sink in until the banquet which brought members of both teams together for a meal. After the Friday morning pep rally on the Compton campus, both teams and their supporters were bussed to Pasadena for registration at the Hotel Constance. At noon the entire entourage, including their ardent followers, had lunch at the Huntington-Sheraton Hotel as guests of the Pasadena Junior Chamber of Commerce and the Pasadena Quarterback Club.

The players were greeted by both opposing coaches as well as Jess Hill of USC, Red Sanders of UCLA, Jordan Olivar of Yale and Lisle Blackbourn of the Green Bay Packers.

While much had been written in the papers and amplified a great deal on every radio station in Mississippi, reality did not set in until the players actually faced each other across the luncheon table. Although Red and a couple of the other Jones boys had played against Negroes while in high school, none of the other players, nor the coaches for that matter, had ever played a team that had even one black player. And needless to say, never had any of the Jones boys ever dined at a table with Negroes.

While some would want you to believe that everything was hunky-dorrey, it wasn't. The blood pressure of the Mississippians began to rise, and while nothing was said out of order during the luncheon, the mixing of the races certainly played an integral part on the field. There was no doubt the Jones boys wanted to win and win big. They had little interest in returning to Mississippi with a loss that could be taunted in their faces for years to come. Perhaps their desire to win so completely overshadowed their playing ability and skills, it had a devastating and detrimental negative effect.

THE WEATHER WAS near perfect. The fans had paid $2.50 for reserved seats or $1.50 for general admission. All 57,132 were ready to get it on. Both JCJC and Compton fielded a full squad of fine athletes with no injuries. Accompanying the Mississippi team were their cheerleaders, majorettes and the largest band from their state. Compton was equally represented by their fine band and a great supporting cast.

AT HIGH NOON the captains of each team met on the fifty yard line for the toss of the coin. Ken Schulte and Paul Hathcock were the co-captains for JCJC. Jones won the toss, and Compton elected to defend the north goal line.

CBS radio was broadcasting the game around the country and across the world through the Armed Forces Network. Local television and the national wire services had a multitude of correspondents covering the game.

Jones County Junior College came into the game undefeated through its nine regular season games. Compton brought a ten-win record and also was undefeated. There was no question in anyone's mind that Compton was far more experienced. A number of their starting players had already been in the military and had two or more years of military football experience that did not count toward their junior college eligibility.

The JCJC coaches feared their team was also at a greater disadvantage as they had sent game films of each of their games to Compton but had received in return only a single game of Compton's.

SCHULTE FUMBLED THE kickoff but recovered. On the first play he pitched out to Ronnie who also fumbled but recovered. Fullback Jerry Johnson had a couple of nice runs, Gebara was thrown for a loss, Ronnie again fumbled a pitch out but recovered. On fourth down and four to go Johnson kicked the ball away.

On the first offensive play by Compton, its star running back, Jimmy Waddell, was injured and left the game for good. Compton generated little offense and punted the ball back to Jones.

With Jones gaining little, they again had to kick it away. All the action thus far seemed to be in the kicking game.

After a couple of short Compton pass completions, Charles McNeil tallied on a 74-yard romp around left end. Pete Flemming blocked the point after, and Compton led 6-0 as the first quarter ended.

On the second series of the second quarter Schulte delivered a beautiful pass to Ronnie who scored on a 68-yard reception. The PAT was no good. The game was tied 6-6.

Jones kicked off, and Compton's fullback, Neal Wagerle, took the ball on their 14. He darted in and out, left then right. Picking up strategic blockers, he was off to paydirt 86 yards down the road. Aldrich made the conversion which put Compton in the lead by 13-6.

Schulte received the kick for Jones and did a beautiful job of scrambling until the ball was torn from his arms and recovered by Compton at the Jones 29-yard line. After a couple of short gains Charles McNeil carried the ball to the 2-yard line, and on the next play a quarterback keeper by Bunny Aldrich gave Compton another six points. Aldrich again made good the extra point, and Compton led at the half 20-6.

AFTER A TREMENDOUS halftime extravaganza by the bands of ten junior colleges from across the country, the teams were eager to resume their contest for the National Championship.

JONES KICKED OFF and Compton returned it to its 39. They pulled a couple of reverses, completed a short pass and missed two others, then punted back to Jones.

Schulte pitched out to Ronnie on a sweep, and he was caught

well behind the line for a six yard loss. On second and sixteen, Schulte completed a pass to Pete Flemming who carried it to the 25 for first and ten.

Schulte opened up with a terrific pass which led the finger tips of Ed Garris by a single inch as he crossed the goal line. Schulte then completed a six-yard pass to Flemming, but on fourth down Jones again had to give up the ball.

Compton couldn't move the ball on its next series and kicked it back to Jones. Schulte found Ronnie scooting down the side-lines, wide open and in the clear. He laid a perfectly beautiful pass right into his hands. As he did in the second quarter, Ronnie, with a quick shoulder motion, faked the Compton secondary out of position and cleared himself for the wide open reception. This touchdown carried for 59 yards, and with Stribling's conversion the Jones boys cut Compton's lead to 20-13 as the third quarter ended.

Little offense was generated by either team until late in the fourth quarter. Compton was driving when Ronnie intercepted a pass clearly two yards inside the end zone. Compton's massive lineman, Bob Gudath, picked him up and literally threw him out of the end zone where the officials called the play dead on the one foot line.

The call, without question, had a horrendous attitude-challenging effect on the Jones boys. You could definitely see the difference in their mannerism, the way they walked, as compared to their lively temperament just moments earlier. It clearly was a missed call by the officials, one that perhaps cost them the game and the National Championship.

With the clock running down, Schulte handed off to Ronnie who was caught in the end zone for a safety. The game was over. Compton Junior College had won the National Championship.

WITH THE GAME being over, JCJC Head Coach Jim Clark faced a band of reporters. "The California heat was just too much for us. Compton has a fine ball club. They're good, but I believe there are two or three teams in our conference who would give 'em a good go. The thing that ruined us," he continued, "was the terrific power in the line and their ability to move the ball."

JCJC line coach B.A. Howard added, "The heat bothered us for sure. And their outstanding line and depth hurt us most of all. But we fought and we're satisfied."

Ken Schulte, who tossed both of Jones touchdowns, complimented Compton's line but added, "We have faced much better backs in our own conference. And we didn't get much of a break with our receptions. Had we held on to a couple of the passes, it may have been a different outcome."

Ronnie also put his two cents worth in saying, "It was a little hot out there. Compton's huge line simply overpowered us. I think we're their equal, but I've got no excuses."

"Compton didn't hit as hard as a lot of other teams in the South," stated Hamburger Harrison the 265-pound barrel who walked like a full grown man. "They play rough, and they're a mighty fine ball team, but we just didn't have it today."

"They're a great team and rugged, but not any rougher than others we faced this year," said 6'3" tackle Tony Roper. Only Pete Flemming, a Jones end, felt different. "I think they were real lucky."

THE JONES BOYS did lose the Championship Game 22-13 to the powerful Compton team coached by legend Tay Brown. And the Compton Tarters emerged that December 10th as the only undefeated and untied junior college football team in the country.

With the game having been played, many thought the South would never again be the same. For those, it was different because a Mississippi team actually competed against an integrated opponent. And the players from the tiny, rural city of Ellisville felt the complete brunt of venom from a multitude of Southern hatemongers. But while Compton's claim to the National Championship was undisputed, thousands upon thousands thought that Mississippi perhaps was the real winner that day after all.

RED WEST, THE tough, scrappy center, had grown up playing football with blacks on the dirt playgrounds in and around the rough housing projects in Memphis. He was to say years later, "From my perspective, I sometime feel that things today are even worse than it was back in 1955. Things have changed but changed for the worse. I think that as bad as things might have been in '55, they were not as bad as they are now. We're living in a very volatile time. I just hope it all comes around and gets better for our country."

With the uproar created by the hatemongers, the Klan and those wanting to cause trouble, you would think that game officials would be looking for racial overtones from the players during the game. This did not happen. Race simply did not raise its ugly head.

Compton's star running back and future All American, Jim Waddell, was knocked out of the game within the first three minutes and sent to the hospital. He was kicked in the head and suffered a fractured nose, cut eye and concussion. He would later say, "It was a good, hard, but clean hit. There was no sign of intentional roughness and most certainly no racial overtones."

And Edis McNeil, a black player and twin brother of Charles McNeil, a Compton end who was named the game's most valuable player, would say, "It was a good, clean-played ball game. I did not see or was not aware of any purposeful roughness or racial problems."

Years later when asked about the game, one of Jones assistant coaches, A.B. Howard remarked, "There was a lot of sportsmanship in the game. You didn't hear any of the jawing back and forth at each other like you do today."

IN ALMOST EVERY game, no matter the sport, there often is one outstanding controversial play. The most meaningful one of this year's Junior Rose Bowl Game was the play described in the last two minutes of action. When the officials called Ronnie's interception dead on the one-yard line, it caused the Jones team to have to work from deep in their own end zone. An almost impossible task for any team. On the first running play, Ronnie was hit hard and dropped behind the line for a safety. That was the final score of the game.

Had Ronnie's interception been called correctly by the officials, then the Jones team would have had the ball on the 20 yard line with the score 20-13 and a minute and a half to play.

The game film would prove the officials made an error on the call, a very costly error for the Jones Bobcats. Perhaps their error may have altered the team name on the National Champion trophy that year. Perhaps the winner would have been the Jones County Junior College Bobcats from little Ellisville, Mississippi. Who knows!

After the contest was over, the field was flooded by family members, friends and fans. Every player, those who won and those who came out on the short end of the score, were hounded by hundreds of spectators for autographs or anything they could toss their way as a remembrance of the occasion.

Compton's head cheerleader made it a point to find Red West and begged for anything he could offer. The only thing that came to mind was his helmet he was carrying. He tossed it to her and with a kiss said good-bye. The equipment manager was not real pleased with the loss of a helmet; however, the value would never be recouped as Red left for the Marines shortly after returning to Ellisville.

Within days, Red would chide his best friend Elvis Presley by ribbing him that while he was touring the southern Bible Belt, playing before high school sock hop crowds numbering perhaps only in the hundreds, he had just returned from sunny California where he played in the historical Rose Bowl before more than 57,000 spectators.

BACK IN MISSISSIPPI, the tiny community welcomed their heros back home. Of course winning matters, but the hometown crowd readily adopted the old saying, "It doesn't matter if you win or lose; what really matters is how you played the game." The Jones boys had done the school, city and the state of Mississippi proud. The trip to California had made history and instilled in each player, those from Jones and Compton, fond memories that would be carried with them throughout their entire lives.

8

THE UNWANTED GIFT

RETURNING FROM CALIFORNIA, the team had only a single week before leaving for Christmas vacation, and it would be taken up with cramming for exams. Although they had lost the game, every player was still on cloud nine because of the wonderful trip and the grand experience they all enjoyed.

This holiday vacation would be an extra long one as Christmas Day fell on Sunday. This year the students would be leaving school on the 16th and not returning until the second of January. Before he left for California, Ronnie's dad had committed that he would drive to Ellisville and bring him home for the holidays. He looked forward to having some leisure time to visit with his oldest son. However, unbeknownst at the time of the promise, this date conflicted with the day he had to meet with E. Dixie Beggs, his attorney, to finalize corporate papers setting up his new company, Dixie Grading and Paving.

When the conflicting dates were recognized, he asked Billy if he would drive up for the purpose. This presented no problem. Billy was delighted to have the opportunity to take a trip, especially if he could use his dad's brand new Pontiac of which he had taken delivery only two weeks earlier.

Billy's car would have made the trip, but he occasionally borrowed his dad's for special events, although very much aware just how meticulous his father was about his automobile. His dad was from very humble beginnings and prided himself on taking care of everything he owned, be it a car, tools, clothes, any and everything. And Heavens to Betsy, if someone left a ring on the dashboard from a Coke can, it could wreak havoc, bring a scolding and perhaps minor bodily harm from Daddy Williams as he was fond of thumping the guilty briskly about the head and shoulders. No, not really; he just wanted to make sure that all in the family took care of their belongings, especially his.

THE PLAYERS WANTED to have a party before they left for the holidays. Their plan was for each to entice their number one muffin into planning the party, buying the food and booze, and they in turn would grace them by showing up. The party was set for Friday, the night before they were to leave school the next morning.

About four o'clock Thursday afternoon Red came pouncing down the steps into the basement of the Bull Pen looking for Ronnie.

"Roper, where is Rod?"

"While ago he went outside with a pail of water. Said something about washing out some britches or something. He's out back."

Hustling back up the dark, narrow stairs he rounded the building. "Man, whatcha doing out here in the cold. You crazy?"

"Gotta wash my new pants."

"Put them in the cleaners for God's sake. You don't know nothin' 'bout washing clothes, you idiot."

"Look, Red, this is my best pair of slacks. Gonna wear them to the party tomorrow night. They're brand new. Polyester. Ain't gonna trust them to no cleaners. KnowwhatImean?"

"Hoss, its freezing out here. Let's go over to Nub's for a brew. Got something to talk about."

"All right, all right, hold your horses, just a second. Let's go back downstairs so I can hang these up to dry. Think Roper'll steal them?"

"Steal what? Yore pants? You gotta be kidding me. Come on, let's go."

"Listen, Red, go get that 45 record by your buddy Elvis and bring it here."

"What for? Man, what for?"

"Just go get it. Crap."

Returning with "That's All Right," Ronnie put the 45-rpm record on his small black and red RCA player, turned up the volume full blast and locked the door behind them. For the next two hours nothing was heard around the dorm but the same song, over and over and over. The coaches were furious.

OF ALL RONNIE'S friends at JCJC, he and Red were almost the perfect match in personalities. Both full of themselves, witty, always looking for more fun. Even when overloaded and completely occupied with a fine muffin at their side, their eyes still scrutinized every young sweet thing who happened to stroll into the room.

The barkeep at Nub's knew they were not of age to partake, but as long as they behaved themselves and kept quiet nothing was said. They isolated themselves around their favorite table where Bo'Deen made sure they didn't want for anything. She, a tall, strikingly beautiful, leggy brunette who was once runner-up for the Miss Mississippi crown, had lost her battle with the bottle a few years earlier. Shortly after the pageant she moved to Nashville in search of a country music singing career, but as close as she ever came was Tootsie's Orchid Lounge, just across the back alley from the Old Ryman Auditorium, home of the Grand Ole Opry. After three years she finally threw in the towel and returned to Mississippi.

Although she was entirely null and void between the ears, she somehow managed to retain all her prodigious, bodacious and quite magnificent dimensions. It had long been suspected around the JCJC campus the description of the character in the prank known as "going to see Miss Lilly" was, in fact, the exact description of Bo'Deen.

"Hoss, the damndest thing is happening to ole Elvis. Man, it's wild! I don't know if he's going to make it big time or not, but he's shore giving it his best shot. Since he signed on with the Louisiana Hayride, he's been on it every Saturday night. Tomorrow night will be his 41st straight week, can you believe that? I don't know if he's just a flash in the pan or not, but they really seem to like him, 'specially the girls."

"Man, I like the cat," said Ronnie. "The other day that dumb dumb Susie said that Pat Boone was a much better singer and a better performer than Elvis. Jeez, Pat Boone's just a zombie who stands around like an old damp mop, while Elvis has more movements than a 21-jewel Elgin.

"Didn't he grow up in Memphis?"

"Naw, man, he's from Tupelo. I done told you that! They moved to Memphis about six years ago. Had nothing. Very poor. They moved into public housing at the Lauderdale Courts. He told me that his dad had even served some time in prison for bad checks or something like that. His folks couldn't find work in Tupelo, so they came to the big city."

"What's he like? Stuck up? You really like him?" Ronnie questioned.

"Heck yeah, I like him. He's a great guy. I'll take you back to Memphis again after the holidays, and we'll get with him and have us a party. If you like me, then I guarantee you'll adore Elvis.

"Anyway, Rod, let me tell you what I wanted to talk about. Some of the students found out that I was jam up and jelly tight with Elvis back in Memphis. So the school newspaper wanted me to write an article for the paper before I check out of here. Something about him and me. I didn't know what to write, but I put this together. What I want you to do is to read it, and tell me what you think."

They moved to another table where an overhead light swagged from the ceiling reflected its beam directly over the yellow legal pad with light, scratchy pencil lettering.

THE UNWANTED GIFT

From the small town of Tupelo, Mississippi, on January 8, 1935, the world was given a treasure. During his formative years Elvis Presley was the typical barefoot Southern kid who, dressed in tattered clothes, could be found playing in the streets and school grounds with other kids his age. Ideas or dreams were seldom voiced by anyone in the Presley family as their plight of poverty forced them into a day-to-day existence with little hope or reason to reflect on the remotest possibility of a brighter future.

Approaching his eleventh birthday, he had pestered his parents unmercifully for a .22 rifle, but Gladys and Vernon Presley explained time and again they could not afford the expensive $28 gift. Nearing his birthday, he and his mom

> visited the Tupelo Hardware where she decided they could afford a nice guitar. The price, $7.75 plus two percent tax. Elvis pitched a real hissy fit after finally realizing that a rifle was not to be. For months "The Unwanted Gift" stood silent in the corner of his room.

"Wait a minute. Wait just a minute. Red, what is a hissy fit?" Ronnie wondered.

"You know, man, you know what I mean. He was teed, pissed. You know. Go on read the rest."

"BS," Ronnie mumbled and then continued.

> Still living in Tupelo and not having money to afford lessons, over the next year or two Elvis occasionally banged on the guitar more in a playful manner than in earnest.
>
> Just four months shy of his fourteenth birthday the Presleys decided to move to Memphis in search of employment and a better way of life. They moved a couple of times within the same neighborhood and were finally accepted for a stint in public housing at the Lauderdale Courts. With each move the guitar was tossed around, abused, mishandled and shown little care or concern.
>
> When Elvis entered Humes High School as a freshman, he was somewhat different from the other students. He dressed different, looked different, talked different and, in general, was different. This would create problems with some of the bigger tougher guys, fellow classmates that were more rugged than he. Some boys sought to change his lifestyle by often creating personal trouble for him.
>
> It was at Humes where Elvis and I became friends. I was the center on the football team and was heavy into Golden Gloves competition. For my size I was physically well built and a powerful athlete. I learned early on how to take care of myself, being also raised in public housing.

"Well, now, Mr. Red West," Ronnie said, "you really poured it on yourself with massive doses of all that macho crap. 'A powerful, physically well built athlete,' my fanny! You just wait 'til the boys hear about this back at the Bull Pen."

"Rod, its just a story. Keep on reading, and hush yo' mouth," Red scolded. "Anyway, you remember that I kept my word and haven't told anyone about how everyone called you a 'Strutter' back at Pensacola High."

"All right, all right." Ronnie noted, then continued with the text.

On more than one occasion I had to intervene between Elvis and those who wished him harm. From such happenings came a deep bond of friendship between him and me. We visited back and forth in each other's homes, "drug the main" through the streets of Memphis and often doubleddated. These were good times, just days of pure innocence. Two young boys who had very few material things in life, but we had a wonderful outlook and attitude. It was a place and time when "yes" and "no" was always followed by "sir" and "ma'am". This was our upbringing, our Southern heritage.

Sometimes at nights or after school I would go to his apartment, and we would take turns picking his guitar. He was always strumming and beating it but hadn't the faintest idea about how to do anything more than just bang away. In fact, he had beat on it so fiercely he even knocked the pick guard completely off.

After graduating from Humes in June of 1953 Elvis began to earn his own living. After short employment periods with Parker Machinists and Precision Tool, in November he hired on full-time with Crown Electric Company. Life for Elvis, me and our friends was very, very simple. After a day's work we just kinda tooled around the city at night with our buddies.

Within a month after graduating from Humes, Elvis put his guitar into his old car, an 11-year-old 1942 Lincoln Zephyr that his dad had saved $35 to buy, and drove to the Memphis Recording Studio on Union Street. He said he paid a lady $4 to make a disc of "My Happiness," a gift he gave to his mother. With a whole lot of luck, that $4 investment just may turn out to be a good one. When I found out that he had paid the studio to make a record for his mom, I really got on his case. I kept asking him to let me hear it, but never, never would he play it for anyone. He kept saying that his mom wouldn't let him.

For the next year or so nothing much exciting happened for us around Memphis. We just cruised the city, stopping at drive inns, taking in a movie and occasionally slipping down on Beale Street and peaking into the blues clubs.

In June of last year Elvis had started tinkering around

with a couple of other Memphis musicians introduced to him by Sam Phillips. The day after Independence Day he went back into Mr. Phillips' studio where the three of them recorded what was to become his very first commercial record, "That's All Right."

The release of the record created a lot of attention on Dewey Phillips' radio show. Elvis started making a few local appearances in Memphis clubs, then quickly expanded his routine to include some high school gigs and other small venues not too distant from home. I always tagged along.

During the year he would record two additional records between our whirlwind trips across a small portion of the South. After his second record he was invited to appear on the Grand Ole Opry. I couldn't hardly believe it. It blew my mind to know that my friend was on the world famous Grand Ole Opry of all places. Man, this was really uptown. Two weeks later he was invited to appear on the Louisiana Hayride and has returned there every Saturday night since. Maybe this will be the real beginning of something big for Elvis Presley, who knows. I think perhaps his appearances on the Hayride may mark the beginning of a schedule which may someday lead him down the road to fame and fortune. You just never know. Could be!

With all the traveling on his agenda I signed on fulltime to accompany him as driver, assistant, companion and, most of all, as a close personal friend. Someone to be close by when the hours of loneliness and apprehension set in, and believe me there were many struggling hours for him. While he was on the road, he truly missed his parents, especially his mother.

I continued traveling with him for the first eleven months of this punishing and laborious schedule until last August when I reported to football camp here at Jones. For some reason or other, I had a craving to try to capitalize on whatever football talents I may have and do so at the college level. Maybe I was just thinking of my future in case Elvis didn't succeed in the tough music business, which at best was a very long shot.

Elvis told me several times how much he admired me for wanting to continue my education but more so my desire to compete in football. He really loves football. It's his most favorite sport.

After he bought me the Model A, he gave me his old, somewhat tattered guitar to keep me company. Heck, we both were just learning how to play a guitar. At least I had some music experience by being in the band. He had none at all. I tried my best to teach him how to read music, but that was next to impossible. He just kept on banging away on the old guitar, breaking string after string with his heavy strumming and beating.

When he would play a gig, he was so rough and beat his guitar so hard it became a habit for me to stand in the stage wings so when he broke a string he would slide his guitar off stage with a swift kick and I'd kick another one back to him. With or without a guitar, he never missed a note, never missed a word, just kept on singing. Needless to say, I replaced a whole lot of strings that first year.

When he gave me the Model A and guitar, I guess he was thinking about the times I came to his rescue in high school. Perhaps the gifts were not only a token of appreciation but a reminder that he had not forgotten my willingness to be there when he needed me the most.

The giving of something personal was, and is, a Southern tradition, especially when its done for the purpose of showing true and loyal gratitude to a close friend. When Elvis gave me his old guitar, it signified, comparatively speaking, a similar gesture of a young boy who may give his playmate friend a worn-out baseball glove or perhaps a well-used bat when he was fortunate enough to get a new one.

I threw the old guitar in the back seat of my Model A and headed down the road to my first day of college. When I arrived here at Jones, the coaches assigned me quarters in the "Bull Pen." I looked forward to playing college ball with great anticipation. Even the Bull Pen had that old stale, musty sports odor. This was going to be fun!

Over the last five months we have made good use of the old guitar. Many were the nights someone would pick it up and strum something that somewhat resembled a tune, and we all would pitch in and sing along. It was handled, used, picked at and abused by most of the athletes who lived in the dorm as well as other students who dropped by.

I have truly enjoyed being here at Jones and most of all having a great undefeated year, then going to California to play for all the marbles, the National Championship, in the Rose Bowl. Man, that was a real treat for me and all the guys. After the game Compton's head cheerleader asked me for something as a souvenir. Having nothing more, I simply tossed her my helmet. I guess this guiltless act of giving reflected the unselfish attitude and daily way of life for us good ole Southern boys. The equipment manager, however, was teed for sure.

Last week when we got back to Ellisville, I made a decision not to continue with college. I was broke and had to do something immediately to make a living. I sold my Model A sedan to a teammate, Steve Perkins, for $50.

And before we leave for the Christmas break, I will give the old guitar to Ronnie Williams, my closest friend here at Jones. I just want to give him something to express my appreciation to him for having a good season and a great Rose Bowl game. But most of all, for just being my friend. The same reason that Elvis gave the guitar and Model A to me a few months ago.

By Red West.

"Man, this is good. You didn't write it, now did you? Fess up, who wrote this for you? Did Becky write it, huh?" Ronnie questioned.

"Well, Hoss, I gotta admit, I wrote it myself. What'd you think?"

"Still don't believe you wrote it, but if you did or didn't, Red, it's pretty special. Did you mean it? You going to give me that guitar?"

"Yeah, if you want it." Answered Red. "I have no use for it."

"That's great. I appreciate it. Heck, I may just record me a tune or two. Thanks, man. Where is it? Back at the Bull Pen?"

"Yeah, I'll give it to you before we take off in the morning."

THE DAY WAS absolutely beautiful. The weather man was right in predicting crisp, cloudless days with the temperature in the mid 40s. Billy arrived in Ellisville late Friday afternoon and called Ronnie from a service station only to learn that he was off with Red somewhere. He left a message that he would pick him up in the morning at 9:00 o'clock sharp. A teammate promised to stick the note on his door. Just a short ride northeast Billy located the El Patio Motel, about halfway to Laurel. Ronnie had made him reservations earlier in the week.

On Saturday morning, much to his surprise, Ronnie was johnny-on-the-spot and raring to ride.

"Morning, Ron, or is it Rod today?"

"Good morning little brother, and either will do, thank you. How'd you cope last night?"

"Slept like a feather, but that El Patio ain't much of a motel."

"Well, you look rested. Must've been okay," Ronnie offered.

"Yeah. Right. Okay was about all you could say for it. Hey, ain't that Red's old Model A? The one ya'll drove to Pensacola last month?"

"Drove? We damn near pushed it the entire way. While Red steered the thing, Flemming, Roper, Sam Burkett and I pushed our tails off. Didn't get to Pensacola until 2:00 in the morning and we left here at 4:00 in the afternoon.

"Last night we had a little party, and after a few beers Red sold it to Steve Perkins for $50. We told Perk he paid way too much for the wreck. But I guess ole Red came out of the deal all right since his buddy Elvis gave it to him. Didn't cost him anything."

The brothers had breakfast at a popular corner cafe on Ellisville square, then hit the road. They found their way over to Highway 15, turned south and headed for US-98 which would connect down near Beaumont, Mississippi. From there they would hammer down towards Mobile and then just an hour drive to Pensacola. A few miles out of town Ronnie ordered, "Man, pull over."

"What you need? What you wanna stop for?"

"Little brother, just pull over. I want to get something from the trunk."

Finding a side road, Billy stopped the car and punched the truck release button. Quickly retrieving the guitar, Ronnie returned again to ride shotgun.

"What you gonna do with that? Where'd you get that old guitar?"

"Red gave it to me. Said Elvis gave it to him in August just before he reported to football camp. Thing's pretty ragged, huh?

Red tells the story that Elvis' folks gave it to him years ago and he moaned and groaned and threw a real fit over it.
Seems like he wanted a .22 rifle or something like that. But had to settle for this. I really don't know the exact story.

"Red's real tight with Elvis. You know he's got two or three records out, don't you? You been listening to him, little brother?"

"Yeah, some, I kinda like him. But the country stations in Pensacola won't play him. They say he's not country. Big LeRoy Morris won't play him at all. Says he sings like a black man."

"Oh, yeah! Big LeRoy! Has he lost any of that lard he's been totin' 'round for years?"

"Naw. I guess he still weighs more than four hundred and fifty pounds."

"That fat he's carryin's gonna kill him one day, and probably sooner than later," Ronnie proclaimed.

"Anyway, Red is Elvis' best friend and says he's really a neat guy. They went to high school together and bummed around a lot in Memphis. Red keeps hoping that he continues to do well 'cause he's thinking of going to work for him, or either going into the Marines. But he really thinks it would be exciting to travel around the country doing those shows.

"Every Saturday night Red hits up ole Connie Boykin, one of our teammates, for his radio so he can listen to him on the Louisiana Hayride. He's on it every weekend.

"Red is always giving things away. After the Rose Bowl he gave his helmet to some cute little muffin who chased him across the field. The coach could have killed him for doing that. They said he would have to pay for it, but my guess is they'll never see a dime. I guarantee you that."

"Last month when you brought your friends home, who was the guy from Panama City?" Bill asked.

"Oh! That was Sam Burkett. Roper's from Bay Springs, Mississippi, and of course Red's from Memphis. You know Pete's from Pensacola."

"Yeah, I know Pete."

"Mamma shore fixed us a fine meal that next afternoon. The guys are still talking about her fried chicken, turnip greens, black-eyed peas and great Mexican cornbread. I guess she must've fried four or five chickens. And the best thing about it was we didn't have to pluck 'em. Said later that we acted like we hadn't eaten in a week. Man, that was a great meal."

"Sounds so. Wish I could have been in on it."

"Where were you?"

"I stayed over at Cleve Lovelace's for the weekend. Don't you remember I saw y'all at the Surf Club Saturday night?"

"Yeah, I forgot. I fixed Red up with Pat Hearn, Tony with Patsy Elliott and I was with Tennie. That was a fun night."

"What about Sam? Who was he with?"

"Oh, he hitchhiked on to Panama City. We left him up on 98 about 2:30 in the morning. Said that he finally got picked up just before dawn. That must have been a long night for him. We tried to get him to stay over with us and go home the next morning, but he was eager to get on down the road. Musta had something waiting.

"LOOK OUT! He's turning in front of you!" cried Ronnie.

Along a three-mile straight stretch of State Road 29, a two-lane road, somewhere between Runnelstown and New Augusta in Perry County, Mississippi, with great weather, and perfect vision, Billy eased into the left lane and hammered down on his dad's new Pontiac. Rather than ease up behind the old truck as he should have done, then slip around it, he chose to change lanes and pick up speed first. About the time his front bumper was about even with the rear bumper of the truck the driver decided, without a signal, to turn left.

Billy's only chance was to try to beat the truck down the dirt road, a sandy road with three-foot-deep trenches on either side. He bore down on his power brakes while turning left at the same time. The right rear end of his Pontiac slapped the left rear end of the old truck, sending it into the ditch.

The dilapidated truck was well overloaded with nineteen people aboard. There were kids, men and women and older folks. All going to the field to begin their work day. How or why no one was injured had to be an absolute miracle.

Within the hour a Mississippi Highway Patrolman, a heavy-set, stereotypical officer, like often depicted in movies, came to the scene and scribbled a detailed report. He estimated that Billy had to have been traveling in excess of 80 miles per hour as skid marks were measured for more than 280 feet, damn near the length of a football field.

The old truck suffered little damage, the Pontiac didn't do as well. The right rear fender was torn off, and the trunk lid would not close. The rear bumper lay dead center of the highway.

The trooper wrote a ticket and told the boys they would have to follow him into the county seat and talk to the judge. They were somewhat surprised to learn, especially on a Saturday morning, that a judge, any judge, would be holding court.

The boys followed the trooper into town, then to a weather-beaten general store where an elderly man with a thick, white beard, a true-to-life "Boss Hogg," was summoned from the back. Standing in the middle of the squeaky, wooden floor, the trooper began to tell of the accident but was stopped when the judge asked all three of them to come into his office.

Standing in front of nothing more than a neglected and dusty formica-covered business desk and the judge who had reclined comfortably in his old rickety high back chair, the boys told their side of the story.

"Well, because of your speed I find you guilty of causing an accident. I impose a fine of eight dollars. Five for causing the wreck and three for the judge's fee. Can you boys pay the fine or will you want to come back to court after the holidays?"

"Sir, can we go outside and discuss it?" Billy inquired.

"Certainly. Take as long as you like and come back in when you've made your decision."

They walked outside to the Pontiac where Ronnie asked, "How much money you got?"

"I got about ten dollars, but we're out of gas. You got any?"

"No, man. We all pitched in last night for that party. Hell, I'm broke."

"What we gonna do?" Billy fretted.

"Let's go back inside and tell him we just don't have any money."

"Ronnie, he might stick us in jail."

"Man, he ain't gonna do that. He ain't gonna do that for causing a silly wreck. Come on."

They found their way back into "His Honor's chambers" and

Billy spoke first. "Sir, we have only nine dollars and some change and we're out of gas. We're from Pensacola and we'll have to fill up to get home. We also need to buy some tape or something to tie down the trunk of the car. We just don't have the money to pay the fine."

"You got anything of value you can leave with the court to insure that you will come back after Christmas?"

Billy again asked the judge if he could step into the corner and talk with Ronnie. He agreed.

Billy softly whispered, "How about the guitar. Can we leave it?"

"Now, what would that old codger do with a worn out guitar?" Ronnie asked. "Anyway, Red gave it to me, and I want to keep it."

"It matters little what he will do with it; what matters is being able to get outta here." Billy harked, somewhat anxiously.

"Let's just tell him we have nothing to leave. Yeah, that's what we'll do," ordered Ronnie. "Just tell him we have nothing of value to leave."

Returning in front of the desk, it was Ronnie's turn to speak. "Sir, we can not pay the eight dollars, and we have nothing of value to leave with you. We will promise to come back when you say we must, but that is all that we can do."

While Ronnie moved his arms back and forth, as was his habit and mannerism while talking, the judge spotted the shine of his watch as it glittered brightly when the glow of the naked bulb dangling from the ceiling hit it just right.

"How about that watch? Will you leave it?"

"Sir, this watch was given to me last week in California, in fact, just a week ago today when our football team played in the Rose Bowl. Each player received a new watch and I treasure mine very much."

"You were on that Jones team, were you? The team that played those niggers?"

"Sir, I don't like to put it that way, but, yessir, that is correct."

"Well, you had better leave the watch with me. Do that, and you boys can be on your way."

In their haste to leave the judge's chambers, they failed to

get a receipt for the watch—or any other paperwork for that matter. Stopping briefly at the store counter, they quickly purchased
two rolls of masking tape, secured the trunk lid tightly and headed
for the Florida line. Happiness was the state of Mississippi in
their rear view mirror.

THE MORNING TRIP had turned from a beautiful, joyous,
crisp December day into a journey which would not end on a
happy note. Billy was very concerned about the rear end of his
father's car, but even more so about his own. A ring left from a
coke can on the dashboard would be of inconsequential significance when measured against the wreck!

Just west of Mobile Ronnie spoke up. "Listen, Billy, let's
tell Dad that I was driving the car."

"No dice, nothing doing. I was driving and I'll face whatever happens. That's the way it is."

"Well, now just listen to me, smarty. Pay attention. You've
got to live at home, I don't. It would be much easier if we just
told him that I was driving."

"Ronnie, you know he'll find out differently. How many times
have you ever pulled anything over on him? I mean ever?"

"Not many. You're right about that. But he won't find out
this time. He won't know the difference," Ronnie pressed.

"I just don't want to take the chance. No. I was driving, and
that's the way it was and is."

Arriving at home, they immediately told their story. Their
saving grace was, although their dad was furious with them, that
he was really more teed with the Mississippi judge than with
them. Billy got chewed out thoroughly, but it was light as compared to the phone conversation Daddy Williams had with the
judge the first thing on Monday morning. He was told in very
strong northwest Florida language that the watch had better be
on its way to Pensacola in Tuesday morning's mail and that he
was sending an eight-dollar check direct to the judge's attention
no later than noon the same day.

The watch arrived overnight by Greyhound bus.

OVER THE LAST couple of years The Unwanted Gift had
done wonders for Elvis Presley. But as fate would dictate, it

would became both a lifesaver as well as an anchor to Ronnie. For the remainder of his life, he would treat it as his personal crutch. Something he possessed. Something he owned. Something that no one would ever take away from him.

In years to come it would symbolize within his mind an entire world unto itself. Something that he would hold onto tightly, something that even a king's ransom could never acquire. To him it was his personal connection to someone who had pulled himself up by his boot strings and made a terrific life for himself. A life from the poorest beginning, a life from the streets of the ghettos to the very tip of the highest mountain. A life of glamour, headlines and importance. A life that Ronnie could only dream of accomplishing. A set of circumstances and events straight from the world's stage where it is mandated that everyone is required to play the hand that life had dealt them.

The Unwanted Gift would be around to see both men succumb to depression, loneliness, agony and despair. Their two lives were now set in motion where nothing could change them. Where no amount of money or great numbers of friends or millions of fans could make one iota of difference.

RETURNING TO SCHOOL after the holidays, many of the players were ready to visit senior colleges in an effort to further their football career and continue their education. Ronnie and several teammates gladly accepted any invitation to visit any school that was interested in their talent. Any school that would pay for their transportation and cost of the trip could expect them to show up on campus.

Most of the traveling was done at night where they could arrive on campus the following morning. The boys were fond of nighttime traveling so they could listen to the all-night disc jockeys from WBAM, WCKY and Del Rio, Texas. The DJs were most entertaining, especially Dixie Hatfield, Joe Rumore and "John R'Ra."

After making several visits, Roper chose Memphis State. Red opted to join the United States Marines and get his service behind him so he would be free to start a career with Elvis. Several others chose the University of Mississippi or Mississippi Southern.

Eddie Gebara wanted to join the Air Force, but after two tries at the induction center the recruiter found him a quarter of an inch too short according to their regulations. Since there was little he could do to make himself any taller, he finally gave in to listening to his buddies in a vain effort to overcome the quarter inch.

Ronnie, Pete Flemming and Gayle Winchester saw to it that their fellow Pensacolian stayed in bed and relaxed the entire weekend. It was their assumption that walking around or joggin' as he often did, was a factor on compacting his body, therefore, packing it downward into a shorter frame. Their plan was to eliminate this possibility in its entirety.

Monday morning, while he remained flat on his back in bed, they eased his sweat clothes over his frame then gently lifted him onto a cot they borrowed from the training room. Placing the cot in the rear of a pickup they carefully drove to the side entrance of the induction center.

When the line was clear, they carried him on the cot into the building. He slowly lifted himself from the cot and walked gently towards the tape that hung limply on the south wall.

He braced himself against the cold cinder block and stood as erect as he possibly could stretch, while keeping both feet flat on the floor. The measuring doohickey gave its reading. It didn't work. He was still a quarter inch too short!

"Thank you for your letter and inscribed copy of 'RONNIE'. I appreciate your taking the time to inform me about your brother's plight and your memoir of him. Alcoholism among our youth is a tragedy and your efforts to educate the public about it are most commendable. Your powerful message on this important issue will hopefully prevent other young people from experiencing the dangers of alcoholism. Please let me know if I may be of further assistance."

Charlie Crist, Florida Attorney General

9

DROPPING LOUISIANA STATE
FOR FLORIDA STATE

AFTER TWO SEASONS of starting in the backfield at Jones and with only one loss and a great Rose Bowl game, Ronnie was heavily recruited for his final two years of eligibility. During the season JCJC Coach Clark had tried in vain to get him to attend the Mississippi State-Ole Miss game. Both head coaches had voiced their interest in having him sit on their bench during the game as a guest of their team. But for some reason he just was not interested in another Mississippi school.

He would be a transfer student-athlete and found the rules at some colleges more rigid than at others. It appeared the grades of transfer students were analyzed more strictly; therefore, a couple of the major colleges who had recruited him were not able to offer a full scholarship.

Among the schools which showed interest in his final two years of eligibility were the University of Louisville, University of Florida, University of Alabama, Furman University, Wake Forrest, Louisiana State University, Southeastern Louisiana, Memphis State and Florida State.

A couple of the letters he received would cause pure hell within the ranks of the NCAA today. One of noted interest, dated November 21, 1955, was on a letterhead which read "Baptist Brotherhood of South Carolina."

123

Dear Ronnie:

We want you at Furman! We offer you a full scholarship, all expenses, plus $15 per month. And, those
folks in Greenville will "take care" of your other needs,
you needn't worry about that. Please keep this to yourself, however.

"You and Ken (Schulte) work out your affairs so
you can come to Greenville on December 2nd. You
can leave Laurel at 9:19 a.m., and arrive in Greenville
at 5:30 p.m., same day.

"P. S. We want your entire backfield. Are you interested in that?"

And, underlined, it instructed, *"Please do not show this letter to
anyone!"*

LOUISIANA STATE UNIVERSITY chief recruiter, Carl
Maddox, had enlisted the assistance of Barney Poole to hit the
road and do some heavy, and if necessary, expensive recruiting.
They were looking for new talent and were most interested in
those with proven abilities. Those who could provide a lightning fast backfield, fleet runners who could carry the payload.

Poole had a great personality that helped him immensely in
becoming a top-notch recruiter. While playing in college, he had
been named All-American at three different schools—North Carolina, Ole Miss and Army—where he was a teammate of the great
Glenn Davis and Doc Blanchard. Perhaps desperation set in when
it appeared that LSU was in bad need of reshaping its backfield
after the initial season of their new Head Coach Paul Dietzel.
His discouraging 1955 record produced only three wins, five
losses and two ties with three of the losses and one tie within his
Southeastern Conference. It was very obvious that overzealous
fans, financial backers and boosters at LSU would not put up
with two or three losing seasons in a row.

The first day JCJC students returned for classes after the
Christmas Holidays, a call came to Coach Clark's office from
Poole. According to protocol he would first make his interest
known to the coach before approaching his players.

"Hello, Jim? Barney Poole, here."

Phone 2-0247 & 2-1847 (Residence)

CHRIST
EVANGELISM
STEWARDSHIP
CHURCH LOYALTY
BAPTIST DOCTRINES
PHILIPPIANS 1:20

JOHN A. FARMER, DIRECTOR

Baptist Brotherhood of South Carolina

1301 HAMPTON STREET, COLUMBIA, SOUTH CAROLINA

November 21, 1955.

CONFIDENTIAL MATTERS.

Mr. Ronnie Williams,
Jones Junior College,
Ellisville, Miss.

Dear Ronnie:

That was a good game you played last Saturday night in spite of that
bad leg. It takes a lots of guts to play like that. I'm for you, boy!

We want you at Furman! We offer you a full scholarship, all expenses,
plus $15.00 per month. And, those folks in Greenville will "take care"
of your other needs, you needn't worry about that. Please keep this to
yourself, however.
I have found out that none of the other schools can take you boys for
spring practice. You must graduate first. Perhaps Coach Griffith can
work out something for you, we'll see. This is true in both the Southeast and the Southwest.

You and Ken work out your affairs so you can come to Greenville on Dec.
2nd. You can leave Laurel at 9:19 a.m., and arrive in Greenville at
5:30 p.m., same day.

Please let me hear from you.

Yours faithfully,

John A. Farmer,
1301 Hampton Street,
Columbia, S.C.

P.S. We want your entire backfield. Are you interested in that?
Please do not show this letter to anyone!

"That we may present every man mature in Christ Jesus" — COLOSSIANS 1:28 b

*A letter from Furman University dated 11/21/55. You
would never see a letter like this today.*

Louisiana State University "L" Club

BATON ROUGE, LA.

January 10, 1956

Mr. Ronnie Williams
12 Boland Place
Pensacola, Florida

Dear Ronnie:

We are forwarding under separate cover, a small token of appreciation from this organization for you having selected Louisiana State University to further your education. We are proud to know you as a future Tiger.

I wish to take this means of welcoming you to L. S. U. and wishing you the very best scholastically as well as in your athletic endeavors.

Sincerely,

Geo. W. May, Jr.
President

GWM:hb

ONCE A TIGER ALWAYS A TIGER

A January 10, 1956, letter from Louisiana State's "L" Club. This type of letter is a relic from the past.

The Florida State University

Tallahassee

DEPARTMENT OF
PHYSICAL EDUCATION FOR MEN

August 21, 1956

Mr. Ronald Williams
c/o James Crabtree
300 North 12th Street
Pensacola, Florida

Dear Ron:

This is your official invitation to report for football at
Florida State University.

The first training table meal will be served at 6:00 P. M.
on August 30. It is most important that you get here sometime on August 30.

On the 31st of August the photographers and newsmen will
begin their work. Pictures of each member of the squad will
be taken for their home-town paper and that day will be known
as Press Day. You will also have your physical examination,
be assigned a room, and be issued your football equipment.

We are all looking forward to seeing you at the evening meal
on August 30.

Sincerely yours,

Tom Nugent
Head Football Coach

P. S. As you know, it is necessary that each man bring his
own towel and bed linens for a single bed.

TN:vc

Florida State Coach Tom Nugent's letter dated 8/21/56.

"Hey, Barney. How you been?"

"Fine Coach, how's things with you?"

"Well, after that California trip, we are about settled down again."

"That was a great game. I hated to see you and the team come out on the short end of the score," Poole eulogized.

"You know how it goes. Win a few, loose a few, few rained out."

"I heard that. Say, Coach, I would like to discuss LSU football with a couple of your players. That all right with you?"

"Absolutely. How can I help you?"

"I need to reach Ronnie Williams."

"Barney, he should be in class at this hour, and there's about a fifty-fifty chance that he is. I can have him in my office at 3:30 this afternoon. Can you call again?"

"Yes, sir. You can expect my call at 3:30 sharp. But if you got a minute, tell me a little about him."

"Barney, you should be looking at our entire backfield. We got some fine ones here this year."

"Yeah, Jim, I know that you do, been following your progress all year. But we're looking for only one more running back. One that can pass, receive and run like Speedo."

"Barney, that's Ronnie to a tee. He's fast as greased lightning, and he's also a pinpoint passer. He scored both our touchdowns in Pasadena, and both were receptions. He can take a hit and understands that goes with the territory. However, let me tell you up front, he really does not like playing defense. Jeez, I think he only weighs 147 pounds," explained Clark.

"Thanks for the points, Jim. Tell Ronnie I'll be calling him at 3:30. Thanks again. Good-bye."

"See you, Barney. Hope you have a good recruiting year. Remember, we got some mighty good ball players looking for another home for the next two years. So long."

"So long, Jim."

Coach Clark filled Ronnie in about Poole's football career, both college and the pros. Ronnie was most impressed with his background and experiences. At exactly 3:30 the phone rang, and Coach Clark turned the phone over to Rod and left the room.

"This is Ron Williams."

"Hello, Ronnie. How was your holidays?"

"Great, Coach Poole, and yours?"

"We had a terrific Christmas. One of the best. Say, let me congratulate you on the Rose Bowl game. I've seen film of the game, and your two touchdowns were a thrill to watch."

"Well, Schulte got the ball to me. All I had to do was run under it. That was the easy part."

"Yeah! Right! Listen to me, you had a terrific game. A game which you will always remember," said Poole, pouring it on hot and heavy.

"Thanks for the comment, Coach."

"Ronnie, the purpose of my call is obvious. Coach Dietzel wants you in the LSU backfield. You interested?"

"Always interested in talking, you know that for sure. However, me and some of our other players have made plans to visit several campuses during the next few weeks. Tell me what's on your mind?"

"Ronnie, we just signed Jim Taylor from over at Hinds. You know him?"

"Do I know him? You bet I do. That tornado comes through a line at about 300 miles an hour. Coach, when I'm plumb full of beer and haven't peed in three days, I don't weigh 150 pounds. When that mother is headed straight towards me and hauling his 200-pound rear end, his is a name you don't easily forget. Yeah! I know him all right."

"Well, he'll be playing for us next year. Wanna be in the backfield with him?" Poole bragged and urged at the same time.

"I had rather be on the same side of the line, that's for sure and for certain. And let me tell you while we're talking smash mouth football, I want you to thank Coach Dietzel for taking that monster tackle, Earl Leggett, away from Hinds. I have had about all of that lard bucket I need. I had little success getting Red, Roper, Perkins and, for that matter, any of our linemen to stop him. They would let him through and leave the task all up to little ole me. Some of the time I swear they did it on purpose. Yes, I know him well 'cause the last four years I've played against him. He played high school ball in Jacksonville when I was at Pensacola High. What a monster."

"Ronnie, when can I come to sit down and talk with you? I

guarantee you that you can start next year in the backfield. Probably dividing your time between quarterback and half, much like you did at JCJC. I need to get you pledged up. How 'bout it."

"Coach, let me ask you something. Is there any problem with me transferring from Jones to LSU?"

"Of course not."

"I mean transferring and playing when I get there. You know my grades aren't the best in the conference."

"Ronnie, very few of our players are great students. Don't you worry; we'll take care of that. Don't you worry one bit. Now, when can I come sit down with you?"

"Coach, I want to visit some of the other schools first. You understand, don't you? If for no other reason than just to get to do a bit of traveling."

"Of course I understand. How about in two weeks?" insisted Poole.

"How about a month from today? That would suit me better."

"You got it. It's confirmed. I'll be in Ellisville four weeks from today. Right?"

"Agreed," Ronnie confirmed.

"Thanks, Ron. Good-bye."

"Coach, I'll see you in four weeks. So long."

Ronnie's memory about the powerful running of Jimmy Taylor was well founded. The two had met head-to-head many times during the '54 and '55 JCJC vs. Hinds games. JCJC's only defeat in two seasons had come at the hands of Hinds and was due much to the powerful running of Jim Taylor.

BEFORE POOLE RETURNED to Ellisville, Ronnie had received a letter from the president of the Louisiana State University "L" Club dated January 10, 1956. It, too, by today's standards, would create havoc within the NCAA:

Dear Ronnie:
We are forwarding under separate cover, a small token of appreciation from this organization for you having selected Louisiana State University to further your education. We are proud to know you as a future Tiger.
I wish to take this means of welcoming you to L.S.U.

and wishing you the very best scholastically as well as in your athletic endeavors.

A month later while visiting Ronnie at Jones, Poole signed both him and their fullback, Jerry Johnston. Although Johnston had two great years at JCJC at LSU, he would find himself in a backup role behind Taylor, who would be selected All-American in 1957, his last year of eligibility.

FOR COACH DIETZEL, it appeared his recruiters had found some great backfield experience as well as exceptional linemen. Their good fortune and appearance quickly took a different turn which at first glance seemed dreadful, but in time it would prove a Godsend, if only to LSU.

Unbeknownst to Ronnie, Barney Poole was only assisting LSU in its recruiting efforts on a part-time basis. Shortly after Ronnie signed with LSU, a full-time staff position opened up at the University of Alabama, and when offered the job Poole accepted on the spot. When Poole left LSU in early '56, Ronnie instantly decided that since his coach had bailed out on him he was no longer interested in moving to Baton Rouge in the fall.

When he declined the LSU scholarship, it left an open slot for another running back. LSU recruiters reviewed their options and decided to offer the position to a little-known Baton Rouge high school senior by the name of Billy Cannon. Hard times at LSU would soon be changing.

RONNIE PLACED A call to Florida State University Head Coach Tom Nugent and discussed his situation. Coach Nugent asked him to come for a visit the following weekend. While there, he succumbed to Nugent's wit and fast-talking salesmanship and immediately became a Seminole.

Coach Dietzel's 1956 record at LSU proved to be even worse than his first year. There were only three wins against seven losses. Five of the losses came at the hands of conference teams.

Although Coach Dietzel's record in 1957 was nothing to write home about, it did improve to five wins and five losses. Four of the wins and four of the losses were within the conference. Much of the success was due to the powerful running of All-American

Taylor and the ever-improving Billy Cannon. During the off-season Coach Dietzel and his staff were looking forward to 1958 with great expectations. They were not to be disappointed.

For years, LSU fans eagerly anticipated the coming of each new football season with talk of the two Tiger teams regarded as LSU's national champions—the great 10-0 team of 1908 and "next year." After fifty years, "next year" finally came about.

Much credit went to the rugged defensive play of the "Chinese Bandits" and the forceful and dominating power drives of Cannon. The LSU Tigers went undefeated in 1958 and outscored their opponents 275 to 53. They defeated Clemson 7-0 in the Sugar Bowl and were crowned the best of the best, National Champions.

Cannon was named All-American both in 1958 and 1959 and was awarded the Heisman Trophy after the 1959 season. It was thought by many that his selection as the Heisman winner was due to his magic run in the Ole Miss game. Top-ranked LSU trailed the third-ranked Rebels 3-0 early in the fourth quarter. Cannon fielded a punt on his 11 yard line and broke seven tackles on his way to pay dirt. To most, this 89-yard run remains as the single most important play in LSU football history.

Ronnie's decision to shun LSU in favor of Florida State was perhaps his first gut-wrenching decision and for sure his most atrocious football error. He would have played in the backfield with both Taylor and Cannon, two All-Americans. Since fate was not on his side, we shall never know what hand he may have been dealt had he made a different decision.

IT WAS NEVER determined if the "token of appreciation" that Ronnie received from the LSU "L" Club was ever returned. Fat chance that it was. All intelligent bets said it wasn't.

"WELL, LOOKIE HERE, BOO. We done got us a letter from ole Red. Guess he got my note. Says on the envelope it came from Tallahassee. Wonder what in the world he's doing in Tally?"

"Well, open it and lets take a look, goofy."

"Hey, it's on Detroit Tiger letterhead. Guess he's really going to try out for the team. He must've figured his friend Elvis wasn't going to make it in the music business. Red's a hellova a catcher. He'll do well in baseball."

"Read the letter, Ronnie. Read the letter," Boo scolded.

"Hi Hoss," it opened.

"That Red's a real wordsmith, ain't he Boo?"

"Yeah, yeah, but what's he having to say?"

"Let's see. 'I guess you got my address from coach. I sure would like to come up Easter, but the first is when I'm supposed to report. I'll be trying out for Donaldsonville, Georgia. I've been working out with Leon High School here in Tallahassee. If I make the team, I'll probably see you now and then.'

"Well of course he'll see me now and then since I'll be living in Tallahassee for two years. What you reckon he means, Boo?"

"Ronnie, Red doesn't know that you're moving to Tallahassee."

"Yeah, you're right. Gotta get back up with him. Let me tell you something, Red's got loads of talent. He was a great football player, now trying out for major league baseball. And you 'member how he would go out at night and play his cornet. Listening to that mother late at night, and as lonesome as we all were, would bring tears to your eyes. Never in my life have I ever known an athlete, a true kick-ass, rough and tumble athlete, who had so much musical talent. "

"Never mind, Ronnie, never mind. Just finish the stupid letter."

"All right, all right. 'Last night my brother had a party. He is going to get married April the second, and we started out at his apartment with a case of beer, and then we went to a little night club out on the highway. We were all drunk, but me and my brother's roommate were about the drunkest.'

"Now, Boo, we know that ole Red can party with the best of them, don't we? Lets see now, where was I. 'He is a highway patrolman and stands about 6'3" and weighs about 210. Anyway, we were dancing around, and he danced over to a table where this guy was wearing a hat. He took it off and put it on his head and kept on dancing. The guy jumped up and grabbed his hat and took a swing at him. The guy missed but Percy, that's his name, knocked him clean over a table. The Negro band that was playing stopped and watched. The guy landed close to where I was sitting, so I took my bottle of beer and poured it all over him.'

"Boo, did you hear that? Red poured his beer on that drunk right there on the floor. Wish I could have been there, I would have loved to have seen him do that.

"Boo, what was that song that said something about don't spit in the wind, don't mess with the Lone Ranger or something like don't screw with Big Jim. Well, every time I hear it, I think about ole Red. Let me tell you, Boo, you don't screw with Red West. He'll knock you on your rear. 'Member that time we were down in Hattisburg and that smart-ass, hippy-looking kid with the long hair said something to Red about the two muffins that were with us. 'Member I had that fine luscious blonde? Man, what a fine muffin. What was her name? Boo, what the devil was her name?"

"Wasn't it Lannie? Ronnie, didn't she call herself Lannie, or something like that. I think it was Elaine something, but she kept calling herself Lannie, I believe."

"That may have been it. Anyway, Red had that great-looking brunette. 'Member she wasn't a student but was visiting her friend who was. I think I 'member that she was from somewhere in Arkansas.

"Anyway, that dumb hippy said something like, 'Where'd y'all get that blackhead and that whitehead?' Well, the next thing I knew, Red had hit that creep twice with his right hand before he could blink his eyes and then cold-cocked him with a left uppercut. He was wearing glasses, those kinda little ole round silly looking ones. When Red hit that mother, they completely disintegrated.

"We were at some student hangout down near the Southern Miss campus. That fruit, I mean to tell you, he hauled butt after Red popped him that third time. No one fooled with us the rest of the night, that's for sure. That Red can be a mean rascal when he has a mind for it. You better believe."

"What else, Ronnie? What else did he write?"

"Okay, okay. 'The bouncer came running over to break it up, and Percy pulled out his police badge, so they threw the other guy out. I never laughed so hard in my life.'

"Man, I wish I could've seen that. Boo, we're missing out

on a lot of good times just sitting out here in Ellisville. We need to get on to Tallahassee. I hope Red sticks around there for awhile. Man, you remember all the fun we had last year. I guess that was the best year of real fun that I've ever had. Ole Red is one of a kind. A mighty good man. A man among men, and you don't see many good ones come by very often these days," Ronnie noted, then continued to read.

"'By the way, did Jones play a spring game this year? I'd like to know how it came out,'" the letter asked.

"Of course, they played a spring game. What's wrong with him? Just because he and I have finished playing, did he think the world of football at JCJC was washed up? I'll give him a call and report in, huh, Boo?"

"Sure, Ronnie, the man wants to know. You just need to give him an answer, and don't be so smart-ass about it. Read on, read on. What else?"

"Okay, let see what other words of wisdom he has for us. 'I'm sorry I didn't introduce you to Elvis that night, but I was in such a rush trying to get squared away that I forgot to. I happened to think about it after I left.'

"You know Boo, that Elvis guy may have something going for him. But that's a goofy name, ain't it? Who ever heard of the name Elvis? But Red says that he is one of us, so that's good enough for me. KnowwhatImean? But he sure wears some strange looking clothes. All that pink and black stuff. But I gotta idea he just might do pretty well though.

"Red was talking about that open weekend we had last fall when we drove his Model A up to Memphis. 'Member the night we went to the party and Elvis was there?"

"Yeah, I remember all right. That was the night that you and Red had that mamma and daughter combo going real good."

"Man, we didn't know they were mamma and daughter. Anyway, Red had the mamma. That weren't none of me. But let me assure you, that mamma was much more of a woman than was her daughter. I swear you couldn't tell them apart. Apart as in a big age difference I mean. Mamma had taken real good care of herself, very good care, I mean to tell you.

" 'Member they didn't think much of us college boys running around in the big city in a Model A while they scooted around in that new pink two-seater '55 T-Bird. Boy, was that ever a sharp car!

"Boo, we gotta go back to Memphis. And where was those girls from?"

"The mamma and daughter potpourri?"

"Yeah. It was potpourri all right. Where were they from? Boo, you 'member where they lived?"

"Carenco, I think. Yeah, Carenco, Louisiana."

"That's right. Why don't we call Red and see if he can meet us?"

"Ronnie, you spastic or something? You just read where he thinks he has to report for training. What's wrong with you, man?"

"Well, I'm gonna ask anyway. Maybe he can get away."

"I wish you much success with this book and your personal appearances. The fact that athletes and students do not always prepare themselves for real life experiences is certainly a problem. I hope this book will help them to not only see the problem but give them ideas for success."

Coach Frank M. Beamer, Virginia Tech

10

I SHOULD HAVE GONE
TO HOLLYWOOD
WITH BURT REYNOLDS

NEAR THE END of January in 1851, the members of the Florida Legislature finally got their heads together and created a couple of schools of higher learning. They had divided the state, and one school was to be located east of the Suwannee River and one west of it. The East Florida Seminary was placed in Ocala and began to take students in the fall of 1853. Four years later the West Florida Seminary was opened in Tallahassee.

For a very short time in 1865, the West Florida Seminary was renamed The Florida Military and Collegiate Institute for an apparently good reason. In March of that year the cadets of the school were called into emergency action for the Confederate States of America. Although they were heavily outnumbered, they fought gallantly at the Battle of Natural Bridge, just a few miles south of Tallahassee. This encounter played a critical role by repelling attacking Federal Troops, and the victory assured that Tallahassee was the only Confederate capital east of the Mississippi never captured by Union forces. About as quickly as the school's name was changed for emergency military reasons, it promptly reverted to West Florida Seminary.

While alumni would become desperately ill even to think of such absurdity, by legislative decree in 1885, the fact remains that among the many name changes the West Florida Seminary later had was "The University of Florida." However, the school never really publicized the name, and in 1901 it was again changed, this time to Florida State College. Two years later the Legislature transferred the title "The University of Florida," the distasteful name that nobody in Tallahassee desired, to the state's agricultural college at Lake City.

Following the lead of other distinguished universities, the time had arrived to bring football to FSC. The first football game ever played at Florida State College was in 1902. That year a total of three games made up the entire schedule. FSC defeated South Georgia Military on November 21st by scoring only a single touchdown. Later in the year it twice played the University of Florida with the outcome being that each team won a game and by the same score of 6-0.

The following year FSC doubled its schedule and played six games. At season's end it had an impressive record of 3-2-1. The highlight of the season was the defeat of the University of Florida by a score of 12-0.

Their third season, in 1904, would mark their last football game for 43 years. But the season proved to be a great one although their record was only 2-3. They were crowned "State Champions" by easily defeating the University of Florida 23-0 and on Thanksgiving Day won a decisive victory over Stetson 19-6.

For the next 43 years they continued to hold their record number of wins over The University of Florida by 3-1. Never again will either team be so lucky.

AFTER A HARD winter on the upper Gulf Coast, late spring brought about gorgeous, chamber-of-commerce type weather. Ronnie and the Strutters were happily mixing and mingling with all their old friends who were home for the summer. They were delighted to be together again and to share another couple of months lounging and playing in the marvelous sun and surf. As usual throughout the summer they could most often be found spending their time hanging out at the Surf Club or the Beach Casino. A few even reminisced about their high school summers, causing them to invade one of the house parties in an ill attempt to go back in time. To do it all over, just one 'mo time! But quickly and wisely, they found the kids now were too young. Wow, how time marches on, they thought.

Way too soon would come the late summer call to report again to training camp. While every one of the Strutters truly enjoyed his football activities, none was ever overly eager to put on pads and helmets in the scorching heat of Florida's August weather.

ARRIVING ON CAMPUS in Tallahassee, Ronnie found a message that had been left for him to report to Coach Nugent's office first thing the following morning. Late last week the school registrar had advised the coaching staff he had learned, upon receiving Ronnie's transcript and other records from Jones, that he did not bring with him enough transfer credit hours. The news from Coach Nugent was that he had no alternative but to red shirt him his first year. He would remain on the team with a full scholarship, but until he earned additional credits the rules would not allow him to participate in any game.

The news was devastating. The one thing he fought so hard against after graduating from high school now confronted him head on. Riding the damn bench!

Being saddled with FSU's strict probation rules pushed him into a deep hole of non-responsive, personal depression. Learning of his predicament, later that night at Senior Hall he became more frustrated than ever.

"Boo, we've made a great big mistake. How in the world did you let me get myself into such a fix? Here I was all primed and cocked to move to Baton Rouge and ready to play some real college ball. Barney Poole assured me that I would have no problems with transferring grades and he promised that I would be a starter for sure. Boo, what happened? What? What? What? What the hell's so different in LSU rules than FSU?"

"Listen Ronnie, you never stop to give anything any thought. You jump from pillow to post, from one quick decision to another and never think of the pending consequences. Man, you need to slow down. Pay attention. Look at all the angles," Boo preached.

"Now, here I am, my butt stuck in Tallahassee, red shirted and with a team that has had only marginal success. They play in front of perhaps 12,000 fans, great fans mind you, but small numbers. Just last December I played before 57,000 in the Rose Bowl. Boo, it seems that I'm going backwards," Ronnie declared. "Have I peaked out already?"

"No man, you've not peaked out. Ronnie, first of all you, don't have a great deal to concern yourself with this year 'cause you ain't gonna play. Face it. You already know that for sure. Had you worked on your grades at Jones like I warned you time and again, you wouldn't be in this miserable position. So it's your own fault. There is no one else to blame but your own lazy self.

"Let this year pass. Count it as being gone, finished. Get over it, but start working on your grades for next year. Anyway, since they've red-shirted you, you still have two years of eligibility left. Everything is going to be all right. Trust me. Just trust me, my friend."

"Boo, I'm just pissed," he hawked.

NEEDLESS TO SAY, Ronnie's years at Florida State offered much more social life both on campus and around Tallahassee than was ever dreamed of in the tiny town of Ellisville, Mississippi. As Pete Flemming would say, "It was much like a young country farm boy being thrown into a barrel of molasses."

The general consensus was that for every one man on campus there were three women. Assuming that perhaps half of the boys on a bet couldn't get a date with anyone, that would improve the odds to about six to one. Further assuming, if the football players caught the eye of the darling muffins by a two-to-one margin over the other students, then they would command a ratio of perhaps twelve to one. Obviously, those who were intent on having a grand time had all the companionship they could handle. There is no question the combined social life at FSU and that of the big city of Tallahassee played a great part in Ronnie's personal life, attitude and ultimate misfortune. Not only did it affect his football abilities, but it also had a profound effect on his grades and eligibility requirements.

The social distractions, now coupled with his knowledge that he was not going to play at all his first year, contributed greatly toward the beginning of the end of what was once a fine-tuned football player.

HIS QUICK DECISION to abandon LSU for FSU proved not to be of sound judgment. This wrong choice surely advanced the loss of his self-worth and the deflation of his attitude and personal ego. However, the detrimental effect could not be blamed on any actions or inactions on the part of FSU. For sure, it rested solely on his personal inabilities to conform with the standards that were acceptable in accordance with the schools rules and regulations.

It was tough on him experiencing only a single loss in the last three years and now joining a team which was playing only their tenth year of competitive college football and having only one winning season over the past four years. To top it all off, now he had to ride the bench for a full year. Adding salt to his wounds, insult to injury, he kept close watch on the success of LSU where he should have been in the backfield with Taylor and Cannon.

AFTER SITTING OUT 1956 as a red-shirt and watching the team from the sidelines, led by senior quarterback Lee Corso, he was much concerned about the season record of 5-4-1. He committed himself to be ready, to get up for the '57 season. He recognized there had to be vast personal improvements made on his part to raise his grade point average, and he was ready to set things right.

ON THE 26th day of September, ATO inducted him into that fraternity. This sprung loose a new dimension of activities and opened doors to many new friends, male and female. His fraternity brothers soon would learn that while in high school he held the State of Florida sprint record for the 100 yard dash for two consecutive years. And now, two years later, he was still considered one of the fastest running backs on the football team. The brothers quickly decided just how best to use his talents. He was promptly assigned the task of dumping paint on the pearly, whitewashed, SAE lion. Many were the nights he barely made it back to the house with his scalp intact.

The brothers also made use of his skills as an artist. Late one Saturday night it was decided that tomorrow he would use his talents to paint a mural on the back wall of the party deck. Taking all day, and with a shaky hand towards sundown, the mural was finally finished. For several years it was enjoyed by all.

It was during this time that Ronnie began to invite Pat Hearn, the beautiful petite blonde from Pensacola whom he once fixed Red West up with, to visit him for ATO weekend parties. Often she would come for a ball game and return to Pensacola late Sunday afternoon. Soon their relationship would begin to jell.

With all the real action being played out on Saturdays, being able to participate only as a scout squad member began to take a toll on him. Although he made it through the season, his attitude was somewhat bitter, but at the same time his grades did show signs of improving. However, at the turn of the new year he began to have doubts about whether or not he wanted to return to school after the summer. Knowing he still had two years of eligibility remaining, perhaps this was the dominating factor which led him to at least wait until after the Spring Game to make a final decision.

WHEN SPRING PRACTICE began, there were four quarterbacks who battled each other for the starting role: Ronnie, a junior; Jerry Henderson, a senior from Pensacola Catholic; Joe Majors, a sophomore and younger brother of Tennessee All-American Johnny Majors; and Bobby Renn, a junior from Henderson, North Carolina. From all accounts, Coach Nugent was depending heavily on this foursome, knowing that any of them was capable of leading the Seminoles to what surely would be a better season than last.

The Spring game went well. The players of both teams performed at full throttle and were most eager to showcase their talents. The coaching staff was delighted with what they had seen and was looking forward to the fall with great expectations.

DURING THE SUMMER of '57 Ronnie and his cronies mellowed somewhat. The partying was limited, and much more attention was directed toward getting in shape for the coming season. He had his work cut out for him, knowing that if he was going to play collegiate football again he had to get it together, study hard and perform as this would be his very last opportunity. This year when time came to report to training camp, he would be mentally and physically fit. Ready to take on the world, ready to challenge all comers for the starting quarterback position.

Over the summer he had a part-time job alongside his brother, who had worked after school and weekends at WEAR-TV Channel 3 since the station opened three years earlier. Ronnie, Billy and a couple of other young men did odd jobs around the studio and ran all the errands. Knowing of Ronnie's PHS and junior college football activities and his potential for the upcoming season at FSU, the Sports Editor, Earl Hutto, interviewed him one night on his mid-week sports program. Ronnie was delighted to have the hometown exposure. Interesting enough, Earl Hutto would later become a long-standing member of the United States House of Representatives from the First District of Florida.

RONNIE THOUGHT HE may have remembered the name of Buddy Reynolds as a running back for the South team in the 1953 State of Florida All-Star Game but wasn't sure. He could not recall whether or not Reynolds had made any outstanding contributions or accomplishments during the contest, although his team, the South squad, came away with the victory. He dug through his scrapbook and reviewed the newspaper articles of the game; Reynolds wasn't mentioned. While leafing through the articles, he recalled that the spark for the South team came from Dick McGehee, a 143-pound scatback from Miami Edison. His hard-charging drives, coupled with those of Miami High's Ellis Baker and Jim Roundtree from Miami Jackson, proved too much for the smaller North defense, he remembered.

The entire North team, individually and collectively, accomplished little to write home about. Being out of Florida for the last two years, Ronnie had all but forgotten about Reynolds. While chatting with a teammate at the training table, he was brought up to date about Reynolds playing for the Seminoles back in 1954 as a freshman. It just hadn't registered with Ronnie.

Reynolds had first signed with the University of Miami before finally deciding to come to Florida State. During a casual visit by Reynolds to Tallahassee for other purposes, Tom Nugent sweet-talked him into staying. Ronnie was well aware of the salesmanship abilities of Coach Nugent. The records indicated that as a freshman Reynolds saw limited action and carried the ball only sixteen times, scoring two touchdowns. Once, coming off the bench at Auburn, he had a 54-yard sprint only to be caught by Fob James, a great ballplayer who later became Governor of Alabama.

The 1954 season eventually proved to be the lone full season that Reynolds would play college football. During the second week of fall practice in 1955, his knee went out. Returning to Palm Beach, he underwent emergency surgery which looked as if it was performed by a butcher as noted later by a famed surgeon who tried to repair the damage. While recuperating, his life took a meandering turn toward little theater work. Soon his new interest led him to change his name to "Burt" Reynolds and hit the road in a long shot search of a career in movies, first New York, then Hollywood.

Unsatisfied and struggling as an actor, he took some time off to travel around the South. A side trip along his journey brought him back to Tallahassee in search of an old girlfriend. With football still on his mind, he could not pass up the opportunity to drop by for a visit with Coach Nugent. Once again, being persuaded by Nugent's slick words, he decided to return to FSU for another try at college ball.

At the first squad meeting, Ronnie was pleased to see his fellow teammates again and quickly became friends with the new players. While Reynolds could not be classified as new, he was new to Ronnie.

THE FALL SEEMED to be getting off to a good start. Ronnie was pleased that his old friend, Pete Flemming, from Pensacola High and JCJC had signed on with the Seminoles. Their friendship dated back to the sandlot leagues around Escambia County. Pete had proven himself to be a dependable teammate and great friend, someone who could be counted on when the going got tough. In their spare time they would often rent a boat and fish Lake Talquin or Lake Jackson. They enjoyed each other's company immensely, and it was good for both of them to be together again.

When they could sneak away, they frolicked with other players and brothers at the ATO house. Parties were always the order of primary interest, especially on weekends. Years later they would often reminisce about the ATO party at Panama City Beach where the women outnumbered the men at least three to one.

However, the party that got them in dutch was the ATO Dog Island weekend. They both were called before the Student Council with the ultimate outcome being their dismissal as members of the fraternity.

The morning of the Dog Island weekend started off like many others: with bad timing. The boys had stayed up all night to "prepare" themselves to leave for the island bright and early on Saturday. They had made plans to pick up their muffins at 6:00 o'clock only to learn upon arriving at their dorm they would not be permitted to leave campus until 7:00. Obviously, this put an immediate crimp in their design for the morning.

Arriving at the ferry boat landing they loaded up and started their 30-minute float to the island. Approaching the pier, Ronnie dared Pete to jump from the boat and race it to shore. The boat captain had already reversed its motion and was backing into the pier to unload. Over the side went Flemming. Needless to say, the captain was not very pleased. The report he wrote to the school detailed the entire episode. Pete was in a jam.

All it took that weekend to get anything started was a dare or a bet from anyone. Other reports detailed, whether true or not, that Pete again acted on a bet. This time for a fifth of V.O. if he would do the "dirty bop" with a wife of one of the coaches. She was willing. He was willing. They were willing. And so it goes. And on Ronnie's part, it seems that he was somewhat careless for leaving his bedroom door unlocked to unexpected visitors.

DURING THE LONG days of practice, every team member, under his breath, would rave and rant about the military type, regimented, extremely tough drills required by Coach Nugent. Reynolds would say of his freshman year, "There were an awful lot of excellent football players out there. It was a question of who was standing after the first four or five weeks. A lot of really good football players were run off."

It was around this time that Coach Nugent inquired of Bob Harbison about who the stocky lineman was that Harbison brought on campus from the Midwest. Before Bob could an-

Above: A February 18, 1957 Pensacola Journal *photo of the four Florida State quarterbacks who were in a race for the starting position: Joe Majors, Ronnie, Jerry Henderson and Bobby Renn. Left: 1957 Florida State fullback Joe Holt.*

Action shot of Ronnie in his Florida State uniform # 17.

swer, Nugent scolded, "Get that fat slob out of here." Well, as directed, Harbison sent Alex Karras on his way. He immediately left for Iowa where he made All-American and later played for the Detroit Lions where he was All-Pro. Much was beginning to happen around the Florida State University campus, some good things and some bad.

JUST DAYS BEFORE the first game of the season, once again the hammer fell with a crushing blow. The coaches were advised that Ronnie and several other players, including Joe Majors, had not reached the appropriate grade point average and, therefore, had become academically ineligible to play.

It was very obvious that FSU officials were beginning to clamp down hard on athletes who were on scholarships. There were, as at every college, professors who cared little about the athletes who were given a free education in exchange for playing sports. While the blame for the deficiency of achievement had to be laid at the feet of those who failed to perform, still the toughness of the FSU administration was beginning to have a dynamic, negative impression on student athletes.

Given the news, Ronnie and the other players were devastated and in shock beyond belief. The coaches excused those involved from the day's practice and scheduled a meeting with them the next day following the noon meal. Shaken to the core, Ronnie felt the need to get away by himself. He borrowed Pete's car and all alone drove south to the coast at Panacea where he secluded himself in the stillness of a small waterfront bar.

"When's it going to end, Boo? I can't take this crap any longer. I'm going to drop out of school. I've had it. That's it. That's what I'll do, I'll drop out."

"No, no, you won't either. Man, you can't quit. You need this education and it's free. Can't you see that?"

"Education, crap. I don't seem to be doing too well in that department, ole buddy."

"You just gotta hang in there, Ronnie. Education will mean dollars in your pocket. You need it so we can go places, see the world, do things together. If you quit, your folks are going to be mighty upset."

"Boo, I ain't just going to hang around the field and play the dummy part of the scout team. I ain't staying there just to get trampled every day so others can take the field on Saturday and play in the real game. That's stupid. KnowwhatImean?"

"Ronnie, forget about football for once, and think about your education. I think that you should go in tomorrow and talk with the coaches and see what can be done. Do that, my man. Do just that."

The following day, before the team meeting, Ronnie talked with Coach Nugent, the result being that the coach urged him to stay in school, and he promised that he would remain on scholarship for the full year provided he got his grades in order. Nugent bragged on his athletic abilities and how intelligent he was, but in the same breath criticized him for not applying himself.

The coach stopped short of guaranteeing him a starting position next year but certainly hinted he was in the driver's seat as first-string quarterback. By this time, promises had become foreign to Ronnie's ears. However, he did commit to hang in until the season was over, then make a stab at a sensible and reasonable decision about next year.

As the season progressed he became more and more disenchanted with himself and the team in general. Watching from the sidelines just wasn't his cup of tea.

AFTER THE DICK Christy incident, an All-American receiver at North Carolina State, Reynolds, himself, was devastated. Nugent would tell the team at halftime, while pointing his finger directly at Reynolds, "If you lose this game, you can blame it on Reynolds for letting Christy get behind him." Christy had caught a long pass for a touchdown, the only points of the game. FSU lost 7-0.

The next day the game film would clearly show that Christy had gone several steps out of bounds which, without question, made him an illegal receiver; then he came back on the field and caught the pass. However, the loss for FSU stood, and Reynolds was humiliated. A few days after the game, Reynolds decided that he was not the player he was back in 1954 and beat down the door headed for Hollywood.

KNOWING HOW DISENCHANTED Reynolds was, how

badly he felt about something that really wasn't his fault in the first place, Ronnie listened to him and at the same time confided in him about his own displeasure. While Reynolds had made up his mind to leave in search of greener pastures, Ronnie was fearful of again making a wrong decision, although the invitation was wide open for him to come along.

No one will ever know what may have been. But as Ronnie would come to believe over the years, the future had already been written, already been cast in stone. What was going to be, was already in the cards. There was nothing he or anyone else could do to change his destiny.

HIS TWO YEARS at FSU were obviously very disappointing. The team finished the 1956 season with a record of 5-4-1. And in 1957 it won only four games, beating Furman, Abilene Christian, Virginia Tech and Tampa while losing to Boston University, Villanova, North Carolina State, Miami, Southern Mississippi and Auburn.

After the season and in a effort to sooth and try satisfying the boosters, Coach Nugent made sure they understood that '56 and '57 had been rebuilding years. The '58 season, he assured them, would most certainly bring better results. But how could anyone actually believe this when just over the horizon loomed the very first game between FSU and the University of Florida?

THE DAY RONNIE left Tallahassee and drove to Pensacola for the beginning of the holiday season marked a day in history that was unknown to everyone, everyone, that is, except the dealer of the cards. This date marked exactly, to the day, the halfway point of his life. While the first half had been enjoyable, except for the last months at FSU, the second half would be absolute misery and everlasting torment.

"Thanks for sending me a copy of 'RONNIE'. I'll enjoy it - it will help revive some fond memories I have of FSU". Thanks again.

Lee Corso, ESPN Sports

11

THE INFUSION
OF HANK WILLIAMS' SPIRIT

WHEN REGISTRATION BEGAN in mid January, Ronnie was standing in line with other teammates to sign up for classes. Assistant coaches and a couple of faculty members made sure they selected the appropriate courses that would be required for graduation. Neither his attention nor his attitude was anywhere near the FSU campus. Midway of the third week he began to cut classes. More and more he was spending time hanging with friends who, like himself, had rather party than study. He fully realized that his class attendance would be reported to the coaches in a matter of days, and when that time came he would deal with it the best he could. Sooner than he had expected he was confronted and asked to explain. He simply had no logical answer or alibi to offer.

Now, for certain, his football days were behind him. Knowing that he had royally screwed up by coming to Florida State in the first place, he began to search for a reason to blame the school. But he knew deep inside the problem lay only at his own feet. Late that night, his final night in Senior Hall, we talked at length.

"Boo, you 'member what Mom said to me the day before I left for Mississippi?"

"Your mom said a lot of things. Whatcha talking about?"

"She said that there would be three milestones in my life that I would have to conquer. 'Member that?"

"Think so. What about it?"

"Is this one of them? Is this the first? Or is it the second or maybe even the third? Have I already been past two of them without knowing it?"

"No, my man. You ain't seen nothing yet. Believe me, you'll know it when they happen. And yes, this may well be the first."

"What we gonna do, Boo? Where to next? You know life's a gamble. You pays your money and you takes your chances. But what are we gonna do now?"

"You're right. Life is a gamble. But you gotta be real careful about what you wish for or dream about because you just may get it. Ronnie, you gotta be careful with your choices from now on. Be careful of things that you just want them to be. Sometimes, my man, they just don't work out. You've really made some horrible decisions as of late.

"Ronnie, you just don't make the best of situations. You don't understand how to use your God-given talents, how to take advantage of your attributes, your personal assets. You just keep on, day in and day out, doing it all wrong.

"You know how you're sometimes fond of quoting Elvis. Well, do you remember that he said, 'To get ahead, you gotta be different.' That's where you are, my friend. You're different from many others. You have unique abilities that you and only you possess. Don't let life throw you. Get up off your rear end and conquer it. Only the strong survive in this wicked world. You need to get with it my friend."

"What can I do? Boo, just pray tell me what can I do? Talent? What talent?"

"Football isn't the only thing you're good at. Man, you got loads of talent in your art work. You can draw, paint, design. All sorts of things. You can make a great living with your talents, so don't give me none of that 'what talent' crap. You made your own bed. Now you gotta sleep in it. You gotta live with yourself."

"Boo, I'm miserable. Have been for months on end. Lonely, unhappy, discontented, unsuccessful. You name it, and I have been there. Man, the loads getting heavier each day."

"Now don't you dare go getting happiness and success confused," Boo warned. "There is a great deal of difference, you know. Happiness is wanting what you get. Truly wanting all the little things that come your way as you travel through life. Being pleased with what fate sends in your direction.

"Success, on the other hand, is getting what you want, things that you strive for, things that you personally deem to be important. Yes, there is a great difference between the two.

"You've been there. You've been on the playing field when you were happy beyond belief. Perhaps you don't remember those wonderful times. Happiness shows itself in many different and magnificent forms. And often as not, it's just a fleeting few minutes of time. A very special few moments when you may be so tightly wrapped up in the excitement of the moment that you actually do not recognized what you've seen, experienced or enjoyed.

"The biggest thrill, the moment of great happiness, is something that is a long time abuilding. It comes of making up your mind about what is important and pursuing your own sense of values completely independent of others. Independent of pressures and social mores with which you may not always agree.

"You can't live your life for the benefit of others. You have to live it in accordance with what you deem to be right and correct for you as an individual. To find true happiness, you have to be absolutely free from doubt. But presently, you are totally consumed, completely engrossed with extra heavy doses of self doubt every day of your life. Ronnie, you must understand that you gotta be tough to be happy. That's a requirement of the first order. Now you listen to me, pay attention, because this is most important."

AS IT OFTEN happened, Ronnie awoke with the spirit of an ultra successful entrepreneur. A belief that he could truly conquer the world. A "deal cried the loser; the next card just may be an ace" attitude. A mental thrust that channelled him into the assurance that he had an opportunity to go about making things better, putting things into their proper perspective.

However, just as quick, self doubt flooded his mind and forced him to think only of the dark back alleys of life. Back alleys of comfort to those who had rather give up than fight to live another day.

For the better part of the two weeks he stayed with friends around the Tallahassee area. Rather than be concerned about a job, he spent his time loafing around St. Marks, Panacea, Alligator Point, Dog Island and Carrabelle. It was while he drifted in and out of coastal towns and other smaller nondescript waterfront villages that he almost decided to chart the rest of his life as a fishing guide. A couple of his close friends owned charter boats. He marveled at their loose, carefree life style. Such a kicked-back atmosphere and attitude were tempting and appealing to him. But by now he was completely shellshocked, absolutely fearful that he would again take a wrong turn, make a wrong decision. Apparently, he had never heard the saying, "not to decide, is to decide." A few days later he thought better of the idea and eased on westward down Highway 98.

HE RETURNED TO Pensacola where he used up several days leisurely surf fishing up and down the beaches of Santa Rosa Island. When he finally got around to it, he interviewed with a few companies, then accepted a sales position with John Hancock Insurance. Over the next six weeks he would spend a couple of hours each night studying for his apprentice license and working days at the new car lot of Hill Kelly Dodge.

While in college he was forever representing one company or another, constantly hitting up his teammates with specials that he could order direct from a variety of catalogs. Whether they needed pots or pans, shoes, sport coats or a multitude of other items, he could get them at a fair price and most of the time have the item delivered to their front door in two days. He was a natural born salesman, and, if not that, he was one of the best convincers that ever lived. Perhaps just short of Coach Nugent.

IN EARLY SPRING he and Pat, his longtime lady friend, decided to tie the knot. She, a lovely blonde of small stature, was known to be a perfect lady and stunningly beautiful. Their friends were convinced they would make a great couple. Both families were very pleased and excited for them.

A couple of weeks before Christmas, Kym, their first child was born. What a gorgeous baby. Beautiful curly blonde hair and an angel face. Ronnie, although mighty proud, was really not much help to Pat around the house and most certainly of no value at all about helping out with a newborn.

Things rocked on about as well as could be expected for the young family of three. He stayed with John Hancock through 1959, then moved his family to Mobile where he became general manager of a Western Auto store. It didn't take him very long to figure out this job was also a big mistake. He again changed jobs, this time accepting a sales position with Mobile Fixture & Appliance Company. This job would last an even shorter period than the others.

Daily, Ronnie would spend an hour or so after work having a few drinks with his buddies, but as often as not he would drop into a small, out-of-the-way tavern where he could be alone. It was times like these when he always opened up and talked freely to me.

"Boo, what'll I do? Man, I'm stuck here in this sorry city. I hate my job. Married. Have a baby. Kym is six weeks old to-day, and I already feel like an old man. When's it gonna end? Boo, when's this crap gonna get better?"

"Ronnie, you don't need to feel like you're stuck. Man, you're married to a fine woman and have a beautiful daughter. Look on the bright side. You're healthy. Young. You have loads going for you. You just need to buckle down. Get your crap together."

"Boo, look what Elvis has done. Man, we're the same age and look at him."

"Screw Elvis! Ronnie, screw Elvis! Man, that ain't you. The guy can sing. He got a lucky break. Quit trying to compare yourself with Elvis, for God's sake. If you want to compare your-self with someone, then pick that other dummy sitting on the stool next to you. Elvis is the exception to the rule; man, forget about him and the money he's made. You hear me, stop all that nonsense," Boo preached.

"How 'bout Red? How 'bout Burt? They seem to be doing all right. I see them all the time on television. But look where I am."

"Ronnie, crap! Come back to the real world. Son, listen, come on back down here were the rubber meets the road. You need to accept yourself for what you are. Your picture-in-the-paper-days are gone and gone forever. You need to realize this. You have to accept your role as a common man, a man just like millions of others who have to work for a living. And didn't someone once say that the good Lord must have loved the common man 'cause he made so many of them? Accept it man, life has changed for you. You need to get on with what you have and make the best of it.

"Anyway, remember just yesterday when that plane went down killing Buddy Holley, Ritchie Valens and that Big Bopper guy? They were only, I think, 23 years old. Look where all their fame and fortune got them. Man, straighten up and get on down the road. Get with it 'fore it's too late."

THROUGHOUT HIS LIFE Ronnie always paid special attention to the news of the day. The morning paper was a must as was the evening television news. With mountains of distractions flowing lackadaisically through his life, it was hard to imagine that his personality afforded him the opportunity to pay attention to news stories which seemingly would be foreign to his interest. But he did. And furthermore, when bad things happened around the globe, or right here at his back door, he repeatedly dwelled on them to a point where he permitted each to have a direct influence on his personal life. It seemed as though he searched for things to worry himself sick over.

A WEEK AFTER Kym turned two and five days before Christmas, the stork brought Paige into their lives, another beautiful daughter. Now, there were four mouths to feed in the Ronnie Williams family.

The 'what to do now' question was rapidly answered. A better job had to be found and found quick. Suddenly, his luck, for the first time, changed for the better. An acquaintance told him of a tremendous position which had recently opened with a national firm, the Revlon Corporation. Of the different jobs he held, most likely this was the one he truly worked hard at and even seemed to enjoy. The pay, benefits and hours were all good, but as things always seemed to happen, it too, all too soon bored him to death.

Since the birth of Paige, he spent a little more time and effort trying to help out around the house, although his presence was about all that was noticed. For awhile rather than stop off with his buddies for drinks in the afternoon, he would beat it on home, bringing with him a six pack of his favorite brew. Sitting in his old squeaky chair, he would take turns rocking each of the girls while eyeing the evening news.

Pat would explain that it was somewhat difficult at times for her to show real anger at him. Frequently, in the middle of an uptight, heated argument, he would start laughing, then spit out some weird words of wisdom or tell a joke that made her stop in her tracks.

This night the family was celebrating the one month birth date of Paige while the TV blared away news stories about the noontime swearing in ceremonies and inauguration of President John F. Kennedy. Watching the new president give his address to the nation, Ronnie noted, "When he smiles, his teeth look like the front grill of Fred Levin's mother's '52 Buick." To this, Pat cracked up.

There were times of happiness and joy sprinkled throughout the marriage, but far too few. The marriage was beginning to crumble. Almost overnight it went from bad to horrible. His inability to find or keep a job, coupled with the lack of attention he paid Pat and the girls, opened wider the gap which had until now been just a crack. His weak and unhappy demeanor pushed the small family further and further apart. He would confide in me that on many evenings, even at home with the family close by, he still had deep and haunting feelings of being totally alone.

As if another child in the family would somehow become the glue which would hold them together, another arrived. In May of '62 their third child and only son, Vince, was born. Ronnie would tell his buddies that he begged and pleaded with Pat to name him Clint, the character that Elvis had played in his first movie, "Love Me Tender." However, Pat would offer a completely different saga as to the choice of "Vince."

Be that as it may, having a son made Ronnie chest-thumping happy. With his vocal chords in full blast, the entire west wing of the hospital quickly became aware of the arrival of this chubby, healthy and handsome boy child. Now, thought Ronnie, there were five!

Ronnie's parents, brother and sister were all pulling for the survival of his marriage and family. They all hinged their hopes on things becoming better now that there were three children, especially since a son had come along. However, Ronnie's personality continued to change. He seemed to have become totally absorbed in himself, for himself, within himself. He seldom let anyone inside the bubble that encased him. As if the invisible buffer shielded him completely from the rest of the world, he lingered in a suspended twilight of life as if he was there all by himself, totally alone.

No one ever questioned the fact that he did not want to accept responsibility as a father and husband, but everyone soon realized that he simply did not know how. And few were his attempts to exhibit any hardcore evidence that would lead anyone to believe that he was willing to take his responsibilities more seriously. Apparently, the responsibilities of accepting fatherhood had become absolutely oblivious to him.

SHORTLY AFTER THE birth of Vince, Ronnie moved to Montgomery and again accepted employment with Western Auto Stores as a district manager. Pat and the three children returned to Pensacola where a decision would have to be made concerning their marriage.

Soon, fate would again intervene by bringing another oddity into Ronnie's already confused and unhappy life. As if his friendship with Red West and the association with Elvis and Burt Reynolds were not enough to confuse a person, especially someone who already had his mind working at full capacity, a new wrinkle was added.

Until the death of Hank Williams on New Year's Eve in 1952, Ronnie had counted him as his most favorite singer and performer. It had only been two weeks since he moved to Montgomery when a friend who knew of his fondness for poker asked him to sit in on their Wednesday night game. That night he would make friends with Charles Carr, and within days they would begin to share expenses of a large furnished home that Carr had recently leased.

It only took a few days for Carr to realize the affection Ronnie had for the music of Elvis and the sad songs of Hank Williams. One evening over a few beers Carr haphazardly revealed that it was he that had been hired by Hank to chauffeur him to a show date in Canton, Ohio. It was he, on New Year's Eve 1952, who found America's most popular country singer dead in the back seat of his Cadillac on a lonesome country road somewhere in West Virginia. Ronnie could hardly believe his ears. Now, there was yet another personal connection with a famous person, and, at that, one of his most favorite entertainers.

"Boo, not again. Man, not another one."

"THERE AIN'T ONE damn thing I can do about it. Boo, if she wants a divorce, we'll let her have it. Just let her get on with it. If she wants her freedom PDQ, she can divorce me COD. You see, my man, I too, have just about had enough of this crap. Just get it over with. Like the man said, 'Pride is the chief cause and the decline in the numbers of husbands and wives.' Let's get it done. Go ahead and throw me right in the middle of that briar patch, and get it over for God's sake. Divorce hurts, but I guess that's what good-bye's are all about."

Ronnie had proven time and again that he was thoroughly terrified of failure. He found himself unsatisfied with, but trying hard to accept, the minor role he was to play the rest of his life. This detrimental attitude began when he left Florida State. When he knew for sure the days of football glory was finally over.

He absolutely refused to accept or to deal with adult situations and responsibilities. The marriage was headed for divorce because to him this was the better alternative. He would get out of it rather than continue to believe every day of his life that he was a failure. A failure due to his weakness of not being able to be an acceptable husband and a good father to the kids.

Now, the only life he really desired was just to be left alone. He would often tell me that happiness to him was a cane pole, a rusty can of worms and a six-pack to tote down to a river bank, any river bank, anywhere.

NEAR THE END of November the divorce had become final. Ronnie continued to live in Montgomery but stayed in touch with his kids by phone and occasionally with a note through the mail. It had now become his lot to play the role of an absentee father.

Late into many restless and sleepless nights, he lay awake cursing himself for the hurt he had caused his wife and children. He longed to do some of the things that he should have been doing for the family since Kym was born. Still, he knew deep inside that it was too late. The bell had been rung, and there is nothing more heartbreaking than a situation where someone is totally helpless to do anything about it. He absolutely had no options left.

He knew that his failed marriage could never be salvaged, and perhaps neither could his life. In a few short years he had become a man who was literally scared to death to try again. Completely terrified to make an effort at anything. To him, giving up was much easier and a hell of a lot more simple. Like it or not, he was now truly alone. Alone, as if he were a ship adrift at sea.

ON A DAMP and freezing Sunday afternoon in early December, feeling as if he had been discarded by everyone, Ronnie grabbed his old slouch hat and hurried outside to the curb where he found his Nash Ambassador covered with snow and frozen ice. After he pumped the accelerator for what seemed like forever, then prayed even longer for the weak battery to turn over and engage the starter, it finally did. Sitting inside the frigid car on its cold, brittle, plastic seat covers, he trembled with the car as it belched and burped a few times, then once again came to life. He eased away from the curb for a leisurely drive around the city just to kill some time, having nothing else to do.

Without a planned route in mind, he began to amble first this way, then the other. He pulled up beside a traffic officer at a red light and inquired if he happened to know the location of the cemetery where Hank Williams was buried. Surprisingly, the cemetery was nearby, just off Wetumpka Road. In five minutes or less he was pulling slowly through the old-fashioned, rusty, double wrought iron gates. From this single visit to honor and pay his respects evolved a pathetic and conceivably dangerous precedent. One that would follow him into his own early grave.

Trying hard to focus his eyes through glasses misted over by chilly moisture being windblown directly into his face, he stood silently for more than an hour in front of the gigantic marble monument that marked the graves of Hank and Audrey Williams. Known only to him were his innermost thoughts.

Although standing there alone, he was sure he wasn't. He could sense that something very strange was happening. He could feel the presence of someone, and for the first time in years he felt that he was not alone. Perhaps he had been searching for this place of silence, peace and solitude for some time. A place where no one would bother him. A place where he was alone, yet not alone at all. Within that hour something highly unusual transpired. It may have been caused when his memory, for a brief moment, drifted back to a distant, long ago incident that had returned to haunt him on this strangest of days.

He thought maybe it was a reflection of something from his past, a horrible instant from another lifetime. A former life experience that had sneaked back into his present memory without him being able to separate this day from back then. Or perhaps the strange feeling could have been summoned up by the eerie motions and sounds of the dead and wilted leaves. The cold wind was sweeping them into a continuous swirling design as they were gently blown back and forth across the grave sites. For sure something occurred that afternoon that was indescribable. A feeling which could not be explained, nor did he really seek or crave an explanation.

While visiting this peaceful and untroubled place, a bizarre but warm sensation tantalized his entire body. The feeling surrounded him with warmth as a blanket would protect a child, wrapping snugly around, submersing its unseen remains passionately within his soul. Standing still, cold and silent, the shiver he experienced was not from the weather but felt more like another person, a great friend, had entered his physical body and began to use his eyes, ears and senses as if their own. While this was the first, there would be countless numbers of other visits. Many would be the times that he and his companion, a fifth of Lord Calvert, would come to visit and sit silently, far into the night.   To him there could be no better evidence than the words and markings chiseled into the marble headstones. These symbols justified and bolstered his belief that fate was now, and had forevermore been, in complete and absolute control of all earthly moments.

Every phrase, all the songs written and sung, and each word spoken by Hank Williams had been taken as true gospel by Ronnie. Every syllable had found its way into the mainstream of his personal, downtrodden existence.

His first visit assured him that whatever is to be will be. And we mere humans have absolutely nothing to say about the direction, timing or final outcome of life's already designed plan. From this first visit he felt guaranteed, he knew for certain, the plot had already been written, and the only thing left undone was for each of us to act out our role for the remainder of our life.

BY NOW EVERYTHING in Ronnie's life had become very unstable, unsettled and occasionally volatile. For him, there seemed to be no purpose in life. Each day it was get up and go to work, drop by a lounge, come home, watch the tube and do it all over again tomorrow. He found himself slipping backwards and getting further behind, even with his financial obligations. In short, things were not going well at all. This terrified him. But terrified him less than thinking about having to make another decision, another change in jobs which he knew would again be another great mistake.

NEARLY FOUR MONTHS ago Marilyn Monroe had been found dead in her bungalow in California. The networks were beginning to run nightly news specials and stories of her life, including alleged sexual associations with powerful politicians. His dislike for politics in general and politicians in particular set him clearly on the side of MM. But still, while not really caring one way or the other, nightly he continued to permit the news commentators to permeate and control his mind with all sorts of stories, be they true or otherwise. He was beginning to have trouble keeping true-to-life stories apart from those that were fiction.

Over recent weeks he had also lived with the tense details of the 13-day missile crisis in October when Russia tested the will of the American people and our young President Kennedy. The afternoon the Russians finally relinquished and turned their cargo ships around headed away from Cuba, Ronnie had every television set in the Western Auto store tuned to the ABC news affiliate and was glued to the unfolding event. That evening he was in rare form.

"Boo, you know just how close we came today to getting into a real war? And I mean a real war? Huh, Boo, you know that? I'll tell you something. That Kennedy is a tough mother. And smart! Whoa, I mean to tell you he's smart! But you can have Bobby, that punk little brother of his. He is absolutely worthless.

"Boo, what we gonna do with those nutty Soviets, huh, tell me? All they're trying to do is scare us to death. 'Member last year when Kennedy went on television and told everybody to go out and build a nuclear fall-out shelter in their back yard? Jeez! Now ain't that real protection?"

"You 'member? You 'member when Levin built that big old drum-looking thing in his back yard? Can you really imagine Fred Levin actually getting down under the dirt in an old drum and sitting there just waiting for the freakin' world to blow sky high? What a joke of a plan Mr. Kennedy came up with this time for our national security defense. Jeez."

"Ronnie, wait a min...."

"Boo, don't interrupt me while I'm talking. Now what about Kennedy and MM. Think they fooled around? I think so. Perhaps they did. Maybe. Possibly. But not that runt brother of his. No sir. That squirrelly looking, buckteethed, squatty mother, couldn't make out with my roomy, Mr. Carr.

"Can you imagine Bobby Kennedy with Marilyn Monroe? For God's sake, my man. MM was okay in my book. She shore gave old DiMaggio a fit though. Kept that ballplayer running the bases all right.

"You know, Boo, I really miss Pat and the kids. Done made a horrible mistake this time. Ain't I friend? Think we could get it back together, huh? Think so? Well, I don't. Misery loves company, so tonight you're just gonna to have to sit here and listen to ole Rod.

"Gonna quit this awful job, Boo. Gonna go south. 'Member when ole Huey Long had all his problems over in Louisiana? He was just sitting there in Baton Rogue. I love that name, Baton Rouge. Just rolls off your tongue, doesn't it? Anyway, he was sitting there in Baton Rouge when a reporter asked him what he was going to do next. He answered, 'I'm going south!' Hell,

Boo, how much further south can you go from Baton Rouge? Know where he went? Went down to Galveston. Ain't that a lick? Going south, bull!

"Yeah, Boo, going south. Little brother Billy wants to open a branch office in Leesburg. I'm thinking about going down there to my old birth city. Great fishing, I mean great fishing. Whatcha think Boo?"

"Yeah, that may be just what you need. Sounds like you would enjoy that area."

"Would enjoy it. Surely thinking 'bout going south. But Billy Boy done got his pilot's license; guess he'll be coming down to check on me. Think he would, Boo? Think that would be a big problem? I just don't know. Boo, I just don't know 'bout that part."

"I would like to thank you for sending me an autographed copy of your book RONNIE -'there just ain't no light'. I'm certainly looking forward to reading about this fascinating and true story of your brother. This book is a welcome addition to my personal library, and I appreciate your thoughtfulness. Although my Senate schedule leaves little time for non-legislative reading, I plan to make time to read this particular book."

Senator Trent Lott, U.S. Senator

12

THE REAL ELVIS PRESLEY

NO MATTER THE time or place, when Ronnie read or heard news accounts of Elvis, and especially if it involved his friend Red, he took notice. Over the years he would keep news articles, magazines and pictures of these two special men. While moving his personal belongings to Montgomery, he had misplaced an article that he often read when he was in the dumps. Tonight, once again he needed to hear the words and was determined to find where he had placed it.

After a light dinner of hot chili, crackers, coleslaw and a few drinks, he inquired of Boo, "Now, old buddy we gotta find it. Where in the world could it be?"

"Apparently, it's somewhere you haven't looked."

"Don't you get smart with me," Ronnie scolded.

"Well, ain't it obvious that it certainly must be somewhere you haven't looked?"

"Of course, it's somewhere I haven't looked, you nut. But where?" Ronnie wailed.

"Pick up something you never move around. You'll find it."

"My man, my man, you hit it right on the head. I betcha I can go right to it." The Bible, thought Ronnie.

"See, I told you it was a place you seldom looked."

"I done told you once to watch your mouth. Too much of that sass will do you in, my friend."

His mother had seen to it that each of her three children received their personal Bible, the one that had been part of the ceremony when they were baptized at the Brownsville Baptist Church. Folded neatly within the rarely turned pages, the article lay silently.

"Now, Boo, I want you to listen carefully. This is one of the most moving stories that I have ever heard. And best of all, it's about my old friend."

He sat in the large overstuffed dark green Naugahyde chair that had seen much better days. The imitation leather was badly cracked, and one leg only occasionally touched the floor. He recognized and accepted the minor, lopsided rocking motion as a help, not a hinderance.

"Boo, the name of the story is "FROM THE HEART" and is subtitled "Man to Man.""

IN JUNE OF 1958 Elvis rented a home and moved his folks from Memphis to Killeen, Texas, so they could be close to him while he was in boot camp at Fort Hood. About six weeks after arriving, Mrs. Presley became ill and had to visit a doctor on a couple of occasions. Shortly after, her condition worsened to the extent that Mr. and Mrs. Presley were forced to return to Graceland the first week of August. Elvis escorted them to the train station, promising to fly home the day basic training was over.

Her condition continued to go downhill. On August 12th Elvis was granted a pass to visit her, who by now had been confined to the Methodist Hospital in Memphis. Every hour she grew considerably weaker from her bouts of liver problems and perhaps hepatitis. She passed away two days later on August the 14th.

Elvis needed to have his best friend, Red West, by his side during this most trying of times. When he was inducted into the Army, Red joined the Marines so that he could get his military obligations behind him at the same time. Red was in training at Camp LeJeune, North Carolina.

Elvis placed a call to Red's commanding officer and pleaded his case. Seldom does the military grant leave under such circumstances unless the death occurred in a soldier's immediate family. However, Elvis prevailed, and permission was approved.

Red was able to hop a free military flight from Camp LeJeune westward to Huntsville, Alabama. From there he had to wait patiently on standby status to board the next commercial flight into Memphis.

By the time he finally arrived, he worried that he might be too late even for the final minutes of Mrs. Presley's services. Hurrying to a pay phone, he called his home to inquire if his father could rush to the airport, pick him up and drop him off at the services. Finding no one at home, he then called his uncle's house and asked if his dad was there. He was told that he was not, but was at the Memphis Funeral Home. Obviously, he thought his father was visiting with the Presley family. He explained to his uncle that he was trying to locate him to see if he had time to come to the airport and pick him up. Without knowing, between the time Red had left Camp Lejeune and the time he had arrived in Memphis, his own father had unexpectedly suffered a fatal heart attack.

Reading between the lines, his uncle finally realized that Red had no idea and proceeded to tell him that his father had died early that morning. The death of Gladys Presley had weighed heavily on Red; now the shock of learning of his own personal tragedy brought this rugged man to his knees. He abruptly fainted, crouching almost in a folded position on the floor inside the small cubical phone booth.

Receiving no response while continuing to talk into the silent phone, his uncle hung up and located Red's brother, Tom. After hearing the details and being concerned about what he feared, Tom raced to the airport. Inquiring of several bell captains if they had seen a Marine in uniform wandering around, one finally reported seeing a serviceman using a pay phone just a few minutes earlier but didn't know what had happened to him. Tom rushed to the battery of phone booths and instantly found Red, still unconscious, cramped and wadded up lopsided on the floor of the small booth.

THE DAY FOLLOWING his own mother's funeral, Elvis attended Mr. West's services at the same funeral home. He was seated alongside other family members on the front row, he next to Red. In the crowded chapel several pews had been reserved for the large family. Tom and other relatives were seated in the second row, directly behind Red and Elvis. During the quiet moments of meditation just prior to the beginning of the service, Elvis put his arm around Red's shoulders and whispered something silently. Red turned toward Elvis and when he spoke, Tom heard him say, "That's all right, man, don't worry about it."

Later that evening Tom cornered Red and explained that he heard his response to what Elvis had said to him during the service but wondered what Elvis had whispered. Red told him that Elvis had said, "A little over four years ago I borrowed two dollars from your dad. I just remembered, I never paid him back."

"**GOOD STORY,** Ronnie. Very good story," Boo agreed.

"Boo, it's moments such as this that amplifies the closeness of true friendship. It matters not how important, how wealthy, how internationally known a person may have become or how many millions of adoring fans they have. What really matters is their personal inner feelings. Feelings and thoughts which are theirs and theirs alone. Emotions and passions which are tucked safely away and are rarely shared with anyone in today's busy and fast-paced society.

"Their true and personal demeanor radiates outward only at times which they deem to be an especially important moment. Times are seldom when they allow others into their very private world. They maintain their own set of values for personal reasons known only to them. And when they choose to display their true soul it's only at the most private of moments. Moments which are reserved for only their closest, special friends."

RONNIE HUNG IN with Western Auto until the middle of May the following year, then turned in his resignation letter which was to become effective on June 1st. While he thought a two-weeks' notice was the proper and business thing to do, his Regional Manager had other ideas. With this being the second time he had left the company, his boss quickly explained that company policy in such cases was immediate termination. Little did this faze Ronnie. In fact, he was delighted after learning from the personnel director that he was still going to be paid for two more weeks although he was officially terminated at once.

Since he was not to report to his new job in Leesburg until

the first of June, he seized the opportunity for a short vacation. He began wandering southward and eventually stopped to spend a week in Cedar Key. This delightful seacoast town, about 40 miles southwest of Gainesville, was just what the doctor ordered. Each time he visited the area he seemed to enjoy it even more.

Early mornings he would either stand on the bank and fish off the jetties or rent a small John Boat and make the short trip to Horseshoe Island, just minutes from shore. On the island he would find the fishing much more to his liking. This laid back way of life was exactly his style.

Some afternoons and most every evening he divided his happy hour times between Frogs and the old Islander Hotel. It took him only two trips to Cedar Key to place the hotel lounge on his all-time favorite list of watering holes. Its ambiance would draw him back to the area dozens of times throughout his short life.

HIS JOB IN Leesburg seemed to be working out very well. He found a nice apartment just off Highway 441 between Lake Harris and Lake Griffin, two of the best large mouth bass fishing lakes in the country. His new job allowed him to set his own schedule and be off every weekend and any day it rained.

As customary, it was easy for him to make friends. This smooth personality trait had worked well in his favor since moving to Leesburg. A couple of new lady friends had made the last several days very enjoyable and the evenings even more memorable.

He had indeed relished his first seven months in Leesburg and typically he adopted a brand new watering hole. He frequently visited the Cane Patch Lounge, just a block off Main Street and only five football fields or so from where he was born, at Doctor Holland's Hospital.

EARLY THURSDAY EVENING it came a young flood across most of Lake County. Heavy, stormy rains continued through most of the night. Knowing his schedule was open for the weekend, he was delighted that it was still misting when the alarm clock blasted him awake at 6:00 Friday morning. Now, he assured himself, he had at least a three-day rest period. He snuggled back under the sheet and didn't stir again until almost 10:30.

No fishing today. He would shower, dress and then practice his required elbow-bending exercises down at the "Patch," as he now called it. But first, a quick lunch at Hazel's Top Hat Grill. A misnomer of a name if there ever was, but Hazel served the best hamburger steak smothered with onions in the South.

After settling down on his favorite stool, the one he chose the first afternoon he visited the Patch, he ordered up a cold long neck bottle of Bud. To his front left, hanging high in the corner, the television gave him the best view in the pub for watching weekend football games. Earlier in the week he had confirmed a date with Valarie Jammison to meet here tomorrow at noon to watch the Alabama-Auburn game. He was looking forward to a great weekend. She was quite the looker!

Valarie, a ravishingly beautiful sandy-haired blonde had taken great pains to preserve and maintain all the equipment Mother Nature had provided. And all of it, as everyone could plainly see, was the exact right proportions. High cheek bones, little if any eyebrows, thin lips, occasional dimples, blue eyes, long legs, narrow waist, just-right hips and a wonderful warm smile. At least, that's the description he had noted on a scratch pad after meeting her at Doug's Bait Shop three weeks earlier. But much to his dislike, she also had the highest pitched voice on earth. One that simply drove him bananas. But, in this, his non-culling days, there were just some things he knew he had to put up with.

He had ordered another long neck and left his stool for a visit to the men's room. While washing his hands, he could plainly hear Claire, the barkeep, and the other few patrons screaming bloody murder. At first he thought there might be a robbery going down because, just as quick, the place became deathly quiet. He opened the door slowly and peeked out. Everyone was frozen, staring at the television in disbelief. President Kennedy's limousine was speeding away from Dealey Plaza in Dallas on the way to Memorial Hospital.

He left a five spot on the counter, and without touching his second beer or saying good-bye he suddenly walked out the front door. Arriving at his apartment, he flicked on the television and settled in for what was going to be a long night. A long weekend.

Early Saturday morning he phoned Valarie to break their date.

She insisted that she drop by his apartment, but he sloughed off her self-imposed invitation explaining that he would see her early next week. He wanted and needed to be alone.

While he detested politics, the death of a president, a world renowned figure of gigantic importance, got his full attention. He would later tell Valarie that his knowledge of history always portrayed a president as an older person, but remarked how impressed he was with Kennedy's young age and noted that "Perhaps we're going to participate in this generation after all."

Always there existed great tenderness, warmth and special feelings deep within Ronnie that were seldom shown to anyone. When a friend was hurting or someone lost his life, even someone remotely removed from his personal life, it bothered him immensely. Throughout the weekend he barely left the sofa.

OVER THE CHRISTMAS holidays he came to Pensacola to spend time with his family. Pat brought the kids over to Ronnie's folks where they shared Christmas morning and a wonderful dinner prepared by his mom, an excellent cook.

Understandably, the morning was not easy for anyone as there was much emotion shown by all. Christmas mornings around the Williams' home had always been filled with love and kindness. This morning was no exception. Within the last two weeks, Kym, the oldest of six grandchildren, had just turned five; Paige, three; and Vince was not yet two. To everyone it seemed as though his kids were especially pleased and very happy to have this unique time to once again visit with their father.

Ronnie's brother and his wife Jean with their two children, Billy and Ashley; his sister Sandi and Wendy, her firstborn, joined in to make this an endearing family holiday that all enjoyed, especially the grandparents. It was good to have the entire family all together once again.

HE HAD SHOWN no discontentment about his job while at home for Christmas or over the next five months; however, in the spring of the year he was ready again to hit the road. While he enjoyed living in central Florida and sharing in all it offered for those who loved the outdoors, his job had become a burden to him. He imagined that it was taking much too much of his time away from what he deemed to be more important matters. After putting in a full year, he opted to return to Pensacola where he would find work at a variety of jobs.

It turned out to be a good thing that his brother had kept him on the company insurance roll an extra six weeks, although Ronnie had no idea that he had. Only two days after arriving back in Pensacola, he came down with horrible stomach problems and other related illnesses. He was most pleased to learn that he was still covered by insurance as his stay in Baptist Hospital lasted the entire month of June.

One of the nurses assigned to his floor was an old friend he had known since high school days. They talked several times daily, and it was she who suggested that he may want to look into a job opening at the company where her husband was employed.

The job description, sales manager for an upholstery company, sounded good so Ronnie climbed aboard. However, it was a new start-up operation, and the owner was completely incompetent. He was a good ole boy, and his heart was in the right place and he meant well, but he hadn't a clue as to what he was doing. He had no knowledge of how his business should operate, and, furthermore, he was totally under-financed.

OVER THE NEXT five years Ronnie earned a reputation as an excellent salesman in the furniture business although he hated every minute of it and was always looking for an escape. During these years he worked at the four leading companies in the city, and with each change of jobs he received a raise in salary and always an increase in his commission percentage.

And, somehow, in between job changes, he found time to marry Frances, a hard-working girl that he had met when he first moved to Mobile some years earlier. As was everything else in his life, marriage was something that was on a trial basis, a hit and miss proposition at best. Apparently, she knew him well and was well aware of his situation, habits and life style. In due time she would learn that she had her work cut out.

THE LAST THURSDAY in January of '69, he was scheduled to work but swapped off with a co-worker for a future day to be determined. With Thursday free, coupled with his off-days of Friday, Saturday and Sunday, he now had a four-day week-end. Since Frances had to work he would "go fishing" Thursday and Friday and be home when she got there after work on Friday afternoon.

Leaving mid-morning on Thursday, he drove to Montgomery. When visiting the city, he always stayed at the Governor's House Motel on the southern by-pass. It was close to several barbeque restaurants and not too far from the point of his main interest. It also maintained a super cozy lounge.

He knew that he had found a true friend to confide in, someone who would listen and not rebuke his thoughts and intentions. A man who truly understood his dire predicament. He would again go to the cemetery and visit the burial site of Hank Williams. He always planned his arrival at nightfall, knowing that all other visitors would have left by then.

At first he stood quietly for several minutes at the foot of the marble slabs. In stone silence he appeared to be absorbing the undivided stillness of the moment. Then, easing to the ground he rested on the corner of the slab and gently set his small cooler nearby in the grass.

"Boo, this day, this very day, I am 10,698 days old. Have any idea what significance that is? Huh, Boo? Huh? Well, let me tell you, ole buddy. Today, right now, I am exactly the same age as was ole Hank when he bit the dust. How 'bout that, Boo? If I live until tomorrow, I will have outlived my main man, at least one of my main men. Ole Elvis will live forever, I'm sure of that. I know I'll beat his narrow butt into the grave. Just wait and see."

"Ronnie, stop talking like that. Man, you got lots of living to do. Don't even think about dying; what's wrong with you anyway, Goofus?"

"Boo, ole Hank did it right. He got out while the getting was good. Didn't have to go through all this crap. What's the world coming to anyway? What we gonna do about all these problems? Huh?"

"What you mean, Ron? What you talking about? What's going on? I mean, like what?"

"Can't you see, you idiot. The whole world is collapsing all around us. The hippies are taking over California. Out in Kansas some wild man went crazy and murdered a bunch of people."

"Now, Ron, you can't do anything about those things, so stop thinking about them."

"Well, how 'bout my kids being adopted? Can I think about that? Is that okay to think about, huh? Was that the second miserable milestone that's coming my way? Is it Boo?"

"It may be, Ronnie, it just may well be a gigantic milestone unlike none other. But don't forget, what happened to your kids was your fault. Don't start blaming your shortcomings on someone else. You are the one that signed the papers for the adoption. Ain't that right?"

"No, that ain't right. She sent me some papers to sign giving her custody, not adoption," Ronnie screamed.

"Should have read the papers more carefully. Ain't that the way you see it, my man?"

"How many times have we got to have this discussion you idiot? She asked me if she could have custody since she was getting married and was moving away. This is how it was, and don't give me any more crap about it. I thought the kids would be better off without joint custody. Now, get off my back. You hear me? Get off."

"You're the one that brought it up. Remember?"

"Yeah, I 'member. Boo, the whole world is screwed up, me included. You paid any attention to what's really going on outside our little few square miles of the planet, say over the last four or five years? Huh, have you? Just listen, my friend, and see if you can make heads or tails of any of this.

"The Democrats and all those other farts are trying to burn down Chicago. Mississippi and Alabama are letting the blacks in their schools. Can you imagine that? Marching Luther King got his ass shot to death up in Memphis. Now, two of the Kennedys have been assassinated.

"I'm telling you, things are beginning to happen that we have no control over. As it is written, so shall it be. We can't fix it my friend, we are doomed. Everything is planned for us. Everything is already worked out. Can't you see that? There was nothing, nothing at all that I could have done about my kids being adopted from me. Nothing. It was in the cards. 'Deal' cried the loser.

"Strange things are happening, strange things indeed. You know something? If that guy Ryan de Graffenreid had not been killed in that plane crash, we would never have heard the name George Wallace. It was all in the cards, planned in advance. It just had to be that way. It was written in the Great Book. Understand?

"Now, can you visualize, right here in Montgomery, just over that hill, right over there, a woman is Governor of Alabama. How in God's name did that happen? And ole George thinks he can be elected president. Brother Billy and his political cronies even had him come to Pensacola last week for a lunch meeting out at Martines. I tell you, Boo, very strange things are happening all over this crazy world, and you better get ready. It's coming.

"Even closer to home, Billy took some friends on a fishing trip on some island and crashed his airplane, for God's sake. Hey, on my birthday at that! And let me tell you about another sad story. Back in high school a good friend, a teammate and an all-around great kid that everyone called "Sonny," Ray Able, just up and died. And get this, he also died on my birthday. He was practicing football with us one day and gone the next. Boo, this is scary."

"Ronnie, don't you think you've had enough to drink. Let's go back to the motel. What you say?"

"Take it easy. Hank and I got things to talk about. Just take it easy, Boo; sit down over there and relax. Take the load off.

"Boo, don't you see what's happening. I feel so sorry for folks who don't understand that there is nothing they can do about the future. As hard as they try, there is nothing going to change the great plan that has already been drawn up for all of us. It's all in the game. All in the stupid game, don'tcha know.

"NASA will soon put a man on the moon. Can you imagine that? Now my grandma says that will never happen. Says it ain't in the Bible, so it ain't gonna happen.

"Anyway, they have done marvelous things with rockets and space and all that stuff, but you know what? 'Member those three astronauts who lost their lives while just sitting on solid ground? Just sitting there testing one of those explosive rockets. Now, it looks like to me if we can go to the moon, we ought to be able to make our spacecraft safe. At least safe enough where men won't be burned to a crisp while sitting on solid ground as stone still as I sit on this cold marble slab. KnowwhatImean?"

"Boo, can't you see that we can't do anything about all this stuff going around us? We have no say so. My friend, we have nothing to say about what's going to happen to us. Hank was lucky. Don't you think?"

"Ronnie, we best go. Let's go back to the motel. Okay?"

"Boo, 'member when we were in Biloxi that time and read about Jane Mansfield being killed in a car crash just down the road? Now pray tell me why she had to be taken away? A beautiful actress in her prime, and all of a sudden she wasn't here any more. Is there a good reason? No. No, there isn't.

"And two months later a good friend, Reinhart Holm, Pensacola's mayor, just dropped dead. Is there a reason? Of course, there is not. There is also absolutely nothing that we mere mortals can do. It has been written. Can'tcha see that? This is why Hank's songs are so real. So important to us. He understood better than us. He wrote about things that we could not visualize. Understand? Ya'see what I mean?

"Politics, God, how I hate politics. Don't understand them. Don't understand why those folks in politics do the stupid things they do. Why on earth would the most powerful man in the universe, President Lyndon Johnson, give up his presidency? Doesn't make sense to me. He had worked for years wanting to be president then the idiot quits. Then next time we were stuck with that moron, Nixon. How in the world did we elect such a fruit? And by the way, I still think Johnson had something to do with Kennedy's assassination."

"And did you read where Jackie married that rich Greek, Onassis? All she wanted was his money. Let me tell you something, I think there is a very special place in hell for women, or men for that matter, who live off the money of others. Those who feel no love whatsoever for their partner but have material things as their only motive.

"Didn't ole Hank say, or did I read it in the Bible, that 'it is harder for a rich man to enter the kingdom of heaven than it is for a camel to go through the eye of a needle.'"

"Ronnie, I think that came from the Bible, not from Hank."

"Wherever it came from, it's probably true. I think that Jackie

O, considering all her schooling, must have been absent the day they taught the lesson about 'Beware Of Greeks Bearing Gifts.' She'll soon learn; the lesson will come back to haunt her. Just wait and see. Boo, can't you understand what I'm talking about? Do you even see what I mean?"

"Yeah Ronnie, things are tough all over. What you gonna do about it my man?"

"Me? Hellfire, there ain't nothin' I can do about anything. Anyway, I didn't cause these problems. Wasn't none of me."

"Just hang loose, Ronnie. Just hang loose. Things will get better, I promise. Now, don't you think we should pack it up. Let's go."

"Boo, I'm afraid to go. I just don't want to go back. I need to call and check on Sandi but I'm afraid. Her accident was just horrendous and I can't do anything about it. She's bad off, perhaps on the verge of dying. Mom and dad are hysterical, and I only add to their problems. I just needed to get away, get out of their hair. Boo, you need to understand this for me."

"I understand, but let's go back to the motel, get some rest and go home in the morning. How about Frances? You miss her don't you?"

"Of course I do. She'll be there when I get home."

"And what about Celeste. What we gonna do about her?"

"Jeez, I almost forgot about Celeste. I forgot to even remember her. Didn't even tell her that I was coming up here. Well, its always easier to ask forgiveness than permission. You know something? Celeste is going to be all right. Ain't she Boo?

"Alcohol and drugs are major problems among students today, including our athletes. Hopefully, RONNIE will be of help to many of these...."

Coach Tommy Tuberville, Auburn University

13

THERE JUST AIN'T NO LIGHT

RONNIE'S PARENTS, his wife, his brother and sister and all of his close friends had long been concerned about his personal attitude and outlook on life in general. Recently, things seem to have grown even worse. Rarely did he want to spend time with his friends or family. More and more he had withdrawn himself into his now all too familiar hiding place, the invisible shell that sealed him away from everyone who loved him.

Although he was highly intelligent, the things he was doing seemed as if he were acting them out for the benefit of others. This within itself would have been better for the family had it been true. But they realized what was going on and knew it was not an act at all. The crazy stunts that he pulled were genuine in nature and reflected in his mind exactly what he thought was real. Ronnie's life should have been about an All-American, small-town athlete who conquered the sports world. However, what the family had feared and now was seeing in his daily actions was that of a former player who could not let go of the past.

He had been a dynamic young man who captured the hearts of sports fans and countless numbers of ladies during his heyday of prep school, college and throughout much of his life. He also self-destructed after the days of football glory had left his world, after the athletic days of attention were over. He carefully stored his glory days of playing in the Rose Bowl into a special compartment only to be pried open when he himself wanted to look inside.

178

Perhaps it was during this time that Ronnie cultivated an aversion for political authority because Mississippi politicians had threatened to keep his team from playing the game. He and his teammates were just a group of good ole country boys who wanted to play football and cared less about partisan politics, either black or white.

When the glory days of football were over, he simply could not cope with the style of life that was left for him. He evolved into a person who could not grasp or hold onto reality. The last half of his short life was lived in his own private world. A world of torment and destruction which he kept hidden deeply within himself without sharing his misery with anyone but me.

HE DREAMED OF success, yet could not understand that in reality it would have to be himself and no one else that would be solely responsible for any prosperity that might come his way. He failed to comprehend that accomplishment and abundance of life would forevermore be fleeting until such time as he could put his mind, body and soul into a greater positive mode than the negative one which haunted him daily.

His life in many respects was so different from the great masses of humanity who seldom, if ever, had his opportunities. Chances to experience, to reach out and touch and to know personally the lives of a handful of men who would make such an indelible and lasting impression on him. Impressions that would eventually capture and control his mind through his self-doubt and personal failures. Impressions that would conjure up spontaneous negative thoughts, thoughts that would absorb so much of every hour of every day for the greater portion of his short 44-year life. Creating within his mind, without his knowledge, an avenue of thought patterns that produced nothing more than a drive toward complete and total voluntary destruction.

Perhaps his mental state of mind and his ever-increasing alcoholic attitude evolved because of the success of a few very special people. Everything he did on a daily basis was in part due to unforseen, sub-conscience reactions of his belief that life itself held no real meaning or purpose because of his self doubt and personal status as someone with little self worth.

The pressures within him were great. He questioned himself

continually as to why he had been allowed to come so close to those who would become personalities of gigantic magnitude while he was left behind.

He could not shut down his mind, to be absent or relieved from thoughts of these extraordinary people. Or the many phenomenal, uncanny situations concerning each. These special and sometimes eerie circumstances haunted him daily. However insignificant to others they might seem, they were of major importance, of dominant proportions to him.

The success of these friends, acquaintances or performers, all near his same age, generated within Ronnie's mind a set of circumstances that would conjure up mountains of memories as each of them made it big while he was left behind. Circumstances, anecdotes and stories when mixed with alcohol formulated a destructive lifestyle for himself. Unquestionably, he lived his daily life vicariously through the personalities of these uncommon men.

His inability to cope with, control or harness the demons which dominated his every waking hour would play a monumental role in the loss of his life. A loss which perhaps might have easily been prevented. The loss of his life was nothing more than a simple case of murder.

So many young athletes find out too late that after the days of their sports glory are over, when the publicity extolling their talents has dried up, they often wake up to learn they have not prepared themselves for the next step: real life experiences. Many never find their second niche, so they continue through their daily lives by dreaming of the success of their achievements in earlier years. Still others live their lives through those they have known in the past. Sometimes these are former teammates who went forward with their careers and accomplished great personal goals.

When the glory days are finished, many turn to alcohol to sooth their personal pain and perhaps deal with ghosts from their past. The spirits of alcohol create free thinking and offer to them a means of continuing to meditate on the past without having to confront or concern themselves about what really awaits them here in the real world.

During his seven years of high school and college football, Ronnie depended solely on others on the team to block, open holes and lead the way. He demanded so much of them yet demanded in return so little of himself. When it finally registered that the time had come for him to fend for himself, it was shocking. A real chore that he was not ready to accept. The team wasn't there any longer to be the massive force in front of him, to be the factor which allowed him to find his way to glory.

IN THE SUMMER of 1969 two of Ronnie's friends, Fred Levin and Fred Vigodsky, purchased the Chick's Bar B Q Restaurant operation. Their goal was to expand the restaurant business across Northwest Florida, into South Alabama and perhaps even into a much wider market area. They set about remodeling some of the older establishments and constructed their first new restaurant in Pensacola on East Gregory Street, just a few blocks west of the Bay Bridge. Shortly after opening, Ronnie was employed as their night manager, although his knowledge of the restaurant business was limited only to the fact he knew this was where folks dined when they chose not to eat at home.

Nonetheless, the opportunity quickly developed into a pleasant position for him. He was easygoing and ecstatic to see many of his old-time friends and classmates who came in to patronize the restaurant. A large percent came by just to renew their acquaintance with him personally.

Since the owners were longtime friends, everything melded into a congenial atmosphere and happy workplace. Everyone got along well together, and never was there a cross word between any of them. But soon it was learned that Ronnie really hated to make decisions of any real importance, especially if it involved personnel problems. Perhaps this came about because of the various and sundry jobs he had held and the variety of reasons that he kept moving from place to place. Knowing just how unpleasant it was to terminate someone, he detested this phase of his job description.

The company had kept its eyes open for any opportunity to expand its restaurant operations. When it became known that Carpenters Restaurant was available, the owners quickly purchased the popular landmark, a favorite dinning place of Pensacolians for many years.

Shortly after the acquisition, Ronnie was transferred to the

Self sketch of himself as a gunslinger.

*Ronnie drew this composite sketch around 1962. It re-
flects his personal evaluation and comparison of how he saw
Elvis Presley and himself. They were both handsome men.*

*Left: Elvis as "Charro."
Below: two pictures of
Ronnie as "Charro."*

new restaurant as co-manager, sharing both night and daytime duties. The restaurant and its popular "Side Bar Lounge" did quite well for a number of months. Businessmen and women filled the dining areas with clients during the noon hour, while several civic clubs held their weekly meetings in the comfortable side rooms. In the evenings reservations were necessary.

However, for reasons unknown, the restaurant just did not continue to retain its old line customers. After a couple of years the new wore off, and it rocked along doing little more than a mediocre amount of business over the next several months.

The decline in diners presented a challenge to the owners as to which direction to take the establishment. A new menu, chef, motif and complete facelift were ordered. Soon after came the new name of "The Nut Club," then even later another name change to "Hank Locklin's." Nothing seemed to help. As the business continued to decrease, management finally closed its doors. For the next several months Ronnie was unemployed while Frances continued to make the living for the both of them.

RONNIE SELDOM TALKED openly to his friends about what he thought of the Elvis movies but opened up to me constantly. While some he deemed outright silly, others he really enjoyed. He proclaimed that "CHARRO!" was perhaps his favorite of the 33 movies. His choice may have been because Elvis was acting, not singing, as there was only a single song which was sung over the opening credits. Or maybe it was the beard and the tough guy image he portrayed. Ronnie would soon grow a similar beard and pose for snapshots in a variety of images that depicted him as an eerie likeness of "CHARRO."

In 1972 Ronnie's parents bought a new home north of Pensacola and allowed him to move into their former residence on New Warrington Road. One night in late November he went to the movies to see Elvis's last film, "ELVIS ON TOUR." Returning home, he rumbled through the old storage house in the backyard and uncovered The Unwanted Gift which he had wrapped securely in an old army blanket. He made a roaring fire then threw himself comfortably on the sofa. With a drink in hand, his mind rewound backwards, reminiscing about the past.

By now, most of Elvis's movies were commonplace on late

night television. With each showing he would search diligently for his friend Red. In most of the earlier movies Red had only bit parts, but in later films he was awarded speaking roles. Speaking parts or not, all, every appearance, were important to Ronnie.

"Boo, while ago at the movies, didja see ole Red riding in that limousine and talking to Elvis? Didja, Boo, didja? Man, what memories things like that bring back. You 'member that time we saw on television where Elvis and Red were leaving that concert and Elvis said something to Red about the girl he was with last night? Ole Red busted a gut laughing. 'Member that, Boo? They must be having a hellova good time."

Over the last seventeen years he had kept the secret of the old guitar to himself and had admonished his brother never to tell the story to anyone. It was to be kept a personal secret between Elvis, Red, Ronnie, Bill and obviously, me. No one else in his family, including his former wife Pat, was aware of its history or importance, although occasionally everyone had seen it. When Ronnie felt the urge that he needed special companionship and personal uplifting, he would drag it from storage and gloat over years gone by. Never without a drink in hand.

TONIGHT HE THOUGHT of the millions upon millions of words written and stories told about Elvis Presley. Since his rise to become the most famous entertainer in the world, much had been written about the many friends and acquaintances who shared a good deal of his time. The special group of men, who had been tagged by the media as "The Memphis Mafia," were close associates, advisors and personal friends. Men who looked after his every need. Ronnie revered the fact that his friend Red was also Elvis's oldest and closest companion.

"Boo, we got us a secret that we ain't ready to tell yet, but someday we'll let the cat out of the bag. KnowwhatImean?

"Around the world ole Elvis has millions of adoring fans, but they only know today's story. Most don't 'member the early days, the very early days before the mafia came into being. They don't know that long before the world ever knew there was a Memphis Recording Studio, Sun Records or Sam Phillips, and before anyone ever heard of Scotty Moore, Bill Black or D.J. Fontanna,

Red was already a part of Elvis's life. And I feel privileged to know that Red is also a part of my life. Know that, Boo?"

"Ronnie, he's been with us a long time. It's been more than seventeen years now. Friends like Red West are hard to come by. You ought to be proud of that relationship."

"Yeah, I know. Long before the world would come to know the name Elvis Presley, Red and ole Elvis were neighbors, just teenage friends. Red used to tell me how they visited back and forth in each other's homes, 'drug the main' through the streets of Memphis and double-dated. Boo, I told you that Elvis was best man at Red's wedding didn't I?"

"You may have mentioned it, but somehow I just seem to know those sort of things."

"Well, anyway, Red married Pat Boyd, Elvis's secretary. Elvis gave them a new Mercedes for a wedding gift. Now can you imagine what Red and I could have done with a Mercedes when we were in school in Mississippi? The good Lord knew what he was doing when Red got that Model A instead of a Mercedes. But guess what? We did all right though!"

SHORTLY AFTER RED and Pat's wedding, Elvis invited Mrs. West, Red's mother, to Graceland to join Red and his new bride for an evening meal. It was during dinner when she, in her low and humble voice, observed just how far Elvis had come with his music and popularity. Then recalled several times when he and Red got into some minor mischiefs back when they lived in the courts. She couldn't resist reminding them about the day they sneaked two girls into her home at the Hurt Housing project, thinking she would be gone all day. She returned unexpectedly, and they were caught red-handed. The table had a good laugh with Elvis taking the lead.

Ronnie would often try to imagine just how Red's and Elvis's early friendship had developed and how their teenage relationship broadened as Elvis became more and more an international, household name. Since the world knows the rags-to-riches story, it's hard to imagine from the beginning how theirs was just a simple story of two neighborhood friends sticking together, enjoying life to the fullest. Just two young men having fun.

Ronnie spent countless hours reminiscing, not only thinking

of the past but hoping that lightning would strike and propel himself onto the world stage. Certainly not as a performer, but in some responsible and important role, perhaps in the business community. And never were his dreams more meaningful and intense than after watching an Elvis movie, especially those where he identified Red as a character.

He often recalled, sometimes vividly, sometimes vaguely, the story Red told about Elvis giving The Unwanted Gift to him. And how pleased Red was when he passed it on to him. Back then not a single person could even dream of what was to become of the skinny, timid kid from midtown Memphis public housing.

When Red brought the guitar to the "Bull Pen," Ronnie would recall how it was picked at indifferently by his teammates. It was strummed, then thrown around from one bed to another. No one had a clue! Those were good, clean and happy days. As the years began to slip by, he would recall them as the very best days of his entire life. He often thought about the day Red sold Steve Perkins his Model A, the day before he gave him the guitar. Memories. Such lasting memories.

He remembered that Red told him the guitar was already more than nine years old when he gave it to him, and now it had to be at least 26. The touch, the feel of the old instrument always brought back warm and fuzzy sensations to him. If ever there was a crutch that a man leaned on for moral and mental support, this was it. On many occasions he thought of selling the guitar, but no matter how strapped he got for money it was always his decision to keep it close by. After all, there would never again be another "first guitar" owned by Elvis Presley.

Ronnie always dreamed of something big happening to him as it did to Hank, Burt, Elvis and a few other close friends. Each fall he delighted in watching Lee Corso, his former FSU teammate, live on television giving his opinions and predictions for the day's games.

He set aside a huge place in his memory for former friends who had made it big. He put them on a pedestal, and there they would remain. He always put them way above himself as if he wasn't in their league. He could never quite grasp that life still had much to offer him if he would only grab hold and hang on. For him he knew that life was all but finished.

And to him, the acceptance of Elvis in the homes of millions of Americans was a fantastic phenomenon. It was uncanny and most difficult for him to comprehend just how simple life was for this young man of only eighteen before the massive explosion. What life was really all about before he burst on the scene with his abundance of raw energy and uncontrolled excitement. He soon captured the entertainment world, live national television and starring roles in 33 movies. The ticking time bomb named Elvis had erupted and had done so in just a very brief few months. Still, Ronnie was left at the starting gate waiting patiently for something big to be handed to him on a silver platter.

LATE NIGHT HAD slipped into early morning hours. It now had become commonplace for him to stay up all night without sleeping.

"Listen, Boo, I want to read you something that mom cut from one of her ladies' magazines. She made me promise to read it when I was troubled. Listen closely, maybe it's important although I don't understand it. It says a lot, and maybe it's kinda like all the decisions I've been making."

After fixing another drink he scooted his dad's favorite chair closer to the dying flames and read.

YES or NO

All through life we must keep choosing. Destiny hangs on "yes" or "no." As we look back, it is to wonder what would have happened if we had gone the other way when the road forked.

On life's bargain counter are wares piled up for the pleasure of all tastes. We marvel that some eagerly select what we reject. Our tastes are as diverse as our natures. What one person takes for granted, someone else would give his all just to have and hold.

How can nature originate so great a variety of patterns? We speak of the mass of mankind as if it were all one. But it presents a bewildering variation. Human beings are as different from one another as their parental influences and their environments, and their personal natures are different. Flesh and blood can never be run in a mold of monotonous uniformity. The fascination of travel is in the endless and varied personalities of mankind that one encounters, more than in silent buildings or inarticulate scenery.

The choice of personal associates is the all-influencing choice. To go wrong here is the likeliest way to cripple one's chances of eminence or of plain, everyday success. A man goes into business with partners guilty of malfeasance, and they pull him down.

A woman marries the wrong man, and though her courage may keep her at the sticking point and may enable her to preserve the appearance of domestic felicity, all that makes for the ideal relationship is absent. The basis of happiness is not in things, but in people whom you truly desire and need. A person who is able to show you the correct way to a happy life, realizing that it could have been different had the other decisions been made rather than the road that you have chosen, is a person worthy of a relationship which should never cease. Those of us who are completely normal cannot get along without congenial society. The kind of persons we choose to be with is the first and surest indication of character. The worthiest must be uneasy and unhappy in the company of the worst; and the best will naturally seek the best. What a person chooses, he is.

Happiness depends upon a number of things. There are two basic ways of being happy; we may either diminish our wants or augment our means. Either will do, the result is the same. And it is for each man to decide for himself, and do that which happens to be the easiest. If you are idle, sick or poor, however hard it may be for you to diminish your wants, it will be harder to augment your means. If you are active and prosperous or young in spirit or in body, or in good health, it may be easier for you to augment your means than to diminish your wants.

"Now, listen closely to this part, Boo."

But if you are wise, you will do both at the same time to achieve happiness and yet run your normal course of life. And if you are very wise, you will do both in such a way as to augment the general happiness of others, while assuring yourself of the goal you wish.

There can be no real and abiding happiness without sacrifice. Our greatest joys do not result from our efforts toward self-gratification, but from a loving and spontaneous

service to other lives. Joy comes not to him who seeks it
for himself, but to him who seeks if for other people whom
he loves, while not considering his own feelings.

"Boo, what does all this mean? I wonder what it really means.
I have spent a lifetime making wrong decisions. Does it mean
that life is over for me? Is there no way to change? To go back?
To make good decisions? I just don't understand," Ronnie com-
plained.

"Ronnie, anyone can change. Anyone can alter his lifestyle
and do things different and better. You can. You, my man, can
make a lifetime of change overnight if you wish to do so."

"Boo, you know I'm broke, don't have a pot to pee in. How
can I possibly do anything better, anything different? Tell, me.
Boo, just tell me how?"

"I'll tell you how. Remember that time you, Red and Roper
went down to Biloxi and ran into those girls from Little Rock?
Remember that all of y'all started talking about rich folks and
how they did things that the poor folks couldn't do? Remember
what the blonde girl said to you? Well, if you don't, I'll tell you.
She said, 'The richest person is not always the person with the
most money, but, it is always, without exception, the person with
the most options.'

"Ronnie my man, you gotta work on your options. Forget all
this junk about crying over happiness. Get your options together,
and happiness will find its way into your miserable life."

"I ain't got no more options. You know that, Boo. My life is
over, man. Completely over. You hear me?"

"Stop with that attitude, you idiot. Your life is a long way
from being over. If you don't think so, then crawl over on that
sofa and lay there until you die. You got enough alcohol in your
veins that your family won't even need to have you embalmed.
You can just lay there until some of the neighbors began to notice the smell. Then it'll be all over. You won't have anything
more to be concerned about. Ronnie, I swear, you just take the
cake."

"Boo, just kiss off.

"You know, if I can just get through today's tough problems,
then maybe everything will be okay. If, and that is a huge 'if,'

but if I can get through them, I will be a much better man for conquering my demons just one day at a time. KnowwhatImean?"

"Ronnie, you remember what Ralph Bunche said about that? I know you remember; we've talked about it several times before. He said, 'God sends us trials and tribulations to test us. But He arms us against them with hope and faith and dreams. Nothing is ever lost until they are abandoned, and then everything is lost. Don't ever let anything take away your hope, your faith or your dreams.'

"That is such a good lesson for you, Ronnie. You should pay attention, but guess what. You need to believe in all three goals, and thus far you have only concerned yourself with 'dreams.' You gotta have them all, my friend. You gotta have hope and faith to compliment all your dreams. Can't you see that?

"With hope, faith and dreams, you can overcome this drudgery of depression. You can overcome the horrible and difficult problem of your drinking. You have to change your ways, and you need to do so now before it's too late. That's the bottom line."

"Boo, there just ain't no damn light at the end of the tunnel. I've tried so hard, you know that. Boo, there just ain't no light. Maybe it's already too late. I just don't see a way to fight it any longer. Maybe I've traveled the road too long. Boo, you know that I have fought it, don't you? Please know that."

"Let me remind you of one of your mother's favorite sayings. She is so fond of quoting Norman Vincent Peale. It goes like this, 'The tragedy of life is not that it ends so soon—it's that we wait too long to begin it.'

"Ronnie, you just gotta get off your rear end and get with it. You gotta reach down with both hands and pull up your boots and start wading through all the crap. Life is a long way from being over for you. You gotta work hard at something. Put your mind to doing a job and get it done. You can either wait for a fish to jump into your boat, or you can go after it. Sure, one may jump right in, depending on just how long you are willing to wait. But most likely, it'll never happen. You simply must go after it.

"Ronnie, you can do almost anything you make your mind up to do. No, you can't sing like your buddies Elvis or Hank, but on the other hand you are as good looking as Burt. Maybe you should have given that a try."

"Yeah, I've often thought about that. Sometimes I really think that I could have been successful. But out in the world there are hundreds of folks that could be good actors. But guess what? Most of them are just like me. They don't want to take the chance of being rejected, being told they don't have it. Just last month Billy even told me that he would back me for a full year if I wanted to give it a try. Boo, you know that if I tried and failed it would kill me.

"I realize that my potential has all but vanished. I never did fully reach my capacity. Never felt the full impact of my capabilities. I never had the nerve to try, to stretch forward, because I was way too scared of failure. I never have wanted to hit a single; it always had to be a home run. I was never satisfied unless I was on the top, the winner. If I couldn't win, or think that I had a chance to win, then I wouldn't even try. I was never satisfied with anything small. It had to be big. The entire ball of wax."

"That's right Ronnie. That's a great attitude. Just sit on your dead rump and do nothing but dream. I'll swear I've never seen anybody like you. Okay, what you gonna do? You have got to work at something. My God, man get with it."

"What I need is a good luck charm. If it wasn't for bad luck, I'd have no luck at all," Ronnie said in a meek voice.

"Ronnie, luck is for the Irish. Hard work never killed anyone, not even John Henry. You remember when President Kennedy's mother said, "To whom much is given, much is expected." Perhaps she had you in mind. Perhaps she was talking directly to you in reverse. Nothing should be expected by you, especially since little has been put out by you in the way of an effort."

"Well, harp all you want, Boo. I'm not overly proud of the things that I have done, but there have been a few. I am satisfied with some of my accomplishments. How many folks you know that has scored two touchdowns in the Rose Bowl? Huh? How many?"

"Ronnie, jeez! Man, when it's over, it's over. Completed. Done. Finished. No more. Get past that time of your life, and move forward. You can't dwell on the past forever. There is nothing from the past that will help you now. Can't you see that? It may not be over until it's over, but my man, you need to open your rose-colored eyes and recognize that it-is-truly-over!"

"Boo, let's face it. I don't really want to think about the future. Life has already been decided, you know that. Life's just like a deck of cards. They deal the hand and you play what you get. There is nothing I can do to change it. Nothing is worse than having a door slammed in your face. Nothing worse than a situation that you can do absolutely nothing about. That's the way it was when I lost my kids. How do you think I feel living with the fact that they now call someone else their daddy? How do you think that makes me feel down deep inside? You'll never know. Boo, you'll never, never know.

"Believe me, there is nothing sadder than a grown man with a broken heart. Nixon spoke of having experienced the excitement and serenity of being on the highest mountain. But he explained that he didn't realize just how wonderful that most magnificent feeling was until after having come from the shadows and bowels of the lowest pit. You see, I'm still in a crater, a very deep hole. It's been a long, long time since I have known the highs and peaks of exhilaration. Or cameras and flash bulbs. Or pictures in the paper.

"Perhaps Hemingway said it best in *A Farewell To Arms,* when he noted, 'The world breaks everyone, and afterward many are strong at the broken places. But those that will not break, it kills. It kills the very good and the very gentle and the very brave impartially. If you are none of these, you can be sure it will kill you too, but there will be no special hurry.'

"Boo, think ole Hemingway was right?"

"Could be, Ronnie. Sounds good to me."

"Boo, life for me is absolutely void of any degree of fulfillment. I'll have a good out-of-town weekend with a lady friend, then I always have to come back to this cold and lonely house. No matter how much money or prestige you have amassed, if you have to come home to a lonely house it's still the pits. Why go fishing when there is no one to share the catch with you?

"Recently, Mother Teresa said, 'Loneliness is the worst disease known to man.' I don't think of it being a disease, but, by God, it's something very close."

"Ronnie, you need to find yourself a good woman. That's the key to your life. Someone to share your life. Love never loses, it always wins. Don't ever forget that. Love always wins. And by the way, Mother Teresa said 'The lack of love is the worse disease known to man,' not loneliness."

"Well, whatever, they're one and the same. No difference."

"That's not true, my man. That's not true at all. There are many people who love you. You know that. They can share their love with you, but the loneliness part you have to take care of yourself. Happiness overcomes loneliness. But happiness comes from within oneself. It's not given to you by someone else. It's not a reward that someone can bestow on you. It's something that you have to create for yourself."

"Boo, you say that love always wins, and perhaps you're right. Be that as it may, I have my own personal thoughts about women folk. While they surely can be traps and burdens, they can also be the very best thing available for overcoming loneliness. I just don't know about the 'love always wins' thing.

"Boo, I guess the bottle is the second best thing. And I hope those who lurk in the shadows of dim-lighted saloons and prey on poor and ignorant drunks will be cursed with sleepless nights and eerie early mornings, just like me."

"Ron, you're bitter."

"Yeah, I'm bitter, but not stupid. And I argue with you on your 'love always wins' position. Tom T. Hall said it best, 'the only thing in life worth a damn is old dogs, children and watermelon wine.' Old dogs care about you even when you make mistakes, and little children are too young to really understand this wicked world. And wine? Well, wine just does what wine is supposed to do."

"Your letter to Governor Underwood was referred to this office for response. Thank you for your concern and your efforts to keep youth alcohol and drug free. I am requesting that your message and web site be shared with each county level Safe and Drug-Free Schools Coordinator."

David Stewart, State Superintendent of Schools WestVirginia

14

IF THIS IS VEGAS, THEN ELVIS IS SURELY SLEEPING

FOR THE BETTER part of the next two years Ronnie was unemployed. And as the old saying goes, "Empty hands are the devil's workshop." So it was with Ronnie.

His marriage was on and off. Making up and tearing apart was the order of the day. And making it even harder for her, Frances continued with her employment with his father's company. It was most difficult for her to do her job and continue to feel that she owed Mr. Williams some allegiance by keeping him informed about what was going on in her and Ronnie's personal and private life. She was a loyal employee, but the combination created a tremendous hardship on her.

During the down periods of their marriage, he would spend time around Cedar Key and several spots up and down the St. Johns River. He was especially fond of the Jungle Inn Lodge, a laid-back place north of Daytona Beach. It was here that Celeste and he had spent many happy days. With little more to do than relax, sit by the pool and fish when he felt like it, this lifestyle was almost perfect for him. Here he could be at ease and let his mind conjure up whatever thoughts it deemed appropriate.

Naturally, he continued to be subjected to the news and national events. And as customary, any negative story would set his mind wondering in an empty vacuum. He tried very hard to always associate the story with a predicament entwined in his own personal life. Every piece of adverse news seemed to drive him back into another silent state of despair.

In his weaker moments he and I often talked about shutting the news down, leaving it outside his private world completely. But just as soon, he would rally back as if from a daze and have no part of such a conspiracy, as he called it.

"Boo, listen to this; it was in the morning paper. What the world does it all mean? Where are we going?" he wondered.

"Whatcha got there, Ron?"

"Some smart-ass senator in Washington made a bunch of comments. Comments like he knows what's going on. Just listen to what he said. 'The average life of each of the world's greatest and best civilizations has been about 200 years. And during that lifespan, it has progressed thought a number of special and important sequences.'

"Now listen closely, Boo. He said, 'First there was bondage, then spiritual faith, from spiritual faith to great courage, from courage to liberty, from liberty to abundance, from abundance to selfishness, from selfishness to complacency, from complacency to apathy, from apathy to dependency, then from dependency back to bondage again.'

"Can you believe that? I suppose since the United States is more than 200 years old and because what's been happening over the last several years, it would appear to me that we certainly are in the last period he described. What you think, Boo?"

"Could be, Ronnie. What you gonna do about it?"

"OhHellfire, man, there ain't nothing I can do about anything. Just go to sleep; leave me alone. Take a hike."

A POTPOURRI OF what he determined to be personal problems were constantly bouncing through his mind. Some had national or international implications, others were regional in nature, and still others of interest only to perhaps himself. However, they all bothered him equally and seemed to come on the scene in droves, all within a very short span of time.

Four college students lost their lives on the Kent State Campus when attacked by the National Guard. Janis Joplin overdosed in a Hollywood motel room. Marshall Renfroe, a longtime neighborhood friend and fellow baseball player, was seri-ously injured in a wreck on the Bay Bridge and succumbed just two weeks later. Karen Askew, the wife of a card-playing buddy, was killed in a car wreck on a quiet residential neighborhood street.

But on the lighter side, Elvis showed up unannounced at the White House and demanded a visit with President Nixon. After a bit of confusion he indeed was granted a lengthy audience. Ronnie doubled up with laughter when he read a comment the one-time timid boy from Memphis made to the President. Presi-dent Nixon had said to Elvis, "Son, you dress kind of wild, don't you?" To this, Elvis returned what he thought to be a compli-ment, "Mr. President, you got your show to run; I've got mine."

Not everything was exploding all around him. There were some lighter and better moments from time to time. In Pensacola the community was exceedingly glad that its favorite son, Reubin Askew, had been inaugurated Governor of Florida. This pleased Ronnie because he knew it was a highlight in the Levin family's life since Askew had been a senior member of their law firm.

But still, Ronnie had become shellshocked by believing that, for every good thing in his life that happened, a bad one was sure to follow. In early spring the miserable cycle continued when Ronnie Shaw, another close friend and neighbor, was slaughtered in an automobile wreck on Scenic Highway. He had almost re-signed to the fact that horrible personal problems, as he deemed them to be, were never going to cease. He knew for sure he would never be free of them. He had been at Sir Richards Lounge the night of Shaw's car wreck and spoke to him just minutes before his car failed to make a dangerous curve. Everytime something unpleasant happened to a friend, he became more despondent, which always drove him into another heavy drinking binge.

His father, assuming that Ronnie was apparently borrowing from friends to fund his drinking sprees, first called Fred Levin to inquire. The call was right on target. Fred assured him that no more dollars would be lent to Ronnie for any purpose.

Mr. Williams was concerned that his comments to Fred may have been taken the wrong way and phoned again the following morning. He explained that he knew just how close he and Ronnie were and did appreciate so much his care and concern for him when in need; however, he wanted to make sure that Fred understood that the funds were being used to Ronnie's detriment. Both men voiced their genuine concern for Ronnie's health, happiness and safety.

Not having the slightest idea which road to take next, his father gave Ronnie another job in the family paving business. Steady work and a weekly income seemed to lift his spirits and return a tad of the self worth that had so long been absent.

Most of his evenings were spent alone at home. After a light meal, the uneventful nights were nothing more exciting than watching the tube until the early morning hours. A new weekly television series, "Wild, Wild West," starring Robert Conrad and his buddy Red West, had earned a national following. He was most impressed with Red's acting abilities and never missed an episode.

As the new year rolled around, the papers were full of disappointing stories concerning the apparent breakup of Elvis and Priscilla. On his 37th birthday Elvis announced that both Priscilla and Lisa Marie would be leaving Graceland. Within six weeks they had abandoned Elvis and his mansion.

Things remained, for the most part, somewhat rocky. There were good days followed by horrible ones. But occasionally, a bright blue sky was on the horizon, and the sunshine filtered through what had become a very dull existence. And while it was somewhat sensitive that he and his estranged wife worked in the same building, they were more than civilized to each other and got along well. It became routine for them to patch it up for a short time, then tear it all down once again.

RONNIE, STILL HAWKISH about world problems, showed great concern that George Wallace had been shot during a political rally in a Maryland shopping center while campaigning for president. And that former President Harry Truman had passed away, as did Lyndon Johnson just five days before the official end of his nemesis, the Viet Nam War. And two more popular performers had lost their lives. Jim Croce was killed in an airplane crash on takeoff from a small airport in Natchitoches, Louisiana, while Bobby Darin died on an operating table from complications of heart surgery.

Vice-President Agnew had resigned from office for allegedly taking bribes, and Congressman Gerald Ford was appointed to fill his unexpired term. And as other events occurred, all of which he believed to have a direct hand in shaping his personal life, he took special note of each.

Shortly thereafter, his maternal grandmother passed away as did a close lady friend and still another entertainer, Mama Cass Elliot.

These deaths, to the great masses of humanity, would perhaps move them to only the briefest moments of respect. And while national personalities were known to Ronnie only as individuals seen on television or in the papers, they still drenched his innermost emotions. Time and again he accepted their plight as his personal problem as if they were close kin.

EVERYONE WAS PULLING for him to come around and pick up the pieces of his scattered life. His brother was very concerned and decided that perhaps a weekend trip would do Ronnie some good. A trip to somewhere new. Some place that he had never been. And why not include their wives? After talking it over thoroughly with Ronnie, the plans were completed. Bill agreed to foot the expenses for a four-day trip to Las Vegas.

Since both Ronnie and Frances were working for the company, plans had to be made for their leave of absence for a Friday and the following Monday. That would be no problem and was quickly worked out. The trip was on go.

The four flew out of Pensacola to New Orleans where they would catch a wide body L-1011 to Vegas. Although the two-hour layover in New Orleans would be quite boring, it was the best flight schedule that could be arranged.

No sooner had they deplaned in New Orleans than came a question from Ronnie, "Brother, how much time we got to kill between flights?"

Bill, who was paying for the trip, had assigned the role of tour guide to Frances who responded, "Two hours and twelve minutes."

"Look here, little brother. There's a place down in the French Quarter that I'm crazy about. Why don't we run down and have us a small little baby drink? We got plenty of time. Whatcha say?"

"Ronnie, you know what time it is right now?"

"Certainly," he said looking at his wrist only to see that he had left his watch on his dresser at home, but glancing at a wall clock he hastily responded, "It's exactly two minutes past nine in the morning."

"Kinda early for a drink, wouldn't you say," chided Jean, knowing of the fondness of her brother-in-law for his early hour splashes of courage.

"Times awastin,' Jean. Now, y'all done spent ten minutes just standing 'round here talking. Let's get a taxi, and be on our way. Whatcha say?"

"Well, I'm game," voiced Bill, noting that they were, after all, on vacation. "How about it ladies?"

With a two and two vote, the men announced they would be back in time for the flight, but just in case they missed it the ladies should go on to Vegas and when they arrived check in at the MGM. The men would be along as soon as possible.

Jean and Fanny, as Ronnie tagged her, quickly realized, as the men were assured they would, that this arrangement was certainly not to their liking nor in their best interest. Rightfully and wisely so, they were the first to hop into the cab for their hasty trip into the Big Easy.

"Where to," grumbled the cabby.

"The Old Absinthe House," came Ronnie's reply.

"You sure you want the Old Absinthe House and not the Old Absinthe Bar?" inquired the cabby.

"I don't know. What's the difference? I thought they were the same."

"The difference is two blocks. One's at 400 Bourbon Street, and the other in the 200 block."

"Listen, cabby, just take us to the one that's got whiskey. That all right with you?" Ronnie snapped.

"Quite all right with me, boss."

"Jeez, I wasn't sure the place was still there or not. I haven't been in the quarters in five or six years," Ronnie remarked.

"Yeah, it's still there," said Bill. "Jean, you remember going for drinks there last year after the Sugar Bowl?"

"Sure do, and was it ever freezing outside. They had three or four heaters with open blazes in the rear. How in the world someone didn't get burned is beyond me. The place was packed. People bumping into each other, pushing everyone. It was really dangerous."

Fighting the heavy Friday morning traffic from the airport to downtown left little time for anything more than the simple purpose of the side trip. After a round of Bloody Mary's and one to go for the men, it was back into a cab and a dash to make their flight.

Bill was the only one of the four who had flown an L-1011. As they boarded, the other three were amazed at its size. In fact, this was only Ronnie's second flight, his California Rose Bowl trip being his first. The plane was only half booked, affording them plenty of room to ramble around and stretch out. Drinks and food were served throughout the flight causing Ronnie, in his prevailing mood of happiness, to wonder if he had actually died and gone to heaven.

The accomodations at the MGM Grand were superb. The men quickly headed for the blackjack tables while the girls dropped several coins in the slots. Service unsurpassed was at their beck and call. The first night they had tickets to the Kenny Rogers show and tried in vain to get Elvis tickets for Saturday night, but typically the show was already sold out. They settled for an evening of entertainment at Circus Circus and a sideshow featuring Lou Rawls.

Bill knew that Ronnie could call on Red West for tickets to the Elvis show for Sunday night, but he steadfastly refused. "Why don't you want to call him?" Bill pushed.

"Naw, man. He's too busy."

"Well, let's call anyway. All he can do is say no. I'm sure he'd love to see you. Don't you think?"

"They're probably sleeping. You know you read all the time that Elvis sleeps all day, so I guess Red and the guys do also."

"Ronnie, let's try anyway. I bet Red will even get us backstage passes. Maybe invite us up to the suite after the show. Come on, man, let's try it."

"No. Red's busy. Just let it be, Billy."

The four had a great time on the trip. Even the endless drive up to Boulder Dam was magnificent. Ronnie talked about the Vegas night life for some time and always mentioned that he was

in vogue without his watch, noting that he was well aware before leaving home that no one in Vegas ever wears a timepiece.

He told all his friends that he had won some big-time dollars
on the blackjack tables and a few more shooting craps. The truth
of the matter was that he, like everyone else who puts up his
money, was so foggy from the complimentary cocktails he could
barely count the spots on his cards or dice.

ABOUT A MONTH later, Bill picked Ronnie up for lunch.
They drove out Gulf Beach Highway to Rusty's Seafood Restau-
rant, a favorite of theirs. It was here that Ronnie brought up the
Las Vegas trip once again.

"Little brother, you know why I didn't want to get up with
Red when we were in Vegas?"

"Obviously, I don't," Bill responded, still somewhat perturbed
over the incident.

"I had been thinking about calling him from the time we
planned the trip until we landed in Vegas. What if he had asked
us to come upstairs after the show. Know what I was worried
about?"

"I can't imagine. Have no idea. What?"

"I can just see ole Red asking Elvis if he remembered meeting me at a party in Memphis and how Red and I played football
in Mississippi. I can imagine Red telling him I was the friend
that he gave his old guitar to when he left JCJC."

"And what about it? What's so horrible about that?"

"What if he had wanted it back, dummy?" Ronnie replied.
"What if Elvis had wanted his first guitar back? Now that he
was so popular, what if he really wanted his old guitar back, the
one his parents raked and scraped to buy him when he was a kid?
Huh? What would I have said? What could I have done?"

"Naw, he wouldn't have wanted it," Bill counseled.

"But, what if he had? What in the world would I have done?"

"Well, you could have told him that you would sell it back to
him."

"Oh, be real, Billy. What would I have done? Really?"

"Well, I'll tell you Ronnie. I don't know what you would
have done at that moment, but for sure that moment is long past.
Why don't you quit worrying about it. It's over. It didn't hap-

pen and that is that. So just get it out of your mind for now and forever.

"Speaking of a 'it's not going to ever happen kind of story,'" Bill noted, "it's kind of like what Joe Blackenship, one of our laborers, said to me one time. It had rained us out for the day, and I was just standing around with the men when I asked Joe if he wanted to go flying with me. He said, 'Na sir, Mr. Bill. Can't get in no airplane.'

"I told him he shouldn't be afraid because, when it came his time to go, that was it. He could be at home taking a shower and slip on a bar of soap because, when it was his time to go, he'd go. He answered me with a bucket full of wisdom that far exceeded his fourth-grade education and said, 'Yessir, I understands. But, Mr. Bill, what iffin I'm up there flying 'round wif you, and it comes yo time to go. What's I gonna do?'

"Anyway, Ronnie, just like Joe was trying to say, when you have no control over a situation, you just don't have any control over it. In short, stop your damn worrying over something that's not going to ever happen. You got your plate loaded with real things that could go wrong. You certainly don't need to be concerned with 'what ifs.'"

"RONNIE" is a powerful book with a tremendous message to the youth of today, and a wake-up call to the coaches who help build the dreams of today's young athletes. Unfortunately, often too many athletes view their sport as the only road to success. RONNIE makes it blatantly apparent that coaches and athletes need balance in their lives. After reading this book I hope every coach in America realizes the tremendous responsibilities and the great opportunity that we have to impact the direction of the athletes we work with."

Butch Davis, Former Coach University of Miami

15

MY THIRD MILESTONE

SHORTLY AFTER THE beginning of the new year in 1976, negotiations between Bill and his father were finalized. Bill had purchased the family paving business, lock, stock and barrel. Since January many changes had been made around Dixie Grading and Paving Company, and many more were coming. Some for the better and perhaps some not so good, but changes were in the works.

His dad now had the free time he needed to pursue another dream of his, a dream of creating another new business from scratch. He was making great strides in putting the finishing touches on a home/business security company that he knew was much needed in the Northwest Florida area. The new enterprise was something he really looked forward to developing to the fullest extent. To him it was most satisfying to plant a seed, nurture it, and watch it grow into something meaningful.

Starting out each morning at full throttle, he went about his daily routine without giving a bit of thought to the pressures of starting a new business. However, the effect of the unforeseen stress was building rapidly within. The enormous amount of hours he was devoting to his new challenge, combined with the personal transformation of his lifestyle in a different direction, totally unlike his entire adult experiences in the highway and road construction business, would take its toll.

THE WEEK HAD been a tough one for everyone. On Friday, the day after April Fools' Day, Bill and Jean left Pensacola for a weekend visit with their friends, Jim and Betsy Leware, who lived in Leesburg, Bill's birthplace city. The Leware family was also in the road construction business, specializing in bridge construction.

After a relaxing weekend they returned home, arriving at dusk on Sunday to be greeted by their four children, Billy, Ashley, David and Malcolm. The kids were aware their parents had been in the vicinity of Disney World all weekend, so they expected their gifts to be from Disney. They were right.

Before retiring, Bill called his folks to see how things had gone over the weekend. This would be the last time he and his father ever talked.

BILL ARRIVED AT his office a few minutes after 7:00 the next morning and was handed the phone when he came through the door. The call was from his mother, who sounded breathless. Her speech was incoherent, almost unintelligible. His father had experienced a massive heart attack.

From what he gathered, his parents had awakened early as usual and were laying in bed reading the paper and chatting. Suddenly, his father gasped for breath. Death came immediately.

Bill rushed to their home in Pine Forest, arriving at the same moment as did the emergency ambulance. The attendants tried their best to revive Daddy Williams, but there was nothing that could be done. The county coroner insisted that an autopsy be performed, but after several strategically placed phone calls that was not to happen. Mr. Williams body was promptly released to Oak Lawn Funeral Home where he would be prepared with the greatest of care.

MID-MORNING ON Tuesday flowers began to arrive, filling the huge chapel with hundreds of bouquets and cards. Both sides of the chapel and every wall throughout the public rooms of the home were covered with floral arrangements.

In the early afternoon Mrs. Williams, her daughter Sandi and her sister Mabel came to Oak Lawn to join with Bill and his family for private moments with their father. Ronnie was urged to join them but declined for the time being. He could not yet face the reality of losing his father, someone he dearly worshiped, although he kept his feeling, for the most part, quietly to himself.

Beginning at 5:00 o'clock the family received hundreds of friends who stayed late into the evening to visit and pay their honor to this very special and most decent man. In late afternoon the family again tried in vain to get Ronnie to join them at the visitation, but neither their influence nor their persuasion found any success.

Everyone knew he wanted to be a part of the services but also understood that he wouldn't, at least not in the traditional way. The death of his father left a void in his life, a vacuum which they knew would never fill. This was another of life's horrible experiences that was added to the mountain of other abrasive negatives stored solidly within his mind. As stated before, the Williams family loved deeply, and, when suffering losses, defeats or rejections, it always took a dramatic and grievous toll. But as normal, even in times of sorrow, they kept their feelings much to themselves, buried deeply within.

"BOO, IT AIN'T fair."

"What isn't fair, Ron? What isn't fair, my man?"

"For days now the entire planet has been keeping up with Howard Hughes just because he's the richest man in the world. They've been flying him all over the globe in his multi-million-dollar private jet. Guess they were trying to keep him alive for some reason or another. Trying to find a way, a place, where he could find peace of mind. Daddy was talking last week of how rich the old grouch was and also just how miserable he must have been. Then the old fart just had to go and die the same day as Daddy. And, Boo, you know something, you don't have to be rich to be miserable. I know that for sure.

"It ain't fair, Boo, it just ain't fair. Daddy was the second greatest man to ever walk the face of this earth, and he's laying out at Oak Lawn in a casket with nobody paying any attention to him."

"Dammit, Ronnie, that's not so, and you know it. You need to get yourself cleaned up and go to the visitation. Billy will pick you up or send a car for you. You need to go, you hear me?"

"Yeah, yeah, yeah, I hear ya. Look at me. A nobody. I can't

go and face those people. What will they think? Look at me, Boo. I'm embarrassed. Mother knows just how I feel about myself."

"Ronnie, let me tell you exactly what they will think. They will think that you, his eldest son, are there to pay your respects to your father. A father who loved you unconditionally. One who cared for you and worried himself sick because of your self-destructive attitude and self-imposed lifestyle. Now, you get your crap together, and get it in gear, my man."

NEARING 8:00 O'CLOCK a member of the staff whispered to Bill that Ronnie was on the phone and wanted to talk with him. Knowing the conversation might become hostile or at the least difficult, he retreated into his private office and lifted the receiver.

"Hello."

"Little brother?"

"Yeah, Ron. What is it?"

"I gotta come out there."

"No, you don't have to come out here or out anywhere. But if you want to come out, then that's what you should do. Make no bones about it, you don't have to do anything."

"Now, just take it easy, Billy."

"Listen, Ronnie. This is your decision. Mother has her hands full, and so does the rest of your family. If you want to come, then I'll send a car for you if you can't drive."

"Well, I want to come. But, brother, I want to wait until they have all gone. I want to come over later this evening. Can I do that? Can I come over later?"

"What do you mean, come later?"

"I want to come when all the others have left. I want to come at midnight. Can you arrange that?"

"Ronnie, I can arrange anything. Anything within reason, that is. Why is it that you want to wait until midnight?"

"Brother, I just want to come at midnight. I can't explain why, so don't ask me. Can I do that?"

"Sure, Ronnie. You want me to pick you up? Or have someone else pick you up so you don't have to see me or any of the family?"

"Now, brother, don't say it like that. Crap man!"

"Ronnie, when would you like to come see daddy?"

"At midnight like I said."

"Well, that's four hours from now. I think that I had better have someone pick you up. You gonna be ready when I send them?"

"Yeah. I'll be ready."

"Okay, be looking for a white, four-door Cadillac sedan to be there at 20 minutes 'til 12:00. You want me to stay here and meet you?"

"No. I want to be alone."

"That's fine with me. Are you going to come to the services tomorrow?"

"Yes, of course I am."

"Ronnie, what's all this 'of course I am' crap? You know perfectly well that none of us know anything about what you will or will not do. I'll have the same car and driver pick you up in the morning at 9:30 for the services. Okay?"

"Sure. Listen, when I come out tonight, who will be there?"

"I have already requested the staff to have someone here around the clock all night. Daddy will not be left alone. I'll have Zona pick you up, and Sam will be here when you two arrive. Both of them will be in the building for as long as you want to stay. And you can stay as long as you like; then one of them will drive you back to your apartment."

"Will there be any music?"

"What do you mean, will there be any music?"

"Will there be any of that sad music playing when I get there?"

"Only if you want it, but it doesn't sound as if you do."

"No, no. No music."

"That's fine, Ronnie. What else? Got any more questions?"

"Can I stay there all night?"

"You mean you want to spend the night here at Oak Lawn?"

"Can I sit there with daddy all night?"

"Ron, you can if you like. But I think a visit for the purpose would be what you should do, and then let me have someone take you back to your apartment. Don't you think that best?"

"I guess so. Will the casket be open?"

"It has been open all evening for dad's other friends. Does this bother you?"

"That's not the point. I want to see daddy."

"Well, you will be able to see him. Would you like me to be there with you?"

"No. Like I said, I want to be alone."

THE DRIVER MADE sure that Ronnie arrived at Oak Lawn at the stroke of midnight. A fresh pot of hot coffee was awaiting him. He fixed a cup and, placing it securely on a saucer, carried it with him into the chapel.

For the longest time he sat on the back row staring straight ahead. After an hour or so, he came to his feet and eased down the aisle. He stood silently and reverently in front of his father for perhaps 15 or 20 minutes. Then, choosing a seat on the front row,he sat alone until almost 4:00 in the morning.

When he was ready to leave, a staff member drove him back to his apartment and reminded him he would be back at 9:30, just five hours later. For the first time in many years, he won the battle this night and did not have a drink.

"Boo, don't know if you've been keeping up with them or not, but if this ain't the third milestone there won't be another, ever. You know, I really don't think that I want to go on any further. There's just nothing left."

"Ronnie, don't give up now. Your mom and family need you. They need for you to be strong and show your respect for your dad. Don't cave in now. If you gonna think about that, then do it later, not now."

ARRIVING AT OAK Lawn, Ronnie looked immaculate. He was dressed in a tailored business suit with a new white shirt and beautiful tie. His hair looked perfect, not a strand out of place. His eyes, while appearing tired, seemed to sparkle. He had brought himself around in perfect fashion, a well-dressed and most handsome man indeed. But inside there was a sad son who hated the thought of having to pay his last respects to his father. This was the last place on earth he would have chosen to be, given the choice.

The services were as large as any seen around the Pensacola area in years. Mr. Williams had led the kind of a life that was a shining example to those he came in contact with, and each fondly respected him. The chapel, vestibule and every nook and cranny of the public rooms of the building were overflowing. The exterior speaker system had been activated so those who had to gather under the long carport could listen to the service.

After all were seated and at the completion of the first music selection, Bill walked down the aisle and stood silently for a couple of minutes directly in front of the casket. On signal, a staff attendant came forward and removed the spray of yellow roses. Bill gently and neatly folded the satin cloth around the sealed glass encasement, then carefully lowered the heavy solid copper lid into place. Slowly he engaged, then turned a handle which tightly sealed the massive casket forever from air and moisture. The attendant replaced the spray of roses, and the service continued.

After the last prayer the family was escorted from the private seating area through the rear door and led to the waiting sedans and limousines, parked directly behind the funeral coach. Those in attendance, out of respect for the family, waited for a few moments, then quietly filed out through the front door, taking their place in their own cars.

After being seated with his family in the lead limousine, Bill made an instantaneous and very personal decision. He would reunite with his family at the cemetery as he decided he would drive the hearse. This would become a ritual for him much too soon, time and again.

The funeral procession stretched for several blocks. It was escorted by a cadre of police and sheriff's vehicles.

BILL KNEW THAT Ronnie was going through a mental firestorm and that little could be done to extinguish the resentment and anguish that was building up inside him. Bill and several other of Bob Graham's close friends had been invited to Washington to have dinner with President Carter at the White House. Thinking this might help in getting Ronnie's mind off his misery, he placed the call.

"Yeah," came the greeting.

"And good morning to you Mr. Williams. What's all this 'yeah' stuff you're putting out this morning?"

"Hello, little brother. What's shaking?"

"What you got planned for early next week?" Bill inquired.

"You know I don't have any plans. Whatcha got going? What's on your mind?"

"Wanna go to Washington?"

"Washington what?"

"Washington, D.C. You know, like in the Capitol, the Federal City."

"Why? Why would I want to go to Washington?"

"Because I'm inviting you. That's why."

"Billy, what would I do in Washington?

"Well, I have been invited to the White House by the president and I can bring along a guest. I thought that you may like to go. Wanna go?"

"Why are you going to the White House?"

"To visit with the president. He invited me and some other friends."

"And what you gonna do when you get there?"

"We will visit. Just visit and talk with President Carter."

"What in God's name would I talk with him about?"

"Ronnie, you're being difficult. You want to go or not?"

"What's it gonna cost. You know that I can't afford to take such a trip. You mean the real White House? I'll be damned."

"Yes, the real White House, and it will not cost you anything. I'm inviting you as my guest. Now, do you want to go or don't you?"

"What's it gonna cost you? How much?"

"Ronnie, I don't know, for God's sake. Maybe three thousand dollars for the both of us. We'll stay at the Mayflower for two nights. We'll be gone for three days. This is getting a little old. You're invited, and you need to tell me if you want to go or not. Do you?"

"Three thousand dollars, huh?"

"About that. Approximately that. Somewhere in range of three thousand. But that's my problem not yours."

"Let's see. Three thousand divided by two. That's about fifteen hundred each, right?"

"Well, I guess. Yeah, that's about it." Bill confirmed.

"Tell you what little brother. I'll make a deal with you. Hold on just a minute; let me get a pencil. Now, let's see. Yeah that'll work out just fine. Here's my deal. If you go to the White House alone and leave me here with my share of the cost, I will take the fifteen hundred dollars and I figure that I can eat about 250 meals at Hopkins Boarding House. And if I sweet talk Eddie and if I pay him the whole amount in advance, he probably will throw breakfast in for free each morning. Whatcha say?"

"Ronnie, just forget it. I thought you may like to get out of town and take a rather historical trip."

"Little brother, the last time I dined at the White House I didn't much enjoy it. Don't really want to go back again."

"Crap, you've never even been to Washington. Get out of here. I'll see you."

"Now, don't go away mad," Ronnie cautioned.

"I'm not mad, but this has almost turned into a game show of sorts. I just called to ask you a simple question, and we're still discussing it. Tell you what I'm gonna do. For your consolation prize I'm going by Hopkins this afternoon and buy you a seven-day-per-week, one-month meal ticket. How about that?"

"Can't do that. They're closed on Mondays."

"Okay, all right! I'll get you a meal ticket for a full month no matter when they are open or closed. Good-bye."

"See you, little brother. So long."

I was invited to Marianna Middle School, Marianna, Fl., to bring "A Message from RONNIE" to their eighth grade class on the last day prior to Spring Break. After the assembly I was gathering my things and chatting with the principal and a couple of teachers when I noticed a young girl who was holding back and not leaving the gym with her classmates.

When I glanced at her she looked away. After my second glance she sheepishly walked over to me and in a frail voice said, "me and some of my friends were going drinking this weekend to celebrate Spring Break but now I'm not going". I congratulated her on her decision and asked how old she was, she responded "14."

As she walked away it appeared that she was stepping just a little bit lighter. Conceivably, could it have been that some of the weight had been lifted from her shoulders? This is what our program is all about. And remember, this was an eighth grade student, just fourteen years old!

16

I'M DOOMED IN DEATH
JUST LIKE HE WAS

AS BAD AS things were for Ronnie, no one suspected they could turn even worse. He closed himself off in his apartment and refused to see or talk with anyone. He even chose to remain at home rather than patronize his favorite lounges. Reports confirmed that he had visited his father's grave site at Bayview Cemetery on a number of occasions, usually late into the night.

Dave Johnson, one of his father's friends, had made a remark to him after the services which did not register at the time. Later, after he was sure of the meaning, it horrified him. Mr. Johnson, a solid citizen in every respect, well-liked, compassionate and full of wisdom, spoke briefly to Mrs. Williams, then individually to Ronnie, Bill and Sandi.

Time and again Ronnie would broach the subject with me. He could not get it out of his mind. Mr. Johnson reminded the two sons and daughter that losing their father was obviously a great loss, but they needed to pay special attention to their mother. Take care of her. See to her needs. And he assured, he preached, "As much as you loved and will miss your father, when your mother is gone, you will have lost the very best friend you have ever known."

"Boo, what'll I do about it? What can I do? What can I do for mom; she spends her day taking care of me?"

214

"Be patient, Ronnie. Be patient. Things will work out. Take it easy, and get some rest. Leave that vodka alone long enough to get your mind thinking straight. You'll find a way to be of comfort to her. Be patient."

Things would never be the same again. The guilt feelings were mounting. The few times of late that he had spent with his father were not enough. He had planned for some time to have a man-to-man talk but never got around to it. It was too late; others were now in charge.

RONNIE ABSORBED THE story of Elvis firing Red West as if it were a bad dose of medicine that had to be taken. Following the accounts closely, he would not believe that after all these years it had to come to something like that.

Just a week earlier he had read in a trash tabloid where Red, the only mafia member with the courage, had gone into Elvis' bedroom at Graceland and gone through his packed luggage. He had removed a large supply of drugs and flushed them down the toilet.

Arriving in Palm Springs for a vacation, Elvis was furious when he began searching for the drugs. He called his father and warned that it had to have been Red who did something with them. He knew no one else had the guts to go into his bedroom and ramble through his personal things.

Vernon Presley confronted Red, and he admitted doing it, saying, "Someone around here had to do something about the miserable problem before Elvis kills himself." The episode gave Vernon all the reasons he needed to fire him. And he did.

The primary stabilizing influence by the only person who was man enough to stand up to Elvis was now out of his life. In an almost eerie comparative set of circumstances, the lives of Elvis Presley and Ronnie Williams had once again come together. Both were completely lost in their own private and lonely world.

For the most part, Elvis had almost always been able to do the things he wanted to do. Now his closest friend was no longer at his side to prevent him from taking harmful and dangerous incidents to the extreme.

Many were the times that Ronnie had thought about Red running interference for him the entire length of a football field and how he must have run interference for Elvis through all sorts of trials and tribulations. No one could ask more of a friend.

Elvis must not have been thinking clearly, or he would have never terminated the person who was most emotionally aligned to him personally. Surely, something horrible had taken hold of the mind and spirit of a very sad and lonely Elvis Presley.

THERE WAS AMPLE time on his hands for Ronnie to take special interest in the death sentence case of Gary Gilmore. Gilmore had been on death row in Utah for a number of years during the time the United States Supreme Court had halted all executions. This all changed on July second when the Court suddenly reinstated the death penalty.

With the stay lifted, Gilmore immediately petitioned the governor to send him before a firing squad. He had long ago decided that he would not spend the rest of his life behind bars and made himself a promise that he would be the first person executed in the United States after reinstatement. Confusing Ronnie more than ever, Gilmore won his cause but lost his life by so doing.

Why do some people choose to live and some choose to die, he wondered? Confusing and befuddling issues were clashing like time bombs going off inside his brain. A week later, 23-year-old Freddie Prinze, star of "Chico And The Man," chose to take his own life with a pistol blast though his skull. Confusing issues. Yes, confusing indeed.

AS IF THE long lines at the gas pumps weren't bad enough, interest rates were climbing at an all-time skyrocketing pace. Jimmy Carter was in total control in Washington. The country seemed unstable. Workers were dissatisfied, businesses were going down the tube. New rules and regulations were bogging down businesses and causing devastating losses. OSHA came into being, and its safety dictates were compounding losses even further. Insurance rates were on a steady incline.

Bill had to make a decision concerning whether or not to keep on fighting the red tape. The new state and federal government rules and regulations had horrendous effects on all aspects of the road building business. He made a hard, conscientious decision to liquidate the company although it would prove to be a personal and financial hardship on him and many of his loyal employees.

FOR THE FIRST time ever, Ronnie had left a message on an answering machine. The message was somewhat garbled, and the reason for the slurred words were apparent. It had been left at 4:13 on the afternoon of August 16th.

Bill and some buddies were downtown at the End Of The Alley Lounge at Seville Quarter doing some nailbiting of their own. Bill's divorce from his wife of seventeen and a half years was to become final in just two weeks. He did not retrieve his messages until he was almost ready to cross the Bay Bridge on the way to his townhouse on Pensacola Beach. The message, while not urgent, sounded important. He was to call Ronnie right away.

By now the entire world was aware that Elvis Presley had been found unconscious at Graceland and had been pronounced dead a couple of hours later at the Baptist Hospital in Memphis.

He pulled his car to the shoulder and made the call. He knew exactly what to expect.

"Yeah."

"Hello, Ronnie. Bill."

"Where you been?" Ronnie questioned with an inquisitive and authoritative voice.

"I've been down at The Alley with Stokes, Swearingen, Bobby Stephens and some of the guys having a beer."

"Going through your middle-aged crazies, huh?"

"Afraid so," Bill admitted.

"You'll regret it, little brother. I promise you."

"Now, you didn't call me to preach to me, did you?" Bill responded.

"Naw," Ronnie assured.

"How you doing? You okay?" Bill asked.

"Me? Yeah, I'm fine. Guess you heard about E?"

"Sure, everyone has by now. Great career move," Bill emphasized.

"Whatcha talking about? Whatcha mean?"

"Oh, never mind; you'll soon learn. Mark my word. How's it with you? You doing okay?"

"Done told you I am. You already asked me that once."

"Just checking. That's all. You want me to come get you so you can stay over at the beach tonight?"

"Naw, gonna sit here and watch the tube. Oughta be interestin'."

"You sure you don't want me to come pick you up?"

"Mother called and wanted me to come to her place, but I'm gonna sit right here, little brother. I want to tell you something strange. Why don't you come by before you go home. Where are you now?"

"I'm on the parking lot at the Kings Inn Restaurant."

"Then you're just around the corner. Come on by. How 'bout it?"

"Sure, be right there," Bill confirmed.

BILL EXPECTED THAT he would find him in a somber but very talkative mood. He was right. Ronnie had never given up his role as the older brother, and Bill never expected he would. As Bill walked up his drive with a beer in hand, Ronnie met him at the screen door. "You shouldn't be driving a car while drinking. You know better than that. Haven't I taught you anything, Billy?"

"Taught me a lot, Ron. A whole bunch. What's happening?"

"Sit down. Got something to tell you. You ain't gonna believe this. Wanna 'nother beer, little brother?"

"No thanks, had plenty."

"Like I was saying, you ain't gonna believe this. Last night I had a dream that he died."

"Elvis?" Bill asked.

"Well, who else would we be talking about?"

"All right, okay, tell me about it."

"Brother, I've never had a dream like that before. It was weird, but as real as you are sitting on this sofa talking to me. It was about four o'clock this morning. I sat straight up in bed, eh, straight up on the sofa, and could see the whole thing clear as a bell. Plain as day, it happened right in front of my eyes."

"Tell me about it. What'd you see?"

"I dreamed that he was drugged out. Far out. He had fallen face down; now get this, he had fallen face down in a thick, I mean really thick, carpet. It was like he was paralyzed. Well, not really paralyzed, but kinda paralyzed. He was laying flat on his stomach, but he couldn't get up. I mean his body was paralyzed, but his arms and legs were moving. Strange huh?"

"You got that right. How could he be paralyzed and at the same time his arms and legs be moving?"

"Bubba, it was so strange. His big body, big belly was laying flat on this deep, deep carpet. His arms and legs were moving like you see skydivers when they leap from an airplane. You know how they float through the sky with their arms and legs spread out? Well, that's how he looked. Flat on the carpet with his arms and legs stretched out and waving. But he had no control to move his body.

"He couldn't lift his head from the carpet. He was gasping for breath. He was trying to breath and had sucked in a wad of carpet into his mouth. His mouth and his nose was filled with the thick fibers. He couldn't get any air.

"He was fighting to get up, but could move only his arms and legs in a waving motion. It was horrible. He was making terrible grunting, inaudible sounds, but no one could hear him. Until he died, for several minutes he was miserable, going through real hell. Just laying there trying to move, trying to get his breath.

" 'Round his neck, under his robe was a heavy thick towel. It was much like a horse collar, and the thickness of it wouldn't let him move his head right or left. He was face down in the carpet. Little brother, he simply smothered to death. The carpet caused his death. I'm sure of that. I saw it with my own eyes.

"Billy, can you believe that? You reckon that's how it happened?"

"Don't know, Ronnie. Perhaps. Anyway, it's a real shame. Whatever happened, it's a real shame. Such a waste."

"Wanna 'nother beer?" Ronnie asked.

"No. Gotta run. Why don't you come to the beach with me?"

"Wait a minute. Sit back down. Let me tell you the rest of the dream."

"You mean there's more? That wasn't it?"

"Now, listen to me. In front of him, directly in front of his head, although he couldn't see 'em 'cause his head was buried in the carpet, were some cards."

"Cards? What kind of cards?" Bill inquired.

"Playing cards. Just plain playing cards.

"It was as though he had been in a card game. His three cards were facing up; all were spades. There was a six, a ten and a five. In that order from left to right. Count 'em. Twenty-one. Right?"

"Yeah. That's right, twenty-one," Bill agreed.

"As if he were the dealer, there were three hands in front of him. All of the cards were face cards. The hand on the left was an ace of hearts and a jack of diamonds. The middle hand had an ace of clubs and a queen of spades. And the hand on the right was an ace of spades and a king of hearts.

"Now, little brother, pray tell me what does all of that mean?"

"Ronnie, I have no earthly idea. None whatsoever. What's it mean to you? What do you make of it?"

"Don't know, Billy. But I've given it a lot of thought. Maybe it means he can't win. Maybe it means all the cards are stacked against him. Like I've always told you, you have to play the hand that life deals you. Maybe it meant that, while he also had twenty-one, it just wasn't good enough to win. It's strange to me. Bubba, it's really strange, don't you think?"

"You got that right. Listen, why don't you come to the beach with me, really?"

"Don't think so. I'm just gonna hang out here."

"Now, don't get yourself in any trouble. You sure you want to stay here by yourself tonight?"

"Yeah. Oh, yeah. I'm just fine."

"All right. Let's talk in the morning. I'm going to the beach. Call tonight it you need me. Good night."

"Billy, you think that is what happened to Elvis?"

"Ronnie, I have no idea. Could have been. We'll know sooner or later. We'll get the right answer some day. So long, Ronnie."

"Night."

THE NEXT DAY late in the afternoon, Ronnie called Bill and told him he had a question but didn't really know how to ask it. Didn't know if it was ethical or not, but he needed to have an answer. He had been up all night thinking about it and knew that Bill could find out what really went on. With him being in the funeral business, certainly he had the correct connections to get the real scoop.

Ronnie wanted him to call the Memphis Funeral Home and talk with someone who would know for certain if Elvis was in fact really dead. Bill thought this preposterous but would make the call if it would settle his brother down.

In a couple of hours he reported back. A full autopsy had been performed, and for sure and certain Elvis Aaron Presley was dead. To further satisfy his doubts, he gave to him the names of the two embalmers, Paul Howard and Ken Stockstill. With this, his skepticism seemed to subside.

OVER THE NEXT several days the world mourned the loss of America's most popular entertainer. It was no more evident anywhere around the globe than in Memphis where large crowds gathered around the music gates of Graceland and continuously bottlednecked traffic up and down Elvis Presley Boulevard. Movie stars, dignitaries, fans and common folks gathered to pay their last respect to the home-grown boy who had captured the entertainment world, although it cost him his life at the tender age of just 42 years.

Since learning of his death, the next three days and nights Ronnie had stayed alone in his apartment. As normal, when he went on a hard drinking binge, he completely shunned all food. This added to his troubles. He and I would go over and over the events that might have lead to the death of Elvis Presley. In his mind he was absolutely sure he had the correct answer.

"Ronnie, don't you think you've had enough to drink this morning? How 'bout it? Come on. Let's give it a rest. Whatcha say? Why are you drinking so much anyway? Huh?"

"'Cause I can."

"Now that ain't much of an answer. How 'bout it? Let's let it rest. Okay?

"Such a waste. Boo, his death was such a waste. Don't you agree?"

"Ron, someone once said, 'The tragedy of life is not that it ends so soon—the real tragedy is that we wait too long to begin it.'"

"Don't know 'bout all that philosophical stuff, Boo. Just don't know. You're just trying to confuse me."

"No I'm not, Ronnie."

"Yeah you are, just trying to get in my head again. Listen to me. Matters of life, matters of my personal life and my soul, are between me and Jesus, you hear me? It ain't none of your business. He and I will work the deal out. Now, matters of the world are a different story. They aren't confidential. They are everyone's perception about how they see the world based on their own life's experiences. These, you and I can talk about. Otherwise, my personal matters are off limits. And I don't want no more of that foolish talk."

Sometime between Elvis's death and the sixth day after, Ronnie had purchased a small, perhaps fourteen-inch-long miniature guitar. Holding it against the east wall of his bedroom, he took a fairly large nail and drove it through the guitar and tightly into the plaster. With a shaky hand he had scribbled on the wall just below his memento, EAP, August 16, 1977. From that date forward, the number twenty-one played a significant role in Ronnie's life.

On the sixth day someone, perhaps a person he talked with on the phone earlier, had summoned the police and an ambulance to his apartment. Around 1:10 in the morning they arrived and found him in a highly agitated state, almost incoherent. While their report indicated that he had attempted suicide by taking a large overdose of pills, there was no physical evidence to support their claim. He was taken to a detox center and released two days later.

THERE WAS LITTLE seen of Ronnie by his friends over the next three months. He had chosen to seclude himself from the outside world and limit his time only sparingly to Celeste, his mother, and an occasional visit to the beach to see Bill. Because he kept mum and talked little about anything important, his family could only guess what was going through his mind and how this most recent tragic event was affecting him.

During his reclusive time he had convinced Celeste to drive him back to Montgomery where he again would visit and pay homage to his friend, Hank Williams. And without success he tried as hard as he could to get her to continue the trip on to Memphis for the same purpose.

In an effort to lessen his bruised inner feelings and ticking

The small guitar that Ronnie nailed to his wall in memory of the day Elvis died, August 16, 1977. Below: At Hank Williams' grave.

Above: Sitting on a river bank with his .44 pistol. Below: Relaxing, having a cool one.

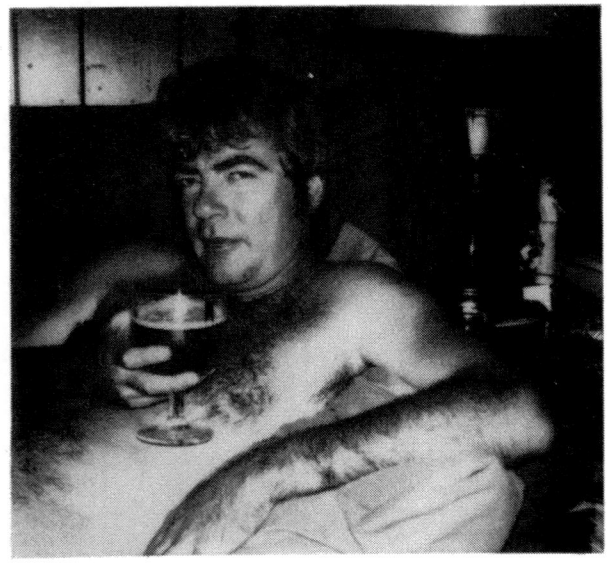

Above: Ronnie standing outside one of his most favorite watering holes, the Islander Hotel, Cedar Key, Florida. Below: The barkeep at the Islander hotel.

emotions, all of which were weighing heavy and bogging him down, Celeste planned a four-day trip back to Cedar Key. She knew this was a place he could relax. A place he could void his mind of the cluttered problems he dwelled on so intently.

AS SOON AS they checked into the Gulf Front Motel, he insisted they have their happy hour an hour early at the old Islander Hotel. The small bar accommodated only eight stools and two tables of four chairs each. Seldom had there ever been sixteen customers bending their elbows at the same time. This afternoon he, Celeste and a stranger who occupied the last stool at the bar to the far right were the only customers.

It was evident by his physical being, not his silence, that the man had gotten a running start on happy hour. Although he mumbled to himself spasmodically, he spoke to no one. Ronnie even noticed that much too often he raised his empty glass and without uttering a word it was reloaded by the barkeep. Within the hour he paid his tab, and without leaving a tip or saying a word he felt his way out the door.

With the two of them being the only customers remaining, and as if they cared, the barkeep began to verbally denounce the man unmercifully. Said he drove a trash truck and wished he would find another bar to patronize. She kept on and on as to how he was the sorriest sumbitch in town. Continually, she raved her anger without letting up.

Ronnie finally had enough and cut her off, "Lady, you should not put the fellow down like that. Hell, maybe he's just lonesome and needs some company. He's just enjoying hangin' out. Let him alone, for God's sake."

"That's all he does all afternoon, just hang out. He's been in here for three hours. I tell you, he is worthless. No good for anything," she continued.

"You shore seem to know a lot about the man," said Celeste.

"I should. Been married to the bum for 26 years."

THE FIRST WEEK in December Ronnie emerged from his shell to be among those celebrating the Bar Mitzvah of Martin Levin, Fred's son. Dressed in his best, he attended the ceremony and the reception. The Jewish event was a first for him. Not knowing what to do, he sat silently in the back of the temple and followed others the best he could.

It seemed that his attendance at the ceremony, just getting out in public again, gave him a renewed sense of being a part of something, anything. It was as if he had again broken out of his cocoon. Later that night, for the first time in months, although alone, he went to the movies to see *"Saturday Night Fever."*

Over the next several weeks he began to come alive, to venture back to the beach where he spent considerable time at Bill's gulf front home. When Bill's kids were there for the weekend, they could readily tell just how much Ronnie enjoyed a family atmosphere. Maybe the bubble had finally burst.

In early January he was approached by his old friend Fred Vigodsky and offered a new job. Fred was expanding Sam's Style Shoppe, and a position was opening at the new warehouse. Ronnie seemed to fit the job description and fell right back into a work mode as if it had been his daily routine for months.

No matter his state of mind or his personal problems, he never lost his exceptional propensity for wit and wisdom. Perhaps his carrying on and his continued foolishness were his means of expressing himself without really letting anyone into his private world. When he wanted to tell someone something or express an idea, he had a knack of finding a roundabout way of doing so without coming right out with it. Without going right to the heart of the matter, he had his own particular manner of getting his point across.

He had painstakingly handwritten a birthday card to his brother on a single sheet of yellow legal paper. Several words had been scratched through or altered. They were never erased but replaced with another word captioned above.

> Yes, yes, May 18th, I remember this date rather distinctly. I was a mere boy at the time, only 19 months old if I recollect. I strolled up to Dr. Holland and asked, 'Well, Doc, is it a boy or a girl?' He answered, "Well, son, I think you've got yourself a brother.' And I said, 'Well, good, I was getting damn tired of shooting marbles all by myself. I beat Mamma so bad she won't play me no more. Happy b'day Brother.'"

Through all these many years Bill has kept the "card" well preserved among his other mementoes.

IN LATE FALL Ronnie found himself in a new part-time voluntary role as an emissary. The campaign for governor had heated up over the summer, and soon the electorate would be selecting their candidate as the Democratic nominee to face the Republicans in November.

For the last eighteen months or more Bill, along with eleven other members, had served on the initial finance committee for the election of Bob Graham for governor. The race had boiled down to a heated battle for the Democratic nomination between Graham, a state senator, and Florida Attorney General Bob Shevin.

Sometimes it happens that friends, occasionally, will find themselves on the opposite side of a political campaign. The Williams family and the Levin family were in different camps in this race. For the last eight years they had been hand in hand with Governor Askew but did not see eye to eye on this year's contest. Ronnie had been asked by Fred Levin to see if he could persuade Bill to jump camp and join the Shevin team as the run-off primary neared. Ronnie quickly pointed out that Graham had spent every night while in Escambia County over the past several years at Bill's home, and he didn't see a chance for a possible switch occurring, but he was game to try.

It was during a Saturday afternoon family cookout at the beach when Ronnie made his pitch. As he predicted, there was no way the suggestion would even be considered. In fact, Bill turned the table and asked him to invite the Levins into the Graham camp. This, too, was to no avail. The friends had to take their best hold in their respective camps and fight the good fight.

Late in the evening of the primary the voter results indicated that Graham had been victorious. Bill and his northwest Florida team were ecstatic. However, being of a good sound political mind, he knew not to rub salt into the wounds of those who had supported Shevin.

The following morning, after a victory breakfast at the Miami Lakes Country Club, Bill called Fred and politely asked him to join hands with the Graham team against the Republicans in

November. Levin, very professional and political, congratulated him on their victory and not only accepted his invitation but also stated a sizeable check was on its way to him for Graham's general election campaign. Furthermore, he would see to it that a fundraiser would be planned by the local Shevin supports in behalf of Bob Graham.

"I have received your letter and a copy of your book, 'RONNIE', about the life and struggle of your older brother. Thank you for writing to me regarding your nationwide campaign against underage drinking. RONNIE'S story is one that will touch the lives of many people who have been stricken with the terrible disease. You have taken a tragedy and turned it into a well-directed mission and for that you should be commended. I admire your initiative to promote awareness and hopefully prevent our teenagers from falling into the trap. "Our children are our most important natural resources and we must do everything we can to protect and educate them about the dangers of alcohol abuse. Again, thank you for taking time to write to me and good luck in spreading your message."

Mike Foster, Former Governor of Louisiana

17

THE STRAIGHT
AND NARROW ROAD

IN THE SPRING of '79 Ronnie went to his brother and inquired of the possibility of him speaking to Governor Graham about a job in Tallahassee. Being careful not to lean too heavily on his friendship with the governor, Bill put into motion alternate means of accomplishing the same goal.

During Governor Askew's first term of office, Bill had been appointed by the governor to serve as a charter member of the Northwest Florida Water Management Board of Directors. Since he was in part responsible for the hiring of the executive director of that agency, he thought it more politically practical to inquire about a position with the District rather than lean on Graham so early in his first term.

After Graham was elected, Bill had resigned from the board of directors as he assumed it to be a conflict of interest since he was now serving on Governor Graham's staff. However, he retained close ties with the staff and management of the board.

It so happened the district, headquartered in Quincy just west of Tallahassee, was about to advertise for a permitting specialist in the Pensacola area. The position would fit Ronnie's background and qualifications to a tee. In May he was hired and advised to report to the district office for training.

Knowing he would soon be transferred back to Pensacola in

his permanent job assignment, he chose not to give up his apartment there. While in training in Quincy, he leased a small one-bedroom apartment at The Stonegate in west Tallahassee.

Ronnie had finally made up his mind to kick his demonic habit and work hard at this new opportunity. For sure he did not want to let his brother down, did not want to put him in a position of being sorry for recommending him, especially since he was a charter member of the board of directors.

The evening of the very first day after completing his move into his apartment, he settled down for a single drink and a heart to heart with me, his ever-present soul mate.

"Boo, we gotta make this work. We gotta get our crap together. There ain't too many more chances we're gonna have. Start out right. Start out strong."

"Ronnie, let me tell you something, and don't you forget it. A man has to be of use. He has to have a goal. You have tons of talent and character. You have to prove yourself a man. In this world a man is here to be useful not only to himself but to others. You have a fine brain. You are highly intelligent, so put that asset to the best use. Set that goal and set it high, then stretch forward, reach out and do it. You can, my man."

FOR THE FIRST two weeks everything was exactly on track. He was at work every morning right on time and quickly picked up the details of his job. He was pleased with himself and knew exactly what was expected of him when he returned to the regional office in Pensacola.

Until!

About the middle of the third week he was driving home from Quincy, his bright red AMC humming quietly down Highway 90. All was in order, everything right with the world. That is until he missed the cross street off Tennessee which led south to his apartment. Knowing he had gone too far, he searched for a place to turn around. As if a giant magnet attached itself to the front bumper of the small car, destiny took him onto the parking lot of Fred's Back Door Lounge.

The next morning he missed work. Did not show at all. Bill McCartney, the executive director and personal friend of his brother, called his apartment. No answer. He called again shortly before noon. No answer. By mid-afternoon he tried once again.

"Hello."

"Ron? McCartney. Where were you this morning, man?"

"Hey, Bill. Son, I was sick as a dog last night. Had to drive myself to the emergency room. Stomach problems. They just let me out about an hour ago. I'll be back to work first thing in the morning."

"Well, let me know if I can do anything for you. Just checking. See you tomorrow."

"Thanks, Bill. See y'all bright and early in the morning. Good-bye."

He hung up the phone and went back to bed.

"Boo, been thinking."

"You know that always gets you in trouble. Need to stop your motor from running, Ronnie."

"Shut up and just listen. Please. Boo, if I sold the guitar, I wouldn't have to go back to work. I could retire. Know that?"

"No, no, Ronnie. You can't do that. You can't do that for two reasons."

"And what are the two reasons my friend," Ronnie demanded.

"First, you'll drink yourself to death. And if that wasn't enough, then remember you said that you would not sell the guitar until 21 years after Elvis passing. Remember saying that?"

"Yeah, yeah. But that was just what my dream was all about. Those cards laying all over the floor in front of him."

"Well, Ronnie you can't have it both ways. Either the dream was real or it wasn't. Now which way you want it this time? Were the cards there, or weren't they? Was he dead, or wasn't he? Make up your freakin' mind. You simply can't have it one way then the other when you feel like changing it."

"Okay, fine, get off my butt. All right, already. Anyway I know he's dead 'cause Billy called the funeral home and spoke with the two men who embalmed him. Sure I'll wait 21 years. All I got to do is work with the stupid state for another 21 years. That's all. Boo, I can't do that. I cannot waste all of that time when I could be enjoying myself. In 21 more years I will be 65 years old."

"And is any thing wrong with that, Ronnie? You could retire, then sell the guitar and live comfortably for the rest of your natural life. Anything wrong with that, my friend?"

"Yeah, as a matter of fact, it is. Why not sell it now and use the money to live on while I can enjoy it. I'm only 43. If I can get a good price for it, then that's what I should do. Billy will help me find a buyer. He knows how to do things like that."

"Go to sleep Ronnie. You got a busy day tomorrow."

THE FOLLOWING TUESDAY the district held a Water Resource Conference workshop at the Wakulla Springs Hotel. After the morning session they gathered for lunch in the quaint dining room overlooking the crystal clear waters of the magnificent springs. The hotel and Springs were known to be the pride and joy of its owner, Mr. Ed Ball. For years he had worked diligently, in the open and behind the scenes, to make certain his pristine corner of the earth was not disturbed by those seeking to harm the environment.

Although his campaign was expensive, he had the proper resources necessary to fight even the state of Florida for what he deemed to be only right. Without his financial abilities, certainly it would have been a losing battle with the bureaucratic establishment. But he won as he always did.

The Springs and hundreds of acres up and down the Wakulla River had been retained as Mother Nature intended them to be. Such a magnificent sight. The crystal clear springs had long been the favorite setting for countless numbers of movies, including several "Tarzan" features.

THE WORKSHOP INCLUDED the staff of the district as well as members visiting from other water management boards and pertinent agencies from state government. About midway through lunch Rich McWilliams nudged Ronnie on his left shoulder, "Now, if you want to meet a classy lady look to your right at the far table in the corner. The girl in the black slacks outfit. She's a real looker."

"You can say that again. Who is she?" Ronnie asked.

"Her name is Amanda. She works at the Department of Environmental Protection in Tallahassee."

"Married?"

"Nope. And very available. And I don't mean that in a negative way at all. I mean she is very single and a peach of a lady. Very calm, polite and classy."

"Well, don't just sit there; introduce me to her."

"Will do. Will do before we go back into session."

THE CONFERENCE BROKE at 3:30 sharp. Amanda had given Ronnie her state business card and agreed to have lunch with him one day soon. He was simply mesmerized by her: her demeanor, attitude, presence of self; even her perfume was delightful.

Leaving the Lodge, he searched her card for a mobile phone number thinking they could talk more freely without the crowd around.

"Hello," came the nice voice with a Southern flair.

"Well, hello again to you. This is Ron Williams."

"Hi, Ron. Such a quick surprise."

"Just wanted to catch you before someone else did. How about dinner this weekend?"

"Can't Friday. Can Saturday."

"Listen, I'm headed for the Gibson Hotel in Apalachicola for the weekend. How 'bout joining me?"

"Can't do that. Wanna have dinner here, can do."

"You mean you would make me cancel my weekend plans?"

"For some strange reason I thought it was you who called me," she responded.

Sharp lady. Real sharp, he thought.

"No, I don't want to cancel your plans. Just don't want to go off with someone I met two hours ago. Understand?" she made clear.

"You're right. Of course, you're right. How about dinner on Saturday night?"

"Great. I accept."

"I'll make reservations. Have a favorite spot?"

"Sure. Several. I like the Talquin Inn, Joe's Spaghetti House or the Slipper. Either one suits me."

"Make a choice," he pushed.

"How 'bout the Slipper," she coaxed.

"Slipper it is. I'll be in touch and pick you up."

"Why don't I just meet you there. Will that work for you?"
"Fine with me," said he. "How about 8:00 o'clock?"
"See you at 8:00 on Saturday night at the Slipper," she confirmed.
"Have a great week. See ya Saturday night."

LATE THAT NIGHT his mind was swirling recklessly. "Boo, think this is the one? Is this who we've been searching for? I've never had this happen to me so fast; she's the lady of my dreams. I can't believe that I just met her, and I feel so good about this chestnut beauty. Reckon this is the one to walk me away from this messy life I've been living? Boo, I think so. I really think she could be the one."

It had only been two days, and he knew he had to see her. Just before lunch on Thursday, he called her office and asked her to meet him for a drink after work. She agreed to meet somewhere for coffee but not a drink, explaining that she did not partake during the work week. His mind was in a daze. He wanted to say something romantic but still did not know how to approach this lady he had known for only 48 hours. He quickly scribbled a note and placed it in his shirt pocket. After their brief meeting he handed it to her, noting that it was not meant to be read until she got home.

Later that evening she read, "My attitude has experienced a tremendous uplifting since I've known you these two days. I think that you are simply beautiful. I look forward to spending time with you Saturday evening."

DINNER AT THE Slipper was fantastic. She had a couple of glasses of wine and he double that many cocktails. They spent most of their time talking about his past, his marriages, kids, family. She, divorced only two years earlier, shied away from talking of her lengthy ordeal with her former husband. She had two children, a girl who was married and lived in Alabama and a son attending Florida State.

"Were you offended by the note I gave you Thursday?" he asked.

"No, not at all. It fact, I was honored. Flattered. There is one thing I can say about you; you come right to the point. You don't dilly-dally around."

"Can't afford to. Too old," Ronnie assured her.

"Yeah. Right! How old are you?"

"I'll be 44 in October."

"October what?"

"15th."

She jotted the date down on a napkin and slipped it into her purse. "Wanna dance?" she asked as she rose from her chair without giving him any chance to say no.

"Not much of a dancer. You'll have to excuse my two left feet," he explained as she pulled him towards the dance floor.

Returning to their table and in a low pitched voice and acting somewhat bashful, he said "I've loved you a long, long time. I just didn't know who you were, your name or where you lived."

"Well now, that's pretty poetic, Mr. Williams."

"How 'bout another?" thinking his humor may loosen the hour. "I could tell you were getting very tired while on the dance floor. You should have been 'cause you've been running through my mind for days on end now."

"So you are a poet?" she stated.

"Not really. Just want to say the right thing. Don't want to make another mistake. I've spent a lifetime making mistakes, and I'm damn well determined that you are not going to be another one of them. I'm really a very quiet person, a bit scared, and a loner most of the time."

OVER THE NEXT three nights he composed a lengthy letter. He had to make her understand just exactly how he felt. He had dreamed for many years about having a woman like her in his corner and was positive he could straighten himself out with her strong encouragement. He just had to give it his best shot.

"Boo, I'm scared to death to send this. I know full well this could be the death knell. God, all the mistakes I've already made. But, Boo, I've just got to try."

"Ronnie, that is the only way to go, my man. Stand up. Be a man. Speak your mind, and say what you want to say. Tell her your true feelings. She might reject you, but on the other hand you will not know until you fly the kite. Go for it. I'm proud of you for taking this stand."

Arriving home from work, she gathered her mail but laid it aside while she attended to her caged dove, her only pet. After returning three phone calls, she picked up the envelope with no return address and cuddled in the corner of her love seat.

Dear Amanda:

Why am I writing this? I guess I'm doing it for me, not for you, but be that as it may, I need and want to do so.

Perhaps my true feelings are that I have nothing to lose by writing. I seem not to be doing so very well with you, and if that's the case then what I think, or write, would matter little. I don't really know where to start; however, I do need to say what I feel. I will not re-edit this so whatever comes out on paper will go in the mail in the morning.

Perhaps you will laugh at the contents. I hope not as I will be only honest with you. This is the only way I know how to be. Maybe this letter will break the ice which I find very difficult to do, or, on the other hand, it may kill the purpose altogether.

For some reason you seem standoffish to me. Maybe your divorce turned you against men. Perhaps you don't want to deal with them again. When we first talked, I asked you if you were involved with anyone and you answered that you were not—it was only you and your dove!

Well, you are and have been on my mind constantly for several days now without ceasing. When we talked those long hours at your home after dinner on our first date, it was so very refreshing to me. Down deep, I have mentally been searching for your image for a long, long time. Having been a part of two failed marriages, I had given up hope of ever again meeting someone whom I would have the slimmest reason to really care for. A lady whom I could trust and she in turn trust me.

Our date on Saturday night was very special. And you need to know, and I'm sure that you will soon learn, that I am honest, sometimes brutally honest, but completely honest. I feel that people should say what is on their mind and get it out in the open for discussion. We did a lot of this on our first date.

So let me say emphatically how pleased I was for the trust you placed in me, and for all the tea in China I would not have broken my promise to you about "behaving myself." For had I done anything different than what I did, it would have meant that I did not do what I promised you.

Had I done anything different, it may have waved a flag that perhaps you could not trust me or believe in what I said. But on the other hand, and let me make myself perfectly clear, in your "jammas" you looked simply exquisite. And cuddling with you all night, while behaving myself, was without a doubt the most difficult thing I have ever done. I hope somewhere off in the future we will be able to look back on that night and smile!

Amanda, I think that you are absolutely gorgeous, and I pray we can find a way, means, desire, comfort level and an abundance of reasons to want to walk into the future together.

Over the past several years I have done little more than exist and dream of what may have been—had some things worked out differently. Sometimes I feel guilty because I don't know exactly what I want to do with the rest of my life. While it may not be important to another soul on earth, to me just having the desire, willingness and possibility to think in terms of having someone in my life again is not only of the utmost significance but also extremely exciting.

Perhaps what I feel and what I think means little to you, but for sure I know how I feel. Yet, you may question as to how I would know what I am feeling in such a short time. Let me answer that just in case you are inquisitive.

I was raised in a strong Baptist family, had great parents, certainly know right from wrong; still, I have strayed from time to time from my ingrained beliefs. An old friend of mine, who died last year in Jacksonville, told me once that I would someday find someone whom I cared about and trusted that would be a special key to my true feelings with the church. His belief was that once a Baptist, always a Baptist. And noting your religious affiliation, I would say that we Baptists aren't too far removed in our beliefs from you Methodists! Perhaps he was right, perhaps not.

I truly believe that we met each other for a reason, and I feel that in time you will be instrumental in making me a much better person. I don't know that I will ever change in such a manner that will preclude enjoying life to the fullest, and as such, I don't think God ever meant us to be a stick in the mud. I don't think that is at all necessary. However, I feel most pleased to know someone with your morals and attitude, and for sure some of it might just rub off on me automatically. Don't you agree?

My mother and I talk often about me attending church. With this I have failed. However, almost daily I do talk with God, and while I am obviously not as strong as you are, I am a believer.

I know not what may or may not come from our friendship, but I haven't the slightest problem with telling you, as I am sure you already know by now, that I want you in my life. I want to spend as much time together as you are willing to give to us. There is no better way to learn about each other than through shared time. Throughout my life it seems that others have always been the "glue" to hold her and me together. Try as hard as one person may, it takes two. It takes two working jointly for a common goal. I can guarantee you that it is much easier that way, and, in fact, I personally would not ask you, or anyone else for that matter, to be the "glue" all alone, all by yourself.

If things work out and we choose to walk down a common path together I promise you, first and foremost, there would never be an occasion for you to question my motives or intentions when we are apart. You will be the only lady in my life, and that is that. And I would expect the same in return. This sentence sounds much like a marriage proposal, it's not. It's just my expression that I would dearly love to begin a relationship with you.

Life for me would again be exciting and happy if you were part of it. Not only do I want to be a part of your world, I also want to be your best friend, and that is of monumental importance to me.

Thus far, I have not written that I love you. Anyway, maybe that word is tossed around much too frequently. And perhaps you would say to me, how could I love you since I have only known you a short while. But the answer to that question was written years ago by someone much wiser than you or I. Someone once wrote, "The answer is in the wind." And the wind tells me there is something very special brewing. I have personal proof that you are a very warm and special lady. And, as said before, I wasn't led to the Wakulla Springs meeting just to be there. I choose to feel that my life is much more important than that.

I must make sure that you understand I have a personal

trait that bothers me considerably. It is called rejection. I don't deal with rejection very well. I love to win, to move forward, to master whatever is ahead for me. I shy away from things that I can't do well—dancing for one—but as promised I'll work on that. I tend to put total emphasis in those things which I do best. There is no question that I have already made a warm, fuzzy and most special place in my heart for you. This I can do well, and quite frankly, the building of that spot came very, very easy.

I have a tremendous amount of love and affection that I hope we can share. When we first talked, you said that you haven't had any fun in three years. Let's work together to change all of that. You also reflected that you asked the Lord to guide you each day. Perhaps, you can mention me a few mornings, and see just what comes about. When I was first divorced, my mother, and you would have loved that Bible-totin' Baptist, assured me that God did not mean for man and woman to live alone. If I ever believed anything in my entire life, I know her words were the truth.

Amanda, there is a great big world out there. A world in which we both previously have loved and lost. But life certainly is not over for either of us, individually or jointly. You have been somewhat vague in your comments about the future. You have mentioned another home, a yard for a dog, and in general other things similar to those. You remarked that you told your mother you would not be in your apartment for long; still you said that you even surprised yourself that you were still there. You've told me little about yourself, and I feel that maybe you have been so hurt in the past that it's hard to really open up and trust again. I do not want to add to your troubles or problems, but I would like to be there to be a part of the solutions if you will permit me to do so.

I have said a lot in this letter, and perhaps it will be the kiss of death to me for being honest, but this is how I feel. I simply do not want to worry myself over someone whom I care greatly for if they have no interest in me. On the other hand, I would adore you forever if you would breathe life into a relationship for us.

You may be surprised just how much love and attention I could and want to give to you. I read somewhere that you're never supposed to love someone for what they can do for you; you love them because you do. This I feel strongly.

Let me wind this up by saying I haven't beat around the bush with my comments. I think you are absolutely beautiful and the person that I have searched for over many years. While I have no intent to lose you, it's really up to you and not me. I am not just looking for someone to take to bed or have a good time with. I want you in my life because we both are good people, and I know we could be good for each other.

So, because this note may scare you off, and I pray to God it does not, let me finish by saying that if I have ever been in love with anyone previously, then I know exactly of what I speak about you.

Again, as in my previous note, I just wanted to share some of my personal feelings with you. I hope that I have not been out of line and hope more than you know you will talk this over with the good Lord and see if there is room in your heart for me. Rest assured that I will be doing the same thing and as hard as I can.

Amanda, if I am to be rejected I need to know it early.

Good night, God Bless, and know that I could love you very much. I hope that you will give me that chance. Now it's your turn to call me.

WHILE HE HAD admonished her to reject him immediately if that was to be his fate, he was astonished to receive a letter by return mail just two days later.

Dear Ron:

I received your kind letter today and had a chance to read it after dinner, and since I like to write I elect to write in return rather than a phone call.

Your letter was a real test, and I don't think I have ever taken one like that before. It literally took my breath away reading your lovely thoughts. The "guilty" feeling started creeping up, however, as I read them. I guess maybe I should have come right out and said so, but I do not have those same feelings that you do. It is regrettable because you do seem to be a very loving man. I am not certain what the Lord has in store for me, but I feel that I will know when I know.

Ron, I am not against men; some of my best friends are men. I just don't have the wherewithal to date for dating sake. I am interested in developing a casual friendship with you if you think that would interest you. I can't see me taking up your time and certainly not leading you on. These words are not what you wanted to hear, but I feel pretty sure you knew in your heart would come.

You are right, and I too believe in brutal honesty if it helps not to deceive anyone. I hope you don,t think I deceived you, because I certainly don,t think I did. I am very comfortable with men, and you are a ver interesting gentleman who I said "yes" to for dinner and to find out if there was something there. The closeness I just did not find, and that is usually a mind and soul thing. So if you will forgive me, all I can say is I wish it was there, too. But it is not in that way. And I still choose to be single.

Fondly,

Amanda

REJECTION HAS ALWAYS been a devastating trait within the Williams family's genes. While things do not always go well, they seem to handle any defeat which comes their way as long as they have an equal, fifty-fifty chance to compete. However, simple rejection of them personally or their ideas always wreaked havoc on their being.

After a couple of hours at Fred's Back Door Lounge, he returned to his apartment and a sleepless night. All night he fought the words of a song he had played time and again. The words kept repeating themselves with each toss and turn.

This world I live in is empty and cold
The loneliness cuts me and tortures my soul
I'm no child of destiny and no fortune's son
I've just chased you so long now I'm too weak to run
A new day is here but nothing is new
All alone in my room I tremble for you
I know I'll return to the back streets again
To find what I need to prove I'm a man
And there I'll treat shame like an old friend from home
That I can lean on 'til my misery is gone
A new day is here but nothing is new
I'm a picture of weakness as I tremble for you

18

ELVIS, HANK AND RONNIE

THE FIRST SIX months of Governor Graham's administration were filled to the brim with his official duties. There was precious little time to do anything else; however, he was always available when any special program involved itself with the youth of Florida. He and Adele had been blessed with four beautiful daughters. Their personal and immense interest always included setting aside whatever time necessary to involve themselves with benefits and special programs for teen-agers.

A group of 40 seniors had won a trip sponsored by the Department of Education to spend the day in Tallahassee on tour of the state capitol. Their schedule included meeting the governor and other cabinet members. The governor had prepared a few comments, and after snacks in an informal setting in the Governor's Conference Room he welcomed these special visitors.

Several weeks later Bill found a copy of the governor's remarks folded between other papers in the basement of his briefcase. After reviewing these, his first thought was that he would take a copy of it to Ronnie. His brother devoured reading materials and was forever searching for new insights about anything which may have a direct bearing on his personal life. Bill was sure the lessons outlined in the speech would be helpful to him. It read:

TODAY, THINGS ARE so much different from years gone by, and unless you've lived in times past it's so diffi-

cult to know, to understand. Unless you have never walked
in another person's shoes, or lived his life, tasted his tri-
umphs and wallowed in his defeats, you really can't begin
to comprehend.

I don't remember precisely and can't quote it verbatim,
but former President Richard Nixon said during the final,
agonizing, and most precious hours just before he resigned
the Presidency something to the effect, "Only if you have
been in the deepest valley can you know how magnificent it
is on the highest mountain."

And once President John Kennedy allowed the world to
peek into his private, innermost thoughts shortly after the
defeat of the United States at the Bay of Pigs invasion on
the shore of Cuba. He noted, "Victory has a million fathers,
but defeat is an orphan."

If you could be exposed to the ways of the past and could
absorb a better understanding of the mentality, mores, goals
and dreams of your ancestors, then perhaps a brighter future would be in store for all of you.

If you could know of the patience, persistence and per-
severance of countless thousands since the first step onto
Plymouth Rock, you would better understand the tough as
steel, strong willed, men and women who dug, clawed,
plowed and hammered this country from the swamps and
wilderness.

They labored and struggled almost beyond reason to
shape and mold this nation from scratch. If you had a stern
awareness and appreciation of the past, then perhaps you
would see where we as a nation are headed today. At times
it seems as through we are driving ninety miles an hour down
a dead end street, traveling a direction which has deviated
completely from whence this nation was born.

A nation that came about primarily because of trust, commitment, a belief in the Almighty and a dream to be more
than we dared to be. A dream to better ourselves through
hard work. A commitment found deep within our ancestors,
quality men and women who did not wait for or demand assistance from others but pulled themselves up to a higher
level.

Presently, much of our 24-hour day is consumed with
CD's, computers, television, cell phones and such. This is
okay, not great, but acceptable. These are progressive tools

of learning, but they teach nothing about the basics of life, yet so much time and emphasis are placed on them.

I want you to learn and make daily improvements in your life. I want you to fully realize that you should be doing things that are hard, not just those things which are easy. Individuals who choose to tackle options that are difficult are the people who, in the long run, create and achieve prosperity through a strong personal constitution buried deep within themselves. A personal, ingrained perception of perfection which commands them to excel in life.

Can things go wrong? Sure they can.

Will things go wrong in life? Surely.

Will some paths of our life be walked that are troublesome? Paths that were not intended to even be there in the first place, let alone traveled any distance? Yes, of course.

Things can and will go wrong. Mistakes will be made but you must always continue.

You must never quit, never give up.

Life is not for timid souls.

Mistakes? Me? Have I made mistakes? You bet I have.

I've made more mistakes than perhaps any three grown men you could name, all put together. Don't get me wrong; I mean mistakes, not crimes, nothing like that. Just plain simple mistakes.

And have I paid for my mistakes? Sure have. Still paying. But I learned from my mistakes, and as hard as it may seem at times, I know that I am a better man today.

I want you to spend some time with me today. I want to reach back and tell you some stories. Let me give you the benefit of my past and those of other men and women that I have known, and in this small way perhaps these stories will have a positive bearing on your future. Perchance you will grasp a better meaning of life, a better understanding of the past. While the past is prologue, it is the guiding light to the future and the basic foundation for what you can accomplish if you choose to do so.

Your past performance in life, everything you've done, is the one direct link to your future destiny. Only you, you alone, can and should be the master of your own house. You can and must shape your own future. Now, settle in with me and listen closely. You may be surprised.

WITH HIS OPENING remarks completed, the governor settled in with the inquisitive group of seniors and spoke to them about his personal life, beginning back in high school. And he told some fascinating stories about the countless numbers of friends that he had encountered along his way to becoming governor of Florida.

RONNIE HAD FORCED a lifetime into 44 years and four months and it certainly would be in order to assume his first 22 years and two months were his happiest. And there is no assumption required to be assured that his last 22 years and two months were pure torment.

Bill suffered and agonized, knowing that he had failed to perceive, to fully recognize or comprehend the extent of his brother's problems and to act positively and quickly on factors which might have saved his life. He continued to study and review every conceivable tidbit of information about not only Ronnie's death but also his life.

Ronnie was burning the candle at both ends and fanning the flame every hour on the hour. Something needed to be done, some action taken to make him realize that he needed to grab hold of himself, take hold of life and turn himself around before it was too late.

He could not get it through his thick skull that there simply were no short cuts and that he was going to have to buckle down to achieve any degree of success at anything. His friends would preach to him that he had to grow up and leave the past behind.

Bill finally came to grips with what he had seen, what he had learned and suspected over the last couple of years. Now, he was assured that his suspicions held much validity, soundness and truth about just how passionately Ronnie actually did live his life through the eyes, voice, acts and deeds of those he admired so greatly.

Unlike hippy groups, who in years to come would travel the country in a cult-like fashion following their musical icons, Ronnie carried to the extreme the same deteriorating lifestyle, but not in public. He sheltered his mental thoughts within himself, all alone in the emptiness of his own home.

It was uncanny, incredible, just how closely aligned were so many aspects of Ronnie's life when compared to the individuals he so much admired. What Bill uncovered was new to him, but not to me as I have been here from the beginning. I had known the truth for years. I was there when these mental intrusions, monsters as such, began to take hold, then unfold.

RONNIE GREATLY ADMIRED his father and accordingly adopted many of Mr. Williams's personal and honest character traits. Yesteryear the virtues of character were seldom praised, yet were expected by society, much more than they are today. Many characteristics of a person, be they good or bad, are passed on to their children and eventually surface through their own personalities. Ronnie adopted good and moral traits as easily as he craved and adored those of individuals who sheltered shadowy, mysteriously concealed ones.

He emulated the considerate, conscientious and honorable character traits of his dad. And like his parents, especially in later years, he mixed infrequently with people outside of his small circle of friends. Possibly this trait shoved him into a life of loneliness. A trait which fostered a desire to spend much of his adult life by himself. An all-powerful and wicked choice that became detrimental to him over the years.

Much had been written about the lonely, sad and secluded life of both Elvis and Hank Williams. Although they were international performers who were in the public eye most of the time, each experienced horrendous bouts of loneliness.

While their lifestyles were light-years apart, Ronnie would tell friends the performers didn't have the market cornered, explaining it was he, himself, who surely must be the Southern distributor for loneliness. He would tell of the many times when he felt absolutely alone even in the middle of a football field with thousands of fans in the stands.

Their habitual and personal streaks of loneliness caused each of these men to search unrelentingly for the adoration, love and companionship of one special lady, although their lives had been super saturated with a variety of women almost from the beginning.

IT SEEMED AS though Ronnie had studied the voluminous

amount of material which had been written about Elvis, Hank and others, then imitated much of their lifestyles. Conceivably without even a clue that it was happening. Unknowingly, he was traveling down a path not created by his own accord, his own volition, desires or wishes, but one built on false hope and false pretenses of dreams formulated within himself based on the acts and deeds of others.

Those whom he felt adoration for, within themselves, had a sullen and lonely side which was seldom seen or known by the public. Certainly Elvis, as well as Hank, had an obscure, dark side to his personality. While the world was in awe of the public persona of these entertainers, Ronnie seemed to live for and adore their total being, their complete personality package, their concealed side as well as their public demeanor.

Perhaps the reason he felt such a strong passion for both of them and complete acceptance of their lifestyle was because each had worked through his personal griefs and struggles during his young life. They did not waver or give up until they made something of themselves. Each projected a strong attitude which Ronnie was painfully lacking. Both of these uncommon men overcame their desperate, beleaguered plight and pulled themselves from the drudgery of poverty to become extremely successful, worldwide entertainers of colossal significance. Ronnie remained in awe.

To a degree, Ronnie must have known how they felt to excel in their chosen field. From his former athletic training he knew for sure there is no better feeling, no better lesson to be learned, than to come from behind in a game and win the contest.

There could be no better sensation of self-worth than exercising your God-given ability to kick yourself in the rump and get the job done that you were there to do. And especially at a point in time when all odds are stacked against you and all the money has been bet on your opponent. A win of such magnitude is the mark of a great team; so shall it forevermore be the sign of a great person.

He believed that men and women who came from nothing, having few material things while growing up, certainly should be afforded the opportunity to conduct their personal lives in accordance to the rules and regulations which they themselves value to be correct. Not archaic and antiquated rules of society which are often forced upon them by the great masses of humanity.

HE WOULD OFTEN say while listening to one of Hank's songs that he knew for certain that ole Hank must have been reading his personal mail. That's the way folks feel about his songs. That's the way Ronnie felt for sure. While playing Hank's records, he would pay ever-so-close attention. As if an invisible hand was writing the words indelibly into his brain, you could almost read the gratifying expressions on his face. The countenance of a man who wished that it had been he who had first composed the lyrics. He knew them well. All of them.

Hank had a remarkable gift for delivering the most simple messages to the common man. Sometimes his words were harsh and crushing, but more often they were words of valued inspiration. No matter the message, his words were always plain, direct and cut right to the heart of the matter. As if an arrow had been shot straight into each person's heart, as if the song had been written for him personally, everyone who listened was touched in a very special way. His were words and stories with which millions could easily identify as their own personal way of life, whether good or bad.

Hank had been born on the 17th day of September 1923 on a tenant farm near Mt. Olive, Alabama. His father abandoned him and his mother when he was a small child. In every song he ever wrote and on every record, you can distinctly identify the lyrics which solemnly illustrate the hard times that had been woven into his fleeting life of only 29 years. Every song he composed was another chapter or perhaps just a week in his personal, sad and lonely life.

Much as it had for Elvis, black music played a great part in Hank's early life as did music from various fundamentalist churches. Hank was taught how to play the guitar by a black sidewalk musician who daily walked the streets of Greenville, Alabama. He would shine shoes and deliver papers, and every time he could scramble up fifteen cents he would give it to "Tee-Tot" for another lesson. He paid his dues by working the streets of Montgomery and multitudes of Southern beer joints, dives, honky-tonks and roadhouses, picking up a dollar or two wherever possible.

In December of '44 Hank married Audrey Sheppard at a service station in Andalusia, Alabama. During these rugged, wartime years countless numbers of couples thought marriage would solve the age-old problem of loneliness and financial difficulties. They were soon to find out differently. Shortly after the simple marriage they moved to Mobile where both found work at minimum wages in a shipyard. You would think because of the hundreds of songs he composed and the gut-wrenching wisdom he possessed, that he would have known that happiness comes from within. It will never come from someone you choose as a soul mate, the person you take as your spouse.

In 1948 the noise of Hank's music began to make a difference. His notable "Move It On Over" took off and propelled him to the stage of the Louisiana Hayride. In February of '49 his "Lovesick Blues" was released. With its success the Grand Ole Opry had no choice but to make him a regular member that summer, although everyone had trepidations concerning his hard-drinking habits. With this new success, his haunting demons were again about to raise their ugly heads.

Hank had been a problem drinker since his early teens. An alcoholic who would start drinking and knowingly continue until he was unconscious. He was a binge drinker who had a low tolerance for alcohol. This affliction caused him to miss a great percent of his scheduled show dates.

It was around this time when Hank took on a sponsor and began doing pitch work for the Hadicol Company. Hadicol, a snake oil if there ever was one, was sold as a super cure-all medicine. From the back of a truck he would mix his songs with the commercial message he brought to those who would gather in the streets of hundreds of small Southern towns. At every stop he was fond of quoting a 30-year-old woman from Pine Apple, Alabama, and would read her testimony: "I couldn't read or write, but I started taking Hadicol and after just two bottles I got a job teaching the third grade."

Hadicol sales were brisk in each hamlet he visited!

HE WAS SOON to learn that success did not buy peace of

mind. Try as hard as he might, things just weren't working for him. In January of '52 he and Audrey were having insurmountable problems and ended the marriage. Then after being sacked by the Opry in August, he moved back home to Montgomery and into his mother's boarding house.

Soon after, he was jailed for public drunkenness in Alexander City, Alabama. Upon his release the world saw a portrait of a beaten man, a man who had only 19 weeks to live. Another offer was made, and he accepted the invitation to return to the Hayride. There, on stage on October 18th, he took another wife, Billie-Jean Jones.

This marriage would be the best investment of Billie-Jean's life. In ten short weeks, on New Year's Eve, Hank Williams would be found by his chauffeur, Charles Carr, Ronnie's friend, dead in the back seat of his Cadillac somewhere on a lonesome road in West Virginia. He was en route to play a New Year's Day show in Canton, Ohio.

Until Ronnie's death he cherished the lyrics and music of this uncommon son of the South. Perhaps it was Hank's difficult life, his drinking problem, or the words of his songs and his mannerism. Or maybe all of these combined in a way that touched Ronnie's soul and naggingly pulled at his heart strings. Creating within him a path of reality that seemed to offer a direction toward personal happiness. A means to avoid his continued journey down the well-traveled road of false hopes and empty promises.

However, after the spin of each record reached its end, the dreams he sought were still not there. The real world awaited him just a few steps past the front door of his apartment. For the most part, his life was now being lived based on events which were true-life experiences of others. The dreams that he would conjure up within his mind were beginning to play a dramatic, personal, but false role. Events which he assured himself were real were nothing more than visions of things that were never to be.

RONNIE COULDN'T AFFORD the luxury of having an in-house swami as did Elvis in Larry Geller. He was on his own to pick and choose his reading materials. The books which Elvis consumed were entirely the choice of his spiritualist, a young Jewish guru. Geller kept the many Presley homes, where the

colonel saw to it he was privately imprisoned, stocked with oc-
cult literature, off-the-wall religious writings and other mind-
bending rubbish.

While Elvis was pouring over such titles as *Sacred Science
of Numbers, The Masters, New Mansions for New Men and Eso-
teric Healing,* Ronnie had yet to get that far off base, although
he did have a copy of *Cheiro's Book of Numbers.*

Between jobs, but as Ronnie would often categorize it as being between opportunities, he spent countless hours reading a
variety of books. As surely as Elvis did, he too, searched for a
new life and a more pleasant and pleasing existence.

Probably, much like he listened to records, he would let his
mind wander while absorbing stories of Mark Twain, especially
the funnier ones. Or *The Source,* by James Mitchner, and Mein
Kampf, the autobiography of Adolph Hitler. He was fascinated
by *Too Young To Die,* a book narrating the life and death of many
actors and entertainers, none of whom had yet passed through
their 40s. He kept on hand a paperback copy of *Elvis—What
Happened,* co-written by his friend Red West. There were other
books about Elvis as well as the life and death of Hank Williams. And a copy of Truman Capote's *In Cold Blood.*

While there was no single book that completely overwhelmed
Ronnie, Elvis on the other hand latched onto *The Impersonal Life,*
a fascinating book that he carried with him everywhere he traveled. Through the years he would give thousands of copies of
the small, black, Bible-looking book to countless numbers of
friends and strangers alike.

ON FEBRUARY 1, 1968, Lisa Marie Presley was born in
Memphis at Baptist Memorial Hospital. Much has been written
about this being the happiest time of Elvis's life. Likewise, when
Ronnie's first child, Kym, was born on December 13, 1958,
Ronnie also was exceedingly happy. She, a beautiful, blonde
child, later had a gorgeous sister, Paige, and handsome brother,
Vince.

However, both men had chosen to remain adolescents themselves, and therefore were not willing to face the real world as
adults. Each would soon realize that becoming a father was most
burdensome. Neither of them allowed his new role as father to

bring growth or a sense of maturity into his sometimes selfish personal life. Times were changing and neither wanted to think in terms of getting older nor taking on the responsibility of fatherhood.

ELVIS WAS ENORMOUSLY impressed with powerful handguns, rifles and shotguns. The more powerful the weapon, the better it suited him. He owned weapons with great historical value, such as his antique Carl Hauptmann-Ferlach double-barreled rifle that was once the prize possession of Hermann Goering.

He owned rifles which could only be described as assassination weapons, such as his .300 magnum which broke down small enough to fit into almost any shallow luggage or briefcase. Perhaps his favorite of all was the Thompson submachine gun that was rumored to have been acquired for him by friends in the Chicago Mafia. In his later years, even while performing on stage, he would often carry a loaded Derringer in a boot. It is hard to imagine that any of his guns would be more favorable to him than the one he carried on his person most of the time.

His collection was monumental, of sufficient volume to hold off a small cadre of law enforcement officers had that ever been a choice or necessity. He and his men kept their keen eyes and agile reflexes trained, and all were qualified as sharpshooters or better. Often his Memphis neighbors would complain about not only the noise coming from the target practice at Graceland but also about the tremendous danger from ricochetting bullets.

As was Elvis, Ronnie too was totally absorbed and fascinated with guns of all types, models and sizes. His dad always kept loaded weapons around their home and for certain at least one in his car at all times. On occasions, he would take his sons into the woods to target practice, but never could it be said that his dad was fascinated with guns as Ronnie would become during his short lifetime.

Ron's family has many pictures of him with a variety of different pistols. Some are photos of him sitting near a riverbank holding a long-barrelled .44, others at home on his sofa posing with a full leather belt of ammunition and a "hog leg" strapped to his side. One of his favorite weapons was a sawed-off shotgun, its stainless steel barrel had been shortened to only 13 inches.

The stock was of light, highly polished wood. A few years earlier, Mr. Williams's friend, Sheriff Jones of Fentress County, Tennessee, had given him the shotgun. The gun, nicknamed "standback," was a gift to Sheriff Jones from his friend, another popular Tennessee Sheriff, Buford Pusser.

WHEN CHEMICAL MACE became available for civilian use, Elvis had bought dozens of canisters and distributed them among the wives of his men and his female staff. This was a new means of protection, and he insisted that each lady carry one with her at all times. Once, Judy West, wife of Sonny, mistook her golden canister, resembling a tube of breath spray, and mistakenly sprayed it into her mouth. The powerful chemical burn left nasty, permanent scars.

On the night of his murder Ronnie tried in vain to explain to the police, those who came to his apartment the first time, that an intruder had broken into his bedroom window and thoroughly sprayed his apartment with mace!

RONNIE AND HIS two alter egos had need for and required female companionship nearby at all times or at least at the snap of a finger. There is nothing wrong with this; it is quite natural. Nevertheless, what is so unreal is the fact, that although none of them ever suffered from a lack of women, still each searched feverishly for that perfect one, someone he could truly love.

Both of Ronnie's marriages ended in divorce. However, both wives, and those whom he dated before, between and after, will attest that Ronnie knew perfectly well how to treat a lady. And he did. He was one of the kindest men you would ever want to meet, ever want to date or be involved with. When he wanted to be.

Everyone will describe him as highly intelligent, having a great mind, clever, witty and bright. And he was. That is, when he wanted to apply himself. He was outgoing, playful and more than generous with his money. When he had any, he would give you the shirt from his back, no questions asked.

All of these were his good traits. However, he could also be selfish, not from a monetary standpoint, but from a personal point of view. He could crawl into his shell and not come out for days on end. And when it fitted his yearning, he could be the most conceited person on the face of the earth.

When he needed no one, he absolutely needed no one. But when he wanted someone, he expected them to be there, Johnny-on-the-spot and ready to take care of his every need.

This description is of Ronnie, but perhaps it just as easily could be an exact and perfect description of Elvis Presley.

WHEN ELVIS LOST his mother on August 14, 1958, he said that life would never again be the same for him. Conceivably, this was the beginning of a completely new and different Elvis. Shortly after the funeral he left for Germany and his tour of duty as a soldier in the United States Army. It was while he was in the Army that some of his entourage began to speak in terms of this being the period in his life when he turned "mean." It was also the point in time when he apparently began using heavy doses of prescription drugs. Possibly the loss of his mother started a chain reaction which ultimately led Elvis to an early grave.

The loss of Ronnie's father on April 5th, 1976, weighed heavily on the entire family. His sudden heart attack had not been anticipated although he was considerably overweight. His father's unforeseen death brought Ronnie much anxiety and unrest. For months he had put off talking with his dad, put off having that man-to-man conversation which he knew he needed to have. The dialogue to confront his drinking problem and address it openly and completely.

Mr. Williams's startling death quickly awoke Ronnie's carefree attitude, an off-the-wall attitude which dominated his daily life. An attitude, a set of shallow values, that convinced him that in time everything would work itself out for the best even if he himself did little to bring about the outcome. However, with his dad's death, reality finally registered.

On the afternoon of his father's death, more than once he gave serious consideration to bailing out of life himself. When the fog finally lifted, it became abundantly clear to him that time was now in control and it had truly passed him by. Forever, any chance to make amends with his father had totally vanished. He fell into the deepest hole of depression which lasted until his own death.

WITH COUNTLESS HOURS of spare time on his hands,

Ronnie filled his mind with the lyrics of hundreds of Hank Williams' songs. He would tell counselors that he knew for sure that he would drink himself to death, as did Hank. He would quickly counter that this was not what he wanted to do, not at all his own decision, but was mandated by fate and completely out of his hands. He knew it was his destiny, a providence over which he had no control.

Hank would write of such torment in many of his songs and say it differently in several phrases. But none of his words could define more precisely exactly what Ronnie was thinking than when Hank sang, "I'm gonna keep drinking until I'm petrified," or in another verse, "until I can't move a toe."

"I am in receipt of the information you sent regarding the program you have initiated to help prevent young children and teens from the abuse of addiction of alcohol. I was also delighted to hear about your book, 'RONNIE', and your personal commitment. In the state of North Carolina there are several ongoing initiatives relative to drug and alcohol abuse. We all have a part to play in combating these most difficult and destructive behaviors in our society. After discussion with the Governor, I will be in contact with you for the opportunity to personally endorse the web site. Thank you for sharing your information and I wish you much success in your efforts."

Dr. Janice Petersen
Governor's Office of Substance Abuse, North Carolina

19

IT DRAWS ME
TO THE APARTMENT

THE COOL, DAMP February day started off for Ronnie as had the last several: miserably. Three days ago on Saturday morning his mother had picked him up for a weekend at her suburban home. She always spoiled him rotten with hot nutritious meals, a most comfortable place to sleep and the greatest thing on earth—a mother's tender, loving care.

Tuesday she dropped him off at his apartment about mid-morning with the understanding that he was to call if he needed her for any reason. With a kiss on her cheek he said goodbye to her for the very last time.

Last week he had been given a temporary leave of absence from his state job. It was noted that one of the stipulations when he was hired and the continuation of his employment would be based in part on his weekly attendance at AA meetings. He had neglected this promise to the state agency, so he was concerned and dreadfully afraid of being terminated. After opening the mail which had gathered for three days, he called a friend, a co-worker who hinted that a termination letter probably was on its way. This disturbed him profoundly.

He made himself a lukewarm cup of instant coffee, had several cigarettes and placed a couple of phone calls to friends. Getting nothing more than their answering machine brought on more anxiety, apprehension and aggravation. He was completely lost as to what to do next. Pacing the floor, he watched the clock and shortly after 10:30 placed a call to his good friend Tony Riha, a well-respected downtown barber.

"Hello," came the busy but friendly voice.

"Whatcha'doing, Riha?"

"Hey, man. What's up?" replied the barber.

"Come on over, and let's play a few hands."

"Ron, I got 'em waiting in line. You drinking already?"

"Naw, man. I just want to play some cards. Get it on over here."

"Ronnie, I gotta work. I can't come over. Maybe on Sunday I'll come by. Or better than that, why don't you come to the house, and we'll cook something on the grill and watch a game. Little Tony would really like to see you."

"Crap," came the reply, and without saying good-bye the phone suddenly went dead.

Tony had become well accustomed to this type of reaction when things did not go exactly as Ronnie wanted. Over the years he had called in the wee early morning hours, late evenings and often late into the night. With every call Tony knew that he was listening to a very distraught friend, a friend who was in trouble and getting worse every passing day.

Hanging up, he searched for another phone number but couldn't find the note he had written Friday night. He loafed around his small, one-bedroom efficiency apartment wanting to do something, but did not have the foggiest clue as to which way to turn. He fought hard to put off having the first drink of the day until finally the struggle was lost. After three drinks of vodka and orange juice he loosened up, relaxed and played a few selections of Elvis, Hank Williams, Willy Nelson and finally lessened the tension with some of Richard Pryor's raw foolishness.

"YOU KNOW, BOO, I've had this little ole problem for a long, long time, and it seems to be getting worse. Nothing more, no drugs, nothing else, just booze. I wish this hadn't happened, but it did and it did big time. It caused the breakup of both of my marriages and the loss of my children. It caused my failure at every job I ever had. It's something that has been with me for a long, long time. Boo, I've tried as hard as I can to lick it but obviously haven't been the least bit successful. All I want is peace and a satisfied mind."

"What you gonna do about it, Ron? Seems as though your friends all enjoy themselves and they have little problem with it. What you gonna do, man?"

"Gotta get help. Since Dad's passing, Mom has worried herself sick over me. It's not her problem, mind you, but mine. She has bent over backwards trying to find the answers, trying to help. My family and friends have done all they can do, but, Boo, there just ain't no damn light at the end of the tunnel. I'm telling you, my friend, there just ain't no freakin' light. This 'tough love' that Mom is always talking about simply adds to my troubles. I know how much she cares, but it's not helping at all."

"Ronnie, you gotta help yourself. Man, get it together before it's too late."

"Yeah. I know. Going to Mom's for a few days always seems to help. A place to dry out, stay off the stuff for a few days. It's always good being there, but then I always have to come back here to this dump. Man, this place is so depressing to me. All I do is lay around here drinking and smoking these smelly Camels. Boo, I get so perturbed, so nervous."

"Ron, why don't you call Pinky, and see if he can prescribe something for you, for your nerves?"

"Think he would?"

"Don't know; try and see. Can't hurt."

"HELLO, IS DOCTOR Permenter available, please?"

"Who's calling?"

"Ron Williams."

"Hold, please."

"Hello," came his laid-back but very professional voice.

"Pinky, Ron Williams. What's happening?"

"Same thing, day in and day out. Just delivering and taking care of babies. What's going on with you?"

"Pinky, I need something to sooth my nerves. I want to try to kick this drinking problem, but man am I uptight. How about writing me a prescription for something, anything. Look, I'm on leave from my state job that Billy arranged, and I need to get myself back to work. I need your help."

"Ronnie, you know that I will help you anyway I can, but I'm concerned for you and pills are not the answer without some continuing professional help and some real help from yourself. You been going to your AA meetings?"

"Well, I went a few times but not regularly."

"You still seeing Doctor Benson?"

"Yeah, I see him occasionally."

"How about Dr. Marshall. Still seeing him?"

"Occasionally, not often."

"Well, why don't you see if one of them will write you a prescription?"

"Pinky, I need something now, and making an appointment to see them will take a week or more. How 'bout writing me one?"

"Okay, Ronnie, all right! I will if you promise me that you will follow the directions carefully and take them as prescribed. Promise?"

"Yeah, Doc, I'll do just like you say. For sure, I'll do just what you say."

"Fine. What drug store are you using? Where do you want my nurse to call in the prescription?"

"Call it into Wayne Adcock."

"His place is the Medicine Shoppe on Twelfth, isn't that correct?" inquired the doctor.

"Yeah. And thanks, Pinky. I appreciate it."

"Ronnie, now you take them according to the directions. You hear me?"

"Sure. Thanks, Doc."

HE WAITED AN hour and shortly after 2:00 o'clock headed for the Medicine Shoppe. He was always concerned about his driving even when he had but a couple of drinks; today his slowness of movement created a hazard itself. Following neighborhood streets to avoid heavy traffic, he turned west on Strong over to Twelfth then took a right. His pharmacist friend had already filled the prescription and had it waiting.

"How you doing, Ron?" Adcock inquired.

"Fine, not great but fine. Win a few, lose a few, few rained out. What's up with you?"

"Same old thing. Work, work, work. No rest for the weary. Now you be careful with these pills and follow the instructions. This is real important. Understand?"

"Yeah, Pinky told me that. Thanks, Wayne. I'll see you in a few days."

He paid with cash, then returned to his AMC where he attempted to read the small print on the bottle. This would have to wait until he located his glasses, somewhere in his cluttered apartment. As directed, he took two pills and washed them down with a full glass of water, then followed the first with a second glass.

Being fond of fishing, he had planned on going to the Gulf and go surf fishing early in the morning. This afternoon, he surmised, would be a good time to get his fishing equipment together, just doing something he enjoyed and simply relaxing.

Within a hour or so, the drowsiness from the pills and the effect of perhaps a full pack of Camels and the vodka forced him into a late afternoon nap. With eyes closed, he began to think of the letter he had received from Amanda. Every time he thought of her, he became soundly depressed.

LAST NIGHT WHEN he talked with Nancy, his Pensacola lady friend, she had suggested they have dinner and take in an early movie tonight. After work she would run by her home to freshen up then pick him up around 6:00 o'clock. They would go to dinner at Morrison's Cafeteria, then take in the 7:30 show.

Although this kind of evening seldom thrilled him, tonight he was at least willing to go along. Sitting still anywhere for a couple of hours or more certainly wasn't to his liking, but he knew that occasionally he had to do something that she wanted to do, something that she suggested.

Looking blankly out his window, Amanda's letter was still spinning wildly in his memory. With each flick of its vision, he had to force himself to pay attention to what was going on inside the car. For some reason an old saying kept coming back into his mind, "A bird in the hand is worth two in the bush."

They arrived at the theater just minutes before showtime only to find a long line stretching down both sides of the building. As was Ronnie's habit, he infrequently waited on anything or anybody. Quite foxy, he knew that if they did not attend the movie then surely they could spend some time having a few drinks down at the Azalea Lounge, the Flower Shop as the locals preferred to call it.

"Nancy, let's get out of here," he pressed.

"Ronnie, the line's not that long. Just take it easy."

"You know with all these people standing in line, if we do get in, we're going to have to sit on the front row, and I ain't gonna do that. Let's go."

Knowing his attitude, she knew that she hadn't even the slimmest chance of changing his mind, so they headed for her car.

"Let's go by the Azalea. How 'bout it?"

"No. I'm going to drop you off and head home. I got a long, tough day tomorrow."

"Oh, bull, woman. Let's go have a drink."

"Ronnie, no. Not tonight."

"Well, just take me to the lounge, and I'll find a way home," he barked.

"No. I'm going to take you home. You don't need to go out drinking tonight."

"Well, hells bells," came his reply with the rocking of his head from left to right in a disgusting motion. She'd heard that hundreds of times when he was disgusted but had learned to ignore him. He'd get over it.

She pulled the car alongside the curb of the narrow, dimly lit street where his door would open directly onto the two concrete runners in front of his apartment.

"I'll talk with you tomorrow. Good night," she said while attempting to kiss him on the cheek as he jerked his head so quickly to the right he slammed it against the glass.

"Ouch, that hurt. Look, let's go have just a couple of drinks, okay, babe? How 'bout it?"

"No. Why don't you spend some time tonight and clean up that dump you're living in. There must be a hundred beer cans and no telling how many empty bottles just sitting around."

"Look, why don't you mind your own business. Anyway, you're the woman; why don't you clean my house for me?"

"Yeah, right. Good night. I'll talk with you tomorrow," she lectured while pushing him gently on his left shoulder. "Get out of the car, Ronnie. Goodnight."

"Don't you want to come in for a little one-on-one?"

"Ronnie, get out of the car. Get out now! I'll see you tomorrow."

With that he bolted from the front seat and slammed the door as hard as possible.

NONCHALANT AS HE went about his every day life, he had forgotten to light the heater in his apartment before leaving. The evening had turned chilly at sunset, leaving the apartment not only cold but humid and hauntingly damp. After striking a dozen matches or more, his trembling hand finally held one steady enough to ignite the pilot. The small space heater came to life with a startling puff. An ash tray on the floor next to the heater attested to the hundreds of matches it had taken him to complete the simple chore.

"Boo, I'm getting antsy, getting restless. Every time I come home to this damp apartment, I get stressed out, nervous. While the house is warming up, why don't we run up to the lounge."

"Now, Ronnie, let's not be drinking and driving. I've told you that a million times."

"It's just six blocks or so. We'll be okay."

It seemed no matter how much he drank, he was always able to comprehend that he was not to drive after having too many. Without question, the number one horror above all others would be that he would have to spend a night in jail somewhere. He shuddered at the thought of being behind bars, knowing it would quickly drive him stark raving mad. For 44 years and four months he had dodged being arrested for anything—not even a speeding ticket.

Tonight he justified the trip by convincing himself that he would go for just a couple of drinks while the apartment was warming, then come home and go to bed.

When talking with the doctor in the afternoon, he forgot to ask him or the pharmacist if he could have a drink while taking the new medication. Since no one specifically said that he could not, then he quite naturally assumed it perfectly all right if he did.

The norm for this time of year on the upper Gulf Coast of Northwest Florida was for fog to roll in around 8:00 o'clock each evening. Tonight the heavy, moist air hung thick, almost at ground level. Being an overly cautious driver, he took it slow, almost to a fault of being a hazard to others without understanding that too slow was probably worse than too fast.

Just a block eastward he crossed over the Bayou Texar Bridge and within sight was Sir Richards, a favorite watering hole for those living on the east side of Pensacola.

Here, he knew he would run into some of his friends, but if not the bartender and the waitresses would offer him comfort and reassurance as they had often done so many times before. Easing through the squeaky door, he found that he was in luck. He took a seat at the bar next to his longtime friend Paul Jasper, one of his favorite feature writers for the *Pensacola News-Journal*. He ordered a Lord Calvert with a splash, lit up a Camel and tried again to relax for the first time today.

About half way through his second drink things seemed to be getting out of sync. Nothing was right. The world was spinning in the wrong direction. He felt very strange inside. Something was tugging at him.

"Boo, what's happening? Something's wrong. I want to go home. I feel like that is where I need to be. Let's go."

His mixed emotions of being among friends and, at the same time, wanting to leave shot contrasting vibes through his brain. The moment was cluttered and confused. His mind was racing, spinning like a selection wheel inside a slot machine. Wherever it chose to land was totally out of his control. While he would normally sit here for several drinks, play the box, chat with Paul and others and in general enjoy himself, tonight he was being pulled back home.

His internal gyro seemed to be bouncing from side to side, bouncing wildly in every direction. His physical body wanted to return to the apartment, back to four cold walls where he would again be all alone. Why, he wondered? Why? He began to see flashes of himself standing in a cold cemetery staring off into the pitch black night. Then, just as sudden, he was back in the lounge among the dim lights, thick smoke and loud music.

He finished his drink, paid the bill and as usual left a good tip. He told Paul and his wife Mary good-bye, not good night as Paul would recall later, but good-bye.

He eased away from the bar and walked slowly to the door, opening and closing it lightly as if leaving the sanctity of a church. He slipped behind the wheel and with great care waited several minutes before pulling onto Cervantes Street. Crossing the bridge, he turned right on 19th Avenue, then took the first left on Strong Street. He was home. No problem. All was right with the world once again.

Arriving, he cautiously locked the car at curbside, opened the screen door and, using an old skeleton key, unlocked the wooden door. He carefully locked it behind him.

He mixed another drink, took two more pills and lit up a smoke. Nervously, he bounced the phonograph needle onto the Richard Pryor album which had been spinning since he left it earlier in the afternoon. A few hours later someone would notice the record still revolving, the needle continuing to rotate around the inner core of the record.

"I hope RONNIE'S story will touch many young people and serve as a deterrent for those that might be considering alcohol and/or drugs."

Coach Phillip Fulmer, University of Tennessee

20

HALLUCINATIONS

IN THE MIDDLE of Johnny Carson's monologue, Ronnie was distracted by a noise which sounded as if it came from his bedroom.

"Boo, what was that? Didja hear that? What was it? Did it come from the bedroom? Didja hear it?"

"No, I didn't hear anything. Just take it easy. There's no noise. It's just some of that bull that Carson's putting out that you're hearing."

Easing from the sofa in the cramped front room, he turned the corner to the right and was standing in the hall. He tugged wildly on a string attached to a ceiling receptacle that held a single naked light bulb. He saw nothing to be alarmed over. The small apartment, for all it wasn't, was compact enough to observe every square foot of floor space from his lookout position under the naked bulb.

Returning to the sofa, his attention was focused on a commercial where NBC was advertising that CNN news would be coming to the nation on June first and would be available across the country through local cable. The commercial told of the owner being someone named Ted Turner.

Talking louder than the television, he asked, "Boo, wasn't that Turner guy someone that we read about one time, someone who won some sailboat race somewhere? Wasn't that where we heard of that big-mouthed fellow?"

After the commercial Carson detailed the death earlier in the day of David Janssen who had been a guest on his show the previous week. Janssen's current television series, "The Fugitive," was making big waves and topping the charts of the Nielsen television ratings. The show and David Janssen himself were long-time favorites of Ronnie's. Ronnie often found some extraordinary and curious comparisons for many events which touched his life, especially concerning the passing of friends or those of importance. Janssen's death perhaps was to be a window of things to come.

For the second time he heard a louder noise coming from the back of the small apartment. And again his search produced no evidence of anything out of order. The sounds were frightening to him.

"Boo, listen to me. There is someone trying to break in on us. You hear me?"

"There's no one here but us, Ronnie. Just take it easy."

"Boo, you see this diamond ring. It's about the only thing I got worth anything. I need to hide it. But where? Boo, where will they not look when they come back?"

"Boo, you know how burglars are. They will look in every drawer, every cabinet, under the bed, between the mattresses. And Boo, don't let me forget to get my guns from between the mattresses. Boo, where am I going to hide this expensive ring? Where, Boo, where?"

"Well, you got that pot of blackeyed peas that has been sitting on the stove since you cooked them last Friday the day before your mom picked you up. Unless you've gotta steel stomach, they've obviously gone bad by now. Why not use 'em for cover? Bury your ring down deep in the peas. They won't find it there."

"Boo, you devil you, you're simply brilliant when you want to be. Yeah! Into the pea pot it goes. Boo, that sounds funny doesn't it? Pea pot. Heck."

"Now Ronnie, push it down deep, cover it up good. Man, put the top back on the pot, stupid."

THINKING OF NANCY'S reprimand earlier in the evening to clean up the apartment, he thought he would give it a shot.

After wiping down the kitchen counter, he made a couple of sweeps with the broom, then left it laying crossways on the linoleum floor. Nancy would tell the next day that it was not there when she picked him up about 5:30.

"I ain't gonna clean this dump. It's okay just like it is. Don't you think, old boy?"

"Ronnie, why not put in a little time and effort in cleaning. You know it could use it and just think how pleased Nancy will be with you."

"Man, the bed has sheets on it, the heater is on and the house is getting warm. That's enough. I can live with it like this. Don't you think? Boo, don't you think this is okay?" he mumbled.

"Yeah. Yeah, Ronnie, it's okay. It looks much like that junky bullpen you lived in at Jones. But if that was satisfactory to you back then, then this dump should suit you just fine today. Not too much has changed over the years, has it, Ron? Look, just don't worry about the house. Leave it alone as you usually do."

"Boo, why don't we have us another drink? Why don't we have us just a little baby drink? Whatcha say?"

"Well, you did sweep up those coffee grounds in the kitchen. That was a start. You really think you need another drink?"

"Why not? Friend, let's have a little shot," Ronnie asked and demanded in the same breath trying to convince himself of the need.

"Yeah, go ahead, sounds good to me, Ron. You got that bottle of vodka opened and I can't stop you. Have at it."

"That'll do. Boo, that'll do just fine. A little vodka, a little water, a little lemon and a whole bunch of ole Hank. That's what we will do, Boo. That's exactly what we will do my man."

"Ronnie, see that dead roach laying over there by the fridge?"

"I see it. What about it?"

"You would scare the crap out of ole Nancy if you pick it up and ease it into the freezer. When she goes for ice, she'll just die."

"Man, I ain't gonna pick up no filthy roach. Boo, what's wrong with you tonight?"

"Just take a napkin and pick it up and put it in the fridge. That's all. Ronnie, just pick it up and put it in the stupid freezer."

"You know I ain't got no napkins."

"Then use anything, Goofus. Just pick it up and put it in the freezer. Use that card laying on the record player. That'll work."

Ronnie was on his knees with the card in hand trying desperately to scoop up the roach when he began laughing out loud and having the best time.

"Boo, this is like being down at Daytona. I feel like Richard Petty racing around. Chasing this grubby, slippery roach across the floor."

A few scoops later he finally hemmed it against the wooden baseboard. Trying to balance it in the middle of the card proved to be an almost impossible task with his hands shaking so badly. The roach would slide back and forth, and each time it came near his thumb he would jerk away sending both the card and the roach to the floor. He finally hemmed it up once again, then lifted it gently. Creeping slowly, he opened the top freezer door of the efficiency refrigerator and slid the slippery critter from the card.

The roach, stunned but perhaps not dead, landed on its back with all legs pointing skyward. Sure enough, there it would be found the next afternoon. Perplexed family members wondered what had prompted him to place it there. It was impossible for it to crawl to its own death as the freezer unit remained tightly sealed. What had he been thinking?

Next, he sailed the card into the overflowing brown paper trash bag tightly scrunched in the corner between the fridge and a partially rusted chrome table leg.

"Don't throw that away, Ronnie. That's your electric bill. Get it from the trash, dummy."

"I ain't planning on paying it. Let it be."

"Ronnie, get it from the trash. Now! Lay it back where you got it. And, yes, you will pay it, sooner or later. Boy, what is wrong with you tonight? Have you gone completely crazy?"

The roach exercise wrapped up the extent of his house cleaning duties for the evening. Glancing at the television, Carson was giving his good night wave to the audience. It was five minutes until midnight.

Not uncommon for him at the stroke of midnight, he reached for the phone and dialed three different numbers. Without getting a human response, he refused to listen and slammed down the phone at the first clue he recognized to be a mechanical message. His disdain for answering machines was unreal. He would never leave a message no matter how cute or professional the greeting on the other end sounded.

"NOW, DAMMIT, BOO, I heard something in the bedroom. Where's my gun? Boo, where are my guns?"

In the stillness of the night the shattering sounds of a glass window broke the calm silence. Hustling out the front screen door, Ronnie screamed at the top of his voice, "Don! Don! Don! Somebody's trying to break in."

His distress call awakened Don and Pat Lewis, owners of the rental apartment sitting just a few feet from the back door of their main house. Hearing his blaring voice and the commotion of the screen door slamming, Don jumped from bed and rushed to the window which had been left open to enjoy the crisp cool night.

"Ronnie, what is it? What's wrong?"

"Someone's breaking into the apartment. Don, they're trying to get me. Hurry," came the terrified voice.

"Ronnie, just stay put, we'll call the police.

"Pat, you best call the law. I guess you need to call 911. Tell them that we have a burglar, someone breaking into our rental unit."

Don hastily threw on a pair of tennis shorts and a pullover shirt, then bounced down the stairs skipping every other step. Before he could get to the first floor landing, Pat hollered, "Don't go outside, the police are on their way. Stay inside 'cause the police want know who you are. They said to stay in the house."

Again, this time even louder, Ronnie hollered, "Help me, man, someone is trying to spray my house with mace. Hurry, Don. Please get some help!"

Within minutes Pensacola Police Officers pulled up to the curb on 19th Avenue and walked towards the main house where Don was awaiting them on the front porch. He explained, "Our tenant, Ron Williams, has somewhat of a drinking problem. I think that you should know that. He may be drinking, I just don't know. He seems to be acting real strange. I don't know if they are burglars or not, but he surely thinks there are and that's what's important right now."

The officers walked through the carport on the south side of the main house and slowly approached the apartment. Ronnie was standing outside near his front door. While he and the officers chatted, another squad car with two more officers pulled up on Strong Street, parking directly in front of the apartment. The officers exited and strolled over to speak with Don, who had walked through the main house onto the rear alcove.

One of the officers remarked to Don, "I think I've been here before."

"Well, I wouldn't know anything about that," Don replied.

"Yeah, we were here once before, and your wife came over and talked to your tenant and convinced him to go to the detox center with us."

"You're right. I remember it now. That's right. That did happen."

One of the officers who had been talking with Ronnie walked to the rear of the main house and remarked to Don and the two officers, "I can't smell any liquor on him now, but he sure is acting real funny. I mean to tell you, he's very emotional."

Officer Chavers asked Ronnie, "What seems to be the matter?"

"Officer, someone's spraying my home with sleeping spray," came his reply.

"What can I do to protect myself? While ago I had to break out a window to let the fumes out. It got pretty bad."

Snapping his head quickly towards Strong Street, Ronnie shouted, "Look, there they go again. Ain't y'all gonna do anything about them? Ain't you gonna arrest them? You just gonna stand there and not do anything?"

The officers all turned in the direction that Ronnie was pointing, and nothing was seen, no movement of any sort.

"Mr. Williams, you just need to go to bed, relax and go to sleep," said Officer Mathis.

"I've got a gun. Can I shoot them outside the window? I could clearly see a man peeking through my window. He had a hat on his head and just stood there looking in. Can I shoot him if he comes back?"

"No, you don't need to be fooling with any guns, or you may go to jail," responded the officer.

Hearing that, Ronnie walked slowly back into the apartment

and took a seat on the sofa. He said not another word and was quiet. With the incident seeming to be over, all of the policemen left except one who lingered just outside his door.

Ronnie walked to the screen door and, without opening it, called loudly over the officer's shoulders towards the main house, "Don, will you come over here a minute, please?"

Don had been waiting patiently on the back porch of the main house to see if the officers had any more questions of him. He hurried to the apartment and, as he neared it, the remaining officer told him goodnight and walked toward his car.

"Ron, what can I do for you? What do you need? How can I help you?"

"Don, they got my pearl-handled gun. My mother's gonna be really upset."

"Who got it, Ron?"

"The police probably got it."

"Ron, they have guns of their own. They are not gonna be messing with your guns."

"Well," was faintly heard under his breath.

Turning away, he motioned for Don to follow him into the cluttered bedroom. He got down on one knee and reached between the mattresses and pulled out a black, long-barrelled .22 Ruger revolver, complete with belt and holster. After looking it over and rotating the cylinder, he threw it on the bed near the left pillow.

"Aw, crap, it's empty. But I got me another one."

With that he retrieved two other guns from the same hiding place.

"Now, Ronnie, you need to put those back under the bed. You know everything is all right, and nobody is gonna mess with you. The police are going to patrol the neighborhood tonight, and if anything happens they'll arrest somebody. They'll get them. You don't need to worry about it. They will get them, I promise you they will."

"But, Don, they've been spraying mace through that window."

Don checked the broken window closer and did not smell or detect any unusual odor in the room.

"Ronnie, the only smell that seems strange in here is all those stale beer cans that you need to throw away. Ron, who are these people who are trying to spray your apartment? You know them?"

"Man, somebody is after me, and I don't have an idea who they are. I just have a feeling that they are out to get me. You don't believe me. I can see that right now. But, Don, a man wearing a hat was staring right there through that window. I don't know who he was. I don't know how many were with him. If I knew, I would tell you. I promise. Believe me. I promise."

"Well, you just need to go to bed. Everything's okay. If you need me, I'm right next door. Just call me, holler out loud like you did awhile ago. I'll hear you. Now please go to bed, and get some rest. Everything's going to be just fine."

WHEN DON LEFT the apartment, Ronnie took the two guns into the living room and sat quietly on the sofa.

"Boo, see this old .22 I got here? It ain't worth two cents. Ain't got no killing power, but it will scare the crap out of 'em. Don't look like much, does it? All this old thick black tape wrapped around the handle. But it'll scare 'em anyway."

Rotating the cylinder, he said, "Got six live ones and an empty."

Laying the first gun down, he picked up the second and noted, "Now this here S&W .38 will knock someone on their tail. Of all the guns I have ever owned, this is my favorite. It belonged to daddy. You see here, Boo, it's hammerless. Daddy liked to carry it with him. You 'member he was a big man, and he could carry this hammerless in one of his pockets. No problem. Couldn't even tell it was there."

Rotating the cylinder, he proclaimed, "We got us four live rounds and also one empty.

"Boo, daddy taught me years ago when I was a kid to always keep a spent shell under the hammer. That's in case if you drop it accidentally it wouldn't go off. When I was married and the kids were around, I would keep two spent shells. One under the hammer and the second empty so if one of the kids happened to get hold of the gun, they'd have to pull the trigger at least twice before it fired."

DON HAD RETURNED to the main house where Pat was waiting at the top of the stairs. In her frightened and concerned voice, she inquired, "Is Ron okay? Is he all right?"

"No. No, he's really not. I think that he's hallucinating."

"Has he been drinking?"

"No, I don't think so, he doesn't seem to be. I didn't smell anything on him. But I think that he is really hallucinating. I have never seen him this scared, this nervous. Pat, something is really wrong with him."

Pat interrupted, "When he was talking to the police, he seemed to be very irrational."

"Yeah, that's about the way I see it."

"Think we should call his mother?"

"I don't know, honey. I really don't know what to do. Why don't we get some sleep. Maybe he'll settle down. Good night."

"Hopefully the youth of the country will be open to hearing what you have to say. This is certainly a story that needs to be told. Once in a while there's a young man like 'RONNIE' who breaks your heart, because he just can't take control of his life. I hope his story will help young people through-out the country make decisions in their lives that will keep them moving in a positive direction."

LaVell Edwards, Former Coach, Brigham Young University

21

POP POP POP—
BOOM BOOM BOOM

IN A FRIGHTFUL voice Ronnie yelled, "Boo, there they are again! Can't you see them outside! There they are! Quick, turn out all the lights so they can't see in."

He yanked at the string attached to the naked bulb in the hall, then tripped the bedroom switch. Dousing the lights left only the flickering amber fire of the small space heater to illuminate the apartment, now bathed in a ghostly incandescent glow. From his lookout in the hall he stared into the dark bedroom and could plainly see the thief who had returned to the window.

"There he is, Boo," he whispered. "See him looking in our window? See his head? He's wearing a hat."

"See him? You can see his head clearly. He's standing still. Looking in the window. Look. Another one is passing behind him. Boo, didja see him? Be quiet. Be real quiet."

Pop.

Pop.

Pop.

"Don't know if I got him or not. This little .22 ain't very accurate. Maybe I hit him. Ssshhh, be real quiet."

Ronnie slipped slowly and cautiously across the cluttered floor to the left side of the window. Hiding behind the loosely hung curtain, he eased it gently towards the wooden casing and peeked out. There was no movement.

"Boo, maybe I killed him, and he's laying on the ground."

Half scared to death and shaking like a leaf, he laid the hot .22 quietly on the chest of drawers. Touching the walls lightly for stability, he slowly guided himself back into the living room.

Whispering, he said, "Where's my .38? Boo, where did I lay my real gun?" Milling around in the eerie glow of the room, his hands searched frantically over the wadded throw cover of the sofa until he finally nudged the handle. Right where he had left it just minutes earlier.

DON WAS PULLING up the covers when he heard the three light popping sounds coming from the direction of the apartment. He instantly reached for the phone, dialed 911 and explained the location to be the one and same where the officers had been less than 15 minutes earlier. He reported that he had heard what may have been gunshots coming from the apartment. This time he was panicky, thinking there really may have been an intruder after all.

Pat hurried downstairs and into the basement bedroom where her 21-year-old son was sitting up in bed, stretching hard to see out the ground level window. She warned him to lay back down, saying there may have been gunshots fired around the apartment. She then checked on their six-year-old son. He was sound asleep.

Leaving the basement, she had to feel her way up the stairs since Don had turned off all the lights to see more clearly what was happening outside. They noticed a plain car turning off 18th Avenue with its lights out. It came to a stop on the south side of Strong Street.

Before the driver got out, Don heard what appeared to be a fourth pop coming from the vicinity of the apartment. The driver had left his automobile but quickly returned to it. Within seconds another automobile arrived and parked across the street from the first. Both men emerged from their cars at the same time and walked eastward on Strong Street, down the south side.

They were sneaking across the neighbors yard when a fifth pop apparently came from inside the apartment. Both men immediately fell to the ground. The Lewises heard what sounded like someone calling out, "It's the police."

From their upstairs eastside front window, Don saw another

automobile ease up and park on 19th Avenue, directly in front of the main house. The driver remained in the car. Don knew for sure that he had to have heard the fifth popping sound.

Pat, extremely uneasy, frightened and very concerned, returned again to the first floor to check on her young son to make sure he was all right. Thus far, all was well with him. He was snoring lightly.

She ascended the stairs and touched her way along the wall to the westside window overlooking the apartment. From her vantage point she could plainly see two men crouching, bending over, quietly sleuthing and sneaking down the west side of the apartment heading south towards the rear of the building.

Ronnie, standing firm at his lookout position in the dark hall stared intently at the bedroom window hoping to catch another glimpse of the burglar.

"Boo," he whispered, "there must be three or four of them. I can see them moving around. But they won't get past this .38, I'll guarantee you that.

"There they are, creeping by the window. See 'em, Boo?

"Didja see 'em?

"They all must be wearing hats. See 'em? Right there they are."

"Pop" came the sound of the sixth shot echoing off the walls of the small apartment.

"Boo, there must be more than a dozen of them outside. I think I shot one. No one is moving. I must've got him. Boo! I killed 'em. I know that I killed 'em. Boo, be real quiet. Listen. Just sit still, don't move. Let's make sure none of them come back."

SEVERAL PATROL CARS with uniformed policemen and unmarked automobiles with plain-clothed officers rushed south on 19th Avenue and slid their vehicles to a stop in front of the main home.

Two plain-clothed men and a uniformed policeman were creeping sheepishly up the driveway of the main house when they heard the sixth shot fired from inside the apartment.

A full minute or more passed since the last shot, then Ronnie came bolting from the apartment. When the screen door slipped from his hand the tension of its rusty, coiled spring pulled it quickly, slamming it hard against the wooden door jam with a loud "whack."

Taking two steps, he then turned left toward Strong Street and almost ran head on into the burglars who had by now worked their way from the back of the apartment to a crouching position in the small front yard.

"Boo, here they are! What are they screaming about? What are they saying, Boo?"

He immediately changed direction and darted the ten paces toward the back door of the main house. From the second floor Don and Pat could hear him mumbling loudly as if he were talking to someone but they couldn't understand what he was saying.

Not able to open the door, he leaped from the alcove, reversed his direction and headed around the southwest corner of the driveway. The weighty sounds of running feet, thundering noises from his heavy leather boots could be heard clearly by the Lewises from their top-floor bedroom.

One of the burglars hiding in the bushes yelled for him to stop. Still he continued galloping, grunting loudly as he rounded the corner, then made a quick left turn to go through the carport, praying that he would find security from the burglars at the front door of the main house.

The Lewises moved to the window of a southside bedroom and could still hear the loud, hysterical, meaningless sounds of their frightened and absolutely terrified tenant, but could not make out what he was saying.

His screaming and the sounds of his muffled words mixed with deep nauseating grunts and horribly strange noises was sickening. He now was shouting at the top of his voice what sounded much like, "I shot 'em! I shot 'em! I got the burglars!"

Reaching the pitch black carport, he ran feet first into a large pile of firewood that had been stacked between an old convertible and a two-foot-high concrete block ledge.

"Boo, what's this stupid wood doing here? Got to get away. Boo, come on, we got to get outta' here, away from the apartment. Crap, I broke my glasses."

"Forget them, Ronnie, let's go."

He knew that he was running for his life, trying desperately to get away from the many intruders. To get away from whatever number there might be, knowing they must be only a step or two behind him. In a bumbling, stumbling fashion, trying desperately to untangle himself from the scattered wood and piles of pine kindling, he slipped repeatedly on rolling logs, then finally regained his balance and rose to his feet. Making a couple of rapid half steps backwards toward the apartment, he impulsively turned toward his left and rounded the corner of the carport, then hustled east toward 19th Avenue.

As he made his turn, he instantly faced a uniformed policeman walking with one of the burglars. His overburdened mind coupled with what he had seen led him to believe they must have captured one of the intruders. Good news he thought!

Officer Pelham, dressed in street clothes, had squirreled his way to the south side of the narrow yard and hid behind the thick leaves of a large white camellia bush.

The Lewises could hear loud, garbled voices being shouted by several people. The confusing sounds were coming from every conceivable direction.

Ronnie was petrified. He could not understand how in hell the burglars could have possibly made their way so quickly from the front yard of the apartment and now confronted him head on. He continued scampering for his life.

"Ronnie! Quick! Look to your right!" I shouted. "One of the burglars is hiding in that bush. See him?"

In a loud and terrorizing voice the burglar screamed at him, "drop your gun."

A horrifying noise overshadowed the voices with a dominating sound that was much like a cannon exploding. A radically different sound, completely unlike the small popping noises heard from inside the apartment.

"BOOM."

The blast from a high-powered Magnum weapon merged with the grunting and groaning sounds of Ronnie's fearful soul. The horrendous noises of gunfire mixed with the shouting voices of the burglars to fill the frigid night with sounds of sheer terror.

RONNIE FELL TO the ground.

"Ahhhh! Ahhhhhh!

"Damn, Boo, they got us. They shot me. Why'd they shoot me? My right leg. It hurts, Boo, it hurts real bad. It's gotta be broken.

"Why did they shoot me? Boo, why in God's name did they shoot me?"

"Drop your gun" was heard.

He tried to hobble to his feet, much like an athlete would do a push-up with both hands on the ground in front of him, but with only a single leg for balance. His pistol remained in his right hand. The gun was forced downward into the damp earth from the weight of his body as he tried to raise himself.

His overactive heart, now beating furiously, pumped a stream of warm red blood from the gaping leg wound. His life's fluid seeped across the wilted, crumpled leaves and quickly mingled with huge drops that oozed from his knuckles, forearm and elbows caused from his fall into the wood pile.

With both hands pushing as hard as possible against the cold earth, he tried in vain to slowly raise his wounded body. His back was grossly arched in an attempt to draw his left leg upwards to his chest so as to lift his weight. His right leg dangled limply, mangled by the exploding force from the Magnum blast.

Lifting his head sluggishly from the ground, he looked straight ahead and screamed at one of the burglars, "Man, why in the hell did you shoot me! You broke my damn leg."

"Drop your gun," someone shouted.

"The gun is empty," came his reply.

"Boo, tell that burglar the gun is empty!

"Boo, my leg! The pain is killing me. Boo? Boo? I can't get up."

While he struggled in vain to raise himself from the frigid ground, trying his best to get to his feet, two more cannon shots shattered the night.

BOOM.

BOOM.

The terribly loud explosions came from very close range. Another Magnum round found its intended target and with a deafening thud tore a hole into the upper right side of his back.

Pelham, hiding himself securely from harm's way, had

wormed himself safely behind the clump of thick bushes. He was much more concerned for his own safety than that of the real victim who had tried desperately to escape from the intruders. From his cowardly position he was the responsible culprit who sent the killing blow directly into the back of this helpless, innocent and completely terrified man.

Pelham was only ten feet or so from his intended target as Ronnie tried desperately to raise himself from the ground. Had he chosen, he was close enough to have handcuffed him rather than deliver the terminal blow. Being only a few feet from Ronnie's back as he struggled to raise up, he instead chose to display his authority, his macho image and use with perfection his deadly, lethal weapon.

"Ahhhh!

"Boo?

"That bastard shot me in the back!"

From his awkward position the hollow point connected with a thunderous blow, knocking him over. He turned his head slightly to the right and whispered as loud as he could, in a slurping, gurgling voice, "What kind of friggin' coward are you? Why in the back?

"Couldn't you see that I........

"Boo, you there? Boo?

"Boo, I can hardly see.

"My eyes are blurred.

"Where are my glasses?

"Boo, I can't move.

"I feel paralyzed.

"What are they talking about?

"Boo, what are they saying?

"What are they shouting about?"

"Hell," said an officer, "you shouldn't have shot him while he was down. You nit-wit! Why'd you do that? You should have aimed to cripple him. Why in hell did you shoot him when he was already down. Why in the back?"

"He was getting up, that's why."

"Getting up, crap. He was just laying there. He couldn't get up. You could see that. Damn."

"There's nothing to worry about. Sssshhh. Just be quiet.

Don't concern yourself. Quiet down, men, just forget it," said the third officer.

HAVING HEARD NO more shots for a couple of minutes, Pat and Don came to the front door. Peeking out, she asked, "Is everyone all right?"

An officer replied, "All the police officers are, yes, ma'am."

"How about Ronnie? Is he okay?"

"Ma'am, you need to stay in the house."

Walking onto the front porch, she asked the question a second time. "How about Ronnie? Is he all right? Is he okay?"

"You can't come out. Please stay in your home. We can't allow you outside."

As the officer made his demand that they remain in the house, their yellow front porch light shown brightly on an emblem pinned on the officer's shirt. The proclamation made Pat sick to her stomach. Proudly worn was his insignia stating, "Sharp Shooter."

WHILE THE MAJORITY OF LAW OFFICERS are truly outstanding individuals who take pride in their profession, there are others who are just the opposite. Sadly to say, scattered across our nation there are too many cops who seek nothing more than to feed their personal ego by portraying a reckless, macho image under the guise of a lawman.

These misfits garner tremendous self-satisfaction by knowing that the public trust has been placed in them. Through that confidence, they feel free to take the law into their own hands and disburse justice in a manner which brings to them great contentment.

We have among us a number of so-called "lawmen" who would never measure up to even the minimum acceptable standards should the public have true knowledge of what is actually going-on behind the scenes. These over-zealous mavericks are those of the sorry sorts, the bad apples, that give their department a reputation which is hard to over come. This night, it was Ronnie's fate to lose his life at the hands of those whose actions indicate that they could have cared less.

It had been less than 15 minutes since the same police force, at the direction of the same radio dispatcher, with the same commanding officers, had been on the scene. Without question, they knew exactly what the situation was all about. Exactly what they were dealing with. They had been there just minutes earlier and knew that Ronnie had been drinking and was badly hallucinating. They knew he had guns in his home because he told them he did. They were aware that he had asked the officers if he could shoot the burglars if they returned.

The officers were directed to the scene by the very same dispatcher who had sent them to the apartment the first time. They knew for certain exactly what they were getting into. How in the world could they have been so adamantly stupid to sneak up on Ronnie's home and do so while wearing plain clothes?

Enforcers of the law? Is that what you would call these men who have supposedly been trained to handle every type of situation? They had the stupidity to place themselves directly in harm's way, to force, to cause a situation which they were dispatched to prevent. But instead, they took the life of a totally innocent man because of their own inferior experiences, inferior training or simply a reckless display of pure machoism.

Ronnie had asked the police less than half an hour before he was killed, "If the burglars come back, can I shoot them?" Yet, without using an iota of mentality, they put themselves directly in harm's way. They, individually and collectively, were the primary and motivating cause of provoking the fear of someone who had already expressed grave concern for his own safety. The police officers had already noted his fear and his erratic behavior. He did exactly what the average citizen would do if he were provoked and concerned for the safety of his own life. In a very correct and most proper manner, he called to his landlord for help, then asked him to summon the police. He wanted and needed the officers to come and check out his private home as he was assured that burglars were trying to do him bodily harm.

APPARENTLY, WHEN A cluster of policemen steals the life of someone, all the top brass from the department have to show up to get in on the publicity. The tiny yard was overflowing with what appeared to be most of the entire police force. Photographs were being snapped from every conceivable angle. A video was made.

Immediately after the shooting, Officers Clayton Ard and Jim Simmons entered Ronnie's apartment to see if anyone else was inside. Their search proved negative. As the brass began to gather, Officer Ard, acting as though he was a ten cent carnival tour guide, escorted the horde of cops through the cluttered apartment. First came Captain Haner, then Lieutenant Beaumont, Sergeant Poe, Officer Rivers, Officer Skip Miller and Bob Grant. As others made their appearance at the scene they were given the grand tour.

"Look at this place. Be sure to take as many pictures as you need. The beer cans, the nearly empty liquor bottles."

A plainclothed cop asked, "Any of you recognize or know him?"

"No, not me," came the reply in unison.

"He must have been a drifter, perhaps just another derelict. He lived like one anyway," an officer announced sarcastically.

INVESTIGATORS TOOK DON, Pat and their children to the station for questioning. Throughout the ordeal each was concerned when the same questions were asked continuously, over and over. They were very uneasy, but completely assured of their answers. However, the constant repetitiveness of the same questions indicated to them the officers were trying as hard as they could to get them to alter their story.

They were not permitted to return home until after daybreak. Arriving, they were ordered not to go into the yard but to remain in their home. Some six hours had now passed, and the body of Ronnie Williams was still laying on the cold ground. The main attraction for the benefit of these "lawmen" had all but been ignored. No one, not one single person, even had the decency to cover his body.

SHORTLY AFTER THE Lewises arrived back home, an officer knocked on the front door. "We need to locate a next of kin. Would you have any information or knowledge of such?

"Yes, I know how to reach his mother. I have her phone number in the house. Would you like it?"

"Yes, ma'am. Do you know if he is married? Does he have a wife? A family? How about children?"

"No, he is not married. He lives alone. He does have children by his first wife, but I have no way of getting in touch with them," she answered. "And officer, you may want to get in touch with Oak Lawn Funeral Home. His brother Bill owns Oak Lawn."

"You mean his brother is Bill Williams? The Bill Williams who's on Governor Graham's staff?" inquired a lieutenant.

"Yes, that's correct, but I know that he is not in town. Earlier, Ronnie was telling us he was with the governor somewhere down in the Tampa Bay area. He's supposed to be back in town tomorrow afternoon."

SUDDENLY THE ENTIRE scene took on a total different appearance. Since his death, the body had been left on the ground in the grotesques position where he had fallen. His fingers and hands had turned a light shade of blue. His knuckles were black and blue where he had tried in vain to push himself from the cold ground before the fatal blast exploded his heart. His hands showed clearly the lasting impression on his left ring finger, although his hands were speckled with dried, caked dark blood. His ring had been well hidden.

With their new knowledge, the police were now assured the deceased was not in fact a derelict or transient and reacted accordingly. As the message quickly spread to every gawker on site, his body was immediately covered and lifted from the ground onto a stretcher. The atmosphere at the scene remarkably changed in a few short minutes.

ON HIS FRONT living room wall Ronnie had thumbtacked a small piece of cardboard displaying a quotation. One which perhaps proclaimed the wisdom of what was to someday come true, the truth of his death. It read, "How can I believe you're telling the truth when I know that if I were in your place I'd lie like hell."

"Thank you very much for the inscribed copy of "RONNIE". You were kind go share your work with me and I appreciate your thoughtfulness. Thanks, too for your moving letter. I admire your determination to ensure that tragedies such as the one that claimed Ronnie's life do not happen to other young people.

Former President Bill Clinton

22

BULLET HOLES
IN BEAR BRYANT'S HAT

ON MONDAY, THE day before the shooting, Bill and his friend Buddy Runnells from Fort Walton Beach had flown to Tampa to join others at a Key Advisors meeting that had been called by Governor Graham. Leaving Tampa on Tuesday afternoon, they flew into Eglin Air Force Base, Fort Walton Beach's commercial airport. At the terminal they were met by Buddy's wife, Bonnie, and Judy, a nice lady friend that Bill had been seeing.

After cocktails and much chatter about their meeting with the governor, they had a fine meal at the Landing Restaurant, then the couples went their separate ways. Bill would spend the night in Destin and take care of some business at a 9:00 o'clock meeting the following morning before driving to Pensacola.

SHORTLY AFTER 8:00 o'clock and two cups of hot coffee, Bill called his office, a ritual each morning after being away from the city overnight. His secretary told him that Ronnie had died. He immediately assumed from natural causes and did not concern himself with any details. He knew the most imperative thing was to leave immediately for Pensacola and drive directly to his mother's home.

As was the norm, he instinctively tuned his car radio to WCOA for all of the up-to-the-minute local morning news. He hadn't the vaguest idea that his brother had been murdered by officers of the Pensacola Police Department until the radio gave the gory details, which not only shocked him thoroughly but saddened him to tears.

He reached for his car phone to call his mother, then, thinking better, he decided against it. He again called his office and told his secretary that he had just heard the details on the radio. He asked her to call his mother's home and tell whoever answered the phone that he would be there within the hour.

When he arrived, there were already several cars in the driveway and twice as many parked at the curb. Sandi had arrived and was helping out around the house and greeting Mother's friends, mainly church members. After speaking to everyone, he and his mother closed themselves in her bedroom where they remained for a half hour or more.

As in the greatest of Southern traditions when someone experiences the loss of a family member, their friends quickly rally to their side. The kitchen was beginning to overflow with food, dishes of every sort brought in by neighbors and friends.

In the afternoon Fred Levin called and asked if he could come over. Mother welcomed him as a lifelong friend of Ronnie's, a friend of the entire Williams family and someone she respected very much as an outstanding attorney. Other of Ronnie's friends called and left word they would visit with the family at Oak Lawn when visitation hours were scheduled.

When Fred arrived, he, Bill, Sandi and their mother excused themselves from the others and moved into the front living room where they tried to put together the pieces of the puzzling events of a few hours past.

"Fred, what can be done? Why did the police have to murder him?" she asked in a quivering and agitated voice.

"Mrs. Williams, I don't know the answers to that. No one does. I can only speculate as to what may have actually occurred. Until the police reports are written and made available to us, we will just have to wonder."

"I want to sue them. Not for the money. I'd just give that away. But I want to sue them for murdering my son. Such a terrible loss. Parents aren't supposed to bury their kids. It should be the other way around."

She wept.

"Can we file suit, Fred?" Bill asked.

"Well, I don't know. If he came from the apartment and shot at them, as the radio was reporting, then there's not a chance in hell that we could win. You know it would be the word of several officers against a deceased person. That's just how the system works."

"But what if he didn't shoot?"

"How you gonna prove that, Bill? How you gonna prove it?"

"We'll see."

LEAVING HIS MOTHER'S home Bill was compelled to go directly to Ronnie's apartment. From his car he called the Lewises to tell them he was coming by and wanted to talk with them; however, that conversation would have to wait until after the funeral. What he wanted now was a key to the apartment.

Don and Pat met him at their back door with the key.

"Bill, Pat and I both are absolutely sick this happened. How is your mother doing?" Don asked.

"As you can imagine, not well. Not well at all. But thanks for asking. I want to sit down with the two of you after the funeral and talk in detail. I know you understand this is not the time."

"Certainly, we understand. But let me say just one thing. I have known Ronnie for some time, and never have I ever seen him so scared. There is no question in our minds that he believed someone was breaking into the apartment. All he was doing was running for his life. The plain-dressed officers did nothing but make the situation much worse. Bill, we'll see you at the services. Please give our best to Mrs. Williams, and tell her to call if there is anything we can do."

"Thanks, y'all. See you later."

AT THE END of a very long and trying day, Bill waited until pitch dark before he returned to the apartment. He wanted to see for himself exactly what Ronnie had seen during his last few minutes.

Arriving at the apartment, he noticed that the postman had left the day's mail. While Ronnie was living in Tallahassee, his

This picture clearly shows six bullet holes, four in the glass and two in the woodwork. The Pensacola Police Department reported only four shots were fired inside his apartment. You be the judge, and count them for yourself.

landlord had been kind enough to forward it to him, but under the circumstances he must not have been sure what to do now. Both pieces had been left as delivered.

The skeleton key unlocked the door with ease. Feeling around in the dark, he flipped on the ceiling light in the living room, then glanced at the mail he was holding. One was a card, a reminder that the electric bill needed to be paid. The other was a letter marked personal and confidential from the Northwest Florida Water Management District. Inside was Ronnie's official letter of dismissal as an employee of the state.

Placing the letters in the vest pocket of his coat, he stepped into the hall and pulled briskly on the stubborn string attached to the bulb in the ceiling, then switched on the bedroom and bath lights.

He was shocked beyond belief to see the large quantity of beer cans, cigarette butts and empty cigarette cartons littering the floor on both sides of the bed. There were three liquor bottles, and each had a tad of spirits remaining.

Even in his sorrow he could not help but smile. He was remembering only a few weeks earlier when Ronnie told him that he never drank the last shot from any bottle. He said that he always wanted to be able to tell anyone who asked him if he had finished off the bottle, he could honestly say "no." This was vintage Ronnie.

Being careful not to touch anything except the light switches, he took note of the entire apartment. Everything was captured in his photographic memory. Standing silently, his mind worked feverishly, wondering what had happened to his older brother during his last minutes on earth.

Walking over to the window, he could plainly see four bullet holes in the glass panes and two more in the wooden trim work. Without touching it, he bent over and examined closer the Bear Bryant's "Hounds Tooth Hat" which was resting on top of the five-foot-tall dresser. He could clearly see where two bullets had penetrated the hat, then continued through the glass.

Turning around, he stepped into the living room and turned off the light then jerked hard on the hall light, then the bedroom and bathroom lights. He stood for several minutes in the bedroom door gazing steadily at the window and waiting until his eyes adjusted to the darkness.

With his vision clearer and thoughts coming together, he wondered if what he was seeing could have been the reason for Ronnie's ultimate and final problem? A set of weird circumstances which caused him the loss of his life. He wondered if this was what Ronnie saw that frightened him out of his wits?

The outline of the black and white checkered hat sitting on top of the wooden dresser was plainly illuminated by the glow cast from a streetlight on the corner of Strong and 18th Avenue, a half block to the west. Clearly, this picture, this scene, could have easily been misinterpreted, confusing and frightening to anyone, especially someone who had been drinking. The view against the dingy glass window panes looked exactly as if a man wearing a hat was peeking into his bedroom window.

LEAVING THE APARTMENT, he again walked to the spot where Ronnie had fallen. Earlier in the afternoon, although he was not ready to discuss with the Lewises the details of what actually had happened last night, he had asked them to point out where Ronnie died. Dried blood had caked the ground. He was shocked and amazed at the lack of sensitivity on the part of the police department for not cleaning up the gruesome evidence of death.

Moving away from the site, he stood in silence for several minutes looking in the direction but only occasionally focusing on the fatal spot. Although he did not wave or acknowledge their presence, he was aware that Pat and Don were standing in their kitchen watching each step he took, each expression on his face.

The Rolodex of his mind was trying to remember an old Hank Williams song that Ronnie often played. It was only vaguely familiar to him, and he couldn't remember the words but bits and pieces of verses kept coming to mind. "His heart went to heaven at the first fall of snow," and something about "surely the robins wept."

Surely with the coming of the morning, the robins would again weep. This time for a man who found that life simply demanded much more than he could give. A man who spent a lifetime chasing a dream that was never to be, a dream way too far.

During his heyday he glistened ever so brightly, then slipped silently into everyone's shadow. Those he cherished and adored became bright lights, far too distant for him to reach. Too far, at least too far within his mind's eye, to even recognize the equality of former friends and teammates. No matter what goals they had accomplished in their life, all of them had outdistanced themselves from this man who never caught up. He was truly left behind in the shadows of those who were once his equal. However, some, if not most, were his lesser lights although he could not personally conceive this to be true.

FLOWERS AND SYMPATHY cards began arriving at Oak Lawn bright and early on Thursday morning. By late afternoon the chapel walls were lined with all varieties of arrangements, some with miniature footballs placed strategically around the buds.

Shortly after 5:00 o'clock, those wishing to pay their last respects began to gather. Many were longtime friends of the family from the congregation of the Brownsville Baptist Church, Ronnie's church since the fourth grade.

Teammates from Pensacola High and their coaches stood outside under the carport and chatted, recalling the glory days when they had won the state of Florida Football Championship in 1953. And just how sweet the victory over Jesuit High!

Friends that Ronnie had known for years and some newer acquaintances talked about his many traits, early accomplishments. And they couldn't forget the countless numbers of opportunities which came his way. All the ones he failed to nurture. Fred Levin remarked that Ronnie was without a doubt the best natural athlete that he had ever seen play the game of football.

Some classmates expressed their sadness that he was not present for his 25th Class Reunion which had been held last fall. They had a great turnout of the class of more than 600.

While such an occasion is never a happy one, the family did enjoy reacquainting themselves with many of Ronnie's friends whom they had not seen in several years. Bill would tell his mother later that evening that he, surprisingly, picked up bits and pieces from the attitude of several friends that they were really not too astonished at his death. Certainly not meaning his death caused by the circumstances which fate dealt him in the end, but not too shocked that his life had ended at an early age.

It quickly became quite apparent that some of Ronnie's friends who were often around him were more aware of his carefree lifestyle than his family had come to realize. Perhaps close relatives fail to observe some of the more obvious traits, mannerisms or characteristics which display themselves so often that they lose a good deal of their meaning or importance.

AN OAK LAWN limousine and two sedans arrived at Mrs. Williams's home to pick up her and the family members who had gathered. Not unlike countless numbers of others who had placed the care of their loved ones with these professionals, Ronnie's family was shown the utmost courtesy and care, nothing more nor certainly nothing less.

Arriving through the rear entrance gates the automobiles eased under the rear portico. The family was taken through the private entrance and escorted into the solitary seating section of the chapel, an area designed especially for only the immediate family members. All three of Ronnie's children, their mother and Crockett, her husband, had gathered with the rest of the family.

Bill, seeing how the west side of the city was rapidly expanding and knowing it did not have a funeral chapel, built Oak Lawn from scratch and opened it six years earlier. Although sole proprietor, he, himself, held no professional or occupational license for its operations. He was blessed with a fine, courteous staff of well-trained professionals who handled the day-to-day operations of the establishment and did so with the greatest of personal care.

By 10:00 o'clock the chapel was filled with friends and family members. Many came to the service who were unable or had chosen not to attend last night's visitation. Tradition finds that a number of people will come to visit during a wake but for personal reasons would not attend a service. On the other hand, many would pass up the routine of visiting the evening before and only attend the service. It's just about an equal number either way.

THE MINISTER SPOKE of Ronnie's life as an athlete and his many accomplishments on the football field. And of his loving family and his many friends who cared greatly for him and were deeply saddened by his sudden loss, especially under such horrendous circumstances.

For the second time in the short span of only 46 months, Bill slipped from the private seating area and eased down the aisle. He paused in front of the casket and first reflected on the funeral of his father, then to the chore at hand. It seemed as though it was just yesterday when the same staff attendant had removed the spray which adorned his father's casket. Now it was happening all over once again and much too soon.

After a few personal moments, he neatly folded the satin cloth from around the edge over into the casket and slowly lowered the heavy stainless steel lid into place. After slowly turning the handle which tightly sealed the unit, he stepped aside while the attendant replaced the flower arrangement.

As he did with his father and as a final honor and tribute to his brother, he would drive the hearse to Bayview Park Cemetery.

ALTHOUGH RONNIE'S LIFE on earth was over, his impact on his family and countless numbers of friends would last for ages. And for the next two years his case, his death and the issue of alcoholism would bounce around the circuit courts, then finally to Florida's First District Court of Appeals.

"I just finished reading 'RONNIE'. After reading it I experienced a feeling I never felt after reading a book. I too play football. I play for Tate. I am in the 10th grade. I received the book free of cost from Coach Leonard; he gave everyone on the team a copy. "I understand the problems of having a person with a drinking problem. My father has a very serious problem with drinking. But reading your book is inspiring to me. I was breath taken by the way RONNIE played footballand the way he conducted (his) life around football. I only can hope and pray that I can play with the authority and skill he had. I only wanted to write this because I felt that God had it in my heart to read the book and write and commend you for the great book. And you and yourfamily's strength during the time of Ronnie's death is inspiring to all. May God be with you and your family."

Student at Tate High School
Cantonment, Florida

23

THE SHOOTING
WAS NOT ACCIDENTAL,
HIS DEATH WAS

BILL HAD INFORMED the Pensacola Police Department that he wanted to come by on Saturday to retrieve Ronnie's personal possessions which they had removed from his body. His attitude, while reserved and cautious, was that of a man who was visiting the very same bunch of trigger-happy cops who blatantly, and completely without cause, had killed his brother just days previously.

Reluctantly, he signed for Ronnie's personal property. Items, of little value, items which had meaning and purpose only to Ronnie. In a cold and deliberate fashion the desk sergeant read the list: one brown wallet with miscellaneous papers, two packs of Camel cigarettes, one key chain with four keys, one watch, one black comb, one BIC lighter, one vial containing 34 prescription capsules from Dr. Permenter, two pieces of candy, $47 in bills and $1.55 in change, one gold-colored money clip, a pair of boots with socks and a pair of undershorts.

TONY RIHA CALLED and volunteered to come to Ronnie's apartment to give a hand in cleaning up or to help out anyway he could. On Monday, he and Bill spent the day loading and hauling off cluttered trash, empty beer cans and such. Ronnie's clothing, bed dressings and towels were donated to the Goodwill Store. His small record collection was placed in storage and his books taken to his mother's home where she would eventually read each, several times. For fear of throwing away something of value, not monetary but sentimental, nothing was tossed until thoroughly examined.

SCATTERED ABOUT THE small apartment items were found that would have meaning only to him. On a small make-shift table was a nondescript record player, not a stereo, and per-haps 20 albums. Some with wellworn covers, some naked. For the last several years these had served as his avenues of escape, the only escape that he really knew. His only deliverance from reality were the sounds within the electronic grooves of the round, black discs. Time and again, over and over, these songs offered to Ronnie a world well beyond his reach, well beyond his grasp. A world way too far.

Throughout his adult life he had never worshiped material things. He never mastered any opportunity which came his way or perfected a personal drive to see a future any brighter than his bleak daily existence. Somewhere along the line he gave up on all possibility of hope except surviving day to day, and that, within itself, was a skillful goal and marvelous undertaking.

Knowing some of his habits, his family knew they should take extreme care before throwing anything in the trash. Not only was every drawer and cabinet gone over with a fine-toothed comb, so was every pocket of every shirt, slacks and other pieces of clothing.

After finding notes and other pictures hidden between the paper fillings of one 8x10 photograph frame, they became even more concerned, suspicious and inquisitive of perhaps other hid-ing places.

Before throwing away any prepared foods from the refrig-erator or stove top, each was gone over thoroughly. His mother was surprised, yet not really at all, when she poured the molded pot of blackeyed peas into a colander and ran steamy hot water over them. The force of the hot water broke up the peas which had jelled together with the grease and oils of the ham hocks. There, shining in the glow of the kitchen ceiling light, she discovered Ronnie's very last secret. His diamond ring was found just where he had hidden it.

The search was not for the purpose of finding anything of value as they were assured there was nothing more expensive than the ring. But they searched in an effort to uncover something, anything, which would shed a glimmer of light on his personal feelings, his private moments prior to his death.

They searched for any clue that would aide them in better understanding just what his mental thoughts and feelings were over the past several months. They searched diligently to find some answers, some reasons, even a single reason; however, they would be denied his secrets because every last one of them was kept entombed deep within himself and shared with no one but me.

ANOTHER UNEASY TASK that Bill had been dreading came about in the middle of the week. He had picked up the necessary insurance papers which had to be executed by his mother. Although the reality of Ronnie's horrendous murder had been accepted, still the signing and execution of the required papers to collect death benefits was something no one faced with comfort.

Scattered over the next few days, several important meetings were scheduled. One was a visit with State Attorney Curtis Golden. The result of the meeting produced some good news, that is, if any good news could possibly come from such a tragedy. Mr. Golden assured Bill that as soon as his investigation was completed, a letter was to be written to his mother detailing the findings. And from what he knew of the situation thus far, he unequivocally stated that, had Ronnie only been wounded and not killed, he would not have been charged with any criminal activity.

Indeed, on March 27th Mr. Golden sent Ron's mother a letter and in part it so stated:

> "It is our opinion that your son was not committing any crime at the time of his death and that the police officers by whom he was shot had no intent of killing him at the time of the shooting.
>
> From our investigation, it appears that your son was un-

der the misapprehension the officers were people trying to kill him and while the officers felt they were defending their lives at the time of the shooting, there was no intent on their part to kill him.

More simply stated, while the shooting was not accidental, it is our opinion that his death was.

RONNIE'S DEATH TOOK a toll not only on his family but also on many of his close friends, friends who had known him since boyhood years. Several phone calls were made to his mom by those who confronted themselves openly about their personal lifestyle. Most of them questioned whether or not they, themselves, perhaps, just perhaps, had also abused the good life a bit too much. His demise weighed heavily on several and perchance changed the personal habits of some.

Of those making comments, some expressed their feelings in very different ways. Some promised to eliminate alcohol completely from their lives while others committed to take a more modest approach of evaluating their habits to make certain they were not going over the edge.

ON SUNDAY, FEBRUARY 24th, Paul Jasper wrote a column in the *Pensacola News Journal* that presented a question that begged for an answer. Maybe Paul's concern was a roundabout way of expressing himself through a comparison. The column read:

> They were just ordinary looking cowboy hats, no different than thousands of others people wear just for fun. Even the silver concho hatband on one of them was not really all that unusual.
>
> Just a coincidence of time and circumstances linked the two hats, in my mind, with a night which began with a tinge of farce and ended in tragedy.
>
> Still, the story may be worth telling, if only as another confirmation of the validity of the parable of the blind men and the elephant.
>
> Most people know the parable where one blind man touched the elephant's tail, one the side, one the leg, one the trunk, and from the touch each man formed a remark-

able different concept of how such a beast must look—like a rope, like a wall, like a tree, like a snake.

Such a concept may be mine.

At least...I hope so.

It began the day I encountered Jack Collins while he was replacing his old hatband with a belt of silver conchos.

Ordinarily, Jack, a handsome, stylishly-coiffed man-about-town, in his early 40s, is impeccably dressed; three-piece suit, cufflinks, the works. This day, he was arrayed in cowboy regalia from head to foot.

I kidded him in the way of people who've known each other, here and about, for years.

"Jackson, who are you supposed to be? Sundance? The Concho Kid? With that outfit all you need is a gun, and you could be Wild Bill Hickok."

He laughed.

"Well, PJ, it makes a change from my usual image. A guy's got to do something a little different every now and then."

"Sure. Why not?"

"But," Jack said, sobering a trifle, "I don't really know why I wear this hat. I don't even own a gun. But every time I wear this hat I get in some kind of trouble."

"Ha," I grinned, "Bub, it ain't the hat. It's you."

So I forgot it. Until a few days later when I again ran into Jack, who was looking considerably chastened.

"What's the matter, Jackson?" I said.

"You remember me telling how I always get in trouble when I wear my cowboy hat?"

"Sure."

"Well, I put it on the other night and went over to the beach and went into this bar, and they told me I couldn't stay there wearing a hat.

"I got mad and left and started back to Pensacola.

"I made a wrong turn, somehow; got in the wrong traffic lane. I decided I'd better not try to back up so I bumped across the divider.

"And sure enough, right there was that blue light.

"He charged me with willful and wanton reckless driving."

The hat. If Jack hadn't been wearing the hat, and banned from the bar for that reason, the whole thing might have happened differently. Still, with this alone, I wouldn't have thought it more than a coincidence, and a rather humorous one. Jack talked one day of his hat getting him into trouble, and it in fact came true not long after.

I just laughed and told him to throw the hat away.

Then I remembered something else, and counted back. And began to wonder.

Jack was given his ticket on February 12th.

The same evening, I recalled, I had been waiting for Mary in an eastside establishment not far from my house when a man wearing a cowboy hat and dark glasses walked in.

I glanced up, thinking, until he spoke, that it was Jack.

"Hi, Paul. Haven't seen you in a long time."

It wasn't Jack. But I knew him. Like Jack, he was a handsome, friendly fellow I've seen around for years, usually well dressed, now just relaxing in his cowboy hat.

"Oh, hi bub," I said. "I didn't recognize you hiding behind all that regalia. You ought to get silver conchos for a hatband, like Jack Collins."

Then, thinking no more of the hat, I added:

"Where you been?"

"Oh, I've been around. I've been working for the state."

Mary walked in. We chatted with him for a couple of minutes longer and then started to leave.

"Mrs. Jasper," he said, smiling, engaging in the raillery that more often than not accompanies a compliment, "I just want to tell you that even though Paul is kind of stupid-looking I think he writes about the best column I've ever read."

I laughed. Mary laughed.

"No telling about some people's taste," I told him.

And, then:

"Goodnight, Ronnie."

"Goodnight, Paul, Mrs. Jasper."

Within hours of this conversation, Ronnie, Ronnie Williams, was dead.

Early Wednesday, February 13, Ronnie, for reasons unknown to anyone, began shooting a pistol in his apartment. When police arrived, he burst onto the street, gun in hand, and was promptly hit by two bullets fired from police officers' weapons.

No news story mentioned it, so I don't know if Ronnie had the hat on when he charged out onto the street.

But since then I've been wondering, off and on, a bit uneasily:

Was Ronnie totally responsible for his actions?"

Or were they, somehow, related to the wearing of an ordinary looking cowboy hat? A hat which, like Jack's brought trouble—and in Ronnie's case more trouble than anyone could handle?

Of course, that's the blind man's concept of an elephant: his mind envisions the whole based upon what he has personally experienced.

The conversations with Jack, the brief connection my mind made between the two men before Ronnie spoke, the fact that the two police-related incidents occurred the same night, do not really make a pattern; they are just the parts I touched.

It was all just a coincidence.

Wasn't it...?

AFTER THE COLUMN was published, Bill again reviewed and traced Ronnie's activities on that fatal night, this time in much more detail and with greater investigative interest. Ronnie, in fact, had been wearing the cowboy hat the night of his death. However, after returning home from Sir Richards, he had laid it on his dresser besides his Bear Bryant hat. While the Bryant hat had suffered bullet strikes, his white cowboy hat was left unscathed.

In the police photos of the murder scene and in the report filed by Officer Pelham, the trigger-happy cop who exploded his powerful .357 magnum into Ronnie's back, it was noted that Pelham had lost his hat. Perhaps it was when he was scurrying around madly trying to cower behind the bushes. The civilian hat was clearly seen in several photos laying on the ground just a few feet from Ronnie's lifeless body.

EVER SINCE THE tragedy, Bill had agonized over his brother's death. Why did he have to die? He never hurt anyone. He kept to himself. Why was he murdered as he was? Hundreds of tormenting questions and shallow, meaningless answers continued to haunt him.

While the Williams family possesses within their genes a

streak of stubbornness, they also have an immeasurable, warm and compassionate, never-ending adoration and devotion for those whom they have loved in the past, both family and friends. Although circumstances and situations may change beyond their control, their true, lifelong feelings for others never do.

Almost daily, since that dreaded night of Valentine's Eve 1980, Bill had been confronted with pestering, agonizing, "what ifs." He had given Ronnie a job on two separate occasions and was directly instrumental for his last employment with the state, yet he still despairs with thoughts of not helping enough. Not being there when it mattered the most. But he also understood that Ronnie would often be standoffish and way too proud to accept any meaningful assistance, especially if it came from his younger brother.

After many years of examining the most infinitesimal clues and analyzing, as much as possible, Ronnie's later years, Bill had grown weary after learning just how miserable, how tormented and alone Ronnie was the last several years of his life. And perhaps even more so his last evening on earth.

Among all the unanswered questions, personal mistakes and painful emptiness, there remained two missed opportunities which haunted Bill every day of his life. One, possibly much more important than the other.

He learned several years after Ronnie's death that a game video of the Rose Bowl was available. While this would be of little significance to the rest of the world, had Ronnie seen it perhaps it would have regenerated some self-confidence in himself.

If he could have again viewed himself as someone in action, someone who was in command of the situation, then maybe, just maybe, he could have recaptured his self-worth which had abandoned him years earlier. Perhaps for the cost of a video and a few cents postage, this could have made a difference. But too late; is forever too late.

The second and perhaps most important mistake was the reluctance of Bill to act on an idea he had thought of many times. Perhaps another missed opportunity to have accomplished something that would have been extremely meaningful to Ronnie. Without a doubt it would have changed his life, maybe for the better, maybe for the worse. But changed it would have been.

While Bill knew that Ronnie was overtaken and in complete awe by the performance and personalities of both Hank Williams and Elvis Presley, he didn't think of the idea until after Elvis's passing. And then, finding the answer after Ronnie's death, it sickened him.

A week or so after Ronnie's funeral he began a search to locate Red West. Using his connections in Governor Graham's office, they located Red's brother, Tom, an employee of the Florida Department of Transportation. From him an address and phone number for Red was obtained. He and his family were living in Ventura, California. The call was placed. Red was overtaken and saddened to learn of the death of his longtime friend and most disheartened to hear of the tragic circumstances.

Bill had to ask the question, he had to have an answer. He explained just how much Ronnie adored Elvis, his songs, movies, lifestyle and, yes, the adoration of thousands of muffins. And just how much he enjoyed seeing television news reports of Elvis's concerts and was always searching for Red. And at times how close he personally felt, as if he was actually there sharing in the moment of excitement. Bill assured Red that Ronnie was indeed there, mentally there in every concert, every movie. Right there walking alongside his good friend, Red West.

He explained that Ronnie had seen all of Elvis's movies and watched closely for Red to make his appearance. Of the 33 Elvis movies Red holds the record of appearing in more of them than does anyone else, well over half.

He told Red that Ronnie saved and replayed, time and again, the video which highlighted Elvis and him leaving a concert and Elvis making a comment which sent Red into a rampage of laughter. Red remembered the incident very well.

Knowing of the closeness of the Memphis Mafia, Bill had to know if Ronnie would have fit-in and would Elvis have offered an invitation had he known of his interest. Given his looks, wit, personality, toughness, his flamboyancy on the football field, would Elvis have welcomed him into this close-knit group of confidants?

While he wanted the answer to be a "yes," at the same time he was afraid it would be. Red assured him that Ronnie was precisely the type person that Elvis wanted around him. Red

Ronnie's great friend Red West and Bill Williams, the author.

expressed a profound personal hurt that he had not known of Ronnie's plight over the years.

He was disappointed that he had not learned in time as he was sure a position with the Presley entourage would have been his for the asking. He furthermore assured Bill that Elvis would have been most pleased to have had someone around with Ronnie's ability to sketch caricatures. Elvis would have loved to have had sketches for the purpose of the moment as well as for his family and heirs.

He also assured Bill that, because of Elvis's great love of football, had the Rose Bowl tape of the 1955 game been available, Elvis would have been most impressed with Ronnie's performance. He would have been delighted to have had him as a member of the group.

Bill got the answer he had dreaded, an answer which left him with a depressed feeling of regret. Regrets that continue to haunt him until this day. Regrets about something that he maybe could have done differently, done better. Feelings and mistakes that forever and eternity can never be corrected. Decisions that he will have to live with forever.

"I commend you for the work you do, and I thank you for sharing your story with me. I wish you the best of luck in your efforts to eradicate the horrors that can result from underage drinking. Our country is fortunate to have men like you working for our youth."

J. Dennis Hastert, Speaker
U.S. House of Representatives

24

LAW ENFORCEMENT OR OTHERWISE?

MRS. WILLIAMS HAD called Bill's office at the capitol in Tallahassee and left word for him to return her call as soon as possible. She had called and asked him to come home to spend the weekend with her. He knew the time was long overdue for her to finally open up and talk about Ronnie's death. On Saturday noon she fixed his favorite meal, then began to vent her anger at the loss of her older son.

"This ordeal has been so very hard on me. I've tried to keep it inside and have done a good job so far, but the anger has built and built. I just had to talk about it."

"I know, Mom. Sandi's accident, then losing Dad not too long ago, your health problems, and now this. I know it's been wearing you down. It's been terrible for all of us, but for you I know it's got to be pure torment."

"How in the world can the authorities call his murder justified homicide?" She asked. "Being killed at his own front door by three, not one, mind you, but three trigger-happy policemen. Honey, all he was doing was running from his own home when he though someone was breaking in through his window. The gun in his hand was for his own protection. The law provides that we can protect ourselves and our property. That's all he was doing."

"I know. I know. We'll get to the end of this, I promise you. It may take awhile, but I promise that we will have our say," responded Bill.

"The first thing he saw when he ran outside was two men in

plain clothes. He had no earthly idea they may have been policemen," she said while fighting back tears. "They had parked down the block and were creeping up on him exactly like a burglar would have done. They were just nosing around his front yard exactly like a burglar would do before he breaks into a home.

"You know as well as I do when you give some officers a badge and a weapon with the freedom to use it, some will do almost anything to show off their authority. This is what happened that night, three trigger-happy, gun-crazed officers doing as they well pleased. That sorry Pelham even shot him in the back. When you have to shoot someone in the back, you are not much of a man, I can tell you that for sure.

"For more than 30 years our family has been in business in Pensacola, and we've contributed to every fund-raising event that law enforcement agencies have asked of us. I would bet you that your dad had given more than a hundred thousand dollars to different and sundry projects and God only knows to how many political campaigns.

"We have always been a law-abiding family. We taught each of you kids to mind the law and to respect the reputation of the law enforcement community; now something like this happens."

"Mom, did you know that at Oak Lawn we have a standing policy that our services are completely free to any law enforcement officer who loses his life in the line of duty? For that matter, we even extend it to any military service personnel who are killed while on active duty. This is one of the ways that Oak Lawn supports law enforcement and the military."

"No, I didn't know that. Son, that's a great idea. I'm glad you're doing it.

"You know, Ronnie had no enemies. None what so ever. Sure he had a drinking problem, but so do many folks around here. And, believe me, a lot of them are walking the streets today, and no one knows of their addiction.

"There is not one medical facility in this city equipped to properly handle the type of problems which haunted and controlled Ronnie's life. Alcoholics are a special breed who need to be better understood. No one tries to understand, sympathize, care for or show these people a true and kind attitude or a concern which is sadly needed. Not a facility in Pensacola has properly trained and educated personnel to perfect a program which is absolutely essential to conquer the cause and effect of the problem. Perhaps this incident, the loss of Ronnie's life, will open some eyes to the problem."

Bill agreed, then hushed so she could continue to vent her anger.

"Ronnie seldom went drinking outside of his own home. He was so embarrassed about his problem that he attempted to hide it by being withdrawn from even his friends. I personally know this is true as he and I talked about it often. Had he been more open and aboveboard, then maybe he could have gotten more help."

"Mother, you did everything in the world that you could have done. I have wished a million times that I had known more about his problems. I confess I really was in the dark as I am sure many of his friends were. How I failed to recognize it is beyond me."

"Our local hospitals just don't want to be bothered with this type problem," she said. "About three days is as long as they will keep someone with the disease. And, yes, without question, it is a disease, make no bones about it. A disease far worse than the dreaded cancer that has the world in turmoil all the time."

"Mother, I may disagree with you on that point. I am not personally convinced that alcoholism is a disease. In my mind a disease is something that you cannot choose to have. To me a disease is something that you have no say so about when it's in control of your body. For instance, you can't choose to have cancer. If you have it, then you have it. On the other hand, again in my opinion, you can choose not to be an alcoholic. At least not be a participating alcoholic."

"Well son, we could argue that point all day. But I choose to think of it as a horrible disease that afflicts millions of people around the globe every day of their lives."

"Perhaps you're right. Mom, I just don't know for sure. But let me tell you something. One time a doctor posed this question to me. He asked, 'If alcoholism is a disease, then why do we have AA chapters?' He obviously meant AA can't change or affect the cause of a disease. And you're right; we could discuss this all day. Sorry for the interruption."

She continued, "Would you think it would have taken six or

seven officers shooting their high-powered guns to bring him down in his own front yard? And shooting him in the back! What cowards. What a cowardly act.

"To my knowledge Ronnie never had even received a speeding ticket. He was literally scared to death to drive drunk knowing the consequences might send him to jail. He would have gone stark raving mad had he ever had to spend a single night behind bars. Being hemmed up would have destroyed him.

"Did you know that he kept the names of several law enforcement personnel in a book so he could call them if he needed help? And he never needed help any more than he did the night they gunned him down. He never had time to make a call. He didn't know that he needed help. For God's sake, all he was doing was notifying the cops that someone was breaking into his apartment. How in the world would he even remotely think they would be the culprits who gunned him down?

"There are no words in my vocabulary to describe the torment and heartache that his tragedy has put me through. I am sick inside. Torn up. A total mental wreck."

"Mother, I know. We will find justice. Somehow we will find the answers. Nothing will bring Ronnie back, and that hurts. It hurts all of us equally; we all loved him very much. You remember the afternoon after the shooting when Fred Levin came to visit you?"

"Yeah, I remember. What about it?"

"Well, Fred said there was nothing from a legal standpoint that we could do because it would be the word of several officers against that of a deceased person. Now, I know for sure that Ronnie did not shoot his gun outside the apartment, and I can prove it.

"When they said he failed to stop when they ordered him to, perhaps he didn't. But I can prove for certain that he did not shoot at them as one of them claimed in his written report. And, by the way, there was only one officer that made such a statement. None of the others said that he fired outside the apartment.

"Mother, it may take some time to prove my point, but I have a lot of time to spare, and I promise you I'll see it to the very end."

"I'm not bitter because I refuse to let myself be," she said as tears poured from her eyes. "But my heart is broken. Neither of the officers who was so quick to pull his trigger that night has even had the decency to come by and talk with me. I think that is a shame. I think it a real shame the taxpayers have no idea that some of the law enforcement officers they are employing have such a low degree of personal pride and self-control.

"It's hard to realize that Ron will not be with us for the holidays. His birthday. Special times and occasions. Never again. His life was taken in its prime. Such a waste. Such a miserable waste.

"None of us will ever know just how many people were actually involved with his death, but I think society in general will have to take some of the responsibility. Then conceivably, hundreds of others who suffer the same affliction may some day be better off because Ronnie lost his life in this sad, dreadful way.

"So much pressure is put on folks by their peers and so called friends to live it up. People often go blindly forward until they decide they are losing control of their life and then suddenly wake up and realize they are out of control and can do nothing about it. And when it's already too late, a life of hell begins. Just a man and his bottle for the rest of his life.

"While Ronnie's drinking problem cost him his life, at least he wasn't robbing a service station or a bank or wasn't mugging someone on the street, thank God. I know the men who were so trigger happy on that fatal night will one day have to meet their Maker and there give an account to the One to whom they will not be able to tell a lie.

"Sure, the officials and the courts can call it justifiable homicide all they want, and, because they do, the wealthy insurance companies won't have to pay double indemnity coverage. But we all, including every last one of them, know his life was an accidental casualty. No doubt about it. Period. End of report.

"You see, it seems that people who try to live correctly and do right are most often the ones who are punished the most. But thanks be to God that one day all the wrongs will be made right, and there will be no wrong decisions."

"Mom, maybe we can do something to help those who need it the most. Perhaps this will open some doors."

"Maybe so, son. I hope I can live long enough to see a hospital in Pensacola that could, and happily would, care for sick people with this awful disease and do so at an affordable cost.

"This may never come about, but I hope the community will pull together to bring those who are sick out of the closet and demand they be treated properly. Perhaps something good will come from his death after all. Maybe so."

"Mother, we haven't talked about it, and since you haven't mentioned it perhaps you didn't realize they did an autopsy?"

"No. No, I didn't know that. Why did they, and who gave them permission?" she asked in a rather stern voice and with narrowing eyes.

"No one gave them permission because in such cases it is mandatory. It's just one of the things they do."

"When was it done?"

"I believe it was done at the University Hospital. I think a Doctor Birdwell did the work. I don't know him, but I think his title is something like the City Medical Examiner or maybe it's the County or perhaps the State Medical Examiner. Anyway, he did a full autopsy about mid morning after the shooting."

"You mean after the murder don't you?" she responded while correcting him.

"Yes, Mother."

"It was murder. A plain and simple case of murder. You mustn't ever forget that. Son, you must not ever, never, forget that. It is most important that you don't," she stressed.

"I understand. Listen, Mom, this morning I went by my post office, and Dr. Birdwell's office sent a copy of the autopsy like I had asked them to do. You need to know, and I have no idea the significance of it, but you need to know that a lesion was found somewhere on Ronnie's brain."

"What does that mean? I want to read the report," she demanded.

"Well, first, I don't know what it means, but you can be assured that I will have it read by a doctor friendly to our side of the equation. And, second, after I read the full autopsy, then I'll decide if you should see it."

"You'll do no sort. What do you mean you'll decide if I should see it. Of course, I'll see it. You know that."

"Mom, possibly there are things in it which you best not be bothered or concerned with. Know what I mean?"

"I'll read the report. Where is it?" she demanded to know.

"It's in the car. Let me take it back to Tallahassee along with the report I've received from the FDLE, then I'll bring it home to you next weekend."

"What's the FDLE?" she inquired.

"The Florida Department of Law Enforcement. I have some friends who work there. I'll get them to make me an appointment with one of their medical examiners, and he can explain the complete autopsy to me. If you insist on seeing and reading it, I'll bring it back to you with a full explanation about what I have learned."

"Yes, of course, I want to read it and any other reports written by anyone concerning my son's murder."

SLOPPY INVESTIGATIVE WORK, perhaps on purpose, by the Pensacola Police Officers who reported they found only four bullet holes where a gun had been discharged from inside the apartment. Any half blind, three-year-old could place his finger tip on six holes with little effort.

Apparently, they thought this number would wash with their superiors and give them the alibi needed to claim Ronnie discharged his weapon outside the apartment, thus firing at them. However, for their report to be valid, it would have to compare and match up with the ballistics report from the Florida Department of Law Enforcement.

The FDLE report clearly identified that a total of six shots had been fired from Ronnie's two guns. The two guns that he used the night of his death.

The arithmetic required was simple. In order to make things work in their favor and in accordance with the reports prepared by the officers of the Police Department, there could be no more than four bullet holes inside the apartment. It didn't take a mental giant to figure that one out.

This was not the case. Ronnie Williams did not discharge his pistol outside of his apartment. They were doing nothing more than creating false reports based on false evidence in an effort to cover their tracks. Trying as hard as they could to find justification for taking his life.

BILL STUDIED THE reports backward and forward dozens of times. He was convinced that after the first visit by the police, when they found the apartment in shambles with beer cans, liquor bottles and cigarette butts thrown about, that they had their minds made up that he was a derelict, a bum, an alcoholic, just a common drunk. If these officers had any degree of law enforcement intelligence, they could have prevented the entire episode from happening.

When they first arrived, Ronnie told them he thought someone was breaking into his apartment because he had seen them looking into his windows. The officers searched the small two-room building and obviously found no one. They knew he was hallucinating. They told his landlord he was. So why didn't these "trained" law enforcement personnel see with their own eyes the hat sitting on top of the dresser with a streetlight down the way lighting it up? This should have been obvious to them. Ronnie verbally gave them every clue they could possibly need. But, no, they hadn't any idea of what they were doing or should have been looking for.

When the police were called and returned to the scene the second time, they could not have cared less about what result the ultimate outcome would bring. They had no concern whatsoever for the person whose home was littered in the condition they had seen just minutes earlier. Ronnie's home, regardless of the physical condition, the maintenance or upkeep or the lack thereof, was his home. It was his castle. And what went on inside his home should not have been the concern of the police or anyone else for that matter.

When he ran out the front door, any policeman with an ounce of professional experience, keeping in mind the conditions that had been found 15 minutes earlier, should have been well aware of the personal circumstances of this frightened and tormented man. Their presence while standing in his front yard in pitch black dark literally frightened him to death. He changed his direction from running north in an effort to stay as far away from the "burglars" as possible. He reversed himself and ran in an easterly direction right into the arms of other plain-clothed officers who were totally concealed under the cloak of darkness.

Attempting to run through the carport, he tripped on a pile of firewood. Stumbling, he hurried himself from the woodpile and started around the southwest side of the carport post.

Officers reported that he "kept running, faster, running" while they demanded that he "stop." The fact is this athlete did not "keep running and running." When he left his home, he was at the spot of his destiny in a matter of three or four seconds. The entire distance couldn't have been 30 feet, or 40 at the very most. They enhanced their official reports by stating he ran a long distance to give themselves an alibi where they could report they had called for him to stop several times.

But with their magnums in hand, the trigger-happy officers exercised the power behind their badges, and in a burst of horrifying blasts they brought down a helpless alcoholic who had no intent of doing anything except protecting himself from intruders breaking into his own home.

AFTER THE SORRY scenario was over, Bill attempted to get a copy of the radio dispatcher's transmissions and other information from the department. But some of the most important and vital information was never provided, including the video tape made at the scene. Throughout the years Bill has retained the opinion that when the officers returned to his brother's apartment the second time, it mattered not what the ultimate circumstance or outcome may have been.

"Thank you for the autographed copy of your book titled RONNIE-'there just ain't no light'. I appreciate your thoughtfulness. I commend you for writing this book that shares the story of the horrors of alcohol abuse and I am confident that it will continue to touch the lives of many. Alcohol abuse among our youth can lead to a tragic end. The pressures faced by our children are greater than ever before. It is important that they receive the adequate tools to fight these temptations. Again, thank you for sharing your book with me. Best wishes and much success as you continue to educate our youth about the dangers of alcohol."

Governor Bob Riley, Alabama

25
THE INCOMPETENT CIRCUIT JUDGE

EVERY MONTH THOUSANDS upon thousands of people pay monthly premiums into trust funds of countless numbers of large insurance companies for a wide range of coverage and benefits. Every 30 days or so, millions of hard-earned dollars are paid for automobile insurance, health coverage, home coverage, business coverage and the like. But when it comes time to collect, some policy holders may be in for a big surprise. Before buying, you had better read the small print!

The policy on Ronnie's life had been in effect for several years, perhaps as long as the family had been in business, dating back to January 1956. The premiums had always been paid; however, when time came to collect double indemnity for Ronnie's accidental death, big, tough New England Life Insurance Company balked at paying the coverage which was obviously due.

For many years additional monthly premiums had also been paid to insure that the policy carried double indemnity benefits. That option had clearly been chosen by daddy Williams's company, the owner of the policy and the remitter of the monthly premiums.

After Ronnie's demise the family sought to recover the value of the policy under the accidental death provisions. However, New England refused to pay the claim by arguing that the policy excluded as a risk any accidental death caused by disease or the insured's commission of a felony.

By their refusing to pay the claim as presented, there was little else to do but bring suit in a court of law. Bill retained an attorney and spent most weekends over several months working with him to prepare for trial. The suit was eventually filed and the non-jury trial was assigned to Circuit Judge William Frye's court. The following spring, on April 30th, the judge heard oral arguments.

The Williams family had three misfortunate experiences in a row; nothing seemed to be going right for them. Ronnie's death being the first, trying to collect from New England the second and, third, by luck of the draw the case being assigned to the most inept, incompetent judge in the entire circuit.

Ronnie's mother was pleased that the hearing was finally scheduled but was unable to attend the court session as she was confined at Baptist Hospital. For several years she had fought a rugged battle with cancer, and since Ronnie's death it seemed to have gotten worse almost daily. Bill had kept her updated on the activities of the hearing as he had done on the trial preparations. Unfortunately, or perhaps fortunately, she would never learn of the ridiculous decision that was to be handed down by Judge Frye. Only five days after the trial, and well before his decision was published, she passed away.

THE JUDGE TOOK six weeks to issue his decree. Why so long was anyone's guess since it was apparent to everyone by his mannerism during the hearing that his mind had been made up while the procedure was in process. His opinion came down, as was expected, in favor of big business, New England Life. In the opinion the judge denied the Williams family any benefits and asserted that Ronnie had been killed because he suffered from an illness or a disease that contributed to his death.

On several occasions during the hearing, Bill had been vocal in his assessment of the cause of his brother's death. For certain he would proclaim, he was killed from the blast of a magnum bullet fired at close range directly into his back. He testified there should never be a question as to what actually caused his death.

However, conversely, the judge's opinion noted, "That Ronnie was an alcoholic and that public policy in the State of Florida is that alcoholism is recognized as an illness or disease and that those who suffer from this illness or disease shall be treated as sick persons."

The judge continued, "That regardless of whether or not alcoholism is a disease, it is an illness that contributed to Ronnie's death. That the bullet wounds that caused his death were intentionally inflicted even if the result of the wounds was not intentional."

He concluded by adding, "That it is not necessary to determine if alcohol is a form of drug, or that the decedent was engaged in a felony at the time of his death."

The judge's final order stated, "That the plaintiffs take nothing by their action against defendant, New England Life Insurance Company, because the decedent suffered from an illness or disease that contributed to his death."

EVEN AFTER THE incompetent judge heard testimony and reviewed a copy of a letter from State Attorney Curtis Golden stating that his exhaustive investigation proved that Ronnie was not committing any crime at the time of his death, he still sided with the giant New England Life Insurance Company.

Bill instantly decided this decision could not stand. Ronnie had been killed by a magnum weapon which was brandished about in a reckless and careless manner by non-caring, ill-trained "officers of the law." He had been killed by a bullet fired into his back while he struggled to come to his feet. He most certainly had not been killed by a disease.

There could be no better evidence than the official death certificate which plainly and appropriately stated the cause of death as being "from gunshot wounds." How much more of an official statement should be required, Bill wondered? And why should an absolutely incompetent judge attempt to change the official records?

Bill was determined to forge ahead, to go to whatever degree necessary to bring to light the true facts while keeping in mind there was no more room for another mistake concerning the life or death of his brother. He asked several friends for recommendations, and after reviewing each he retained a Tallahassee attorney who had a great deal of experience practicing before the Appellant Court. His track record spoke for itself.

Together they spent considerable hours reviewing records, the Circuit Court's decision, and most importantly the merits of the case. As soon as possible all documents were prepared and the appeal filed with the First District Court of Appeals in Talla-hassee.

IN SEPTEMBER OF the following year the case was sched-uled for hearing. The result this time would perhaps be a differ-ent story. Bill was completely confident a different decision would be reached if the Appellant Court based its opinion on the true facts of the case, unlike the decision from a judge who had only borderline knowledge of the law and no compassion what-soever for the true victim of this most horrendous affair.

SO FAR, THE month of July 1981 had been a scorcher. Searching for a cooler place, Bill came home for a weekend to his condo on Pensacola Beach. There probably could not be found anywhere a more relaxing atmosphere and for certain not a more beautiful beach in the world.

As usual he was up early strolling the sugar-white sands at sunrise. After a couple of miles he returned to the pot of coffee he had left brewing. He retrieved the morning paper from the porch and with coffee in hand headed for the second floor bal-cony and the hot sauna bath overlooking the Gulf. The sun had risen just enough to make out the small print.

The Sunday morning paper of July 19th was even larger than its normal bulky weekend edition. After scanning the front page, he automatically bounced over to the editorial section. His posi-tion at the governor's office gave him daily access to every news-paper in the state; keeping up with his hometown editorials was a daily ritual whether at home or elsewhere.

This morning his friend Paul Jasper, editorial director of the *Pensacola News-Journal,* had written a remarkable column about the circuit judge's decision in Ronnie's case.

Reading it quickly, he was pleased but at once knew it required a more careful examination, closer scrutiny. He studied every word and searched for anything which might help with his decision to appeal the ruling by the incompetent circuit Judge. He re-read the column over and over, slower and more methodically each time.

WHEN POLICE LAST year shot and killed Ronnie Williams, it was, much as I regretted the loss of a friend, no surprise to see it labeled "justified homicide."

But I was flabbergasted to discover last week that a circuit court judge has ruled that Ronnie actually was the victim of an "illness."

No, not "lead poisoning." That's the kind of ruling old Judge Roy Bean, the legendary "Law West of the Pecos" might have made.

"Circuit Judge William Frye ruled seriously that Ronnie suffered an illness called "alcoholism." This illness, he said, contributed so substantially to his death that his family was not entitled to double indemnity claims on his insurance.

Now, I've been following the Ronnie Williams case, out of simple curiosity, since shortly after the morning in February, 1980 when he burst out of his house here, pistol in hand, and was shot by police already summoned to the scene and thinking they were under fire.

It was pretty plain that Ronnie was drunk and suffering paranoid hallucinations that "people were out to get him." He'd already shot bullet holes through a couple of his own hats under the apparent assumption they were his enemies. The police had good reason to be jumpy when they arrived on the scene.

So it was a fairly obvious case of justifiable homicide, whether it was a mistake on the part of police or whether Ronnie actually did shoot towards one of them.

But the basis for the civil court ruling is something I'd not heard of before, and it led to what, to me at least, were some interesting trial twists.

I supposed the case would follow the usual pattern:

The attorney for the survivors would argue:

That the slain person had legitimate and legal reasons to come outside with a gun (suspecting prowlers, perhaps), that a door behind him slammed shut with a gunshot bang, and police, wrongly believing they were in danger, fired at him with fatal results. In short, clearly an accident.

Or that the victim was so intoxicated he didn't know what he was doing and so didn't knowingly contribute to his own death; that is, to contend he was temporarily insane.

Whereupon, the attorneys for the defendants would argue:

The slain person contributed so substantially to the circumstances leading to his death that he forfeited claims to double indemnity.

And that taking a drink was a voluntary act which put him at fault regardless of whether he was in his right mind when the shooting occurred.

And both the plaintiffs and defense did indeed use just about those arguments.

For instance, in his brief, the attorney for the insurance companies, Miles Davis, cited a Florida court decision holding that even though the slain person was intoxicated "the rule has been established that, when one who is the aggressor in an altercation from which a fatal injury reasonably might or should be expected to result is killed, the death is not considered to be accidental."

But the defense also added an unusual (to me) element to the case: that alcoholism is a disease and or an illness and that therefore a death arising from this illness cannot be accidental.

This is the one that seemed to me to put the Williams family attorney, James Swearingen, in a curious double bind.

If Swearingen argues that Williams was not an alcoholic, he lost his best crack at a temporary insanity ruling. But by showing Williams was an alcoholic, he proved that point for the defense, leaving only the question of whether alcoholism is or is not a disease or illness.

Swearingen thereupon was forced to take the position that while Williams was an alcoholic, alcoholism is a behavioral problem instead of a disease; no drug can cure it, the alcoholic himself must decide to stop.

But this, in turn, lent credence to the defense argument that Ronnie's first drink of the night was a voluntary act, and that he should be held accountable for subsequent events.

Of course, it seemed to me, as to Swearingen, that the defense could hardly contend on the one hand that alcoholism as a whole is a disease, and on the other that the first drink is a voluntary act.

Said Swearingen in his brief: If the disease of alcoholism sets in only when there is a loss of control to abstain from drinking, as (a defense expert witness) testified was the case, then how could the insured be suffering from a disease when his first drink of the evening was a voluntary act?

In the event, however, the court did uphold the defense's line of argument that alcoholism is an illness, if not a disease, making moot the other questions. If he died of an illness, it couldn't have been an accident. (The decision is being appealed).

Judge Frye's ruling, while strange to me, is not in fact an unreasonable decision to have made, given state law on the subject.

He based the ruling at least in part on a law that mandates all public officials to recognize that alcoholism is an illness or a disease.

Swearingen, however, argued—quite plausibly, I think—that the law was really intended to bring a halt to the once common police practice of putting common, or garden variety, drunks, guilty of nothing else, in jail. These days, if they go anywhere, it's to a detoxification center.

Nonetheless, the law is there and clearly Judge Frye is entitled to interpret it on what it seems to say.

But it seems to me that if this interpretation becomes the general practice of the courts, it's going to mean a drastic revision of past practices in civil damage cases—and maybe in criminal law itself.

THE WISDOM OF Paul Jasper magnified within Bill's mind the great opportunity which not only was possible but also most probable. He felt for sure the Appellant Court would overturn the lower court's decision.

"Thank you for sending me a copy of 'RONNIE'. I commend you for sharing the personal side of your brother's life, all the happy times and accomplishments as well as the times he fought his bouts with alcohol abuse. This book should be read by every student in high school and college. I wish you much success in reaching your goal of telling this story that will benefit and prevent others from similar experiences that ultimately cost RONNIE his life."

Coach Mark Richt, University of Georgia

26

AND STILL ANOTHER TRAGEDY

THE EMPTINESS AND pressures that Bill felt since losing Ronnie, then the outcome of the trial and, more than anything else, the loss of his mother was beginning to take a personal toll. There had to come a victory from some source, from around some corner. Things just could not continue the way they were going. Something had to change; events had to reverse themselves and do so very soon.

Ronnie had lost his life at the hand of a policeman who made the decision to shoot him in the back while he struggled to raise himself from the ground. He most certainly was not killed by whiskey, beer, pills or a combination of any or all. This had to be made known; the true facts must be accepted by the Court of Appeals. Bill knew that he and the family could not suffer any further heartbreaking losses. The truth must prevail.

ON THE 24th day of February 1982, two years and eleven days after Ronnie's murder, oral arguments were heard by the First District Court of Appeals of the State of Florida. The following September 23rd the opinion was handed down.

The Appellant Court's final judgement detailed, clearly and distinctly, the events and facts of the night of February 13, 1980. And it continued with the judges' opinion by stating:

Whether alcoholism is a disease for insurance purposes

is a question that cannot be readily answered, although a superficial reading of Florida statutes would seem to indicate that it is. Nevertheless, we note with interest the position taken by the United States Supreme Court in a criminal proceeding:

The inescapable fact is that there is no agreement among members of the medical profession about what it means to say that "alcoholism" is a "disease." One of the principal works in this field states that the major difficulty in articulating a "disease concept of alcoholism" is that "alcoholism has too many definitions and disease has practically none."

This same author concludes that "a disease is what the medical profession recognizes as such."

In other words, there is widespread agreement today that "alcoholism" is a "disease" for the simple reason that the medical professional has concluded that it should attempt to treat those who have drinking problems.

Debate ranges within the medical profession as to whether "alcoholism" in any meaningful biochemical, physiological or psychological sense, or whether it represents one peculiar manifestation in some individuals of underlying psychiatric disorders.

A careful scrutiny and consideration of Florida Statutes reveals that the legislature intended for alcoholics to be treated, not punished by incarceration in the county jail, or placement in the town pillory, as had been the traditional means of public response to the condition of alcoholism.

Statutes further declares that criminal law is not an appropriate device for preventing or controlling health problems. Dealing with public inebriates as criminals has proved expensive, unproductive, burdensome and futile. Statutes calls for handling alcoholics as sick persons.

It is readily apparent that the term "disease," as used in New England Life's standard policy, is highly ambiguous especially when considered against the facts of this case. If the question were susceptible to a resolution solely upon the conflicting medical testimony, we acknowledge that we would be obligated to sustain the lower court's finding as there was competent, substantial evidence supporting that determination. Yet, the question is not so simply resolved. We are confronted also with the question of whether the insurer, by the language it employed, intended to include alcoholism within the gamut of excluded risks under the policy. We considered that if New England Life had wished to condition its contractual liability upon the insured's conformance with certain conduct, or the exclusion of certain risks, it could have done so in clear, unambiguous language.

As to New England Life's alternative argument that the proceeds need not be paid, because the decedent's death was caused by his commission of an aggravated assault, we have observed that the lower court expressly deferred from ruling on this issue. Since we have determined appellants' right to the proceeds by reversing the finding that alcoholism is a disease, we find it necessary to confront New England Life's alternative argument. Remand of this case will be necessary in order for the court to make a factual finding relating to whether the insured's death was caused by his commission of an aggravated assault.

As a general rule, one need not be convicted of a felony for one's estate or beneficiaries to be denied the proceeds of an insurance policy by virtue of a policy clause in which the insurer excludes the risk of death resulting from the insured's commission of a felony.

In the case at bar there is evidence suggesting that the decedent was involved in the felony of aggravated assault at the time of his death due to the police officer's testimony that the decedent would have been so charged, if he had lived. Of course this testimony conflicted with the state's attorney's statement that the decedent was determined by him not to have been committing a felony at the time of his death and would not have been prosecuted by him for such offense had he lived.

There is substantial evidence before the court for it to find that the decedent was intoxicated, perhaps even hallucinating, at the time of his death. Aggravated assault is considered a specific intent crime, and voluntary intoxication is a defense to a specific intent crime. Consequently, one who is so heavily intoxicated as to be incapable of forming the requisite intent may avoid the application of a clause barring coverage for death or injury occurring due to commission of a crime. Finally, the policy excludes the risk of death and the insured's commission of the alleged felony.

The court's ruling denying the plaintiffs' requested relief as to their action on the New England Life policy on the ground that the insured's death occurred as the result of illness or disease, not accidental, requires more extended discussion. New England Life's coverage excludes accidental death caused directly or indirectly due to a disease, or the insured's commission of a felony. As to the former, we reverse the lower court's determination that alcoholism is a disease.

Accordingly, we reverse the final judgement as it bars the appellants' right to the proceeds from the New England Life policies.

THE LONG DESPICABLE road had come to an end. The double indemnity lawsuit was finished. After losing the case at the circuit court level, the family had finally experienced victory in Florida's First District Court of Appeals. The satisfaction was not about a financial triumph but concerned itself wholeheartedly with the manner and cause of Ronnie's death.

Even before the initial ruling by the incompetent Judge Frye of the lower court, Ronnie's death had been ruled by the state's attorney as accidental. Furthermore, he had given his written opinion that Ronnie was not committing a crime the evening of his murder, and, should he have survived his wounds, he would not have been charged with one.

Such a long journey. Such a struggle. But it had to be done. It had to be done to make everything complete. Bill could not stand the thought of his father, mother and brother laying under the cold blanket of earth without someone looking after the family's business, the business of making everything right with the world. Right in the court of public opinion.

Now armed with the Appellant Court's decision and with the state's attorney proclaiming that Ronnie was not committing any crime, then, apparently and appropriately so, there must be grounds to re-open the case.

Perhaps the governor would assign a state's attorney from another district who would summon a grand jury for the purpose of re-examining the evidence.

Certainly there must be a means of using the truthful evidence to bring charges against the individuals that were grossly negligent and totally responsible for the death of a completely innocent individual.

WITH THE SUCCESS of the appeal behind him and his quest now achieved, Bill thought he could find closure. Find some way and purpose of getting on with his personal life, but he soon recognized this was not to be the case. He found that closure is a word too often used concerning the death of a loved one. For sure, there is never "closure." Never does the hurt or pain fade away. It is always present. And those who think in terms of a final "closure" simply have not experienced or been subjected to the horrendous death of a loved one.

After keeping all the hurt and pain bottled up within himself for a long, long time, Bill knew he had to open up to someone and talk it out, to move forward with his life. All that he had learned from the experiences of his brother's predicament forced him to pay attention to the more minor problems of his own life. He began to look carefully at new directions, new paths to follow which would guide him away from falling into a similar trap. His absentee ownership of Oak Lawn Funeral Home was certainly in the good hands of his very capable staff, and within weeks he was reconfirmed as chairman of the Florida Career Service Commission. He personally scheduled a heavy case load for the commission from one end of the state to the other to insure that he was kept busy and mentally challenged. At the same time and at full throttle, he plunged headfirst into the re-election campaign of his good and faithful friend, Governor Bob Graham.

Things were finally getting back to a more normal routine. But just about as soon as they began to settle down, another tragedy peeked over the horizon.

SOME SAY THE strong can take almost anything. Perhaps that is true; maybe it's not. While the death of a loved one is never easy to cope with, it seems as if some handle the ordeal better than do others. And without question, the loss of a child has to be the most depressing of all deaths. Such catastrophe brings everyone to his knees, and each shares in the heartfelt loss. There never is an exception.

The Williams family, no different than millions of others around the globe, had experienced its share of exceedingly happy days and beautiful memories, but also its share of tremendously horrifying ones as well.

Many friends of Ronnie's dad would say that it was better that he did not live to witness Ronnie's plight; yet somehow or other he made it through Sandi's horrible accident. Perhaps in the end, Mother Williams was the strongest of all. Her exceptionally solid, never-wavering religious beliefs saw her through years of adversities. The sudden death of her husband, the murder of her firstborn and the near loss of her only daughter took its toll, but she never lost her faith.

Ministers will preach that God "out-thinks all of us." And many, but not everyone, will acknowledge that His plan for every man and woman was in place and completely structured long before their birth. Perhaps as Ronnie professed, life truly is a stage, and we must all play our part, the part which is our destiny without any opportunity to alter it.

God's overall plan for our personal, individual future and His conception for the forecast of the entire world for centuries to come is known only to Him. His perfect design is zillions of light years ahead of man's foggiest thoughts. His every notion of things to come, be they large or small, is for deliberate and specific reasons. Reasons not always understood, but a blueprint of perfection well beyond the comprehension of mere mortals.

THE BEAUTIFUL DAY was designed to be enjoyed by the young and the young at heart. The new leaves on the trees were of tender, multiple shades of green. The wild flowers along the roadside had blossomed into golden oranges, bright yellows, fiery reds and royal purples. The azaleas and magnolia trees circling Compass Lake, a small, circular lake only a few miles south of Marianna, Florida, were in full bloom.

Vince, Ronnie's son, and Brenda, his wife of only a single year, had planned this to be a special day on the lake. At daybreak they had packed a lunch of health foods, fresh fruit and bottled water. The dawn opened into a gorgeous spring morning, a day to relax and take in every ounce of Mother Nature's bountiful outdoors. A day to set about mastering the purpose of their recently acquired Sunfish sail boat. The day was theirs to enjoy and remember.

Before their marriage they had planned their future well; they had it all together. Both would work for a few years, and when the time was right they would begin their family, perhaps only two kids. He had a good job as a draftsman with a Marianna construction company. Conceivably, some of the talent Ronnie had for freehand sketching and art work was coming to life through Vince's hand. Brenda held the responsible position as managing editor of the *Floridan,* their local newspaper. Things at that very moment were as near perfect as any young couple could want.

Throughout the day they adjusted the sail to capture the breeze that continued to carry them back and forth and around the edges of the lake. As they slowly cruised here and there, laughing, cutting up, just kidding around with each other, they often posed in mock fashion so the other could snap a picture.

After pausing briefly for a bite of lunch, they eagerly reboarded the small craft and quickly caught the wind. As freak accidents sometimes happen, even during the happiest of times, one did.

Was it their demonic fate that raised its ugly head to cast an evil spirit on this happiest of days, to shower such morbid pain on this young, vivacious couple? Or was it a splinter from the design of a master plan that swept down and immediately altered such a beautiful and loving relationship? As Ronnie so often wondered, was it at all possible for mere humans to change what was going to be, what was already written? Do we really have any say so in the matter? Could anything at all have been done to change the ill wind of fate that was stirring fatally all about them?

As they approached the southern shore, they slowly brought their small craft about and headed northward. The Sunfish, with its aluminum mast, passed under low-hanging high voltage electrical transmission lines. A massive jolt shot down the mast and penetrated Vince's body. Brenda, although suffering second degree burns and shock, managed to swim to shore for assistance.

The loss of a child is the worst thing that can possibly happen to a parent. I have my doubts if Ronnie, although his kids had been adopted, could have survived the loss of Vince. And for sure, it would have been almost unbearable for Ronnie's parents, were they still living.

Vince's parents, sisters and family, Brenda's family and their friends were completely overcome by the tragedy. Still, their strong, convincing, non-wavering faith brought each of them through the days of agony with their heads held high.

There is absolutely no doubt in anyone's mind that Vince is now in a far better, much safer place. Those who knew him best would attest to the high moral ethics of this unique and special young man. An outgoing, well-read, highly intelligent young person who possessed a firm and acknowledged Christian faith years beyond his age. The world in which we remain is worse off for the loss of such a fine person. He would have been 22 years old just 13 days later.

"Thank you for your recent correspondence to my office regarding the publication of your latest book, 'RONNIE'. I read with interest the facts pertaining to the sad, true story of your brother's decline into alcoholism. Peer pressure is a strong and pervasive siren call to our youth, and it leads to many temptations and challenges during the formative years. I praise your efforts in telling your family's story as a means of educating teens and their parents to the dangers of alcohol abuse. I commend you for your efforts."

Roy Barnes, Former Governor of Georgia

27

ONE CARELESS STEP
OR THOUGHTLESS DEED

SHORTLY AFTER THANKSGIVING Bill had gone into his attic to retrieve his stored boxes of Christmas lights and decorations. There were several, and nuzzled among them was a special box, one which contained only Ronnie's personal possessions. After Christmas each year when he returned the boxes to the attic for safekeeping, he would place Ronnie's box among the others so he would not dare overlook it the following year.

Every holiday season he set aside some private time to pause and pay special remembrance to the missing members of his family. Pause to reflect just how much everyone of them always enjoyed this happy and special time of the year. During the hectic days of the season he always chose a particular night, a special time when he could be alone. An hour or so when he and Ronnie could share a few moments together, just being brothers again.

Moving all the Christmas boxes aside, he sat in front of the fireplace with Ronnie's box at hand. Together, the two brothers had their annual talk.

The strong shipping tape was cut and the box opened. As usual, it would again be tightly secured after the visit. It contained nothing more than Ronnie's personal memories. Things that he had kept and treasured.

Pictures of Sandi and him, some of the two brothers and several of their parents. A few football snapshots and some old game-day programs. A story and pictures of him scoring his two touch-downs in the Rose Bowl, pictures that had been featured in two Los Angeles papers. A small photo that had been made in a 25-cent fair booth, a head shot of himself between Red West and Ken Schulte.

A faded polaroid snapshot of his family, him, Pat and their three children, Kym, Paige and Vince. The autograph of Hank Williams that he had kept preserved between two sheets of wax paper since it was handed to him personally in 1952.

Another picture of Sandi, perhaps six years old, dressed in what appeared to be a bathing suit and holding a child's baton. The Bear Bryant hound's tooth hat with two bullet holes. His collection of a few record albums. Two Mark Twain books and one entitled *Mein Kampf.* The boots and belt he wore the night of his murder. A deck of playing cards and a pair of red dice that he had brought home from his only trip to Las Vegas.

And a large brown envelope that Bill had taped securely just days after cleaning out Ronnie's apartment. The contents, known only to him and Ronnie and those mentioned inside, were always treated as Ronnie's most personal property. It had always been that way, and that's the way it would forever remain. Each year on this very night Bill always entertained thoughts of burning the sealed package but could never muster up enough nerve. Perhaps this year he would.

At sunset the weather had turned bitterly cold, something most Pensacolians dream of for this time of year. The double-sided fireplace between the den and the kitchen was in full glow, warm and inviting.

For a moment he let his own personal memories of seasons gone by overtake him. He, himself, had demons within. Many which lingered for years on end and refused to leave. Thousands of memories of his personal past continued to demand a special audition, an exclusive place and time to be heard. A special few minutes to remember, to recall times that once were.

Some memories were great and some fantastic, but many were intense and haunting. Each Holiday Season always brought conflicting thoughts. Memories to be confronted, to be faced and labored over again with the final question always demanding an answer about what might have been done differently, done better.

After touching every item, he carefully repacked the box, making sure each object was placed where it fit the best. In the weeks immediately following Ronnie's death, each item had been inspected gingerly by him and his mother. There was nothing hidden, nothing that had not been noted previously.

He held the thin, well-worn, tan-colored wallet for a few moments, then snuggled it tenderly into a proper place. For some unknown and mysterious reason, he again lifted it out, opened it wide and obviously found the same contents as last year. Ronnie's drivers license. A paid receipt from the Beach Front Motel, Cedar Key, Florida. A polaroid picture of the rustic Islander Hotel and Lounge. A couple of snapshots of an old, dilapidated waterfront home built on pilings that had obviously withstood all but the final of Cedar Key's hurricanes and lesser storms. Although still standing, it was now vacant and lonely. The structure barely remained above the water line, hanging loosely atop its broken and rotting timbers. The pictures portrayed a ghostly and haunting view of something of obvious beauty in past years, but now had fallen into the hands of helplessness and disrepair. Perhaps, Bill thought, Ronnie may have kept the picture as a symbol of what his life had evolved into being.

The wallet contained a couple of phone numbers that were important only to him. The family never inquired. The numbers were never called.

This year, as had not been the case when going through the ritual the last five years, something urged him to be more curious, to examine the wallet more carefully. Almost as if invisible hands were forcing him, he turned the wallet inside out. Lifting the thin leather interior siding from the middle where folding money is usually kept, it revealed yet another compartment. An even better place for hiding more secret, more special things.

He was surprised to find a two dollar bill hidden behind the crease. The bill was folded haphazardly around a small piece of faintly lined yellow notebook paper, the exact same size as the bill.

Written in pencil appeared to be a verse, a poem. The words were difficult to decipher since the paper had been wadded up several times as if it had been thrown away. Perhaps it was, then fished from waste cans and again secured in its secret place. The faded, liquid-blotched words were almost invisible, virtually hidden between the wrinkles of the tattered note.

The verse probably described Ronnie better than could all of his friends and family together. Maybe the carefully chosen words confirmed his personal thoughts of his own life, his own identity. A life somewhat similar to the piece of paper that had been thrown away time and again.

It was never determined if the verse was from his own pen or copied words from another sad soul. No matter the origin, Bill instantly understood its meaning and was sad but pleasantly pleased that he did. It told of the imitation of a life, the life of a person who had given up completely.

You'll meet many just like me along life's busy street.
Men with shoulders steeped, heads bowed low, and eyes that
    stare in defeat.

Or souls that live within the past, where sorrow plays all
    parts.
Where a living death is all that's left, for men with broken
    hearts.

You have no right to be the judge, to criticize or condemn.
Just think, but for the grace of God, it could be you instead
    of him.

One careless step or thoughtless deed, and then the misery
    starts.
And to those who weep, death comes cheap, to these men
    with broken hearts.

Oh, so humble you should be, when they come walking by. For
it is written, that the greatest men never get too big to cry.

Some lose faith in love and life, when sorrow shoots her
    darts.
And with hope all gone we walk alone, we men with broken
    hearts.

You've never walked in my shoes, or saw things through my
    eyes.
Or stood and watched with helpless hands, while the heart
    within me died.

Some of us are paupers, some are kings, some, masters of the
  arts.
But in our shame, we're all the same, we men with broken
  hearts.
Life sometimes can be so cruel, that a heart will pray for
  death.
God, why must we, the living dead know pain with every
  breath.
So help your brother along the road, no matter where you
  start.
For the God that made you, made me too, we men with broken
  hearts.

LAYING THE TATTERED paper on the sofa, Bill was absolutely assured of the meaning of the verse. He knew perfectly
well why Ronnie had carried these words with him, probably for
many years. The line that read, "one careless step or thoughtless
deed" magnified Ronnie's downhill spiral. As Bill had assumed
for years, Ronnie's life of misery, anguish and torment began on
the day he permitted another man to adopt his children.

With moist eyes, Bill carefully folded the note and returned
it to the loneliness of its secret hiding place where it wouldn't be
disturbed for another year, or perhaps never.

Sitting reverently and silently in the warmth of his comfortable den, a chilling but familiar voice was plainly heard. A voice
of unmistakable clarity. He knew it well. As crystal clear as if
he too were sitting on the floor next to him.

"Billy, don't do that. I'm okay. Everything is okay."

THE END